D0323804

DAYS OF THUNDER

DAG ENBERG, SHOTGUN RIDER

DAYS OF THUNDER

A WESTERN DUO

PETER BRANDVOLD

FIVE STAR
A part of Gale, a Cengage Company

Farmington Hills, Mich • San Francisco • New York • Waterville, Maine
Meriden, Conn • Mason, Ohio • Chicago

Copyright © 2017 by Peter Brandvold
Five Star™ Publishing, a part of Gale, a Cengage Company.

ALL RIGHTS RESERVED.
This novel is a work of fiction. Names, characters, places, and incidents are either the product of the author's imagination, or, if real, used fictiously.

No part of this work covered by the copyright herein may be reproduced or distributed in any form or by any means, except as permitted by U.S. copyright law, without the prior written permission of the copyright owner.

The publisher bears no responsibility for the quality of information provided through author or third-party Web sites and does not have any control over, nor assume any responsibility for, information contained in these sites. Providing these sites should not be construed as an endorsement or approval by the publisher of these organizations or of the positions they may take on various issues.

LIBRARY OF CONGRESS CATALOGING-IN-PUBLICATION DATA

Names: Brandvold, Peter, author. | Brandvold, Peter. Shotgun rider. | Brandvold, Peter. Two smoking barrels.
Title: Days of thunder : a western duo / Peter Brandvold.
Other titles: Two smoking barrels. | Shotgun rider.
Description: First edition. | Waterville, Maine : Five Star Publishing, 2017. | Series: Dag Enberg: Shotgun rider | Description based on print version record and CIP data provided by publisher; resource not viewed.
Identifiers: LCCN 2017008108 (print) | LCCN 2017012648 (ebook) | ISBN 9781432836863 (ebook) | ISBN 1432836862 (ebook) | ISBN 9781432834098 (ebook) | ISBN 1432834096 (ebook) | ISBN 9781432834128 (hardcover) | ISBN 1432834126 (hardcover)
Subjects: | BISAC: FICTION / Action & Adventure. | FICTION / Westerns. | GSAFD: Western stories.
Classification: LCC PS3552.R3236 (ebook) | LCC PS3552.R3236 A6 2017c (print) | DDC 813/.54—dc23
LC record available at https://lccn.loc.gov/2017008108

First Edition. First Printing: July 2017
Find us on Facebook– https://www.facebook.com/FiveStarCengage
Visit our website– http://www.gale.cengage.com/fivestar/
Contact Five Star™ Publishing at FiveStar@cengage.com

Printed in the United States of America
1 2 3 4 5 6 7 21 20 19 18 17

For Roberta, Jack, and Sam

TABLE OF CONTENTS

★ ★ ★ ★ ★

THE SHOTGUN RIDER

★ ★ ★ ★ ★

CHAPTER ONE

"There's a good-lookin' woman on the premises, an' look who's playin' billiards," said Cougar Ketchum.

The tall, curly-haired outlaw entered the Diamond in the Rough Saloon in Mineral Springs, Arizona Territory, grinning like a mule chewing a mouthful of cockleburs. He let the batwing doors shudder into place behind him.

He sauntered into the room, heels barking, spurs rattling, and shuttled his vaguely cross-eyed gaze from the beautiful Zenobia Chevere to Dag Enberg just as Enberg pocketed the six ball.

Enberg propped the end of his pool stick on the edge of the table. He picked up his half-filled beer schooner and looked at Ketchum over its rim. He took a sip of the lukewarm ale, then glanced at Zenobia, who returned his look with a cool one of her own, and shrugged a bare shoulder, imploring him in her silent way to stand down.

Zee, as she was known, sat alone at a table on the far side of the saloon/hotel's main drinking hall, away from the long, ornate bar. A long Mexican cigarillo smoldered between the beautiful *puta*'s long, pale, tapering fingers, the nails of which were painted a rich burgundy.

"Times sure do change," said Ketchum as he stood in front of the batwings, thumbs hooked behind his double-cartridge belts to which three big Smith & Wesson revolvers were holstered in pearl-gripped, silver-chased splendor. "Why, there was

11

a time when a fully stoked train engine couldn't have kept you two apart. There was a time when you two woulda been takin' apart *Senorita* Zenobia's crib upstairs a stick at a time, so the whole damn building woulda sounded like it was comin' apart at the seams!"

A flush rising in her sculpted cheeks, Zee glanced down at her cigarillo.

Dag Enberg squeezed the handle of his beer schooner as his ears warmed. He glared at Ketchum, who just then glanced over his shoulder at his burly, beefy sidekick. Raoul Leclerk was entering the saloon behind him, dressed almost entirely in black.

Ketchum canted his head to indicate Enberg. He chuckled to Leclerk, then sauntered over toward Zee's table. The girl regarded the man coolly, her upper lip curled with disdain. She glanced once more at Enberg, her dark-brown eyes flashing nervously, and then took a deep drag from the cigarillo.

As Leclerk walked over to the bar, the apron, Mort Kettleson, pointed a pudgy, admonishing finger at Ketchum. "Zee's off-duty, Cougar. Lay off her."

"You heard the man," Zee sneered as Ketchum slacked casually into a chair at her table. "Some other time, *maybe.*"

Ketchum grinned across the room at Enberg, who stood by the billiard table, silently fuming but trying to keep his wolf on its leash. The last thing he needed was trouble. He couldn't afford more trouble—not here at the tail end of a most troublesome time.

The barman, Kettleson, must have sensed Enberg's anger. He glanced at the tall, blond-bearded, blue-eyed Enberg standing by the billiard table, holding a cue stick in one hand, his beer in the other hand, then gritted his teeth at Ketchum once more.

"No trouble, Cougar," the barman said, his pudgy cheeks flushed with anxiety. He was a little breathless, his lumpy chest rising and falling sharply. "You hear me? Cates don't stand for trouble in here—you know that!"

Logan Cates owned the Diamond in the Rough and half the county.

"Cates is out of town." Still grinning, Ketchum reached into his wool coat and pulled a sheaf of bills from his shirt pocket. He waved the bills in the air, making a flapping sound, then dropped the wad onto the table.

"You robbed another church, I see, Cougar," said Zee, irony flashing in her eyes.

"Nuh-uhh," Ketchum said, slowly wagging his head and casting his leering grin at Enberg. "I don't rob nothin' no more—least of all churches. This collie dog changed his spots. I sold me a small herd of hosses to the cavalry over at Bowie. Bought 'em from a Mexican in Sonora who couldn't afford to feed 'em or trail 'em. I grazed 'em for a few months and sold 'em off for twice what I paid for 'em. This is what I got left after celebratin' down in *Mexico.*"

He stretched his lips back farther from his large, yellow teeth, a couple of which were missing. "That there is the very definition of a businessman—wouldn't you say, Dag?"

"Congratulations," Enberg said, unable to keep himself from imagining smashing his right fist through the arrogant bastard's mocking mouth. "But, like Kettleson said, Zee's off-duty. You'll want to mosey." He glanced at Leclerk leaning forward against the bar. "You an' your friend there."

Cougar Ketchum's brows closed down over his flat, light-brown eyes. "Now, wait a minute—did I miss somethin'? Last I heard you weren't town marshal no more. Last I heard, Cates fired you for—"

"Ketchum, that's enough," Kettleson intoned, again glancing nervously at Enberg. "I told you to leave. Now, leave . . . before I send for Whipple."

Geylan Whipple was the new town marshal of Mineral Springs.

"I got ten dollars says you won't send for Whipple," Ketchum said, plucking a single bill off the pile before him and waving it in the air before Zee's smoke-wreathed face. "Ain't that the goin' rate for a tumble with Cates's top whore, Kettleson?"

"I am not entertaining," Zee said.

"How about if we double the pay today," said Ketchum, "since I'm flush and feelin' all generous?" He glanced slyly over at Kettleson, whose eyes had gotten small as he stared at the money on the table and in the outlaw's hand. "Twenty dollars . . . for just one hour of *Senorita* Zenobia's time."

He cast his mocking gaze toward Enberg.

"You wouldn't mind—would you, Dag? I mean, she's not your woman anymore." Ketchum laughed. "Hell, she's every man's woman. Every man with money enough to pay for it!"

Enberg squeezed the handle of his schooner so hard he thought he could hear the glass beginning to crack. A red haze had dropped down over his eyes. His heart was beating with the force of a war drum.

"She'll never lay with the likes of you, Ketchum," Enberg said, glancing quickly at Zee. "Not if I have anything to say about it."

Ketchum turned to the suddenly greedy-eyed barman, but said nothing. He only smiled enticingly.

"I told you several times now, Cougar," Zee said, keeping her cool. "I am not currently entertaining. Even if I were, like Dag says, I would never . . ."

She let her voice trail off as Ketchum leaned toward her and stuffed the ten-dollar bill down inside her corset, between the rich, creamy mounds of her full, firm breasts.

Zee glared at him.

Ketchum peeled another bill off the stack on the table and

poked it down inside her corset. He slowly removed his right index finger from between the young woman's breasts. He stuck the finger in his mouth, closed his lips around it, and slowly pulled it out as though savoring the flavor.

"Now, that tastes good!" Ketchum laughed. "But, then, you know how they taste—don't ya, Dag?"

He turned to grin at Enberg and then at Kettleson. Leclerk now had his back to the bar, resting his elbows on it. He was chuckling deep in his throat.

"Them enough *pesos,* my *puta* darlin'?" he asked Zee, who continued to glare at him, hard-jawed.

Dag Enberg's heart felt like a red-hot fist battering the backside of his breastbone.

Ketchum turned to Kettleson and arched a brow.

"No?" Ketchum said, turning back to Zee. "My, my—ain't we high on ourselves? All right—how 'bout another?" He stuffed another note down inside her corset. "Now, that's thirty dollars!" He laughed incredulously. "Surely, that's enough for an hour upstairs, *Senorita!*"

Zee drew deeply on her cigarillo and blew the smoke into Ketchum's face. "No amount is enough, *amigo.* Not for you, Cougar. Not ever. *Comprende?*"

"Really?" Ketchum said, reaching for another bill. "How 'bout another twenty?"

He held the note up for Kettleson to see and then shoved it down inside the whore's corset. Zee snapped her head toward Enberg, who strode slowly toward her table.

"Easy, Dag," Kettleson said. "Easy. Easy, now. Go *easy!*"

"No, Dag!" Zee said.

As Enberg made his way to Zee's table, the only other three customers in the place—two shopkeepers and a bookkeeper from the bank—quickly finished their drinks and skinned out

15

through the front door, the batwings clattering into place behind them.

Enberg stopped before Ketchum, balling his fists at his sides.

"Dag, let me handle it!" Zee urged. "You don't need any more trouble from Cates."

"No, I don't," Enberg said, glowering down at Ketchum, who sat back in his chair, knees spread, grinning up at Enberg. "And neither does this gutter rat."

"He's just trying to provoke you, Dag!" warned Kettleson.

"He's done that," Enberg said softly. "Ketchum, you gather up the rest of your money and hightail it."

"Or what?" Ketchum said, an open challenge in his liquid gaze. He glanced at Enberg's right hip. "You musta forgot, Dag. The marshal done took your pistol away. You can't wear a gun in town no more."

His mocking grin widened, dimpling his unshaven cheeks. "And you only get to carry your shotgun when you're ridin' messenger on the stage. So . . . if you'll excuse us, me an' *Senorita* Zee here are in the middle of a business transaction. I got little doubt we'll be upstairs shortly. Then you can just sit down here an' listen to her moan."

Cougar Ketchum gave a slow, lewd wink that was like a knife driven into Enberg's side.

CHAPTER TWO

Enberg placed his shaking fists on the table near Ketchum and said with quiet menace, "Take your money and leave, Cougar."

"Dag!" Zee said, fear flashing in her eyes. Knowing she could not reason with Enberg, that he'd gone beyond the point of no return, she turned to Ketchum. "You've pushed too hard, Cougar. *Leave!*"

She pulled the money out of her corset and slammed it down on the table. "Take it and leave and don't come back. Not *ever!*"

Ketchum looked down at the money she'd thrown onto the table. He looked at Enberg. Then he looked past Enberg to Kettleson and very slowly placed his hand on the sheaf of neatly stacked money.

He slid the sheaf toward Zee, shoving the money from her corset along in front of it.

"There," Ketchum said with self-satisfaction. "That there is five hundred dollars, *chiquita.*" He raised his voice and glanced around Enberg at the bartender. "Five hundred dollars for one hour upstairs, Kettleson. What do you think about *that*? Who pays that much *dinero* for a romp with a Mexican whore? I think Cates would be right pleased!"

"Ah, shit, Zee," Kettleson said, beseechingly. "Cates would say go ahead! Dag, stand down. She ain't your woman no more."

Enberg placed his hand on Ketchum's shoulder, and squeezed.

Ketchum looked down at the man's hand.

"Dag," Zee said, glancing over his left shoulder.

That was when Enberg knew that the big, burly Leclerk was standing behind him. He could see the man's thick shadow on the floor to his left. He could also smell the wild-animal reek of the man. Enberg realized his mistake. Once again, his hot Nordic temper had gotten the better of him.

"Ah, Jesus," Kettleson lamented. "Come on, fellas. Now, don't go doin' anything stupid. Dag, you know the score. If you get into any more trouble . . ."

He let his voice trail off as Enberg turned slowly to face Leclerk. Enberg was well over six feet. Still, Leclerk had three inches on him plus forty pounds. Leclerk gazed at Dag, smiling, eyes glinting devilishly from within their shallow sockets.

"*Mierda*," Zee said in disgust. "You walked right into it, Dag. All along, they were only trying to provoke you, you cork-headed Norwegian!"

It all galloped through Dag Enberg's brain then, as he faced the big man before him. His history with Ketchum and Ketchum's kin. When he'd been town marshal, he and the county sheriff, Glen Sutton, had ridden out to the Ketchums' outlaw ranch to arrest the Ketchums and Leclerk for throwing broad loops around the cattle of other ranchers and selling them across the border in Mexico or to the crooked Indian agent at San Carlos.

One man had died that day—Ketchum's father, Hawk Ketchum, who'd cut down Sutton with a Sharps carbine, paralyzing Sutton, who now wheeled himself around a boarding house in Lordsburg, tended by his only daughter, a school-teacher.

Enberg had shot Hawk Ketchum in the belly, and it had taken the elder Ketchum a good long time to die while Enberg and his and Sutton's deputies had transported him and the other prisoners back to the county lockup in Florence.

By the corrupt workings of the law in Pinal County, Ketchum and his two brothers and three cousins along with Leclerk had gotten only a year in the territorial pen.

Well, they were all back now. A year older, but obviously none the wiser.

And they had a bone to pick with Dag Enberg.

"Pull your horns in, Dag," warned a voice in Enberg's head.

But his anger had built to such a hot lather that the voice had no teeth behind it.

Enberg met Leclerk's mocking grin with a broad grin of his own, showing nearly all his large, white teeth inside his dark-blond beard, which offset the cobalt blue of his fiery eyes.

Then he smashed his forehead against Leclerk's nose. He could feel the warm wash of the bigger man's blood against his own flesh.

"Uhhh!" Leclerk stumbled backward, eyes snapping wide with shock.

Though Enberg was known for his dark moods and fierce temper, apparently Leclerk hadn't expected so sudden an onslaught. Keeping the man on his heels, Enberg followed him, smashing his right fist into the man's left cheek and then his left fist into Leclerk's right cheek.

Kettleson cursed as Leclerk fell over a chair and onto a table, the legs of which broke under the huge man's weight.

Leclerk and the table fell to the floor, taking down two shot glasses and a half-filled bottle of tequila, as well. His face was a mask of red from his exploded nose.

"Dag!" Zee screamed.

Enberg turned in time to see Cougar Ketchum's pistol arcing toward him in a blur of white and silver. The butt caught Enberg across his left temple. He stumbled backward, tripping over the same chair that Leclerk had fallen over. Enberg managed to keep his feet.

Ketchum flipped his gun in the air, grabbing the grips. He started to click the hammer back but then Enberg was on him, punching the gun out of his fist.

"*Ow!*" Ketchum intoned, wincing at the pain in his wrist as his pistol hit the floor and slid toward the batwings.

Enberg drove his right fist against Cougar's face once, twice, three times, turning his face pink with blossoming bruises and sending him flying across the table Zee had recently abandoned. She now stood over by the pool table, still holding the stub of her cigarillo and staring in fateful disgust at the dustup. A strap of her skimpy gown hung down her arm, revealing nearly all of her sloping right breast.

"Stop it!" Kettleson shouted. "Stop it right now! Stop or I'll blast ya, Dag!"

Enberg was too incensed to heed the warning or to even glance behind him. If he had looked over his shoulder, he would have seen the fat barman aiming a double-barreled shotgun at him but looking more frustrated than prepared to trip one of the two bore's triggers and send lead buckshot hurling through the back of a man he called a friend, albeit sometimes reluctantly.

Enberg kicked the table out of the way, picked up the moaning Cougar Ketchum by his coat lapels, and hurled him against the far wall. Ketchum bounced off the wall and into Dag's right elbow.

Ketchum's head flew backward. His boots rose off the floor. He flew back once more against the wall with a sharp bang, dislodging an oil painting of a snowy-skinned, naked blonde sprawled on a red velvet settee, and shattering a bracket lamp.

Ketchum piled up at the base of the wall, yelling, "Enough! For god sakes, enough!"

"Behind you again, Dag," Zee said.

Enberg swung around. Leclerk stood behind him, both eyes

swelling fast behind what looked like a ripe red tomato smashed against his face. He jerked his enraged eyes toward Zee and shouted, "Goddamn greaser bitch!"

Enberg had picked up a leg from the table Cougar had broken when he'd fallen on it. Now he raised it like a club.

"You want more, you stupid bastard?" he bellowed as the big Leclerk turned toward him.

Leclerk grinned.

Enberg swung the leg at the big man's head. Somehow, Leclerk ducked the blow. The table leg whooshed through the air. Enberg grunted as his own momentum spun him around. When he was half-turned away from Leclerk, the big man punched Enberg in the side of the head, just above the ear.

It was a savage blow, knocking Enberg sideways, that ear ringing like a broken bell and his vision clouding. Still, he managed to keep his feet. Swinging back around with a roaring bellow, he thrust the table leg backhanded.

It connected soundly with Leclerk's throat.

The big man staggered backward once more, crouching, eyes growing so wide that Dag thought they'd pop out of his head. Leclerk got his boots under him. Crouched forward, he clutched his throat with both hands as though to remove an invisible noose wrapped snugly around his neck.

Leclerk's eyes grew wider and wider as he fought to remove that invisible noose. He opened his mouth as though to speak but the only sound was a raspy strangling sound. The big man turned to Enberg, a mute pleading in his eyes. Enberg realized that Leclerk was trying to draw a breath but his smashed windpipe wouldn't allow air into his lungs.

Leclerk swung around and, continuing to claw at his throat, ran across the saloon and through the batwings and into the street as though he'd been hurled out of the room by a hurricane.

Enberg stared incredulously toward the Diamond's shuddering doors.

"Christ almighty," said Kettleson, staring in the same direction and slowly lowering his shotgun.

A woman's shrill scream rose in the street.

Enberg dropped the table leg. He strode across the room, pushed through the batwings, and stopped on the saloon's front porch to watch Leclerk kneeling in the street before a woman dressed to the nines in a stylish salmon dress, white shirtwaist, and feathered picture hat. She was taking mincing steps backward, tripping over the hem of her gown as she tried to flee the big man who was clawing at her as though trying to maul her.

She was Constance Norman, wife of one of the county's wealthiest ranchers.

The panicked, strangling Leclerk was only beseeching the horrified woman for help. Which she, of course, couldn't offer.

The best sawbones on the frontier couldn't have fixed Leclerk's busted windpipe.

The woman screamed again as she tripped over her gown and fell to her butt in the street. Writhing in horror of his fast-approaching demise, Leclerk flopped down on top of her, kicking his legs and arms and raking his fingers across his throat. His grisly strangling sounds rose above the woman's shrieks.

Leclerk turned over and over as he fought death, his horrifically swelling face growing bright red and then blue until, after nearly a minute of violent convulsing, with the woman screaming and trying to kick him away, he finally stopped fighting.

The dark angels of death swept over him.

Leclerk rolled onto his back, legs spread wide. He blinked one last time, gave a final twitch, and lay glaring toward heaven.

CHAPTER THREE

"Christ, look what you done," Kettleson said as he walked onto the saloon's front porch to stand beside Enberg and stare out at the body of Raoul Leclerk. A couple of townsmen were helping Constance Norman out from underneath the big man's slack body. "When Cates gets word about this, he's gonna be madder'n a bobcat caught in a piss fire."

"What else is new?" Enberg grunted.

Kettleson stared at him in disgust. "Dag, you're about as sharp as a cue ball—you know that?"

More townsmen were walking out into the street to see what had caused the commotion. Eventually the town marshal, Geylan Whipple, would be here as well. Enberg wondered if he should save the lawman a trip and mosey on down to the jailhouse under his own recognizance, but then Zee pushed through the batwings and said, "Let me take a look at that head of yours, you stupid bastard."

She pulled Enberg down by his shirt collar and scrutinized the cut on his left temple. She sucked a sharp breath through her small, even teeth and grabbed Enberg's arm, turning him around and pulling him toward the batwings.

"Get in here, fool," she ordered. "That needs tending before you bleed to death."

"The doc'll tend it," Enberg said, pulling his arm back.

She gazed up at him with that snooty, obstinate way of hers, rich ruby lips slightly parted, heavy bosom rising and falling sharply. When she wore a look like that, there was no denying the girl. Or woman, as she'd become now, Enberg reminded himself, noting the mature cast to her brown-eyed gaze and the uncompromising set of her plump lips.

"Ah, Christ!" Kettleson said as Enberg let Zee pull him back through the batwings. "Don't you two break any furniture up there, goddamnit! And you're only gonna piss-burn Cates all the more, if he finds out you been together. You're married to his stepdaughter, for mercy sakes, Dag!"

"Even Logan can only get so mad," Enberg said over his shoulder as he followed Zee down the drinking hall toward the carpeted stairs at the rear. On the far side of the room, Cougar Ketchum was climbing heavily to his feet on the other side of the table, which sat at a steep slant now, missing two legs.

Ketchum was breathing hard and cursing under his breath. He looked as though he were trying to gain his balance on the deck of a storm-tossed clipper ship.

One of his eyes was swollen shut, and several cuts on his cheeks and lips oozed blood. He looked at Enberg and pointed. "This ain't over!"

"You'd better hope it is," Zee said snootily, tugging Enberg along by his hand.

Enberg chuckled.

Zee cast him a reprimanding look over her shoulder. That sobered him.

She said nothing more as she lead the big Norwegian—Enberg's father had come from Norway to Arizona four decades ago to hunt for gold—up the stairs and along the hall to her room. Her door was the centerpiece of the second story, situated as it was at the end of the long, ornately papered hall and labeled with a brass nameplate in which *Senorita* Zenobia was fancily scrolled.

Zee kept her door locked. Enberg had always thought the

reason had more to do with creating an air of mystery around the courtesan than because she had anything particularly valuable inside. Her most valuable assets, after all, were tucked so beguilingly and incompletely away in her corset and bustier.

The cool-eyed Mexican beauty plucked a brass key out of a pocket of her silk robe, turned the key in the lock, and threw open the door. She stepped to one side, and looked up at her much taller charge, arching a dubious brow, her lips set as though with anger.

"After you," Enberg said, gesturing.

Zee gave a slow blink and walked in ahead of him. Enberg liked the way her robe so gently caressed her long, lean, finely sculpted legs on which she wore nothing. She wore black shoes with gold buttons and high, slender heels. The shoes had to be uncomfortable and hard on her delicate feet, but no practiced paramour could have walked more gracefully, despite them.

Enberg had always been a little taken aback by the girl's room. Of course, he'd never been inside a queen's quarters, but he thought that Zee's room would have held up well in comparison.

Filled with intimate shadows and caressed by slender beams of sunlight filtering through two cracks in the velvet drapes, it was the size of two large hotel rooms. The chamber boasted a separate washroom as well as a gigantic, canopied bed with a billowy, red silk comforter and red silk, gilt-tasseled pillows.

There were brass fixtures and wood-framed oil paintings on the walls. In the dim, variegated light they were hard to see from even a few feet away, but most of the pictures would have evoked chuffs of disdain from the local ladies' clubs.

"Sit," Zee said as she tossed the key on a scrolled, marble-topped dressing table and stepped through a curtained doorway into the washroom.

Enberg walked over and sat on the edge of the bed. He could

hear water splashing in the washroom. Zee stepped through the curtained doorway carrying a porcelain basin and a handful of cloths.

She stopped, planted her fist holding the cloths on her hip, and gave a reproving sigh.

"I meant the sofa."

Enberg grinned and bounced up and down on the bed. "This is more comfortable."

He allowed himself a devouring look at the beautiful brunette's intoxicating body. She was over twenty, and she'd been working the line for three years. But she still didn't look a day over eighteen.

She didn't have that drawn, jaded look so many acquired after only a few months' worth of trade. Nor was she stricken with that pasty pallor from little or no sun exposure. Despite her penchant for tobacco and bacanora, a favorite drink of the border country, she had few lines around her lips and eyes. The ones she did have gave her exotic countenance dimension and definition—they made her less of a goddess and more of an irresistibly attractive young woman.

Enberg thought she was sexier now than she'd been when she'd first ridden into town from Mexico in her own private coach driven by a liveried butler named Gomez, who'd died in an old-fashioned, Spanish-style duel behind the Phoenix Hotel one soggy night during the summer monsoon.

Zee's father's ancient, sprawling hacienda had been ransacked by revolutionary cutthroats who had murdered her father and stepmother, but not before her father had sent Zenobia away with Gomez to fend for herself in any way she could—preferably north of the border, where she'd have a better chance of survival than in her war-torn home country.

The Mexican beauty had indeed survived. Her stepmother, the former Pilar de la Croix, had been a courtesan trained by a famous madam in Mexico City. Secretly, without Zenobia's father knowing, Pilar—who had been of mixed French and Spanish ancestry—had passed her secrets along to Zenobia, knowing that at such a turbulent time in such a savage country as Mexico in the 1870s, it was important for a girl to have something relatively stable as well as lucrative to fall back on in the event that all hell broke loose.

Which it had.

But Zee had survived in winning fashion, putting her body to artful use in sustaining itself and making a name for herself as the most enthralling and man-pleasing courtesan plying her artistry in the shadow of the Mogollon Rim.

While Zee worked for Logan Cates, she'd worked out a deal where she kept fifty percent of her profits. She worked only when she wanted to and reserved the right to refuse clients she deemed unacceptable—which usually included the severely unkempt or temperamentally undesirable, though most of that ilk couldn't have afforded Zee's steep prices anyway, unless they'd found an especially large nugget somewhere out in their desert diggings.

Such an arrangement with Logan Cates had formerly been unheard of, as Cates was known far and wide as a pernicious, parsimonious businessman. Enberg had often wondered how the girl had managed to finagle such an arrangement, but, while he didn't want to dwell on it overmuch, he thought he probably knew.

Zee had likely proven how rare she was, as well as how essential, to Cates himself, though Cates was married to the persnickety widow of a former business partner. If his wife had found out that Cates had been less than loyal, the formidable Gertrude would likely have taken piano wire to his balls.

The screams would probably be heard as far away as Nogales, Enberg thought now with a grin, though little about Zee's dealings with other men ever gave him anything to grin about. Since the first time he'd met the talented Mexican beauty, Enberg had had to work hard on keeping chained his jealousy, an emotion that he'd formerly never experienced—at least, not with such power as that which Zee evoked.

Theirs, however, had been a short-lived, proscribed relationship, for as the town marshal of Mineral Springs, Enberg was considered as much in Cates's employ as was Zee.

Cates did not allow his employees to "mingle." At least, that's what he'd told both Zee and Enberg when he'd caught the marshal skinning out of her room one night—a night when her "red lamp" hadn't been burning, as it were. When she hadn't been officially entertaining.

Enberg had had little choice but to declare the relationship null and void, lest he should lose a job he'd badly needed and cause problems for Zee, who had nowhere else to go if Cates summoned the courage to cut her loose. Enberg would likely suffer the consequences of his recent indiscretion with Cougar Ketchum and Raoul Leclerk. Zee, however, had become far too valuable to incur anything more than a brow beating for inviting Enberg to her room. Since Enberg had been warned off of her like a mongrel off a blooded bitch, she'd become even more powerful than Cates himself.

Enberg didn't know if she and Cates were aware of this shift in their fortunes. But he and everyone else in Mineral Springs were. Zenobia was the uncrowned queen of Cates's castle.

"The sofa will do," Zee said now, tapping a lovely foot on the carpeted floor. *"Vamos, pendejo!"*

CHAPTER FOUR

"Why the sofa, when the bed's so much more comfortable?" Enberg said. "Cates is over in Wilcox making a deal on horses for the stage line. He won't be home till tonight to get ready for tomorrow's run."

Enberg would be shotgun guard on that run, for that was his job now. How far he'd fallen from his short-lived stint as town marshal. But he had only himself to blame for that. Not Cates, the town council, or anyone else, though it was Cates who'd fired him.

Enberg had swallowed the hard fact that Logan Cates controlled his fate here in Mineral Springs. He had since he'd bought up nearly the entire town and half the county, and he likely would continue his control until Enberg had had his fill and moved on.

The trouble was, he had nowhere else to go. And he'd gotten himself ground in deep with Emily, Cates's stepdaughter . . .

Zee kept her cold stare on him. Such callous eyes for such a beautiful, half-dressed woman who looked as though she'd been well-planned and carefully crafted by the most loving of gods . . . or a god out to destroy every man who laid eyes on her . . .

Enberg sighed, rose from the bed, and walked to the overstuffed sofa in the parlor section of the paramour's chambers. This section of Zee's quarters was outfitted with a small brick fireplace, but there was no need for a fire now in the late Arizona summer, although Enberg was beginning to smell the perfume of mesquite and piñon around Mineral Springs after sunset.

A door led out to a balcony, but the drapes were drawn across the cracked door through which a refreshing breeze blew. From outside came the sounds of a town in the midafternoon—hoof clomps, mule brays, dog barks, occasional yells of men wrestling ranch or mining gear into heavy-axled Pittsburgh drays that would be climbing back into the surrounding mountains before dark, armed with Winchesters against potential Apache attacks.

Enberg sagged down on the sofa with a grunt. His denims had drawn taut across his lap. He groaned with sexual frustration and sank low on the cushions, stretching his long legs out and entwining his fingers behind his head.

Zee folded into the sofa beside him, crossing her legs and setting the basin on Dag's thigh. She leaned toward him, scrutinizing the gash on his temple and the long stream of mostly crusted blood running down that side of his bearded face.

She shifted her brown-eyed gaze from his torn temple to his eyes. "You are a *pendejo,* you know that? A dunderhead. Stubborn as a mule and just as destructive."

"Where's my thank you for coming to your rescue? That scum had his hand in your corset!"

She dipped a cloth in the water and dabbed at the cut. "Why so protective of a whore's tits?"

"You know why. *Ouch!* Easy, will ya?"

"Don't be a crybaby." He liked the way she spoke, putting the accent on "baby." He'd always like the Spanish lilts of her slightly raspy voice. The way she talked always intensified his desire for her. "They were goading you into a fight."

"They know me too well." Enberg grabbed her wrist. "Anyone treats you like that, they're gonna have me to deal with. Cates can go to hell. Anyone, you hear?"

Zee's eyes blazed. Her breasts rose and fell heavily. She lowered her gaze to his lap, arched her brows, and said, "It was a mistake, bringing you up here."

He grinned. "You knew what you were getting into. You know what you still do to me. You like what you still do to me."

Zee's cheeks flushed as she stared at him. Then her eyes sparked with anger, and she pressed her hand against his lap. "We could have run away together, *pendejo!* You had your chance to take me away from here, and you didn't take it!" She stared at him as if to ram the words into his thick skull. He tried to wrap his arm around her and draw her to him, but she pulled away, removing her hand from his lap.

She cursed again in Spanish, dipped the cloth in the water, and dabbed at the cut once more.

"Where would we have gone? What would we have done?"

She hiked a shoulder as she cleaned up the dried blood running in a jagged river down his bearded cheek. She scrubbed at him, pulling painfully on his beard. Somehow, the pain increased his desire. He looked at her well-filled corset, and then reached over and started to slide the strap of her camisole down her arm.

"*Dios mio*—no!" she said.

"Cates is gone."

"You had your chance." She continued scrubbing at the blood, tugging on his beard.

"You're a bitch—you know that, Zee."

She smiled. "*Si.*"

"You like it—don't you? The power you wield."

"*Si.* Who wouldn't?" Then her anger flared once more. "You had your chance, Dag. Now, get it out of your mind. You're married now."

"You don't want me to get it out of my mind. That's why you ordered me up here. You want to keep the flame burning every bit as much as I do . . . in spite of the fact that we had our chance, and now there's absolutely nothing that can come of it. Nothing except frustration."

Enberg shook his head. Anger now burned in his ears as he regarded the alluring, damning creature before him. One breast had nearly pushed out of her corset, exposing half of a tender pink nipple. "Christ, you're a devil!"

She dropped the cloth in the water and slapped him hard. The smack resounded throughout the room.

She jerked up her corset and glared down at him, eyes on fire, chest rising and falling more sharply than before. His cheek burned pleasantly. The blow had kicked up the pain in his temple, a pleasant sensation distracting him momentarily from his physical hunger.

He reached out to fondle a lock of brown hair spilling down her shoulder, but she pulled away from him and rose from the couch. "Go!" she said, pointing at the door. "Go now, Dag. You're right—it was a mistake bringing you up here. See the doctor. That cut needs stitches. I've done all I can do for you."

Enberg chuckled without mirth. "Whatever you say, my queen."

He rose a little unsteadily. She looked down at his pants. She smirked with satisfaction. She took a step back, crossed her arms on her breasts, and cocked one foot out before her, leaning back on her slender hip.

"When are you going to make me stop suffering, *chiquita*?" he asked her. "When are you going to make me stop paying for falling in love with you?"

Zee frowned as though she had no idea what he was talking about. "You've started drinking again, Dag. That was a big mistake."

Someone pounded on her door.

"Zee?"

It was Cates's voice.

She shot a quick, worried look at Enberg.

"Zee, I know he's in there!"

"Ah, shit," Enberg said, scowling at the door. "Wouldn't you know it—he's back early."

"Dag, I'll see you in my office," Cates called. *"Pronto!"*

His footsteps drifted off down the hall.

CHAPTER FIVE

Zee quickly wrapped a strip of flannel around Enberg's head, and showed him to the door.

"Give him my regards," she said, drawing her mouth corners down.

Enberg sighed and started out the door. Zee grabbed his arm, drawing him back to her. "Dag, I'm sorry," she said, shaking her head. "This is my fault. You're right. I enjoy torturing you. I don't know why."

"I know why," Enberg said. "You know why." He gazed at her. She looked genuinely regretful as she stared at his chest. Enberg shrugged and gave her chin an affectionate nudge. "What's the worst he can do—fire me?"

"He won't fire you," Zee said. "You're the best shotgun rider he has. Men fear you. No one would dare try robbing any of your coaches."

Enberg threw a parting arm up as he moved off down the hall. He was acting more nonchalant than he actually felt. The old, self-recrimination he'd experienced during his days of hardest drinking was rearing its ugly ahead again. With good reason.

He'd been a fool to allow Ketchum and Leclerk to goad him into a fight. He should have ignored them. He should have walked away. He would have if he hadn't been drinking, which he'd started doing again roughly a week ago, to lighten the oily darkness that washed over him every couple of months and that felt like a heavy blanket dipped in coal oil.

Suffocating.

During those times, the war and all his past mistakes came up to climb in bed with him every night, yelling in his ears, keeping him from sleeping.

The loneliness of those dark times was overwhelming even when his wife, Emily, lay right beside him, not three inches away. He wasn't worried about losing his job as shotgun messenger for Cates's Yuma Stage Line. Like Zee had said, there was no one better at the job. Besides, he was married to Cates's stepdaughter. While Emily and Cates had little time for each other, Cates wouldn't leave her out in the cold.

He'd have Gertrude to answer to if he did.

Enberg climbed the stairs to the second story and stopped outside Cates's office door, which was directly above that of his prized whore.

He knocked once.

"It's open," Cates said dryly.

Enberg opened the door and stepped into the office, which was as large as Zee's quarters. Cates stood looking out one of the two, partly open glass balcony doors flanking his desk, which was bathed in a trapezoid of golden sunlight. The green shade on his Tiffany lamp shimmered like spring cottonwood leaves.

Cates wore his usual claw-hammer coat and string tie, and he was smoking his usual cigar. Smoke wreathed his craggy, hollow-cheeked face as he glanced toward Enberg and said, "Want a drink?"

At first, Enberg thought he was serious. But then he recognized the glint of irony in the older man's gaze.

"No, thanks," Enberg said with a sigh.

Cates smiled. "Have a seat."

"No, thanks. I prefer to take my blows standing."

Cates chuckled as he puffed more smoke and stared out through the open balcony doors. "How's your head?"

"I've hurt myself worse crawling out of bed in the morning."

Cates continued to stare out the windows. He didn't say anything for a long time.

Enberg moved forward and placed two large, sun-reddened hands on the back of one of the two visitor chairs angled before Cates's wagon-sized, impeccably neat desk. Apprehension pricked the hairs under his shirt collar. Usually, when he was called into Cates's office, Cates laid into him right away, calling out his transgressions in much the way the Union cavalry officers used to lay out the day's skirmish strategy every morning during the war.

Cates taking his time reminded Enberg of a rattlesnake dozing in the shade of a barrel cactus. Sooner or later, he'd strike. And when he did, those hooked fangs would pull extra hard.

"By god, it's just flabbergasting to me," Cates said, and took another puff from the cigar.

"What is?" Enberg said, playing his part.

"How much this town has grown in the twenty years since your old man and my uncle built a cabin here and dug out the springs, started selling water to wagon trains on the old freight road. Two years later, they knocked together a hotel. Of sorts." Cates chuckled, shaking his head. "Who would have thought that hotel would become *this* one, truly a Diamond in the Rough, and there would be nearly thirty successful business establishments surrounding it within fifteen years."

"Didn't hurt that gold was discovered in the Mules."

"Hell, it was your old man who discovered it. Yes sir, your old man was a desert rat through and through. Even after he and my uncle built up several businesses, including a couple of saloons and a livery barn, and then ran the first stage relay station before establishing their own line from the New Mexico border to California, he preferred living out with the coyotes and rattlesnakes."

"He had gold on the brain, the old man did. Never brought it in, though. Was afraid someone would steal it from him . . . or backtrack him to his diggings."

"Hell," Cates said, "Olaf Enberg really didn't want that gold. He had no need for it. He had enough money coming in from the businesses that he and my uncle had established."

"So he stashed it," Enberg said. "Every nugget and grain of dust." He shook his head in frustration. It was rumored that Olaf Enberg had found a veritable mother lode of raw gold in the barrancas aproning the Mule and Anvil ranges, though of course no one knew for sure. He'd never shown anyone a grain of it.

"Too bad he was killed out there." Cates shook his head. "Maybe someday we'll be rid of those damn Apaches."

"It wasn't Apaches that killed my pa, Cates."

Cates turned to him, one silver-brown eyebrow arched with surprise. "Oh? Who, then?"

"I don't know. But it wasn't Apaches."

Enberg had always believed this but he'd never given voice to it. He had no idea why he was voicing it now. Maybe it was because all trails seemed to be converging here, suddenly, as they never would again, and he might not get another chance.

"Pa knew the Apaches. Hell, he was half-Apache himself. Maybe not by blood, but he'd been soaking up their ways, their beliefs, since he first came out here forty years ago. He knew them, and they, him. They respected each other. It was white men who killed my pa. Most likely white men out for his gold."

Cates studied Enberg for a time, as though working out the theory in his own mind. He puffed his cigar, knocked ashes into a tray on his desk, and then cast his gaze out the balcony doors once more.

"You know why I bring all this up, don't you?"

"Your uncle and my old man? I got no idea, Logan, but I

have a feeling you'll get to it sooner or later. But, no—I don't know what it has to do with Leclerk and Cougar Ketchum. If it's about Zee, somehow—she was just wrapping my head."

Cates laughed as though he were dealing with seven kinds of a fool.

CHAPTER SIX

Logan Cates finally stopped laughing and said, "It has nothing to do with Leclerk and Ketchum . . . and Zee . . . and it has *everything* to do with them, Dag."

"I think I will sit down, after all," Enberg said, slacking into one of the chairs fronting Cates's desk. "You're starting to make me a little dizzy, Logan. Never knew you to talk in riddles before."

Cates looked at him. He stared at him for a long time in a serious way that made Enberg deeply uncomfortable. It was as though Cates was staring right through him.

Finally, Cates laid his cigar in the ashtray on his desk, then walked over to a liquor cabinet standing against the back wall, near a potted palm tree and under a map of Arizona Territory that marked all of the relay stations and watering holes for Cates's Yuma Line. There was also an oil painting of the springs when there'd been nothing but the springs, the trail, and a livery barn here, nestled in a broad, chaparral-studded valley between rocky desert ranges.

Cates splashed bourbon into two goblets.

He brought one of the goblets over and slammed it down in front of Enberg, on the edge of Cates's desk. Whiskey splashed over the lip of the glass. Enberg found himself wincing at the waste.

He looked up at Cates, puzzled. Normally, Cates was easy to read. Enberg couldn't read anything in him now except a wash of cluttered, possibly competing emotions.

"Drink up," Cates said. "No point in stopping now, eh, Dag?"

Cates dropped down into the high-backed leather chair behind his desk, threw down half his drink, and leaned far back in the chair, entwining his hands behind his head. He would have been handsome if he hadn't lost the hair on top of his head—all save for a few, wiry stragglers, that was—and if his ears hadn't been so large. He'd lost weight over the years, the skin drawn taut across his bones. He was like an old Indian drum.

Also, his eyes were dull and flat, as though hiding the cunning Enberg knew was always behind them. His cheeks were sunburned from his recent ride to Wilcox. His forehead, which had been covered by his hat, was starkly pale in comparison. He didn't look well. But, then, age and the stress of doing so much business would probably do that to a person.

Enberg didn't touch his glass even though he wanted to swallow all the bourbon in one fell swoop. He found himself avoiding the drink, however, as though the glass were booby-trapped.

"I mention your old man and my uncle to draw a sharp distinction between them and you, Dag."

"Oh?"

"I was trying to draw a sharp contrast between what *they* did with their lives and what *you've* done with yours."

"Meaning . . ."

"Meaning that you ran off to the war, joining the Union forces in New Mexico and looking for adventure because you were tired of tending your old man's livery barn and the spring while he wandered the desert looking for gold. Meaning that the man who came back to Mineral Springs was a mere shadow of the man who'd left."

"For chrissakes, it was a long war. I lost a lot of friends and my old man to boot. I hadn't been expecting that!"

"Come on, Dag. You know the real reason you went downhill. You came home expecting the old man to not only be alive but rich. You thought you'd be rich, too."

"Yes, I did, Logan. I sure as hell didn't think he'd be dead. Nor that he'd left everything to you!"

"Not to me. To my uncle. They were like brothers."

"Let's not split hairs. When your uncle died, everything went to you."

"You know the reason for that as well as I do. Your father was mistakenly sent a telegram informing him you'd been killed at Cold Harbor. In his mind, he had no one else to leave his holdings to."

"That was convenient, wasn't it?"

"What are you implying?" Cates asked bitterly, eyes sharpening.

Enberg had his suspicions about who might have killed Olaf Enberg in the desert, to make it look like Apaches had done the dirty deed. He also had his suspicions about who might have sent his father the telegram erroneously informing him of his son's death in the war.

The telegram could have been a bureaucratic mistake. Or it might not have been . . .

"I know what you're thinking, Dag. None of it is true. You'd like it to be true, but it's not. You'd love to have come home to a rich father, a rich comfortable life. And because that isn't what you found here, you cracked. You became a whining drunk!"

Raw fury broiled up inside of Enberg. He ground his heels into Cates's dollar-a-yard carpet. He picked the drink up off the desk and tossed it back. That made the fury burn even hotter.

"You think you know it all, Cates. You think you do, but you don't. You don't know the half of what I've been through, because you never went to war. You never watched all of your

41

friends, wave after wave of them, die!"

"No, I didn't go to war, Dag. I promised my uncle I'd stay here and help him run his businesses. Lord knows you'd been ready to run out of here since you could walk! As soon as they started calling for troops, you went. If I'd left, too, there'd be nothin' here now but the springs and the Apaches!"

Cates threw his own drink back.

Enberg felt the rage cause his right cheek to twitch. But now his anger wasn't directed so much at Cates the man, but at the truth in what he'd said.

Staying here in the territory, Cates had had to fight his own war against the Apaches. There'd been little army left to prevent the Indians from reclaiming their ancestral lands after the legendary first gunshot at Fort Sumter, so Cates had hired his own militia of sorts.

As the stories went, he and the small militia made up of area settlers and freighters and retired soldiers and native Mexicans had managed to keep the two local war chiefs, Diri and Holds Thunder, from sacking the fledgling settlement of Mineral Springs.

Enberg's father had been of little help. By then, the settlement had grown enough that the silence of the desert had beckoned to the elder Enberg. He'd retreated with his picks and shovels into the rocks and cacti of his hidden diggings. Two years after Dag had gone off to join the Union forces against the Confederates, the elder Enberg's body was found, bristling with arrows and half eaten by coyotes.

A year later, Cates's uncle, Norman Century, had died after a wound from a Chiricahua arrow had turned gangrenous.

With both of Mineral Springs's founding fathers dead, their holdings willed to Cates, Logan had assumed control of their entire empire, still small at the time but growing.

He'd made sure it had continued to grow.

There'd been no one to contest the elder Enberg's will, for Dag was still at war and presumed dead by everyone in Mineral Springs. He wouldn't be back for another two years—one more year of bloody fighting and then another of whoring and drinking his way around New Orleans, Corpus Christi, and Houston, trying to rid his mind of the cannon blasts and the screams of men and horses, and of the smell of gunpowder and spilled human guts.

When he'd come back to find both the old men dead but their little spring developed into a bustling frontier outpost, he'd had little ground to stand on regarding proprietorial rights.

His father's holdings now belonged to Logan Cates. When he'd returned to Mineral Springs, all Enberg had owned were what was left of his nearly shredded uniform, his horse, his saber, his old Navy revolver, and a Sharps carbine forever stained with Confederate blood.

He didn't even know where his father's cached gold was. Olaf had never told him, though he'd assured him there was plenty. Olaf was not the kind of man to lie or even exaggerate. But he had been one to keep secrets. Dag was sure that in time his father would have told him where he'd stashed his gold, but he'd never gotten the chance.

Briefly after returning from the war, Enberg had had Zee. But then Cates had taken her, too.

At least Cates had had the decency to give him a job—first as a saloon bouncer and then as town marshal. But one more thing Enberg had brought back from the war was the bottle fever, so that when the Mineral Springs bank had been held up, he'd been too drunk to hear the gunfire or the screams of the two young girls who were killed, much less to organize a posse to pursue the culprits.

Until the next day, at least. By then, it was too late. The thieving killers had disappeared into Mexico.

Memory of that humiliation seared Enberg all the way to his loins.

He leaned forward in his chair, scowling, his cheeks as hot as irons. "All right, all right—let's just get to the point here, Logan. You gonna dock my pay? Make me pay for a couple of broken tables? Turn me over to Whipple for a couple of days in the hoosegow? Remember, you got a stage comin' in tomorrow, and you're gonna need me to ride shotgun."

He sat back in his chair, emboldened. Everything that really meant anything to him had already been taken away. There was nothing more for Cates to take. "Or . . . you gonna try to coax Emily back into your house with her mother? Go ahead, if you'll think she'll go. Hell, you don't even want her there yourself."

Cates stared at him flatly, slumped low in his chair. His thin lips formed a straight line beneath his pencil-stroke mustache.

Enberg chuckled. "While you think about it, I'm gonna refresh my drink." He grabbed his glass up off the desk and walked back to the liquor cabinet. He poured three fingers of whiskey into the glass, threw back half, and then walked back to Cates's desk.

Cates was still staring at him in that flat, dubious way of his, making Enberg wait. The thing of it was, Enberg wasn't worried. He had nothing left to lose, and Cates needed him to ride shotgun. There was no one better at the job, and damned few had the guts to ride shotgun messenger through a territory still often at the mercy of reservation-jumping Apaches, not to mention owlhoots of every stripe from both sides of the border.

Enberg sagged down into his chair.

He lifted his glass to his lips. Just as the bourbon began to sluice into his mouth, Cates said softly, almost as though he deeply regretted the words: "You're finished here, Dag. You're through. I'm firing you from the stage line. And I'm kicking you out of my town."

CHAPTER SEVEN

Enberg lowered his glass.

He swallowed the small bit of whiskey in his mouth. It clutched at his throat like something solid, choked him, made him cough. When he'd finally cleared the blockage, he blinked tears from his eyes and studied Cates across the desk, his heart thudding slowly but like a powerful fist hammering a table.

"You can't fire me, Logan. You know you can't. No one else is fool enough to take that job."

"I've got someone coming in from Lordsburg. A gunman. He won't be here until the end of the week, however, so you can take tomorrow's run. No doubt you can use every bit of pay you can squeeze out of me. After the run, I'll give you your time for the month. And then we'll be forking trails."

Enberg scowled in disbelief. "You got a gunman coming in from Lordsburg? That means you've been planning this for a while."

"Ever since I saw you drinking a beer downstairs. The first of last week, I think it was."

"You might have said something."

"I've said enough. I told you when I gave you this job that you had it only until you started drinking again."

"For chrissakes, Logan—it was only beer. Somethin' to cut the trail dust!"

Cates glanced at the whiskey glass in Enberg's hand. Enberg set it down. His hand was shaking slightly.

45

"All right, all right—don't forget the bourbon was your idea. But I'll quit with the beer." Enberg hated the fear and pleading he heard in his own voice. But, then, such emotions had become all too familiar. He heard them given voice inside his head every day and every night.

The shrill screams from the fear of what his life had become.

"You can't fire me, Logan. You know I'm good at it. Like no one else. And I need this job. I need it for me . . . and for Emily. She's with child, Logan—you know that!"

"What kind of a father would you make?" Enberg was knocked back in his chair by the chill in Cates's words. "You're a self-pitying drunk, Dag. I can't let you keep riding shotgun. Eventually, you're going to make another big mistake, and the line will suffer. You can't hold a job. You have nothing to your name but a little log prospector's cabin you bought for the back taxes.

"What kind of a life could you possibly provide for Emily? She comes from wealth, you cork-headed idiot! Hell, the only reason you married her in the first place was because Gertrude and I didn't want you to. Emily married you to defy me and her mother. Now you've impregnated her and started drinking again, and I expressly forbade you to do the latter while I'd assumed you were wise enough to prevent the former!"

Cates had climbed slowly up out of his chair until he stood now, leaning forward against the desk, staring coldly at Enberg. "Leave here, Dag. For the last time. Go ahead and make tomorrow's run, and I'll give you your full month's pay. Then pack your bags, saddle your horse, and get the hell out of Mineral Springs."

"You can do a lot to me, Logan," Enberg said, shaking his head slowly, stubbornly. "But you can't kick me out of town. The *entire* town is not yours. Not yet, anyway!"

"I'm not telling you to leave out of spite, Dag. I'm sure you won't believe this, but I'm honestly *strongly* suggesting you leave Mineral Springs so that you can discard all the old baggage that's weighed you down over the years, and start a new life for yourself. Somewhere fresh. Here, you're going nowhere but to an early grave.

"I don't say that merely because Raoul Leclerk has a lot of friends around here. I mean, you have no spirit left. No *real* will to live. You're broken. You've been broken ever since you came back to find your old man dead and his holdings in my hands. A broken spirit is as deadly as any knife one of Leclerk's or Ketchum's boys could stick in your back."

He paused. The two men locked gazes—two bulls locking horns.

"I know I'm partly to blame, Dag," Cates said, his voice pitched with honest regret. "But I had no option but to take over the holdings. If I hadn't, someone else would have. At least, I gave you your chance to work back into the business."

He pursed his lips and shook his head. "But, no, you were too proud to be a saloon bouncer or even the town marshal. Those jobs were beneath you. You wanted everything I had without having to work for it. So you stewed . . . and drank. And here you are drinking again, and I'm not going to watch it anymore. True, you're a good shotgun rider, but I'm sick of you. You've worn out your welcome. I'd rather have my stages held up than continue to prop up the lifeless scarecrow of a self-pitying man."

He thrust his arm out, pointing. "There's the door. I'll see you back here after the next run. That'll be the last time I ever see you again."

Enberg drew a heavy breath and released it. "Forget tomorrow's run. I'll take my time right now, Cates."

Cates straightened, sighing. "Now, huh?"

"If I'm so dispensable," Enberg growled, "I'm sure you can

find someone qualified to fill in for me tomorrow."

Cates nodded, flaring his nostrils. "Yes, I probably can. And will."

He turned to the small safe huddled on the floor behind him, to the right of a broad filing cabinet. He turned the knob back and forth, opened the door, rummaged around inside, then closed the door with a solid clang.

He tossed a small wad of bills down on his desk.

"There is thirty-five dollars. I've even paid you through tomorrow. Consider it your severance pay. Now, take your money and leave. And remember, Dag, I never want to see you again. Understand?"

Enberg gathered up the money. "If you do?"

"I'm going to keep Whipple from arresting you for Leclerk . . . until tomorrow noon." A corner of Cates's mouth curled in a menacing leer.

"All right, Logan." Enberg headed for the door. He placed his hand on the knob and turned back to Cates. "Have it your way, Logan. You always have had it your way, haven't you?"

Fury threatening to cause his head to explode, Enberg left the office.

He trod heavily down the stairs and into the saloon where Kettleson and his half-breed bouncer, Billie Two Doves, were cleaning up the place. Cougar Ketchum was nowhere in sight.

Enberg ignored a glare from the barman and stepped out onto the front porch. A horse and buckboard wagon had been pulled up near where Leclerk had fallen, and the town undertaker, Merlyn Hodges, and Hodges's idiot son, Johnny, were loading the body into the wagon.

A couple of dogs were running around the wagon, barking excitedly. Two small groups of boys watched from both sides of the street, wide-eyed, touched by the same excitement as the dogs.

Death was a thrilling spectacle . . . unless, of course, you'd spent four long years hip-deep in it. Enberg hadn't actually tried to kill Leclerk. He hadn't been aiming for the man's throat but for his head, which was a lot harder to damage.

Oh, well—the world was better off with one less bully in it.

"What do you have to say for yourself, Dag?"

Enberg turned to see the diminutive Geylan Whipple standing to his right; Whipple's shoulder was several inches below Enberg's. Whipple was a steely-eyed, wiry, waxen-faced Texan who'd been quite the regulator in his day, before he'd become a stock detective and then the town marshal of several frontier towns in Kansas and Oklahoma.

He was old now but still ramrod straight and cool-headed. He wore impeccably neat, clean wool suits with a crisp gray Stetson perched smartly atop his gray, bullet-shaped head. He kept his town marshal's badge polished to a high shine.

Commanding a certain respect for his former gun prowess, he was managing to keep Mineral Springs relatively quiet, though the weekends were always a challenge. Whipple had three deputies on his roll, however, and though they weren't cut from the same cloth as Whipple—far from it, in fact—they were so far doing a fair job of keeping the match from touching the fuse of the powder keg that any frontier town could still become, given the right ingredients.

Enberg said, "Talk to Logan about it, Geylan. He'll tell you what I have to say."

Whipple frowned up at Enberg, wrinkling his small, straight nose. "Is that liquor on your breath?"

"Like I said, Geylan," Enberg said, "talk to Logan. He'll tell you all about it."

As Enberg dropped down the porch steps and started moving into the street, Whipple said, "Oh, I'll talk to him, all right. Don't I always? Headin' that way now . . ."

Enberg crossed the main street and headed for a footpath that would take him to his and Emily's shack on the edge of Mineral Springs. He was cursing under his breath as he walked.

But the only person he was cursing now was himself . . . and wondering how he was going to explain the recent turn of events to the young woman who was carrying his child.

CHAPTER EIGHT

The place Enberg called home was an old prospector's shack backed by an arroyo and a fringe of dusty mesquites and willows. It sat at the very edge of town and was flanked by a rocky outcropping of salmon-colored sandstone that rose to an east-sloping mesa.

There had been an old mine in the side of the mesa, but rockslides had gradually filled it in over the years. The area back there was rife with Mojave green rattlers, making perilous to the point of near-suicide a casual evening's stroll along an old path likely carved by the original prospector walking to and from his mine.

Enberg had learned to avoid the area. Occasionally he'd find the nasty vipers slithering into the yard between the outhouse and the cabin, and he'd shoot them and chop them up for the stew pot.

He had a feeling that the original prospector had had his fill of rattlesnake stew. There was probably a nest nearby, but try as he could, Enberg had never found it.

He stopped at the edge of the yard, between two mesquites whose long, slender leaves flashed silver with the slanting afternoon light. Emily was out in front of the cabin, using a metal can to water the two rosebushes that stood to either side of the cabin's door and which were climbing the trellis that Enberg had built for them at Emily's bidding soon after they were married by a justice of the peace in Tucson.

She was a slender girl of twenty-two with a long, pale neck. She wore a plain brown print housedress, and she had pinned her copper-colored, curly hair into a messy bun at the top of her head.

The former Emily Dayton always had an air of serenity about her, but Enberg knew her heart to be troubled. Her father's early passing had left her wounded despite her mother's attempt at distracting her from the pain by shipping her off to a finishing school somewhere in the east—Enberg couldn't recall where, exactly.

Emily hailed from wealth, but it had been a wealth that she had felt smothered by, especially following her beloved father's passing. She hated her mother, and anyone who knew Gertrude—except Logan Cates, apparently—knew why as soon as they met the woman. That she was a demon straight out of hell's bowels had been obvious to Enberg the first time he'd met her. That she'd somehow squandered her fortune on the heels of her husband's passing from a heart stroke hadn't dulled her fangs in the least.

"Dag!" Emily called, having turned to see her husband watching her from the edge of the yard.

She dropped her watering can and strode lightly toward him, swinging her arms and smiling brightly, the spray of freckles across her face looking darker now in the sunlight, her blue eyes as bright and shiny as a pure mountain lake. "To what do I owe the honor, kind si . . . ?" She let her voice trail off as she frowned at him. "My god, Dag—what happened to your head?"

Enberg hemmed and hawed for a moment, fingering the bandage through which he could feel the oily wetness of his blood. "It's nothing, honey."

"Dag, you're bleeding!"

She stopped before him and rose onto her tiptoes to inspect the bandage.

"I just found myself between two drunk miners goin' after each other with shovels—that's all. You can't walk through town without comin' on two or three fights. The place is getting too big for its own damn good."

"You mean you broke up a fight?"

"If I hadn't, those two fellas would have killed each other." Enberg was vaguely surprised at how easy lying had gotten for him lately.

"Instead, it looks like they nearly killed *you*!"

"It's not as bad as it looks, Em. Really."

"Are you sure?"

"Positive."

Emily wrapped her arms around his neck, rose onto her tiptoes again, and pecked his lips. "Well, I'm happily surprised to see you. I thought for sure that after your meeting with Logan you'd find a poker game somewhere along the old wash."

Her mention of his "meeting" with Logan drew Enberg up short. How did she know?

But then he remembered that he'd told her he was walking into town for an afternoon meeting, and it was this mythical meeting she'd meant—not the actual one in which he'd just been fired. He hadn't wanted her to know he'd been going to town merely to drink beer and to play pool.

Her mention of poker had been an allusion to Enberg's predilection for gambling with the old retired miners and prospectors who lived in shacks along Cavalry Wash, just south of Mineral Springs. He enjoyed spending time with the old salts. They reminded him of his father, who'd been the eldest of them all.

Besides, they brewed the best ale in central Arizona . . .

For some reason, Emily's mention of the wash annoyed him. He supposed he felt guilty for so often feeling the need to escape her.

"Well, you can see I'm here, right, Em? So could we let the wash go now?"

"What's the matter? What happened?" Emily reached up to sandwich his face in her hands and to scowl up at him worriedly. She always seemed to be gauging his moods, a habit he found no less annoying for being understandable. She was, after all, deeply sensitive. And he was, after all, as moody as a mountain winter.

"What do you mean?" Enberg asked, trying to smile but feeling as though his face were a mask of clay.

"I can see it in your eyes. Something's wrong. You're troubled."

"Nah, not really," Enberg said. "Just one of those days, I reckon."

"How did the meeting go?"

Enberg stared at her. He opened his mouth to begin to tell her what had happened, but then he closed it. Somehow, he found himself unable to tell his wife that Cates, her mother's husband who'd given him several second chances, had fired him. Again.

Shame blew threw him like a hot summer wind.

He tried again. He had to tell her sooner or later, after all. Again, the words wouldn't come. He just couldn't do it.

"Dag, honey, what is it?" Emily asked.

"Nothin'. Nothin' at all." He felt weak and helpless. Weak and worthless. He couldn't even convey the bad news to his wife. He had to leave town tomorrow, so he had to tell her sometime.

Later . . .

"Right now I'd just like to lie down and take a little nap," he said.

"A nap, eh?" Emily pressed her breasts against his chest and wrapped her arms around his thick neck. In her irritating, little girl's voice, she said, "How 'bout if we go upstairs together and I make you feel all better?"

She pressed her hand to his crotch. It felt nothing like how Zee's hand had felt a short time ago. He found himself wanting to brush it away.

"Do you think that would be a good idea?" Enberg said. "In your condition, I mean . . ."

"I'm only two months along. Your son . . . or daughter . . . won't feel a thing." Emily looked down at her flat stomach, then looked up at him, smiling lustily and biting her lower lip. "That's just like you, though. To always be so gentle with me."

Enberg tried another smile. He did not want to make love to his wife. Guilt hammered him for it. But, what the hell? Spending the afternoon with Emily in bed would buy him some time before he had to face the fact that he'd been kicked out of town. Forced to leave his wife and unborn child.

He felt even guiltier because the truth was that after all that had gone wrong here in Mineral Springs and knowing that Zee could never be his, he was ready to go. On his way over here from the saloon, he'd fleetingly considered just saddling a horse and riding out of town without saying a word to anyone, including Emily.

He was ready to leave his wife and unborn child.

Self-revulsion mingled with his guilt. What kind of a monster was Dag Enberg, anyway?

"Dag?" Emily stared up at him, head tipped to one side, one eye narrowed.

"What is it?"

"You did . . . you didn't see her . . . did you? In town . . . ?"

"Who?" His heart thudded. His ears warmed.

"You know. Zee. You didn't see her in the Diamond, did you? I mean, I know she works there, and all. And I know . . ." Emily glanced toward town, then turned back to him, sliding a stray lock of copper hair away from her freckled cheek. "I know you still carry a torch for her."

"No." Enberg suddenly couldn't have felt more uncomfortable if his boots had been filled with Mojave green rattlers. "No, no, no—of course not. We're ancient history—Zee and I." He kissed Emily's cheek. "Don't you know that?"

Before she could answer, he picked her up in his arms and spun her around, faking lusty laughter.

"Oh, Dag!" Emily cried, laughing.

Enberg carried his wife into the cabin. He kicked the door closed. As he did, three men stepped out of the mesquites and willows at the edge of the yard. All three were armed with pistols and holding rifles.

One was Cougar Ketchum, who peered out through badly swollen eyes.

CHAPTER NINE

Enberg kicked the front door closed. He didn't bother to lock it. No one had ever bothered him out here at the edge of town. There was no reason to. Everyone knew he wasn't riding shotgun for Logan Cates because he'd found his father's treasure.

He was as poor as the most raggedy-heeled Apache.

It didn't occur to him that anyone would try to even the score so soon for what had happened at the Diamond earlier.

He carried Emily up the rickety stairs to the loft over the kitchen, the ancient staircase squawking and swaying beneath his weight. As he did, he looked around their cozy but sparsely, crudely furnished shack. It wasn't much.

Emily had come from so much more. Dag would be doing her a favor by sending her back to Cates and her mother. Emily might not agree, but in time she'd see how much better off she was.

"What are you thinking about?" Emily asked in a perplexed tone as he gained the loft.

He laid her down on the bed topped with a colorful quilt Emily had made last winter. He leaned toward her, brushing stray strands of her hair from her cheeks with his thumbs. "How can you stand living here, after how you were raised? So much money, so many nice things . . ."

"I like it," Emily said. "Because I share it with you. Besides, it's simple. Coming from a life like mine, you come to appreciate simple things. All of those furnishings, all of that money, does not come cheap, you know, Dag. There are many expectations and obligations."

"Expectations like not marrying beneath yourself?"

Emily sighed, scowling at him. She tugged at his ears. "All right, here we go again. The same old conversation about how poor you are. I love you, Dag Enberg, and I always will. You're just in another one of your moods. Now, climb out of those clothes and lie down here and let your wife please you the way only *I* can!"

Chuckling coquettishly, she squirmed around beneath him, igniting his desire.

Enberg rose from the bed. He kicked out of his boots and began undressing. As he did, Emily rose to a sitting position and began shucking out of her dress. She removed the comb from her hair and let the copper tresses tumble to her shoulders.

Enberg watched her lift her thin chemise up over her head and toss it onto a chair. Her pale breasts were small and firm, with inordinately large nipples. She followed his gaze to the orbs, and cupped them in her hands.

"You like me now, don't you?" she said in that little girl's voice again, and looked at his stiffening manhood. She reached for him, caressed him gently, then pulled him toward her by his shaft.

She pressed her lips to it, then looked up at him smoky-eyed.

"Come now . . . come and make love to your woman . . . the only woman who really loves you, Dag Enberg, you moody man."

She pulled him down to her. He slid his hands beneath her thighs and pulled her farther up on the bed. He lay down between her spread knees. She stared doe-eyed up at him as she wrapped her hand around him, and directed him into her waiting portal.

"Oh," she whispered, tipping her head back onto the bed and closing her eyes. "Oh, Dag . . ."

As he thrust his hips toward hers, sliding farther and farther inside her, he stared down at her face, slack with passion. But it was no longer Emily's face. It was Zee's face, her thick, dark-brown hair spilling thickly across her pillow, framing her cameo-beautiful countenance, rich red lips stretching back from her fine white teeth with the passion of their coupling.

As he thrust against her, harder and harder, the headboard battering the wall, Zee opened her eyes. But now it was not Zee's brown eyes but Emily's blue eyes. She stared up at him with vague accusation even as she winced and groaned with each thrust of his hips against hers. It was as though she knew, if only half-consciously, that it was not her he was making love to in his mind.

The hard look in those blue eyes began to distract him, to dampen his passion. He slowed his thrusts.

But then Emily's eyes grew soft and passionate once more. She smiled, wrapped her arms around his neck, and drew his head down beside hers. She moaned into his ear, "Oh, yes! Oh, yes, Dag—*yes!*"

Finally, when their joint spasms ceased, he rolled onto his back beside her. Emily closed her legs, rolled toward him, and kissed his cheek. "There, now," she said, purring like a kitten, running her hand through the hair on his broad chest. "Don't you feel better?"

"Mm-hmmm."

She snuggled up against him. But his desire to be close to her had been spent with his passion. He hated himself for feeling this way. Again, he wondered what was ailing him. Why had he married her? He'd thought he'd loved her. Had he only married her to try and distract himself from Zee?

The thought of their baby coming in seven months gave him

no joy whatever.

Enberg dropped his legs over the side of the bed. "I'd best split some wood so you can get supper goin'."

"We could lie here for a while. It's not too warm up here today."

He inwardly recoiled at the pressure of her hand on his back. As though she sensed his aversion, she said in her little girl's voice, "Do you love me, Dag?"

"Of course I do, Em." He smiled over his shoulder at her.

"Say it, then, please."

"I love you, Em."

She smiled and pressed her lips to his left shoulder blade. "I love you, too, Dag Enberg."

"Now, why don't I bring that wood in?" He rose stiffly from the bed and stretched. "I'm gettin' hungry."

"I'll make you something good," Emily said, striding over to the washstand. "You just wait and see if I don't. I can cook as well as any other woman in this town," she added in a playfully defensive tone.

That her cooking skills were lacking was a joke between them. She'd never learned how to cook while growing up, because her parents had hired others to perform such onerous tasks. While the food had been cooked and delivered on carts to the dining room, the family had milled about on the porch or in the drawing room, reading or listening to Emily play the piano.

While Emily gave herself a quick sponge bath at the washstand, and dressed, Enberg dressed slowly, thoughtfully, sluggish from the effects of the beer and whiskey and the lovemaking. Emily buttoned her shoes, wrapped her arms around Enberg, giving him an annoyingly hard squeeze, groaning with her love for him, and then started down the stairs, her shoes clomping loudly on the steps.

Enberg stomped into his boots.

Downstairs, Emily gave a loud but clipped scream. Enberg jerked with a start. He turned his head toward the stairs.

"What is it?"

She'd probably seen another rat. Somehow, they kept working their way through the loose chinking between the cabin's logs. They were probably running from the rattlesnakes.

It was not Emily's voice that answered him. It was a man's voice.

"Come on down here, Dag."

CHAPTER TEN

Recognizing Cougar Ketchum's voice, Enberg reached for his double-barreled, sawed-off shotgun hanging from the back of a chair by its lanyard.

"Leave the shotgun," Ketchum said, tauntingly.

Anxiety rippled through Enberg as he walked around the bed to peer over the rickety balcony rail into the main cabin ten feet below. Ketchum was slacked into Enberg's rocking chair, near the cold stone hearth on the far side of the small shack. He wasn't holding a weapon. He stared up at Enberg grimly, both eyes blackened, a pale bandage wrapped around the top of his head.

Two other men from Ketchum's gang were down there with Ketchum. None were Ketchum's brothers, though Enberg thought Ray McInally was a cousin. Enberg had heard that the Ketchums had had a falling out in prison. Leclerk would have been down there, too, if he wasn't being fitted for a wooden overcoat.

Ray McInally sat at the crude kitchen table, slowly building a cigarette while smiling up at Enberg. A man appropriately called "Ugly" Tom stood near the door. He held Emily before him, the upcurved tip of a Bowie knife pressed taut against her neck.

Emily stared up at Enberg, eyes alive with horror.

Ugly Tom grinned from beneath his tobacco-brown Stetson. The right side of his face had been badly burned when a peeved whore had thrown a lit lamp at him. That eye was mostly eggshell white with a smear of blue peering out as though through a frosty windowpane.

Enberg cursed himself in silence. He should have locked the door. He hadn't expected Ketchum to make a play on him so soon, if at all. Ketchum wasn't known for his spine.

"You dislocated my jaw!" Ketchum said, pointing angrily up at Enberg. "Get down here!"

"Don't try nothin', neither," warned Ugly Tom, "or I'll cut her purty head off!"

"She is purty, ain't she?" said McInally, a Tennessean who hadn't been playing with a full deck since the war. "Awful purty. Me—I'd like to have a go at her, too!"

He reached under the table and squirmed lewdly around in his chair.

They'd been here the whole time, Enberg thought. Listening to him and Emily upstairs. His heart thudded with fury.

"I said get down here, Dag," Ketchum said, leaning far forward in his chair and jutting his lower jaw. "Or I'm gonna tell Ugly Tom to bleed her dry!"

"Take it easy," Enberg said, starting down the stairs. "Let her go. She's got no part in this."

"She has a big part in this," Ketchum said, fingering the swollen, purple skin around his right eye.

Enberg glanced at Emily. She stared at him, horrified. Ugly Tom had his head thrust up close against hers. The tip of the Bowie knife had burrowed far enough into Emily's freckled neck that a very small bead of dark-red blood shone at the top of the blade.

"Go ahead and take a seat by Ray there," Ketchum said. "And keep your hands above the table."

Ray McInally was slowly rolling his quirley closed, keeping his eyes on Enberg.

Dag walked around behind the table and sat in a chair around the corner of the table from McInally. The chair squawked as he eased into it. He had his back to the black range. He was facing the front wall and Ugly Tom and Emily.

"All right—I'm sitting," Enberg said, placing his hands palm down on the oilcloth-covered table. "Let her go. She had nothing to do about what happened at the Diamond."

"We ain't here about the Diamond," Ketchum said. "We was plannin' on payin' you a visit all along, even before the Diamond. Truth be told, I was surprised to see you over there, Dag. I'd heard you'd given up the bottle. But there you was, drinkin' an' playin' pool and makin' time with—"

"I wasn't makin' time with anybody." Enberg interrupted the man, glancing sheepishly at Emily. "I was just playing pool and nursing a beer."

Ketchum glanced at Emily, who was frowning at Enberg.

"Well, now, you call it what you want," Ketchum said, grinning now as he realized he'd struck a tender nerve. "But you was there, and Zee was there, and you seemed to take it sorta personal when I tried to buy an hour of her time." He spoke to Emily. "In fact, he killed poor ole Leclerk over it. Busted his windpipe, most like. Terrible way to die."

Deep lines stretched across Emily's forehead now as she continued to stare incriminatingly, heartbrokenly, at Enberg, who pressed his hands down hard against the table.

"They were mistreating her," Enberg told his wife. "I would have done what I did for anyone."

"Oh, but the way I heard it," Ketchum said, "you went up to the whore's room afterwards."

"Just to have that notch you carved in my forehead tended!"

"Well, now, you call it what you like." Ketchum laughed and rocked back in his chair, thoroughly satisfied with himself.

Enberg glanced at Emily again. The disappointment in her eyes was a knife to his heart.

He turned to Ketchum, fury burning in his cheeks. "What in the hell do you want, Cougar? Time to settle up for what happened in the Diamond? Or for your old man? Well, Emily had nothin' to do with any of that. Let's you an' me go outside!"

"I told you, Dag," Ketchum said, mildly, "the Diamond ain't what we're here for. That was a good, old-fashioned hoedown. I ain't mad. Serious. I ain't mad about that. Now, about Pa—you an' me will talk about that someday. I'm gonna save it. I'm here today to see about a favor."

"A favor."

"That's right—a favor." McInally snapped a match to life on his thumbnail.

"What favor?"

Ketchum said, "On your way back from tomorrow's run, you're gonna have Charlie Grissom stop the stage at Bayonet Creek, and you're gonna toss down the strongbox you'll be carryin'. There'll be several fellas from my gang waitin' for you. You won't see them, but they'll be there, watchin' from cover. You're gonna leave the box with them in the wash, and ride on."

Enberg just stared at him.

Ugly Tom chuckled through his teeth, his blind eye rolling around like a marble in its socket. McInally drew deeply on his quirley and then blew the smoke out in a gust of laughter. "I don't think he understands, Cougar. You musta scrambled his brains for him!"

"What's to understand?" Ketchum said. "It's really purty simple."

Enberg studied him. Then he looked at Ugly Tom.

"I think he gets it just fine," said Ketchum. "If you don't leave that strongbox in the wash, your darlin' bride—who we heard has a bun in her oven—is gonna be missin' her purty head. Now, I realize you're more fond of one dark-eyed little

whore over at the Diamond, but this one here . . . why, she's gonna bear your child, Dag. Now, ain't that somethin'? One more Enberg in the world!"

Ugly Tom laughed through his teeth. He pressed his hand to Emily's belly. She groaned with revulsion, squirming in his arms.

Enberg turned to Ketchum. He didn't know what was in the strongbox. He never knew what Cates was shipping, often in league with Wells Fargo. It had only been his job to make sure that the box made it to its destination.

Somehow, Ketchum must have found out what Cates was shipping. Otherwise, he wouldn't have concocted the scheme for securing the box. Ketchum's cowardly method didn't surprise Enberg. Enberg had a reputation as a formidable shotgun messenger, and none of Ketchum's men were known for their gun savvy. They didn't want to take their chances with Enberg out on the trail.

They were not the brightest bunch of border outlaws that Enberg had ever known. But he had to admit that Ketchum had concocted a smart if devious plan.

Ketchum said, "Me an' the boys will stay right here with your darlin' bride . . . and her baby . . . until we get word you left the box in Bayonet Creek. Don't worry how we'll know whether you left it or not. We'll *know*, Dag."

Enberg glared at him, his chest rising and falling heavily. "What's the matter, Cougar? Tired of rustling cattle and horses? Of kidnapping Apache girls to sell as slaves down in Mexico? Decided to move up in the world, did you?"

"That's right," Ketchum said dully. "You got it, Dag."

"The money you flashed over at the Diamond ain't enough for you?"

"No," Ketchum said, slowly shaking his head. "It's not."

Enberg flared his nostrils at the ugly, raggedy-heeled outlaw.

"The joke's on you. He fired me."

"What's that?"

"Cates," Enberg said. "He fired me. For drinkin' after he warned me not to."

He glanced quickly at Emily, who did not react to the information. Tears continued to slide down her cheeks as she stared at her husband beseechingly, wanting him to do something, anything, to get that knifepoint removed from her throat.

Ketchum's swollen left eye twitched nervously as he considered the news. "And for goin' up to Miss Zee's room," he said, sneering, glancing again at Emily. "He warned you off of that whore, too, you damn fool."

"Your plan won't work, Cougar. You caused the trouble, and you got me fired. You did all this for nothin'. Now, tell Ugly Tom to ease that knife away from Emily's throat. You boys might as well pack up and head out, go on back to rustlin' cows for a living. That's more your style, anyway."

He knew he was pushing his luck by airing his spleen so venomously, but he couldn't help himself.

Slowly, Cougar Ketchum rose from the rocking chair. He glared hard at Enberg as he walked toward the table. He walked around behind McInally and stopped near Enberg's chair, staring down at him, eyes flinty, his lower jaw jutting.

He stared at Enberg for nearly a full minute before he smashed his right fist into Enberg's side.

"Dag!" Emily cried.

Enberg clutched his battered ribs and groaned in misery, trying to draw a breath. Ketchum had slugged him hard.

"Get them hands back up on the table, Dag!" Ketchum ordered.

Sucking air through his teeth, Enberg placed his hands on the table. He glared up at Ketchum through pain-blurry eyes.

Ketchum stared down at him, giving his chin a slow dip. "You get it back. You hear? You get your job back tomorrow, and you get aboard that stage. If that strongbox ain't in the wash at Bayonet Creek tomorrow afternoon, Ugly Tom and ole Ray is gonna do whatever they want to your lovely, freckled bride . . . and then cut her throat."

Emily dropped her chin, sobbing.

"There's somethin' I'd like to do to her right now," McInally said, grinning goatishly at Emily. "I'd like to have me some o' what Enberg just got. Sure would." He slapped the table and whistled, feasting his eyes on Emily's writhing body. "Look at that!"

Enberg jerked his enraged gaze to McInally. "You try anything like that, you ugly goat, and first chance I get I'll gut you like a fish. There'll be nowhere you can hide!"

McInally's faced turned red. The outlaw rose tensely from his chair and reached for one of the two Colt Navies holstered on his hips.

"Step down, Ray!" Ketchum ordered. "He ain't gonna do us any good dead—now, is he? Step down! You'll get another chance at him. Later."

"He's got a mouth on him," McInally said, fuming. "Always has. And I've always wanted to bust it for him."

"You'll get your chance. For now, fetch some rope and tie him. Tie her, too." Ketchum strode slowly, confidently, back to the rocking chair. "It's gonna be a long night till tomorrow."

CHAPTER ELEVEN

Enberg jerked his head up with a start.

He must have dozed off.

Blinking his eyes into focus, he looked around the cabin. The shutters were drawn back from the windows, allowing in the cool desert air spiced with night.

The sun had long since gone down. Two lamps burned low—one bracketed to the wall to his left, another on a table in the cabin's small parlor area.

Ketchum was asleep in Enberg's rocking chair, head thrown back, snoring. Ugly Tom slept in a chair beside the door, chin dipped to his chest. McInally sat on the short leather sofa against the back wall, to the right of the fireplace. He had one boot hiked on a knee. He held a cold cigarette stub in his right hand, resting on the sofa beside him. His head was canted to one side, and his eyes were closed. He, too, was softly snoring.

A stack of cards sat beside him, near the hand holding the cigarette. The last time Enberg had looked McInally's way, the outlaw had been laying out a game of solitaire.

Hours ago, just before sundown, Ketchum had ordered McInally to tie Emily to the bed in the loft. Nothing but silence up there now. Dag couldn't imagine that she'd fallen asleep, as scared as she was, but he himself had nodded off. Maybe Emily had, as well.

Emily.

He might not have loved her, but he'd be damned if he'd let

these dogs have their way with her, to kill her and the baby. Enberg now wished he'd followed his gut instinct, however lowly it had been, to avoid the cabin and to saddle a horse and ride out of there without saying goodbye to Emily.

They'd have both been better off.

Now, he'd just gotten her in even deeper trouble.

And from Ketchum she'd heard about Zee.

Christ!

Enberg put his head down and, gritting his teeth, worked at the ropes tying his wrists together behind his back. He cursed under his breath. McInally had tied him tight.

As he worked at the ropes, his chair gave a squawk against his shifting weight.

Ketchum stopped snoring.

Enberg looked at the outlaw. Ketchum opened his eyes and lowered his head. He'd removed his hat, which hung off the chair's left arm. His matted hair curled down over his eyes.

Blinking, Ketchum looked at Enberg. His eyes seem to shed the opaqueness of sleep. Scowling, the outlaw rose from the chair, walking quietly over to stand beside the shotgun rider.

"What you up to, Dag?"

"Go diddle yourself."

Ketchum leaned to the side to inspect the ropes binding Enberg's wrists behind the chair. He pulled at the ropes with his left hand. Then he buried his right fist into Enberg's side.

Enberg grunted as the fiery pain bit him deep, hammering the air out of his right lung. Those ribs were still tender from the first punch.

"You chickenshit bastard," Enberg bit out.

Ketchum chuckled and punched him again.

A wave of almost unendurable agony washed through Enberg. His ribs felt as though they were grinding against each other, nerves exposed.

"Don't do nothin' stupid, Dag."

Ketchum walked back to the chair, sat down, yawned, folded his arms on his chest, and went back to sleep.

Enberg didn't sleep for the rest of the long, miserable night.

He simply sat there, charting the very slow, gradual abatement of the pain in his ribs and trying to come up with a way out of this dire situation. By dawn, when the outlaws rose, stretching from their slumber, he'd come up with nothing.

They stoked the stove and brought Emily down from the loft to make breakfast. As she did, she didn't look at Enberg except to cast him a couple of fleeting, accusatory glances. Everyone except Enberg ate the beans and bacon she cooked. The outlaws didn't want to risk untying the big shotgun rider.

That was all right. Enberg wasn't hungry. His stomach was churning with the anxiety of the situation. In order to keep Emily alive, he had to turn over a strongbox when the only thing he'd ever been good at since returning to Mineral Springs from the war was *holding onto strongboxes.*

After Ketchum and the other two men had eaten, they sat around for another hour, sipping coffee. Emily cleaned the kitchen, knocking pans around behind Enberg, who sat in the same chair he'd spent the night in, staring dully out before him, the stoniness of his features belying the storm raging within.

Ketchum must have known that under normal circumstances Enberg would be expected at work at nine. The outlaw checked his tarnished silver timepiece at eight-thirty, and ordered McInally to untie him.

When McInally had cut the ropes, Ketchum grabbed Emily and drew her taut against him, drawing his pistol, pressing the barrel against her head, and clicking the revolver's hammer back.

"Please," Emily said, sobbing. *"Please!"*

Ketchum stared at Enberg, who sat glaring back at him, rubbing blood back into his hands.

"You know what you gotta do, Dag. You do it right, and you'll come home to find this purty little gal waitin' for you. You do it wrong, you'll come home to find her in bloody pieces all around this cabin."

"Dag!" Emily sobbed.

"Don't worry, honey," Enberg said, sliding his chair back and gaining his feet.

He moved over to her, staring down at her. He took her chin between his thumb and index finger. "Don't worry. I'm going to do what they want. You'll be all right."

He looked at Ketchum and shook his head slowly, hardening his jaws. "If you hurt her, so help me."

"Yeah, yeah—you just get your tail on over to the Diamond and kiss Cates's ass nice and soft. If you don't get your job back, that means you ain't followed through, and she's *dead*—understand?"

Enberg drew a deep breath. Ketchum glanced at Ugly Tom standing at the bottom of the stairs, holding Enberg's double-barreled coach gun and leather bandoliers filled with shotgun wads. Ugly Tom tossed Enberg the gun. Dag snatched it out of the air. Then he caught the bandoliers and looped them over his broad chest.

He inspected the twelve-gauge Greener.

"It's empty," Ugly Tom said, gloating, as though Enberg would find that surprising.

Enberg dropped the lanyard over his neck and around his shoulder and grabbed his hat off a wall peg. "If I come back and find you didn't hold up your end of the deal, it won't be." He glanced around at the three outlaws, savage threat in his gaze. "I'll track you down and show you the hard way."

"Enough tough talk, Dag," Ketchum said. "You tuck your

tail between your legs and get on over to the Diamond and hope like hell Cates gives you your job back. *Vamos!*"

CHAPTER TWELVE

Enberg crossed the wash and headed into town.

It was a fresh morning only just now beginning to heat up, though the shotgun rider noted this in only a vague, half-conscious way. His brain boiled with rage and frustration as well as humiliation.

How could his life have gone so wrong?

If only the old man hadn't died out in the desert. That had been the beginning of Enberg's bad luck here in Mineral Springs. If that hadn't happened, he'd be Cates's equal now.

He'd be above such demeaning circumstances.

He took the shortest route to the Diamond in the Rough, meandering around log or adobe brick cabins and stock pens outlying the business section. He walked up through a trash-strewn gap between two business buildings and came out on the main road, Arizona Street, which traced a slow curve through the heart of Mineral Springs.

He paused before Zebrow's Barber Shop when he saw the dusty Concord stagecoach parked out front of the saloon/hotel, passengers just then being helped into the coach by George Wilkes, an ex-miner who worked as a bouncer in the Diamond and as an occasional relief shotgun messenger for the Yuma Line.

Charlie Grissom, the jehu, sat in the driver's boot, arranging the leather ribbons in his gloved hands, while the fresh six-horse hitch stomped and blew and switched their tails, eager to get running.

The strongbox was already in place atop the roof behind Grissom, chained and locked.

Enberg started forward, wending his way through the early-morning traffic. He brushed past Wilkes as Wilkes closed and latched the coach door.

"I'm takin' the run, George," Enberg said, climbing up into the driver's boot.

"Hey—what the hell you doin', Dag?" Wilkes said, scowling. He was nearly as big as Enberg, but he was a good ten years older and he had a game knee from a mining accident. He was a rawboned, bearded man with a badly pitted face and close-set, stupid eyes.

Wilkes had already set his coach gun in the boot. Enberg tossed it to him. "I'm takin' the run. Go back inside. I'm sure Cates will find somethin' for you to do."

Charlie Grissom scowled at him, his broad face appearing as weathered as an ancient rifle stock behind his patchy, snow-white beard, and beneath his low-crowned straw sombrero banded with the skin of one of the rattlers Enberg had killed behind his cabin.

Grissom's hobby was fashioning various articles of clothing, including wallets and women's reticules, from snakeskin and selling them during his off-duty hours from a plank-board booth on Arizona Street. Enberg had furnished the old driver with plenty of snakeskin, though Grissom had traps out in the windy bluffs south of town, as well.

"What the hell's goin' on, Dag?" Grissom said, looking and sounding as though his feelings were hurt. "Cates said you was done."

"Dag!"

Enberg turned to see Logan Cates standing on the Diamond's

broad front porch. The shotgun rider lifted his gaze slightly to see Zee standing on her second-floor balcony, directly above Cates. She was clad in her usual skimpy but colorful attire, a cigarette smoldering in a long, wooden holder.

She gazed at Enberg, her brows ridged skeptically.

Cates was dressed to the nines as usual, complete with freshly brushed bowler hat. He stood glowering at Enberg and holding his bone-tipped ebony walking stick—an ostentatious accouterment brandished out of pure vanity.

"You offered to give me one more day," Enberg said. "I'm takin' you up on it."

Cates studied him for a moment. Then he came down the porch steps, walked around behind the coach, and brushed past Wilkes, who was still frowning indignantly up at Enberg. He stopped beside the coach's right front wheel. "You're relieved, George. Go on inside."

Wilkes puffed out his chest as he glared at Enberg, then wheeled and stomped off toward the saloon.

"Why the change of heart, Dag?"

Enberg hiked a shoulder. "Figure it's the last money I'll likely make in a while. Why not earn it? I do have a shred of self-respect, Logan."

Cates frowned, dubious. Then he drew a deep breath. "Frankly, I'll be glad to have you on the run. The strongbox you'll be picking up in Tomahawk means a lot to me."

Enberg frowned at him curiously.

"Never mind what it is," Cates said. "Just make sure it arrives safe and sound . . . which I know you will."

Cates stepped back and nodded to Grissom.

The old jehu glanced over his shoulder at the coach and yelled, "Grab a handhold, folks—we're about to chew trail!"

With that, he shook the reins over the backs of the team, and the stage creaked into motion. Grissom waited until they'd negotiated the town's morning traffic and were in the raggedy outskirts, the chaparral bristling on both sides of the trail, before he slapped the team into a lunging lope.

Enberg sat back in the seat, shotgun across his lap, and glanced over his shoulder in the direction of his cabin. He couldn't see it from this vantage, but he could see the line of silver mesquites lining the wash beyond which it sat. His gut tightened with anxiety.

He'd left Emily and his unborn child alone with three men who had the dispositions of rabid coyotes. Enberg wouldn't be back until late the next day. There was no telling what those three might be tempted to do in that time, holing up alone with Emily, a desirable young woman. Maybe the fact that she was Cates's stepdaughter would help suppress their goatish urges. Logan Cates had the respect of even the outlaws in these parts.

While Enberg did not feel committed to Emily in the way a man should commit to his wife, he still had strong feelings for her, and not merely because she was carrying his child. She was a sweet, sensitive girl. A good person. She did not deserve to be married to a man of Enberg's lowly character.

Guilt mixed with the anger and frustration boiling inside him.

He turned his head forward. Charlie Grissom was staring at him dubiously.

"You gonna tell me about it?"

"About what?"

"About what?" Grissom mocked, adjusting a wad of Climax plug tobacco in his mouth and spitting over the left front wheel. "About why Cates done fired your broom-tailed butt—what do you think?"

"I had a beer."

"Just one?"

Enberg hiked a sheepish shoulder. "I had a beer and—"

"You turned Raoul Leclerk toe down. Matter of fact, I heard they planted his worthless hide last night. Both the two sky pilots in town refused to say words over him, too, so there's no tellin' where he is now. I hope he don't mind the smell of butane."

"If you know all about it, Charlie, why in the hell did you ask me?"

Grissom shouted over the thunder of the team and the roar of the coach's iron-shod wheels. "Because I wanted to hear it from your own mouth, you raggedy-heeled, broom-tailed, cork-headed fool!"

"Well, you didn't let me tell it, you old reprobate. You just . . . !" Enberg let his voice trail off. He wagged his head and snorted a laugh at the old man, whom he considered his only real friend in Mineral Springs—besides Zee, that was, though she could no longer really be counted.

Grissom had known Enberg's father, Olaf. They'd drunk and caroused together back when Grissom was contracting with the army, hauling freight to Forts Bowie and Chiricahua from the supply depots along the west coast. Grissom had become Dag's foster father of sorts after he'd returned to Mineral Springs to learn that his own father was dead.

"What started the dustup?" Grissom asked him after a time, leaning forward, elbows on his knees, the reins resting lightly in his hands. He was so skilled at his job that he could steer each horse of the six-horse hitch with the slightest pressure on individual lines.

Enberg drew a deep breath.

"It was that Mex whore, wasn't it?" Grissom said. "If I had to count the number of men I've known who were ruined by a set of purty Mexican tits I'd have to take my shoes and socks off!"

"There you go again, Charlie—askin' me questions you

78

already know the answers to. But I'd just as soon you didn't call her that Mex who—"

Enberg cut himself off, for he'd just spied furtive movement off the trail's right side.

"Heads up, Charlie," Dag said, lifting the coach gun from his lap. "Think we might have trouble."

Chapter Thirteen

"What'd you see?" Grissom said, loosening the pistol he carried in a shoulder holster under his long denim jacket.

"I don't know. Somethin'."

"The Dill brothers still in the area?"

"I heard they went down to Mexico after robbing a saloon in Lordsburg, but they might be back. They're slow to learn, them boys." Enberg tensed as he watched a familiar rocky outcropping, bristling with cactus, rising before the stage, on the trail's right side. "If it's them, it might be time to teach 'em a lesson once and for all."

Grissom glanced nervously at his shotgun rider. "What're you gonna do?"

Enberg rose from the seat, spreading his boots to keep his balance as the stage rocked beneath him. "Just keep rollin', Charlie. If they try to stop you, let 'em."

"Let 'em?" Grissom exclaimed. Then, as Enberg leaped off the side of the coach and onto the outcropping sliding past on his right, the old driver said, "What in tarnation . . . ?"

Enberg dropped onto the crest of the outcropping and wheeled back to face the trail, crouching low. The stagecoach rolled on past to his right, dust billowing high behind it.

A passenger had poked his head out the window and, holding his bowler hat down on his head, stared back toward Enberg with a puzzled, leery expression on his face, which was framed by thick red muttonchops.

Enberg backed away from the edge of the outcropping, looked around carefully to see if anyone was near, then hotfooted it down the outcropping's backside. He knew the trail between Mineral Springs and Tomahawk so well that he knew where the Dill brothers would likely strike.

If it was the Dill brothers he'd seen, that was. He'd glimpsed only a couple of man-shaped silhouettes scrambling down the side of a low mesa about a quarter of a mile ahead. But most area outlaws familiar with the route between Mineral Springs and Tomahawk would likely choose the same spot in the trail to stop the stage.

The spot was a crease between buttes, with a steep rise ahead of it that would slow the team considerably. Enberg was always on high alert when rolling through there. Some outlaws wouldn't mess with a coach that Enberg was riding shotgun on. But some would.

When he'd gained the bottom of the outcropping, Enberg ran back across the trail, then traced a circuitous route through mesquites and barrel cactus and palo verdes, taking a shortcut to the place he believed the outlaws would strike. As he jogged, he could hear the clatter of the stage and the intermittent snorts of the team off to his right.

Dust from the stage billowed above the brush and low, rocky hills glistening dully in the late-morning sunshine.

Enberg steered wide of the trail and then followed a narrow gully back toward it. As he jogged, sweating and breathing hard, he heard the rattling of a snake off to his left. Apparently, he'd interrupted the viper's morning nap in the shade of a palo verde. He slowed his pace a little and regarded the ground around him warily. All he needed to sour his fate even further was a rattlesnake bite.

He was ahead of the stage now. He could hear the clomps of the horses and the rattling of the wheels growing louder as they moved toward him down the long, steep slope he knew so well.

When he reached the trail and the slope's' broad, bowl-shaped bottom, he dropped to a knee behind a boulder and peered off to his right.

The coach was rolling down the slope, Grissom hauling back on the reins to slow the team, for the bottom of thc slope was rocky with flood debris washed down the arroyo during spring runoff and summer monsoons. It was a good place to break a horse's leg or to lose a wheel rim.

Enberg looked around. He saw no sign of anyone near the trail.

He was beginning to wonder if he hadn't been seeing things, when two men stepped out of a gap in the brush on the trail's far side, about thirty feet to Enberg's right, between him and the stage. Both men held Winchesters. The taller of the two stepped into the center of the trail, cocked his rifle, and sent a bullet hammering skyward.

The crack of the rifle echoed.

Beyond the two, Grissom yelled loudly as he hauled back on the reins. The horses lifted their heads, and their eyes grew wide, ears pricking nervously.

A male passenger stuck his head out the window on Enberg's side of the stage, his own eyes wide with anxiety. He pulled his head back into the window, and as the stage jerked to a shuddering stop before the two highwaymen, a girl's scream sounded from inside the Concord.

The two outlaws—Dill brothers, all right—glanced at each other and grinned with satisfaction.

Enberg remained hunkered low behind the boulder, drawing deep, steady breaths, urging himself to remain calm. He'd seen only two silhouettes scuttling down the side of that mesa, but before he took down the two Dill brothers standing with their backs to him now, facing the stage, he had to make sure they were the only two.

He didn't want to get caught in a whipsaw.

He looked all around him, both up and down the trail, then stepped back into the chaparral. As he began moving toward the stage, paralleling the trail from roughly fifteen feet away, he heard one of the Dill brothers say, "Well, good mornin' there, Charlie. How you doin', you old bag of lard an' bones?"

"You two best step off the trail if you know what's good for you. Get along, now—I got a timetable to keep, goddamnit!" Grissom cast a sheepish glance down toward the door on his side of the stage. "Forgive my French, ladies!"

"You'll get back on your timetable just as soon as you drop that strongbox down over the side of the coach, there, old-timer," ordered the shorter of the two Dill brothers.

Enberg thought his name was Roy. The other was Franklin. There were two more Dill brothers, and unless they were lying dead in Mexico, their bones being gnawed on by buzzards and cougars, they were likely out here, too.

"You Dills ain't robbin' my coach!" Grissom bellowed, red-faced. "Now get the hell out of the way before I run you over!"

Franklin cocked his rifle again and aimed it at Grissom. "Drop the reins, old man."

"Where's your shotgun rider, Grissom?" asked Roy Dill. "We thought Dag Enberg was gonna be ridin' messenger on today's run." His voice told Enberg that he'd been anticipating more of a challenge.

Enberg was walking, crouching, through the brush near the coach now. Occasionally peering under branches and through gaps in the mesquites and willows lining the wash he could see the outlaws and the coach. He looked around carefully, wanting to make sure that Roy and Franklin Dill were the only two owl-hoots out here before he made his move.

"Dag got himself fired, the cow-headed son of a bitch," Grissom snarled. "So we was short-handed today. That don't mean I'm gonna let you two polecats robs my coach, though—and you can bet the seed bull on that. I got a reputation I don't want tarnished by no scurvy Dill brothers!"

Satisfied that Roy and Franklin were the only two Dills out here, Enberg moved through the brush and crouched behind a mesquite about fifty feet off the side of the trail and off the right hips of the Dill brothers staring up at Grissom. He was about to click both his coach gun's rabbit-ear hammers back when hoof thuds rose from behind the stage, growing louder.

Enberg turned to stare up trail. Two riders were galloping toward the coach. They both had pistols out.

Enberg drew his head back behind the mesquite as the two riders rode up along both sides of the coach.

"Please, don't harm the women!" beseeched a man's voice from inside the coach.

"We'll do anything we want to the women—after we've secured that strongbox!" yelled Franklin Dill above the thudding of the newcomers' horses.

Dag removed his hat and slid a cautious glance out around the mesquite to see both horseback riders moving up to join the owlhoots on foot at the head of the stage. Enberg recognized Curly and Martin Dill.

"Took you long enough," Roy Dill said.

"Curly's horse had a thorn in its frog. We had to stop and dig it out." Martin Dill, a beefy, neckless lad in his middle twenties, looked up into the driver's box, then frowned at Roy and Franklin. "Where's Enberg?"

Franklin said, "Grissom said he got himself fired."

"Bullshit!" Curly Dill said, looking around wildly. "He was on the stage when it lit out from Mineral Springs!"

Enberg rose and stepped out from behind the mesquite.

He clicked both the coach gun's hammers back to full cock

and said, "Curly ain't as stupid as he looks. I'm right here, and you two are gonna be snugglin' with the diamondbacks less'n you toss them guns down and do it quick."

CHAPTER FOURTEEN

The four owlhoots swung their startled gazes toward Enberg, smiling over the twin barrels of his cocked twelve-gauge.

The two horseback Dills checked their mounts down. Dust billowed around them.

They squinted through the dust at the shotgun rider. The horseback Dills kept their pistols aimed skyward. Anxiety showed on their pinched-up faces, all bearing the familial traits of feral eyes and belligerently jutting chins.

Inside the otherwise silent coach, a woman was sobbing loudly. The sobs were muffled as though by a gentleman's shoulder.

"He's only one man," Roy Dill said, testily.

"Yeah, but he's got that blasted scattergun," Franklin Dill said.

Grissom said from the driver's boot, "And I got my trusty hogleg. You dumbasses better take me into account, too!"

"You rancid old coot," snarled Curly Dill. "You couldn't hit the broad side of a barn with that thing!"

"Damn your hide, Dill!" Grissom bellowed, red-faced and aiming his old Remington.

"Drop 'em now!" Enberg said. "Or so help me god—!"

He cut himself off when Curly Dill swung his pistol toward him.

The others moved at the same instant, bearing down on Enberg. Dag tripped the left trigger of his coach gun, lifting a roar like that of a dynamite blast. He tripped the second trigger a quarter-second later and watched as Curly Dill was thrown off the side of his horse as though he'd been lassoed from the far side of the trail.

Both Franklin and Roy triggered their rifles into the air as they went pirouetting toward where Curly had fallen, their upper torsos splattered with buckshot and viscera oozing from holes in their bellies.

As Martin Dill turned his mount toward Enberg, Charlie Grissom rose to his feet in the driver's box and cut loose with his old Remy. His slugs shredded the air around Martin's head to puff the dust of the trail around the last surviving outlaw.

The old man's bullets, wide as they were, served to cow and confuse Martin. The last Dill swung his horse back to the other side of the trail and, crouching low in the saddle, went galloping down the trail along the coach's far side, taking him out of Enberg's view. Automatically, Dag broke open his shotgun, plucked out the spent, smoking wads, and quickly replaced them with fresh from his crisscrossed bandoliers.

As he snapped the shotgun closed, a yelling Martin Dill came galloping up from behind the stage toward Enberg. "You murderin' sonofabitch!" the outlaw bellowed, wide-eyed and crouched low over his horse's neck.

Dag stepped back into the shrubs as Dill triggered two shots at him, the bullets snapping branches in the shrubs off Enberg's side of the trail. As Dill drew up near where Enberg was just then thumbing the coach gun's hammers back, Martin swung toward him, swinging his revolver around, as well.

Dag cut loose with both barrels.

KA-BOOOMMMM!

Martin's head with wide eyes and gaping mouth went flying backward off his shoulders. The man's hat remained attached to the head by a snugly drawn chin thong.

Enberg stepped to one side as Martin's horse with Martin's headless body went thundering past him through the brush.

Meanwhile, Martin's head hit the middle of the trail with a dull smack, pluming dust. It rolled twice and, geysering blood from the ragged neck, came to rest face up, eyes blinking and lips moving as the man—or the man's head, at least—was trying to say something.

Enberg lowered the smoking shotgun.

The woman's sobs rose again from inside the coach.

Grissom got the team settled back down in their collars and stared at the still-blinking head in shock. "If that don't beat all," he said finally.

Grissom glanced at the coach door below and behind him. "Sit tight, folks. You sure as Jehova don't wanna come out here. We'll be rollin' again in just a minute. All's well!"

The old jehu wrapped the ribbons around the brake handle and, grunting and muttering under his breath, climbed down from the driver's box and walked over to stare down at the bloody, hatted head. Martin Dill stared up at him through wide-open eyes. He was no longer blinking. He looked dumbfounded, which was only natural, Enberg supposed.

Grissom looked at Enberg, who had breached the shotgun once more and was replacing the spent wads with fresh. "How far you reckon the rest of him will get without his head?"

Enberg snapped the gut-shredder closed. "No tellin'. He's probably better off without it."

Dag thought he should maybe try it himself. His own head had done little but get him into trouble.

Enberg kicked Martin Dill's head off the trail and into a clump of prickly pear cactus where the buzzards would likely find it soon. He and Grissom dragged the rest of the Dill brothers off the trail, mounted up, and set off once more.

Forty miles of nearly open desert stretched between Mineral Springs and Tomahawk, on the west side of the Whetstone Mountains. Cates had positioned his relay stations, some of which were small ranches, between ten and fifteen miles apart. There were two relay stations between Mineral Springs and Tomahawk.

Grissom stopped the coach at both of these for no longer than fifteen minutes—long enough merely for the five passengers to stretch, grab a sandwich provided by Mrs. Wormwood at the Rebel Canyon Station, drink some water or coffee, and use the privy. The teams were switched out for fresh, and the coach's axles were greased and checked for cracks, the rims checked for bowing.

The dust had barely settled from the stage's arrival, when Grissom gave a bellowing roar, popped his blacksnake over the team's backs, and they were off at a westward gallop once more.

Enberg was always alert for trouble, for he knew it could come from any quarter out here on this vast, bristling desert hemmed in on all sides by distant, craggy mountain ranges. Today, however, he was even more alert and wary than usual. If he hadn't glimpsed the shadows of the first two Dill brothers, he could very easily be pushing up cactus about now.

The brothers might have shot him out of his shotgun messenger's seat as a preamble to robbing the stage. He doubted the Dill brothers could have accomplished that feat, for they weren't known for their shooting, but their attempt on the stage had reminded Enberg to be extra cautious.

If something happened to him before he could turn Cates's strongbox over to Cougar Ketchum's gang, there was no telling what would happen to Emily. If the gang didn't find the strongbox in that wash tomorrow, they could send word back to Enberg's cabin and follow through on their threat.

And they'd probably have a good time with Emily while they did it.

Cougar Ketchum wasn't the savviest of outlaws, and he wasn't known for his gun prowess any more than the Dill brothers had been, but Ketchum was one of the lowliest men Enberg had ever known.

Fortunately, the rest of Enberg's trip was as monotonous as it usually was, the tediousness tempered only by the lurking worry about getting held up.

It was a bedraggled bunch—driver, shotgun rider, passengers, and horses alike—that finally crossed the last arroyo to rattle into Tomahawk ahead of a thickly churning dust cloud. The stage was so coated in dust that Enberg and Grissom had to wipe the passengers' luggage with rags as they handed them down from the rear storage boot.

The passengers slinked dustily off to their hotel rooms while Grissom and Enberg tended their end-of-run business with the supervisor at Cates's depot in Tomahawk, reporting the attempted robbery by the Dill brothers.

The supervisor tapped out a telegraph message about the Dill brothers' demise to the deputy U.S. marshal up in Phoenix and sent out a local sheriff's deputy and two other men and a wagon to retrieve what was left of the bodies.

Meanwhile, Grissom headed off to the nearest brothel for some slap-'n'-tickle with his favorite Tomahawk dove, while Enberg tramped off to Delancy's Tonsorial Parlor for a badly needed bath, but not before stopping to buy a ten-cent cigar at the local tobacco shop.

He awarded himself with such a treat at the end of each run.

As he sat lounging in the copper tub filled with tepid water in Delancy's back cabin, smoking the dynamite-sized cigar, apprehension was a venomous snake slithering around in Enberg's loins. He wasn't as worried now about tomorrow's run as he was about another complication he'd have to find a way to manage.

The stage line supervisor here in Tomahawk had informed him and Grissom that Logan Cates had assigned a second shotgun rider to help guard the strongbox on the trip back to Mineral Springs.

CHAPTER FIFTEEN

After his bath, Enberg headed over to the Santa Rita Saloon, which sat on a side street in Tomahawk and was shaded in the east by a giant tabletop mesa. As soon as he pushed through the batwings, he saw the man he was looking for.

"Boonie Schaeffer, how in the hell you doin', old son?"

Schaeffer had been sipping a glass of milk. Now he set the glass down, turned to Enberg, brushed a fist across his mustache-mantled mouth, and grinned. "Dag Enberg, you old catamount! Cates said in his telegram you'd be the second shotgun."

"Hell, I'm the first one, Boonie!" Enberg laughed as he bellied up to the bar and frowned at the white glass in front of Schaeffer. "Boonie, tell me that ain't milk. Ain't you heard that it ain't good fer a man to drink milk after he's been weaned off his mother's tit!"

Schaeffer looked sheepish. "Yeah, well, I was goin' at the whiskey pretty hard there for a while. Felt like I was losin' my edge, an' you know as good as anyone, Dag, in this country it ain't good for a shotgun rider to lose his edge."

Schaeffer usually rode the relay run from Tomahawk farther west to La Quinta.

Enberg slapped the zinc countertop. "Honor, I would like a shot of your best busthead. I can't afford the stuff on the top shelf, but I don't want any rattlesnake venom, either." He rubbed his belly. "Sort o' sours my stomach, don't ya know."

The apron, Honor Burlinson, looked at Enberg reprovingly askance, then pulled a bottle up from beneath the bar. When he picked up an overturned shot glass from atop the bar near Enberg, a black widow spider went running out from under it.

Enberg smashed his fist down on the critter, laying it out flat.

He made a face as he looked at the black mush staining the edge of his fist. "Honor, I see you haven't gotten any cleaner since the last time I was in here," Dag said, scraping his fist off on the counter.

Burlinson splashed whiskey into the glass and was about to cork the bottle when Enberg said, "Go ahead and leave it. I'll be damned if I don't feel like I got half the Sonora Desert lodged in my throat. It's gonna take dynamite or busthead to blow it out. I believe I'll go with the busthead."

Burlinson gave him a sidelong look of warning. "Go easy, Dag." He drifted off to help another customer.

Schaeffer gestured at the whiskey in front of Enberg. "I heard you was on the wagon your ownself, Dag."

"The wagon broke down, Boonie. Hit a rock called time."

Schaeffer, a willowy, sun-seasoned Texan around Enberg's age and with a gray-streaked handlebar mustache, scowled incredulously. "Say again."

Enberg sipped the whiskey. "Yessir, I got to thinkin' one night about how much time a man has on this earth. All the shit he has to go through and put up with. All the long, hard years addin' up to little more than a pine box—if he's lucky, that is—and a cold, black hole in the ground."

Enberg threw back the last of his shot and refilled his glass. "Sometimes—durin' the worst of times, I reckon—it seems like a *long* time, and sometimes it seems all too *short* a time. Don't really matter, though. Both ways—short or long, good or bad—it leads in the same direction. That cold, black hole. So I got to thinkin' about how important it is for a man to enjoy the simple pleasures. And I personally enjoy nothin' more than the simple pleasure of endin' the day with a shot or two of good-to-middlin' who-hit-John."

He threw back half of the second shot and smacked his lips as though he'd just tasted a nectar lovingly fermented by a benevolent god and poured straight into his glass from heaven. "Mhmmm-uhmmmm! Nothin' better than whiskey after a long, dusty day out in the hot sun!"

"Well, shit," Schaeffer said, glowering enviously down at Enberg's shot glass, then sliding his milk glass toward the bottle. "I reckon I never quite looked at it that way. I sure don't like the sound of that cold black hole at the end of it all. Damn! Pour a little of that in here, will you, Dag?"

Enberg poured a liberal amount of busthead into Schaeffer's glass, then raised his own glass in salute. They clicked glasses, nodded, and drank.

The next morning, Enberg woke with a start.

Something told him he had overslept.

Beside him, someone groaned. There was the soft rustling sound of moving hay. Enberg lifted his aching head to see a little, brown-skinned *puta* with long, dark-brown hair and large breasts roll away from him, naked as the day she'd been born but a whole lot better filled out. Beyond her lay another whore— the taller of the two whom he and Schaeffer had found last night, going hand-in-hand from saloon to saloon in matching red dresses under which they'd worn nothing.

Dag and Schaeffer had taken the girls back here to Cates's barn—an older, seldom used one at the rear of the Tomahawk stage station—where he and Schaeffer had made a night of it with the two *putas* in this very stall.

Now, Schaeffer lay on the stall's far side, his back to Enberg and the two *putas*, snoring softly against the adobe wall. Schaeffer wore only his longhandle bottoms. The top hung down around his waist.

Like the two *putas*, Enberg himself was naked save for a light covering of hay and straw. He and the little whore had had quite a go of it. She and her flopping breasts—and the way she'd straddled him as though she were galloping a broomtail bronc—had been a nice distraction from his life's current predicament.

He sat up, looked around for his pants, and rummaged inside them for his pocket watch. He flipped the lid. Six-twenty-five. He had fifteen minutes to get over to the depot building, where Grissom and the stage would be waiting for him.

He looked at Schaeffer. Dead out. An empty liquor bottle lay nearby.

As Enberg rose and began slowly, quietly dressing, he remembered the several bottles of tangle-leg that he and his partner had knocked back before retreating with the *senoritas* to the barn.

Enberg had thrown every other shot over his shoulder. Still, his head felt like a giant pumpkin split with an ax. Having drunk twice as much as Dag had, Schaeffer would be out for a good, long time. When he did come around, he'd likely roam the town on his knees, begging for someone to shoot him.

Despite his agony, Enberg grinned. All according to plan.

He finished dressing while the whores and Schaeffer slept. He brushed hay from the crown of his hat, donned the topper, looped his bandoliers across his chest, and grabbed his shotgun. He slung it over his shoulder as he cast one more cautious look back at Schaeffer, then eased open the stall door, slipped through it, and closed it just as quietly behind him.

Birds were chirping and the sky was lightening as he made his way across the station yard to the front of the depot house, where the six-horse hitch was just now being backed into the shafts by three hostlers who looked in little better condition than Enberg felt.

"Where in the hell have you been?" Grissom asked him as he tossed a small steamer trunk into the rear luggage boot. "All the passengers are loaded up and we're ready to go. Been waitin' on you to help me fetch the strongbox out of Hagel's office." He made a face. "Christ, you smell like a still!"

"Schaeffer's fault. I caught him falling off the wagon, and he grabbed onto me like I was some sorta life raft."

"Some life raft," Grissom snorted, looking Dag up and down in disgust. "Where in hell is he, anyway? Hagel said Schaeffer's sidin' you today."

"I don't think so, Charlie. Schaeffer's three sheets to the wind. If he's lucky, he'll sleep all day. If he doesn't, he'll probably shoot himself."

"Ah, Christ. If Cates finds out about this—"

Enberg wrapped an arm around his old friend's broad shoulders. "It'll be our secret, Charlie. We'll tell Cates that one of the horses kicked him and laid him out for a day. No point in gettin' him in the same kind of trouble I'm in—right?"

Grissom shook his head and cursed until an old lady poked her head out of the stage and asked him if he'd been born in a barn and ordered him to pipe down. Her granddaughter was asleep inside the coach.

That cowed the bearded jehu.

"Let's go inside and fetch the strongbox, Charlie," Enberg said, nudging the older man toward the depot building.

CHAPTER SIXTEEN

"What do you suppose is in that thing, Charlie?" Enberg asked as Grissom put the team into a gallop, heading into the desert east of Tomahawk. The Whetstone Mountains loomed ahead—remote, purple, and forbidding as the dawn grew behind them.

The white-bearded jehu glanced over his shoulder at the padlocked, steel-banded strongbox chained to the roof. "I don't know, but it must be valuable for Cates to have assigned two guards to it. Maybe one of his gold mines out in Californy showed a good profit this summer, or somesuch."

"If it came from that far, and if it was really valuable, he'd likely have it shipped in a special wagon by an armed escort. I'm thinkin' it's a relatively modest amount—for Cates, anyway—and it came from closer by."

"Yeah, well, modest by Cates's standards could still mean a hundred thousand." Grissom spat a stream of chaw down over the side of the coach and brushed the back of his gloved hand across his bearded mouth. "How would I know what's in it? I never had more than twenty, thirty dollars at any one time in my life, and when I did have that much, it didn't last long. I'll tell you that!"

"That's due to your preference for the more expensive doxies, Charlie," Enberg said. "The younger, better-looking ones that cost a pretty penny."

Enberg laughed.

"Don't I know it," Grissom said, shaking his head. "But I

figure we only go around once, so might as well enjoy the best lovin' a man can find for as long as he can find it!" He glanced sheepishly at Dag. "Uh . . . sorry, partner."

"About what?"

"I just . . . uh . . . hope what I said didn't remind you about *Senorita* Zenobia, that's all. I know how you felt about her. Maybe still do, for all I know."

"She's behind me, Charlie," Enberg lied, again feeling the sharp pang of his loss of what he and Zee had once had. "I'm married to Emily now, though I reckon it won't be for much longer."

"What's that?"

Enberg had said that last so quietly, beneath the thunder of the team and the violently rocking coach, that fortunately Grissom hadn't heard him.

"Nothin', Charlie. Just nothin'." Enberg glanced at the strongbox once more.

"What's the matter?"

"Huh?"

"Why do you keep lookin' at that box?"

Enberg shrugged. "I don't know—just curious, that's all."

"We've carried plenty of strongboxes. Why you so fidgety about this one?"

Annoyance born of guilt rolled through Enberg. "I ain't so fidgety about this one. Christ almighty, I'm just tryin' to make conversation, that's all. Forget I said anything, you old fossil, and just drive this heap, will you?"

Grissom scowled at him, baffled. He shook his head. "You're a puzzle these days, Dag, you know that? A pure puzzle."

"Shut up and drive!"

"I'm drivin', by god!" Grissom bellowed, and turned his head back to the trail unwinding before them.

Enberg couldn't help glancing once more at the box behind him.

How much was in there?

Gold, regular coins, or paper currency . . . or all three?

Like Charlie had said, the strongbox's contents must be especially valuable for Cates to have put two guards on it. Somehow, Cougar Ketchum had found out that Cates was shipping something extra special this run, and had decided to go to extra lengths to steal it.

As he looked around the country sliding idly past him on both sides of the curving trail, ever on the watch for trouble, Dag wondered how Ketchum had found out about the valuable shipment. Enberg never would have suspected that Cougar Ketchum had the wherewithal to uncover such secretive information.

Cates was as secretive about his own special shipments as Wells Fargo was about theirs.

As the miles unwound beneath the team's hammering hooves and the coach's churning wheels, Enberg's nervousness intensified. What he was going to do about four miles out from the last relay station between Tomahawk and Mineral Springs went against his instincts as a shotgun rider, a job that he'd for some reason taken special pride in.

But Cates would understand once Enberg told him that he'd turned the box over to Ketchum's bunch to save Emily's life. Cates would understand, and so would Grissom and everyone else around Mineral Springs.

As soon as Enberg turned over the box, he'd tell Charlie everything and hustle back to town, make sure that Emily was safe, and then report to Cates and Geylan Whipple what had happened.

He probably should have told them what was happening yesterday morning, but there was a chance they would have tried to foil Ketchum's plan prematurely, and get Emily killed.

When they learned about the kidnapping, Cates and Whipple would most likely form a posse right away. They'd hightail it after Ketchum's bunch, who couldn't cover much ground quickly with a box as heavy as the one currently residing atop the coach, and should be fairly easily overtaken.

Then Enberg would be cleared. Cates might even consider reinstating him as shotgun rider after he found out what he'd done to save his stepdaughter.

Stepdaughter . . .

A fresh wave of anxiety washed through Dag. He couldn't help imagining Ketchum being overcome by his baser desires and of dragging Emily upstairs. When he was finished, he'd likely turn her over to McInally and Ugly Tom.

Enberg hardened his jaws and shook his head, squeezing the shotgun resting across his lap. Ketchum better not have hurt her. If he or any of his gang had done anything to harm that girl, they'd pay with their lives.

They'd die good and slow, howling . . .

Enberg studied the chaparral around the coach with an extra sharp eye. He couldn't let the coach get hit before they arrived at Bayonet Creek. He was glad when, around three in the afternoon, they arrived at the Clearwater Station, the last relay station on the trail to Mineral Springs.

He was even more relieved to pull out of Clearwater with a fresh team in the traces.

His anxiety intensified once more when he saw the wash ahead of them, marked by a low-lying area of willows and palo verdes. He squeezed the shotgun in his gloved hands as Grissom put the team down the declivity, through a break in the chaparral, and into the broad wash.

His heart skipped several beats as he turned toward Grissom and said, "Stop 'em here, Charlie."

"What?"

"Stop 'em here."

"What're you talkin' about?" Grissom looked around. "You see somethin'?"

"Just stop the goddamn team, Charlie!"

Grissom bunched the reins in his hands and drew his arms back, chest-high. "Whoooo-ahhhhhh, now, ya mangy cayuuusssssesssssssss!"

When the horses had stopped, shaking their heads—they were fresh and wanted to keep going at a good clip—Grissom turned to Enberg. "What the hell has gotten into you?"

Enberg reached inside the jehu's dusty canvas coat and pulled the graybeard's old Remington out of his shoulder holster.

"Hey!" Grissom said, indignant. "What in the hell . . . ?"

Enberg shoved the pistol down behind his cartridge belt. "Just gonna relieve you of this for a bit, Charlie. You can't stop me from doin' what I'm about to do."

"Just what in the hell do you think you're about to do, Dag?"

Holding his shotgun in his right hand, Enberg climbed up onto the coach's roof. "I'm gonna toss the strongbox into the wash."

"You're gonna *what*?"

"Just trust me on this one—all right, Charlie? Please just trust me. It's somethin' I have to do. It's for Emily." From his shirt pocket he withdrew the key to the locked chain securing the strongbox to two brackets on the coach roof. He couldn't open the strongbox itself, because he didn't have the key for it. At this end of the line, only Cates did.

"I can't quite wrap my mind around what you're doin' there, Dag. But if you honestly think I'm gonna sit here and let you roll that box into the wash, you got another think comin'!"

Grissom started to haul his two-hundred-plus pounds up out of the driver's boot and onto the roof. Enberg swung toward him, bringing the sawed-off twelve-gauge to bear on the jehu's bulging belly. "Stay there, Charlie."

Grissom looked at the two round maws leveled at him.

"What's going on up there?" a man called from the coach. "Why are we stopping?"

"Shut up and stay where you are!"

Enberg's heart was really pumping now. He was sweating, the dust turning to mud on his bearded cheeks. He narrowed his eyes at Grissom. "Cougar Ketchum has Emily back at the cabin. I have to leave the strongbox here for the rest of his gang to fetch, or he'll kill her."

The deep lines around Grissom's blue eyes were dug deeper.

"I have to do this, Charlie, or Ketchum will kill Emily. We'll get it back. Just as soon as I know Emily's all right."

Grissom looked around apprehensively, squinting off into the brush lining both sides of the wash. "They around here?"

"Several of 'em are. Somewhere. They're stayin' out of sight." Enberg turned the key in the padlock securing the chain and the strongbox to the steel brackets. The padlock opened with a raspy click. "They're watchin' us right now. When I get this strongbox into the wash, they'll probably send a man galloping back to town to let Ketchum know. Then, if Cougar fulfills his end of the bargain, they'll ride out away from my cabin, and leave Emily unharmed."

"Christ almighty," Grissom said, shaking his head fatefully. "You sure that's what this is about, Dag?"

Enberg dropped the padlock and both ends of the chain, and looked at his old friend. "You think I'm stealin' it for myself, Charlie? If I was, I'd have a horse waitin'. A horse and a mule with a pack on it, most like. Come on, Charlie. I know I ain't the man I was before the war, but I wouldn't do somethin' like this on my own."

"Ah, shit. I know that!" Grissom cursed and then grunted as

he heaved himself up onto the coach roof. "Here—let me help you with that damn thing."

Together, the two men slid the strongbox over to the edge of the roof. They shared a dubious look for several stretched seconds, and then rolled it off.

The box hit the wash with a clanking thud.

CHAPTER SEVENTEEN

"Good lord!" exclaimed the old lady poking her head out the stage door to stare at the strongbox lying on its side in the dry wash. "What are you two scoundrels up to, anyways?"

"Nothin' to be alarmed about, Mrs. Scanlon," Grissom said as he and Enberg dropped back down into the driver's boot.

He gave Enberg a worried look. Dag returned it and took his seat, looking around cautiously and resting his shotgun across his lap.

"Let's go, Charlie," he urged, wanting to be finished with the distasteful endeavor as soon as possible.

"We're goin', we're goin."

Grissom shook the ribbons over the team's back, and the Concord rolled on across the wash and up the bank on the other side. Soon, the old jehu had the team galloping again across the open desert, heading in the general direction of Mineral Springs.

As he rode, Enberg glanced behind at the line of desert brush delineating the wash, wondering if he could see any sign of Ketchum's men retrieving the strongbox. If his guess was right, they were already scrambling into the draw to secure it. Enberg hoped one was heading back to Mineral Springs to let Cougar Ketchum know that Enberg had fulfilled his part of the bargain.

He stared northeast. That was the most direct route back to Mineral Springs. The stage couldn't take the most direct route, because it was too rough for the relatively fragile contraption.

The stage had to follow the trail, which skirted the roughest terrain, swinging a good mile and a half south of Mineral Springs before careening back to the northeast and on into town.

A horseback rider, however, could negotiate that rough terrain relatively easily. If a rider had left the wash around the time that the stage had, that rider, heading northeast, could reach town in half the time it would take the stagecoach.

Enberg held his left hand up to his hat brim, shielding the westering sun from his eyes as he stared off across the chaparral. It bothered him that he didn't see the dust plume of a rider out there, galloping toward town.

He stared in that direction a good long time, but he saw nothing. No sign of a rider or riders taking that most direct route to Mineral Springs.

That could mean several things. Maybe the gang had left Emily tied in the shack and had already pulled out, betting that Enberg would fulfill his part of the bargain.

Or . . . it could mean that they'd done something far more nefarious.

"Step 'em up—will ya, Charlie?" Enberg urged, leaning forward and tapping his boots on the wooden floor of the driver's boot.

"I already got 'em in a full-out run, Dag," Grissom yelled above the thunder of the team's hooves. "I can't make 'em grow wings and fly. I wanna get back to town as fast as you do, but these animals have done reached bottom!"

Enberg cursed as he fidgeted around in his seat, further frustrated when the trail swung out even farther south of Mineral Springs. He knew it would swing back north but not after another mile or more.

Anxiety was a hundred baby snakes wriggling around inside him. There was nothing he could do but sit here and silently pray that when they did roll into town he'd find Emily unharmed in the cabin. As the coach pitched and swayed and bounced over chuckholes, he couldn't help imagining finding Emily . . . and the baby inside her . . . dead.

He found himself wishing he'd treated her better. She hadn't deserved to play second fiddle to Zee. Emily was a good, sweet girl who'd fallen in love with Enberg, useless ass that he was, because she'd seen something inside him beyond what everyone else, including himself, had seen.

She'd seen a future in him—as both a husband and a father.

And nearly every time he'd made love to her, in his mind he'd been making love to Zee. Even when he'd fathered their baby, he'd been imagining Zee writhing around beneath him.

Frustration beat Enberg all the way to his toes. He knew the horses were galloping as fast as they could, lunging forward in their hames and collars, but to his badly rattled brain they were moving as though mired in quicksand.

The knot in his chest eased slightly when the stage rounded the last bend and swung northeast, and Mineral Springs grew slowly on the horizon before him—shabby mud-adobe shacks loosely surrounding the main business district with its gaudy two- and three-story business buildings, including Cates's especially gaudy Diamond in the Rough Saloon.

"I'll get off here, Charlie!" Enberg said as, grabbing his shotgun, he began climbing down the side of the coach.

"Hold on—you'll kill yourself!" Grissom yelled, hauling back on the team's reins.

He hadn't gotten the team slowed much when Enberg leaped off the iron step ring over the right front wheel. He hit the ground, which was pulled like a rug out from under him, and went rolling in the cloud of dust kicked up by the passing coach.

He rolled up off his shoulder and hip, got his boots beneath him, and ran off the trail's right side and around behind a hog pen and stable. A dog ran out from nowhere to bark at him briefly.

He headed straight out through the chaparral and toward the rocky mesa flanking his cabin, which he couldn't see, hunkered as it was on the other side of the mesquites lining the wash.

His heart hammered heavily.

His boots thudded on the gravelly ground. His breath raked in and out of his lungs like sandpaper.

He pushed through the mesquites, bounded across the wash, and ducked under the arching branches of a palo verde. He stopped dead in his tracks, bending forward slightly, chest rising and falling heavily.

He frowned at the cabin hunched before him, fifty yards away, at the base of the mesa.

"Wha . . . ?" he said, trying to catch his breath, trying to understand what he was looking at. "What . . . ?"

Then Logan Cates turned toward him. So did Geylan Whipple, his badge flashing in the sunlight. Both men had been conferring outside the cabin's open door.

Cates thrust his arm toward Enberg, pointing at him. Whipple drew his Colt revolver, aiming it at Dag.

"You crazy son of a bitch!" Cates shouted. He glanced at Whipple. "Arrest him, Charlie!"

"You got it, Mr. Cates," Whipple said, striding toward Enberg, aiming his cocked Colt straight out from his right shoulder.

"What the hell happened?" Enberg yelled, his heart a runaway train in his chest. "Did . . . did they—?"

He must have raised his shotgun inadvertently, because just then Whipple shouted "Stop!" and triggered his Colt.

Enberg staggered backward as the bullet tore into his upper right arm with a burning fury. He cursed as he dropped to a knee, cursed again as he heaved himself back to his feet and bulled under the palo verde, wincing at the pain in his arm.

Cates shouted.

Whipple snapped off two more shots and then another shot as Enberg gained the wash. The bullets ripped leaves from the palo verde and plumed dust at Enberg's heels as he ran up the wash, crouching slightly as he held his aching right arm taut against his belly.

"There's nowhere to run, Dag, you son of a bitch!" Cates shouted, his voice quavering as he gave chase behind Whipple.

As Enberg followed a bend in the wash, he glanced behind. Whipple was running after him, holding his Colt barrel up in his right hand. As he ran, his gray Stetson blew off his head. He kept running, spectacles glinting in the sunshine filtering through the brush on both sides of the wash.

He had a prissy sort of run, holding his free hand up, palm out, the Colt aimed skyward in the other hand. But his lean, pewter-mustached features were grimly determined.

"Goddamnit, what the hell happened?" Enberg shouted, but he was in too much pain to give the question much volume, and he was not about to stop and let Whipple arrest him. He had to find out what had happened to Emily, and he had to be free to do something about it.

The cold, fist-sized stone in his belly told him that Cougar Ketchum's men had killed her. For some reason, Cates and Whipple thought Enberg was responsible. He had no idea why that would be, but he was not going to allow them to arrest him.

He had to get back to the cabin. If Emily was there, he had to see her for himself.

And then he had to get after Cougar Ketchum and make him pay the ultimate price for his sins.

CHAPTER EIGHTEEN

Enberg ducked as Whipple triggered two more shots behind him.

The bullets screeched through the air around him, spanging off rocks littering the wash. Enberg followed another bend in the wash, heading toward town.

Suddenly, he stopped, glancing behind him once more. He couldn't see Whipple, who was on the other side of the bend. So was Cates, who just then yelled, "Stay with him, Charlie. Don't let him get away!"

Enberg swung to his right and ran up out of the wash, heading in the opposite direction of town. He'd head for the mesa. They likely wouldn't expect him to backtrack to the cabin. Quickly, he used a branch to cover his tracks where they followed him out of the wash.

He drew back behind a cottonwood when he glimpsed Whipple running around the bend in the wash. Enberg held there, crouched, wincing against the pain in his bloody arm, and watched Whipple run off down the wash, following the bend toward town.

Cates was about twenty yards behind him. Logan was holding a small, silver-plated, pearl-gripped derringer. As Enberg watched him from behind the cottonwood, he frowned with befuddlement. Cates wasn't wearing his hat. His left cheek appeared bruised and his right eye appeared to be swelling, as though he'd been in a fight.

While Enberg was mildly curious about Cates's condition, he had no time to dwell on it. When Cates had passed from sight, following Whipple, Dag pushed off the cottonwood and ran back in the direction of the cabin. He held onto the shotgun because it was the only weapon he had, and he'd need it when he encountered Ketchum's bunch.

Ahead of him rose a whining, rasping sound.

Enberg saw the Mojave green rattler almost too late. The snake struck just as Enberg leaped the viper, and the snake's lunging head with savagely exposed fangs passed only two inches under his right boot.

Enberg hit the ground and continued running.

The cabin shone ahead of him. There appeared no one else around. He dashed in the front door and stopped, looking around, horrified by what something told him he was going to find.

"Emily?" he called quietly, his voice drawn taut with dread.

He stepped softly into the cabin, moving slowly, allowing his eyes to adjust to the dark shadows. He swept his gaze from right to left and back again, expecting to find her lying dead somewhere.

But there was nothing. The place was a little unkempt, but otherwise it looked just as Enberg had left it.

"Emily?" Enberg called again.

Then he looked at the loft. His heart began beating faster.

If they'd killed her, they'd likely left her up there . . .

Enberg set his shotgun on the kitchen table. He took the rickety stairs two steps at a time and stood gazing, breathless, down at the bed. It was empty. It looked as it had when he and Emily had left it before finding Cougar Ketchum and the other two outlaws downstairs.

Enberg looked into all corners of the loft.

He went back downstairs and looked into the corners there,

as well. Nothing. No sign of Emily. There was no sign of a struggle, either.

His mind churned with questions. They made him dizzy. Meanwhile, blood oozed out of the ragged hole in his right arm to dribble onto the floor. He grabbed a dish towel and tied it tightly around the wound.

The sound of running footsteps lured him to the front door. He looked out to see Whipple running toward the cabin.

"Hold it, Enberg!" Whipple shouted as Dag drew his head back inside the cabin.

Gunshots sounded. The bullets ripped into the doorframe.

Enberg grabbed his shotgun off the table and ran across the parlor area of the cabin to the back door. He removed the locking bar from its brackets. Hearing Whipple's running footsteps approaching the front, Enberg ran out the back.

"Stop, dammit, you son of a bitch!" came Whipple's exasperated voice behind him, from inside the cabin.

Again, the man fired. The bullet thumped into wood as Enberg ran straight out away from the cabin and into the brush behind it. The mesa and the boulders strewn about its base grew before him.

He wasn't sure where he was headed, but the mesa seemed his best bet. It was a rugged, craggy formation owning all sorts of nooks and crannies he could hide in until dark. When Whipple and Cates gave up looking for him, he could make his way back down the ridge, possibly steal a horse, and go after Ketchum.

He had to find Emily.

He knew he probably wasn't thinking clearly. His head was a storm of contradictory thoughts and questions, and his body was racked with pain. What primarily compelled him at the moment was his own momentum and blind instinct.

Behind bars he could do nothing to change his situation. He

had to keep running until things got clearer.

Looking around to make sure he didn't step on a rattler, he ran up the mesa wall, weaving around cholla plants and cracked and crumbling boulders. A gun barked behind him. He glanced over his shoulder to see Whipple running out of the brush and gaining the base of the ridge.

The town marshal paused, took aim, and fired.

The bullet cracked off a boulder to Enberg's right.

Dag continued running on up the mesa wall.

After only a few more steps, a heavy storm cloud seemed to pass over the sun. The ridge grew dark. Enberg's knees weakened. The ground pitched around him.

He dropped to a knee, cursing.

The bullet in his arm had sapped his strength. He must have lost more blood than he'd realized. As Whipple's pistol cracked again, Enberg threw himself behind a boulder. He lay on his back, breathing hard, feeling sick to his stomach, the ground swirling around him.

A hissing sounded.

He lifted his head with a start. The viper was poking its head out of a crack in the ridge wall about ten feet above.

The clacking of heels on rock rose on the other side of the boulder. There was the rasping of strained breaths. Whipple ran around the boulder, extending his Colt straight out and then slanting it down when he saw Enberg on the ground.

"Hold it!"

An ominously low rattling sounded behind the lawman. The rattling grew louder, shriller.

Whipple jerked as the snake sunk its fangs into his right calf.

"Oh, *shit!*"

Whipple wheeled and fired, but there was only the metallic click of his Colt's hammer falling on an empty chamber.

Another rattling sounded and Enberg saw the viper slithering through the gravel to the marshal's left. Whipple lurched away from the snake too late. The Mojave green rattler flung itself up off the ground to sink its fangs into Whipple's left thigh.

Whipple screamed, stumbled backward, and fell. The second snake bit him again, in the crotch, while another slithered down the slope to sink its fangs in his right cheek.

Whipple screamed and yelled and thrashed his arms and legs, trying to get away from the vipers swarming over and around him. But the more he thrashed, the faster the venom raced through his veins. Soon he was no longer thrashing but lying flat on his back, quivering as though he'd been struck by lightning, his head swelling, lips turning blue.

His dusty, round-framed spectacles hung low on his nose.

Enberg stared in shock at the dying lawman.

He'd looked long and hard for the rattler's nest, but Geylan Whipple had been the one to find it . . . to his everlasting dismay.

Dag looked around. The snake that had rattled at him from above had retreated into a crack in the ridge wall. It had probably fled to the nest, likely swirling with dozens of the deadly vermin.

Enberg pushed himself to his feet and leaned against the boulder to steady himself. He looked down at Whipple, who stared up at him, eyes wide with horror and the worst kind of agony, paralyzed. The snakes were finally slithering away from him toward a long crack in the ridge wall about six feet above him.

Enberg gave a shudder of revulsion.

Whipple's slowly rising and falling chest fell still. His eyes turned to isinglass.

Footsteps rose to Enberg's left. Cates was moving up the ridge, holding his derringer out in front of him. He looked from the still form of Geylan Whipple to Enberg, and stopped, bringing his silver popper to bear on Dag.

Behind Enberg, another man said, "Hold it or I'll cut ya in half sure enough, Enberg!"

Dag turned slowly, heavily, to see the pitted, bearded face of George Wilkes glaring at him from ten feet away. The shotgun rider and sometime-bouncer aimed a long, double-barreled shotgun at Enberg's chest, both big hammers rocked back to full cock.

CHAPTER NINETEEN

"Drop the shotgun," Wilkes ordered.

Enberg leaned his Greener against the boulder. As he did, Cates continued to move toward him, scowling horrifically down at the still, bloating, and purpling form of Geylan Whipple.

"For chrissakes!" Cates intoned, looking bewildered at Enberg. Not only was one of the businessman's eyes swelling up, but there were several cuts and bruises on his cheeks, and his lower lip was split.

Cates's condition was not Enberg's main concern, however. "Where's Emily, Logan?"

"You know very good and well where Emily is, Dag, you good for nothing sonofabitch!" Cates's voice trembled with emotion. Enberg had never seen the man so undone. Even with all that had occurred over the past two days, seeing Cates this traumatized was startling.

"Look, Logan, whatever you think you know—"

"Shut up!" Cates looked at Wilkes. "Drag Whipple down the mountain before those snakes slither back out of their hole."

Wilkes stepped wide around Enberg, who stood clutching his right arm with his left hand. Wilkes looked down at the dead marshal and whistled. "You ever seen the like?" he asked Cates.

"Just drag the poor bastard down the hill!" Cates was speaking to Wilkes, but he cast his enraged glare at Enberg. He wagged his derringer. "Get moving. You're under arrest for robbery and murder, Dag. I knew you were sliding, but I reckon I just didn't know how fast or how far."

Enberg began moving down the ridge, taking mincing steps to avoid sliding on the scree-littered slope. He glanced over his left shoulder. Cates followed from several feet behind while Wilkes picked up Whipple's ankles, giving a sour expression at the body continuing to purple from the poison that had been pumped into it.

"Whatever you think you know, Logan—it's wrong."

"I told you to shut up."

"Just tell me where Emily is. Please."

"They took her, as you knew they would. I walked in on them just as they were getting ready to pull out. I went over to your place to urge Emily to come back to the house, so we could take care of her—Gertrude and I. And I walked right into Ketchum's bailiwick. They beat holy hell out of me! They taunted me about you throwing in with them, about stealing my money and taking my stepdaughter."

"I didn't—!"

"They took her hostage so I wouldn't send a posse after them. They said they'd turn her loose when they were sure I hadn't sent anyone after them. I gather the only reason they didn't kill me was they wanted to avoid a murder charge!"

Cates had fairly shouted the entire spiel. His voice trembled. He was gaunt and pale. He looked nearly as bad as Enberg felt.

By the time he was finished, he and Enberg had reached the bottom of the ridge.

"Those bastards," Enberg said, fury rising in him again, beneath the thundering pain in his upper right arm. "Those bastards promised me they'd leave her. And I did not throw in with them, Logan. They told you that to spite me, because I killed Cougar's old man!"

"What else did they promise you?" Cates asked in disgust. "How much of a cut were you going to get for dumping the box along the trail, Dag?"

Enberg turned around to face the haggard-looking business-man. "It wasn't like that, Logan. I wasn't involved. Christ, if I'd been involved, do you think I would have come storming back to the cabin right after I'd dumped the strongbox? Why would I do that—throw myself right into your hands?"

Cates studied him, flaring the nostrils of his slightly swollen nose. Blood dribbled down his cheeks and his chin, glistening in the late-day light. "I have no idea what compels a man like you, Dag. I thought I did. I thought I was helping you get yourself on the right track. Obviously, I was wrong. You're under arrest for robbery and murder. I'll be sending for the circuit judge just as soon as I figure out what to do about retrieving the strongbox and getting Emily back safely."

Enberg was about to respond to this when running footsteps sounded from the direction of his cabin. Running toward him through the brush were Whipple's deputies flanked by Billie Two Doves from Cates's saloon. All four were wielding pistols and looking harried.

"What the hell's goin' on?" said L.D. Cook, Whipple's head deputy.

He canted his head to see around Enberg and Cates as Wilkes dragged Whipple's body down the ridge behind them. Wilkes dropped the dead man's ankles and, breathing hard, scrubbed sweat from his forehead with a red handkerchief.

"Who the hell is that?" Cook asked. He was a thickly built man with black hair, black mustache and goatee, and snaky gray eyes. He dressed to impress Whipple in neat, conservative suits, but his body was sloppy. "And what in hell happened to him?"

"That's the marshal," Cates said gravely, almost sadly, glancing back at Whipple. "Dag led him up the ridge to kill him." He cast his incriminating gaze at Enberg again, curling his bruised upper lip. "Being new to town, Whipple probably didn't know about the Mojave green rattlers that infest this area. But you did, didn't you? And you lead him up there to get him shed from your trail."

"That's not true, Logan. That's no truer than anything else you believe about me. I ran up the ridge because I was boxed in. I had nowhere else to go, goddamnit. I didn't want to see anyone killed!"

"What the hell is goin' on here?" asked Bryce Tanner, another of Whipple's deputies—a belligerent blond man who'd once served as gambling lookout and bouncer for Cates. "Grissom told us Enberg dropped the strongbox. Then we heard shootin' and come out here to find . . ."

The none-too-sharp Tanner let his voice trail off as he switched his befuddled gaze back to Whipple. Obviously, things were happening so fast for the square-headed, dull-witted man, his brains were scrambled.

"Ask Charlie why I done it," Enberg said. "He'll tell you. He knows the truth!"

Cates scoffed at that. "He knows the truth as *you* told it to him. Or maybe that old reprobate has thrown in with you . . ."

"Goddamnit, Logan!"

"Shut up!" Cates turned to Cook. "You're sheriff now. Take Enberg back to the jail and lock him up good and tight, then send for the doctor. I'd just as soon he bled to death for all he's done, but why cheat the hangman? Stand by for my orders. Cougar Ketchum's bunch is responsible for the holdup. Complicating matters is the fact that they've kidnapped my stepdaughter, Emily. We have to tread carefully. I've little doubt they'll kill her if they see we've gone after them."

"Jesus Christ," said Cook, drawing each word out and shaking his head as he stared in shock at his suddenly dead boss. He gritted his teeth at Enberg. "You no-good sonofabitch—get movin'!"

"Handcuff him, for chrissakes!" intoned Cates.

"Yeah, yeah, I was just gonna do that." Cook looked at Tanner. "You got cuffs on you?"

Tanner reached around to the small of his back, and said, "Yeah, yeah—I got cuffs."

"Heaven help us all!" said Cates, stomping toward town in disgust.

"Wait, Logan," Enberg said. "You gotta hear me out!"

Cates kept walking until the chaparral had consumed him.

CHAPTER TWENTY

A black widow spider made its halting way across the adobe ceiling.

It paused at a fracture in one of the mud bricks, then turned this way and that way, as though looking around for a better route.

Finally, it backtracked a couple of inches and crossed the crack where it started as a hairline, and then continued its way across the ceiling. When the spider reached the opposite wall, it scuttled down the hastily laid, uneven bricks flecked with straw to the barred window. There it began perusing its web for flies though it had finished off the last one earlier that morning.

Enberg knew because he'd watched the black widow, which bore the little red hourglass figure on its belly characteristic of females, slowly and methodically devour the half-alive insect just after Enberg had finished his morning meal of beans, bacon, and coffee.

It had made him a little sick to watch, but for some reason he'd been riveted on the spectacle, which had taken a good twenty minutes.

The spider had begun by appearing to regurgitate some sort of frothy black fluid on the fly. And then, as the fly started to shrivel as though what the spider had thrown up on it were some sort of acid, it proceeded to eat it. The devouring was curious in its own right, because it seemed as though the spider had somehow eaten the fly from the inside out, chewing as well as sucking.

Enberg had never seen anything like it, and now, reflecting back on it, he hoped he never saw anything like it again.

When all was said and done, and the spider hung fat and happy in its web, all that remained of the fly were bits and pieces, mostly from its legs.

Lying on his iron cot that hung from chains from the cell's barred wall, Enberg stared at the spider, his sole companion here in the cellblock of the Mineral Springs City Jail.

"All gone, sweetheart," he said, idly massaging the tender wound that the doctor had cleaned and sewn shut and wrapped with a heavy bandage. "You've done eaten it all. Now you're just gonna have to wait for the next damn fool fly to get caught in your . . ."

He let his voice trail off, for he heard the raspy, metallic scrape of a key in the cellblock door just outside his cell. As the door's steel hinges squawked, Enberg turned to see the door open. L.D. Cook poked his head into the cellblock and said, chuckling, "Visitor, Dag. You ain't too busy, are ya?"

"As a matter of fact, I am, L.D.," Enberg said, dryly. "Could you wait until I'm done burrowing a hole through the wall here?"

"Don't even joke about it, Dag," said the humorless new town marshal of Mineral Springs, who drew the door wider and stepped back.

Charlie Grissom brushed past Cook and started into the cellblock.

"Hold on, Charlie," Cook said, pulling Grissom's old Remy from its shoulder holster, and grinning. "You won't be needin' that."

"Yeah, I will," said Grissom. "I was gonna give it to Dag here . . . so he could shove it up your fat ass and pull the trigger."

Grissom's shoulders jerked as he gave a wheezing laugh.

Cook scowled, pinching up his snaky gray eyes. "Listen, old man—I'm the town marshal now, so you better talk to me with a little more respect."

"Ah, go fuck yourself, L.D." Grissom started walking in his halting, tender way toward Enberg's cell. "I know what L.D. stands for. The ten-cent whores over at old Ricardo's told me."

Grissom snickered.

"Goddamnit, Grissom—you're gonna pay for that!" Cook glared at the old man, who'd turned his broad shoulders away from him, and then stepped back into his office and slammed the cellblock door.

Enberg sat up, swung his feet to the floor, and rose, wincing at the pain in his bandaged arm. He strode to the door as the white-bearded jehu stopped in front of it.

"Any word from the posse?" he asked.

Cates had ridden out with a posse of twelve men the day before. He'd hired a tracker who had once scouted for the army and was now working as a stock detective—Bart Moses.

"Nothin'."

"Figured there wouldn't be. Ketchum's likely in Mexico by now. I thought he might send Emily back, though." Enberg sagged back down on his cot. "Shit!"

"Yeah, shit," Grissom said, pressing a shoulder up against the cell door and reaching inside his denim jacket for his makings sack. "Tell me it ain't true what Cates believes about you, Dag. That you were in on it from the start."

Enberg snapped a surprised look at him. "You know it ain't true."

Grissom let his makings sack dangle from his teeth by its drawstring as he troughed a wheat paper between the first two arthritic fingers of his right hand. "I know you ain't been right since you got home. That's all I really know. I know you been draggin' your ass around here ever since you came back to find your pa dead and Cates runnin' things."

"You think I'm desperate enough to steal a strongbox?"

"Hell, I often feel desperate enough to steal a strongbox." Grissom chuckled dryly as he dribbled chopped Coronado Blend on the wheat paper. "Hell, what's one strongbox to Cates?"

He glanced at Enberg regarding him incredulously. "No, I don't think you done it. You're not fool enough to go in with Cougar Ketchum. And I know you'd never let anything happen to Emily. One thing I do know, though, is that you are desperate for a stake, and you got it bad for a certain *senorita* who's got the kind of curves a man like me can only dream about."

"What—you've never taken a tussle?" Enberg asked, grinning as though to make it a joke though he was genuinely curious and a bit jealous. Most men around here saved up for an hour or two in Zee's boudoir.

"No, never have."

"Don't tell me you think she's overpriced."

"Hell, I've spent that much on whores before."

"I know you have."

"Me—I kind of like leavin' some ground untrod. Especially when that ground is the woman of a good friend—even if said woman's for sale. I reckon I'd kind of feel funny about it. Besides, even if I did have the money, she'd never have me. Oh, she'd take me upstairs and give me a drink or two, and we'd have a few laughs. But in the end she'd kiss me on the cheek, reshape my hat for me, and I'd leave with my pants too tight. But somehow I wouldn't be all that disappointed. That's the kind of girl she is. But you already know that, Dag."

"Yeah, I know."

Enberg put his head down and ran his hand roughly across the back of his neck. He cursed.

"You goin' crazy in here?" Grissom asked, rolling the paper

closed, making slight crinkling sounds as the paper rubbed against the tobacco.

Enberg walked over to the window with the spider web in the upper left corner, and stared out at a Victorian-style, adobe-brick house sitting atop a bluff roughly half a mile away and surrounded by a white picket fence shaded by cottonwoods and a couple of fruit trees that Cates had shipped in from California.

"Hell, no, I got all kinds of company. I got a spider in here somewhere. I call her Betty. Knew a blonde named Betty once in New Orleans. Spider Betty reminds me of blond Betty." Enberg gave a caustic chuff. "And I got Gertrude starin' down at me from that big wraparound porch up there on her and Cates's fancy place."

"You see her out there?"

"From time to time, she comes out all dressed up like she always is, with those high, white collars and her hair done up in that big mushroom bun. She comes out and fires pitchforks at me with her eyes."

"You know—I don't believe I've ever had the pleasure of an introduction to Gertrude."

"You don't want one. I've met her twice, and the second time she was spittin' all over me the way spider Betty spits on the flies she's trapped."

Grissom blew smoke into the cell. "Say again?"

"Never mind." Enberg sighed. "Anyway, I got Betty and Gertrude for company." He glanced at Grissom staring skeptically in at him, the old man's leathery, white-bearded face wreathed in shimmering tobacco smoke.

"Any sign of the circuit judge?" Dag asked.

"Heard he's on the way, is all."

Enberg gave his back to the window. "You think he'll hang me?"

"He's hung men for less than killin' a town marshal."

"I didn't mean to kill him, Charlie. I swear it. I didn't sic those snakes on him."

"Dag?" Grissom drew on his quirley, then pulled it out of his mouth and scrutinized the smoldering coal. "You mind if I give you a piece of advice?"

Enberg walked back to the front of the cell and wrapped his hand around a bar.

Grissom narrowed his leathery lids at him. "If you get out of this thing, you leave here and don't ever come back."

Enberg gave a dry chuckle.

"I ain't jokin', now, Dag. This place ain't for you no more. It went sour on you, and it ain't all Cates's fault."

"Ah, hell—I know that, goddamnit."

"I don't know that you really do. I been wantin' to tell you that for a while, because I just really hate to see what's become of you. I hate to think what your old man would think—you marryin' a perfectly nice girl you don't love just to get your mind off the one you do.

"All your drinkin' an' walkin' around with your tail draggin', driftin' from job to job. I've been wantin' to tell you that, and now, since you can't be in a much deeper hole than you're in, I'm tellin' you now . . . because me an' your pa were friends . . . that if you somehow get out of this cooler and avoid the judge's ten feet of taut hemp, you hightail it and never look back. You make a man out of yourself!"

"Tell me somethin', Charlie."

"What?"

"Did Cates have my old man killed? Come on—you'd know if anyone did."

Both questions had preyed on Enberg's mine for the past two years.

"Ah, fuck—why in the hell do I try to tell you anything?" Grissom rolled his head as though genuinely bereaved, blowing smoke through his nostrils. "Never mind."

He threw his hand out and started to turn away, but Enberg pulled him back.

"Charlie, get me out of here!"

CHAPTER TWENTY-ONE

"How do you propose I do that?" Grissom asked. "You want me to waltz into Whipple's . . . I mean, *Cook's* office, get my gun back, and beef him with it?"

"Slip me a gun through the bars." Enberg glanced at the barred window behind him.

Grissom shook his head, eyes hooded. "Uh-uh. I'll have no part of that."

"I wouldn't ask you if I wasn't desperate, Charlie. I have to get Emily back. She's in harm's way because of me. I've caught her in the same web I been caught in ever since I came back to Mineral Springs. She doesn't deserve any of this. I have to get her back, goddamnit. I have to make it up to her!"

"Cates is after her now."

"Ah, shit—Cates! Moses! What do they know about leadin' a posse? They're both old men—no offense. Hell, I tracked during the war. Wherever Ketchum's bunch is headed, I'll find 'em. And I'll do it without getting Emily killed." Enberg paused, staring at Grissom. "I have to clear my name, Charlie. I have to get that money back! I have to get my wife back to prove my innocence!"

"That better not be the only reason you wanna go after Emily, Dag," Grissom said, anger lifting a deep red flush behind his white beard.

That knocked Enberg back on his proverbial heels.

His reputation was so bad that the old driver, his best friend here in Mineral Springs, had found reason to question his motives, not to mention his honor.

But, then, what honor did he really have?

Since the war—none.

He had to get that back again, too. He'd been far too free with it, he realized now. He hadn't known how important it was.

"Forget it, Charlie," Enberg said, sitting back down on his cot. "Forget I asked you. I had no right."

"Dag, gallblameit, I'd help you if I could."

"I know you would."

"If there's anything else you need, you let me know—you hear, partner?"

Enberg tried a smile. "How 'bout your makin's? I could use a smoke."

Grissom tossed him his makings pouch. "Keep it."

"Thanks, Charlie."

"Dag?"

"Yeah?"

"Don't do anything stupid, you hear? You let Cates get Emily back. You just sit tight and wait for fate to decide your history. There's nothing more you can do."

"I know," Enberg said with an air of defeat, opening the sack. "I've done way too much already."

"Take care, now, partner."

Grissom strode to the cellblock door, and yelled, "Cook, open up!" through the small, barred window.

"Why should I?" Cook said when he finally got around to unlocking the door.

"Fuck you, you worthless son of a bitch!" Grissom glanced once more at Enberg, grinned, and then left the cellblock.

Cook glared at his lone prisoner, then slammed the door, the thunder resonating throughout the block.

Enberg had barely finished smoking his quirley when the cellblock door opened again.

"You got another visitor, Enberg!" Cook yelled, his voice echoing. "A far purtier one than the last one."

Enberg turned his head to see Zee come through the half-open door. She strode down the cellblock attired in a conservatively cut, cream and brown print cambric dress. The kind many housewives wore while dusting their parlors or hoeing their kitchen gardens.

But most housewives couldn't wear a dress like that the way Zee could. Watching her, Enberg felt a hard knot grow in his throat.

She wore her hair down, the long, curly tresses tumbling across her shoulders and snaking around her proud, upturned bosom.

"Hello, Dag."

Enberg rose and walked slowly, heavily over to the door to feast his eyes on her. "To what do I owe the honor?"

"Pity."

Enberg sighed. "Well, at least you're here."

Zee reached through the bars to brush her fingers across his arm. "Does it hurt?"

"Nah. The doctor said the bullet nicked the bone a little, but then it passed right on through the flesh."

"How 'bout your head?"

"Better."

"You never cease to amaze me."

"Yeah?"

"Your capacity for trouble never ceases to amaze me."

"I had a feelin' that's what you meant."

"We should have left here when we had the chance."

Enberg grabbed two bars and fidgeted around, leaning forward and toeing a crack in the floor. "We could have had a wild ride, you an' me. We never really got much of a chance, here in Mineral Springs." He stopped toeing the crack and looked up at her. "But you wouldn't have left, anyway, would you have?"

"Why do you say that?"

"Because you like your work. Maybe not the nuts and bolts of it, but you like control. And you like being wanted. You like the idea of the men of Mineral Springs makin' love to their wives while in their heads they're seein' you."

Zee stared at him, her pupils expanding and contracting slowly, like a cat's.

Enberg shook his head. "Comin' from what you come from— who can blame you? You came here and you made out well. And you'll continue to make out well for another five, six years . . . with a body like yours."

Zee wrapped her hands around the same two bars as Dag was squeezing, above his hands. She leaned forward to gaze at him directly, convincingly. "I would have gone, Dag. With you I would have gone."

"Really?" Enberg studied her, puzzled. "Why?"

Zee drew a deep breath, her well-covered but richly mounded bosom rising sharply. "Because I saw in you what I knew was in me. A wild, broken heart."

She paused, keeping her eyes on him.

"I would have left with you. But you are right. It wouldn't have lasted. We would have ruined each other. And you were right again about . . . my lust for seduction. My stepmother only told me of the rewards, which I've found quite rewarding indeed. But she did not warn me of the perils."

"Which are?"

"You hinted at it a moment ago. Premature old age and loneliness. But, then, the loneliness is already here. I feel it every time I look into a man's eyes . . . and see nothing but his lust. When I looked into your eyes, I saw so much more . . . and I couldn't have it because of who I am and who you are."

Zee slid her hands over his. He closed his eyes to savor the warmth of her flesh pressing against him until he could feel her pulse through his own skin.

"You still have a chance."

Enberg opened his eyes. "How?"

"Get your woman back. And love her the way you should. Love her like a *man*."

Enberg felt a wave of emotion roll through him. Self-loathing. Regret. Loneliness. Heartbreak. Longing for something he wasn't sure was attainable:

Redemption.

Love and honor . . .

He swallowed the knot in his throat. He felt his eyes grow wet. He nodded. "I'm going to. As soon as I figure a way out of this cell."

Zee reached up and began unbuttoning her dress.

Enberg frowned. "What're you doing?"

"Keep it in your pants, *pendejo*."

When she had five buttons undone, revealing a good portion of her coppery, mounded flesh sliding down inside a fringed pink corset, she slid two fingers into her cleavage. She pulled out an over-and-under derringer with gutta-percha grips.

"Cook didn't frisk me very well though he kept his hands on me plenty long enough." Zee winked and extended the pocket pistol to Enberg.

"No." Dag shook his head.

Zee arched a befuddled brow.

"They'll know who gave it to me. I'm sure every man on the street watched you walk over here."

Zee shrugged and glanced at the window behind him. "It could have come in between the bars."

Dag shook his head again. "I won't risk anyone else's life. I'll go it alone." He stared at her. "But when I get out, I'd appreciate it if had a few things waiting for me on the trail out of town. A few things I'll need for a trip down to Mexico, including two horses."

Zee pursed her lips and widened her eyes. "Anything for you, my wild-hearted *pendejo*. You know that."

CHAPTER TWENTY-TWO

That night, when the town outside the jail had fallen silent, Enberg sat up, tossed his single wool blanket aside, and dropped his feet to the floor. He felt around for his boots in the inky darkness, and pulled them on.

He fished a match out of his shirt pocket, firing it on his thumbnail. Holding the match high, he rose from the cot and looked up at the ceiling. The light from the match guttered and expanded and contracted, shepherding ragged-edged shadows around his cell.

When the flame started to burn his fingers, he dropped the lucifer and fired another one. He moved to the barred window. The flickering light glinted on the cobweb in the top left corner. Enberg smiled when he saw Betty there, spinning another web.

"Hello, there, baby," Dag said. "You're lookin' right queenly tonight, if you don't mind me sayin' so."

He let the second match go out and lit three more. He laid them on the edge of the window. They sputtered and popped, smoking and touching his nostrils with the smell of sulfur. He returned his attention to the black widow.

"Come on over and say hi to Dag, Betty. It's just you an' me tonight. Might as well make it a party—don't you think, honey?"

He swept his finger across Betty's path as she spun another web. He caught Betty on his finger and placed her on his arm. Immediately, she ran up his arm toward his elbow, the slightest of tickling sensations.

He brushed her back down toward his wrist. She felt like the lightest of breezes bending the blond hairs on his forearm.

Until she bit him.

Enberg cursed. He waved his arm, dislodging Betty into the darkness of a cell corner.

"Thanks, honey," he said in a pain-pinched voice, gritting his teeth as he felt the poison ooze into him. It was a strikingly painful, burning, numbing sensation that spread out from the point of the bite halfway between his wrist and elbow. "I owe you one, sweetheart."

He sat down on the cot, scrubbed both hands through his hair, mussing it to make it look like he'd been sleeping, though he hadn't slept a wink since sundown. He'd just been lying there, thinking and plotting.

He lifted his head and shouted as loud as he could: "Owww— *goddamnit!* Goddamnit, goddamnit, goddamnit! Tanner, get in here! You got spiders in here, you fool!"

When he heard nothing from the jailhouse office, he grabbed his tin thunder mug, which Tanner had emptied a little before dark, and raked it across the bars of his cell. It made a loud, tinny drumming sound.

"Tanner—get in here!" Enberg roared. "I been bit by a spider!"

"What the hell's goin' on in there, Enberg?" came Tanner's sleep-gravelly voice. Tanner was the night deputy. He wasn't supposed to sleep but he'd been asleep, all right. Enberg could hear it in his voice. "Do I need to shoot you from here, Dag?"

"I been bit by a goddamn black widow, Tanner! My arm's burnin' up! Fetch the doc!"

"Pipe down, Enberg, or so help me I'll take my Winchester and shoot you through the cellblock door!"

"My arm's burnin' up!" Enberg bellowed, staggering around his cell and kicking the bars. "I need a doctor, goddamnit. Fetch him now, Tanner!"

"Ah, bullshit. Just lay down and go to sleep and it'll be all better by mornin'."

"Get me a doctor, Tanner! I been bit before by one of these things, and my jaws locked up and my windpipe swelled so's I couldn't breathe. Ain't gonna look good for you if the judge makes a trip out here for nothin'!"

"Oh, fer pity's sakes!"

Enberg inwardly grinned when he heard the scrape of a key in the lock of the cellblock door. He continued to stomp around, cursing and sucking air through his teeth as the cellblock door squawked open.

A light played along the floor. Tanner moved into the cellblock, holding an old, brass-framed railroad lantern in one hand and a Winchester carbine in the other hand.

The deputy was a vague shadow behind the illumination. The light glistened on the rifle barrel.

"Hurry up," Enberg bellowed. "My arm feels like it's rotting off!"

"This better not be a trick, my friend," Tanner warned. "Or I'm gonna gut-shoot you and leave you howlin'. Fuck the judge!"

"You oughta get these damn spiders out of here, you pinheaded fool. I'm liable to sue your asses. Fetch the doc!"

"Oh, stop carryin' on like a damn pantywaist. Let me see—where'd it bite ya?"

Tanner held the lantern low against the bars. He held the rifle a ways back, the maw about two feet from the cell door. Enberg needed to get it closer, so he could grab it.

Or . . .

He held his bit arm up close to the bars. Tanner lowered the light until the dark-red, egg-shaped swelling on Enberg's blond-haired forearm was revealed by the flickering lamplight.

Tanner laughed. "Holy shit, you did get—!"

The deputy's blond head was closer to the door than the rifle was, so Enberg thrust his spider-bit arm through the bars, wrapped it around Tanner's neck, and slammed his head against the door with a loud, rattling ring.

Tanner cursed.

Enberg wrapped his other arm around the man's neck and slammed his head against the door again, again . . . and again. The fourth time was the charm. Tanner dropped the rifle and sagged down against the cell door with a rattling liquid sigh.

He dropped the lantern, as well, which clattered to the brick floor and tipped over on its side.

Enberg grimaced, staring at the guttering flame inside the steel-banded mantle. He thought for sure the lamp would break and spill coal oil, which would quickly catch fire and give him little time to fish the cell key out of Tanner's pocket and open the door before he was roasted like a pig on a spit in his own locked cell.

Thankfully, the coal oil didn't spill.

At least, not yet.

Enberg looked at Tanner. The deputy sat slumped against the cell door, his back to Enberg, his head tipped to one side. He was groaning, mostly unconscious. His legs were stretched out wide before him.

Quickly, Enberg dropped to a knee and, ignoring the acidic fire in his quickly swelling left arm, reached through the bars, grabbed the lantern, and stood it on its base. He couldn't smell coal oil, which meant none had so far leaked out of the base. He wanted to kill the flame and thus douse the risk of roasting himself alive, but he needed the light to find the key and his way out of the jail.

He felt around Tanner's body for the key ring. It was protruding from the deputy's back pocket. Enberg pulled out the ring and, keeping a nervous eye on the lantern, stood and fumbled the key into the lock.

He grimaced at the pain in his left arm as well as the pain in his right arm. The bullet wound was bellowing now, as well, from his bouncing off the cell walls.

It took him nearly a minute to get the key positioned correctly in the lock. He blew a sigh of relief when he heard the locking bolt scrape and the door give a metallic whine as it sagged on its hinges.

He grabbed his hat, drew the door open, and stepped into the hall.

Tanner's eyes were closed but he was moaning softly, his chest rising and falling slowly. Enberg considered giving him another smack to make sure he stayed out for a good hour but decided against it.

With his luck, he'd likely kill the man and find himself facing another murder charge.

Instead, he pulled the Colt Army .44 from the man's holster. He gave the weapon a quick appraisal, nodding his satisfaction. He slid the gun's barrel behind his wide leather belt. Picking up the lantern, he hurried to the cellblock door, which stood partway open. He gave a snort at the sign, which read in large letters penciled, no doubt, by the late Charlie Whipple: LOCK THIS DOOR BEHIND YOU!

Tanner probably couldn't read.

Enberg stepped into the office, holding the lantern high, spreading a broadening pool of yellow light around him. He looked at the gun cabinet recessed in the wall at the office's far end. His shotgun and cartridge bandoliers were there. The cabinet's locking chain had been snaked through the twelve-gauge's trigger guard.

Enberg flipped through the keys on the key ring. There were only three—one obviously for the cellblock door and another for the individual cell doors. He hoped the third, smaller key was for the padlock on the gun cabinet's chain.

He was right. The lock opened; the chain fell away.

Enberg grabbed his two-bore, broke it open, and filled the empty tubes with wads from his bandoliers. He snapped the two-bore closed, looped the bandoliers over his neck, set the lantern on the desk, and moved to the front door.

He quietly tripped the latch and looked out through the six-inch gap between the door and the frame. The street appeared deserted. The shops on both sides of the street were dark. The only sound was the slow, indolent strumming of a guitar likely coming from one of the Mexican cantinas off to the east.

Enberg moved on out onto the boardwalk, drew the door closed, slipped around the building's left front corner, and jogged down the gap between the marshal's office and a lumberyard, cursing when his right boot kicked a can.

Both his bullet-burned upper right arm and his spider-bit left forearm were barking like sons of bitches. The forearm felt hot and heavy. It felt as though a small rat were inside it trying to eat its way out.

Using Betty had been a hell of a way to break jail, but he hadn't been able to come up with a better plan. This one had worked. As long as the venom didn't kill him. He didn't think it would. He'd lied to Tanner about his jaws locking up. He had a strong Nordic constitution, and his old man, who'd been bitten several times while burrowing into cool, dark desert crevices for gold, had taught him a way to treat it.

First, he had to get to the horses he hoped that Zee had arranged to be waiting for him.

The first horse was there, outside of a little cantina on the Mexican side of town—a sprawling, dilapidated adobe with a long brush-roofed galleria fronting it. There were several horses tied under the remuda.

Enberg moved along behind the mounts. They stiffened

nervously as he approached, arching their tails. A couple whickered as they turned owly looks at the stranger. He found the horse he was looking for—a rangy pinto marked with a red bandanna tied to one of the leather straps holding the bedroll in place behind the cantle of the saddle. The horse was outfitted with saddlebags and a bulging burlap food bag, as well.

So far, so good.

Enberg didn't know who the horse belonged to, or who had left it here for him. Probably some loyal client of Zee's—one whom she trusted and who didn't ask questions.

Enberg cooed to the horse, running his hand down its neck soothingly, as he backed it out from under the remuda. As he did, he heard a girl groaning. He turned the horse in the street and then looked toward the cantina.

A lit window with a thin, pink curtain faced him. On the other side of the window, a naked Mexican girl was straddling a man on a bed. All Enberg could see of the man was part of his belly and his hands on the girl's undulating hips. The girl leaned forward over the man, hair falling and breasts swaying.

From one of the bedposts hung a shirt with a five-pointed town marshal's badge.

Enberg gave an involuntary laugh.

The girl snapped her head toward the window. She'd heard him . . .

The man leaned across the window and looked out. His head was silhouetted against the watery lamplight. Because of the badge and by the shape of the man's head, Enberg could tell it was L.D. Cook.

Dag's heart hiccupped.

"Hey, who's out there?" Cook bellowed through the glassless window, brushing one of the curtains aside with his hand.

Turning the pinto between him and the cantina, Enberg

covered his mouth with his hand and said into his palm, "Sorry, mister!"

"You better scram, you goddamn pervert!" Cook bellowed as Enberg heaved himself into the saddle. "This is Town Marshal Cook here, and if you don't stop peepin' in windows, I'm gonna throw your fairy ass in jail!"

Enberg barely heard the last half of the threat. He and the pinto were galloping on down the street and heading for the west edge of town. Despite the agony in his arms, he allowed himself a laugh at Cook's expense.

He glanced over his shoulder to look at the mostly dark town retreating behind him. "Mineral Springs has hit the jackpot, law-wise!" he said, and snorted another laugh.

CHAPTER TWENTY-THREE

The second horse was waiting for Enberg right where he'd expected it to be.

You had to hand it to Zee. She could be counted on to follow through with everything but a long, loving relationship. But, then, who was he to criticize? She'd come through for him here, and now was all that mattered.

The second horse—a steeldust gelding with a right rear black sock and black tail—whickered edgily as Enberg rode up on the pinto. The steeldust was tied to a cottonwood a half a mile off the main trail, about fifty yards from an old, abandoned Spanish mission church that gleamed palely in the light of a rising quarter moon.

According to plan, the horse was not saddled, only bridled. Enberg needed only one saddle.

He had rendezvoused here with Emily not long after they'd first met accidentally in Mineral Springs, when she'd been taking long walks around the town to escape her overprotective and overly restrictive mother as well as the expensive but staid confines of the Victorian house on the bluff.

Enberg had naturally been curious about the identity of the beautiful, freckled redhead he often saw strolling along the back streets—which could be dangerous even by day—clad in expensive-looking gowns and picture hats. So one day, seeing her on one such back street when he'd been having a beer with Charlie Grissom on the brush-roofed patio of a little cantina, he'd simply walked out and introduced himself.

Emily had been surprisingly receptive to the big, blond-bearded stranger in denims and sweat-stained buckskin tunic. They'd started out by taking walks together round the town, keeping to the backstreets and outlying washes so word about the proscribed get-togethers wouldn't drift to her mother. When Emily had wanted to sneak away for a walk, she'd merely told Gertrude she was retreating to her room for a long nap.

Then she'd escape via a rear outside stairs.

Enberg's and Emily's trysts had gradually drifted beyond Mineral Springs to the little mission church, where they'd made love on blankets spread near picnic baskets, empty wine bottles, and their ground-reined horses.

Dag hadn't had to work very hard at seducing the girl. It had happened on their second meeting at the church. Emily's carnal appetite had surprised him every bit as much as her first receptiveness to him—a shaggy-headed, shotgun-bearing stranger with beer on his breath. Her uninhibited lovemaking, which included an adeptness at, not to mention a proclivity for, fellatio, had told him that when her mother had sent her east to finishing school, it had not only been school she'd learned to finish.

Eventually, he and Emily had eloped in Tucson, to Gertrude's everlasting fury. For some reason or another, marriage had meant an end to their thrilling and lusty trysts here at the old mission church.

A sad thing. It was his own damned fault. He knew now that he'd married Emily to distract himself from thoughts of Zee. But as soon as he and Emily were married, Zee was the only woman he could think about.

"Goddamn moron," he gritted out now as he swung down from the pinto's back, holding his spider-bit arm against his side.

He grabbed the saddlebags off the pinto's back, and sat down on a rock. He rummaged around in the saddlebags and pulled out a small burlap pouch. Inside the pouch was flannel for bandages and a bone-handled Barlow knife.

He set the pouch atop the saddlebags on his lap and then opened the blade of the Barlow knife. He ran a match flame along the blade's steel edge, and then looked down at the spider bite on his left forearm.

It resembled a goose egg half-embedded in the skin. It throbbed and burned fiercely. The venom was eating away at his flesh. It had to come out.

Enberg laid his arm across his lap and, hunkering over it and gritting his teeth, passed the edge of the blade across the egg-shaped swelling, about a quarter of an inch deep. Blood and yellow pus oozed from the incision.

Enberg sucked sharply through his teeth.

He pulled a twelve-gauge shotgun shell from his bandolier and, his hands shaking, opened it with his knife. He poured the buckshot onto the ground, then dribbled the gunpowder into the dripping wound.

The gunpowder would continue to draw out the poison. Olaf Enberg had passed the remedy down to his son. The elder Enberg had claimed that when he'd been bitten in the past, the gunpowder cut in half the time he knew it would have taken the bite to heal on its own.

He thought it had also cut down on any possible lingering damage to tissue and nerves and prevented such reactions as vomiting and debilitating stomach cramps, not to mention suffocation due to possible neck swelling.

Dag hadn't needed to test the old man's cure until now.

He hoped it worked.

He withdrew a length of blue flannel from the burlap pouch that Zee had provided, and wrapped it tightly over the wound.

He tied it off on the underside of his forearm and then shoved the pouch back into the saddlebags. He tossed the saddlebags over the pinto's back, and, a little breathless and weak from the lancing of the bite, walked over and soothed the edgy steeldust.

He'd wanted two horses so that he could switch between the two, allowing him to travel farther and faster.

He untied the steeldust from a cottonwood branch, retied the bridle reins to the pinto's tail, and mounted up. He sagged forward in the saddle.

Fatigue weighed heavy on him. The nervous energy he'd worked up plotting and then effecting his escape from the Mineral Springs jail was waning. Now the poison and the misery from the wound in his right arm as well as general weariness—he hadn't had a decent night's sleep in days—were getting a dangerous hold on him.

But he had to keep moving. L.D. Cook would learn of his escape soon and come after him.

He had to pick up the trail of the robbers—and likely Cates's trail, as well, from where he'd dumped the strongbox—and get after them all. He had to get to Emily before Ketchum killed her, which, since the outlaw had gone as far as kidnapping her, he might very well do. Emily's life meant nothing to Ketchum except short-term security.

He was liable to kill her if only to get back at Dag for Ketchum's father and Raoul Leclerk.

Emily wasn't the only thing Enberg was after. He had to retrieve Cates's strongbox. He had to clear his name. Cates and the men he'd chosen for his posse were likely experienced riders. They were being led by an effective tracker in Bart Moses.

But none of them, including Cates himself, had as much at stake as Enberg did. He had to get his wife and his honor back.

Cates and the posse would tread cautiously. Enberg would

throw caution to the wind and replace it with cunning, killing fury.

"Let's go, hoss!"

Touching heels to the pinto's flanks, hardening his jaws against his misery and fighting to stay conscious, he galloped off into the night.

CHAPTER TWENTY-FOUR

Enberg arrived at the place he'd dumped the strongbox as dawn painted a gray blush across the eastern horizon and the desert birds were beginning to pipe.

The area was scoured by the prints of many horses. Part of Ketchum's gang had obviously been here first to pick up the box, and then Cates's posse had ridden into the wash to pick up Ketchum's trail.

Enberg had no idea how many men comprised Ketchum's gang. He knew it to be a motley unit that varied in number, and they were not always together even when they considered themselves a gang. Enberg guessed there were between five and ten.

The men who'd picked up the strongbox had likely rendezvoused with Ketchum, Ugly Tom, and Ray McInally somewhere along the trail to Mexico.

Cates and his posse were after them now. All the tracks that converged here at the gouge in the wash where Enberg and Grissom had dumped the strongbox continued west. That fact didn't change Enberg's notion that Ketchum had headed to Mexico. There were several routes to the border, and he'd probably chosen one west of here—one of the old freight roads that had been used since the time of the Spanish, most likely.

Enberg resisted the urge to pause here in the wash and take a short nap. He couldn't sleep yet. He had to keep riding until he could ride no more.

As he followed the relatively fresh tracks of the two gangs, Enberg wondered how close Cates was to Ketchum. He also wondered about Emily. There was a good chance he'd find her body somewhere along the trail, discarded like trash after she'd lost her usefulness to Ketchum.

The possibility was sour milk in Enberg's belly. But he had to face up to it so that it didn't tear him entirely apart if he did, indeed, find his wife dead.

His wife and their unborn child.

He'd need some semblance of sanity to continue after Ketchum.

He pushed the pinto hard for another hour, then, when the sun had cleared the eastern horizon, he stopped to switch horses. He'd just unstrapped the pinto's latigo to remove the saddle when he glanced along his back trail.

Far out through the bristling chaparral casting long fingers of morning shade across the desert rocks and cactus, a shadow moved.

"Now, what in the hell?" Enberg muttered to himself.

He stared at the shadow until it suddenly disappeared.

His blood quickened in his veins. Someone was shadowing him. Who?

The new marshal of Mineral Springs, perhaps?

Quickly, Enberg strapped his saddle and the rest of his gear to the steeldust's back. Then he led the horses around to the south side of a low rise. When he'd tied the mounts to a breeze-ruffled mesquite, he jogged up the side of the rise and hunkered down on his belly near the top, doffing his hat.

He squinted off to the north.

It was hard to pick out possible riders because of the gradually lengthening shadows angling westward of the desert plants and rocks. But after five or six minutes of sweeping his gaze back and forth across his back trail, he spied them.

Three riders moving toward him.

They were shadowy figures, the eastern sun lightening only their left sides. But they were riders, all right . . . riding Indian file in Enberg's direction. Following his, Ketchum's, and the posse's trail.

Dag stayed low, fingering the double-barreled shotgun hanging from the lanyard around his neck. He stared along his back trail. The three riders kept coming at a canter until he could see the white stripe angling down the snout of the first rider's horse, a claybank, the morning sun glistening in its coat.

The first rider was dressed in a black hat and a black coat. That would be the newly crowned Marshal Cook. The two behind were likely his deputies, Tanner and Mel Jackson. Tanner was probably feeling a little worse for the braining Enberg had given him against the cell door. And likely a little glum about it.

Gradually, the thudding of the hooves rose, as did the rattle of bit chains and the squawk of tack. One of the horses blew. Another kicked a rock. Enberg heard the rock tumble. The clear sound told him they were within range of his barn blaster.

He rose to his knees, aiming the sawed-off from his right side, and tripped the left trigger.

The thundering boom was like a cannon blast in the quiet morning, causing birds to flutter up from the chaparral. The buckshot blew up a gourd-sized clump of dirt and red gravel six feet in front of Cook's horse.

Cook cursed as the claybank swerved off the trail, violently crow-hopping, head down, tail arched, angrily kicking its rear hooves.

"Goddamnit!" Cook screamed, clinging to his saddle horn.

The clay wheeled abruptly. Cook and his saddle went sliding off down the horse's far side. Cook screamed again as he hit the ground with a thud while the horse trotted off through the brush, whinnying.

Tanner and Jackson stopped their own horses behind Cook, and started to slide their rifles from their saddle scabbards.

"I wouldn't do that," Enberg said, rising from his knees and aiming the twelve-gauge on the deputies. "Just keep those long guns where they are, or I'll blow you both out of your saddles with the same charge."

The deputies sat side by side, about three feet apart, at the base of the hill, scowling up at Enberg.

"Enberg, you bastard!" Cook bellowed, pushing himself up onto his hands and knees. "You son of a goddamn bitch!"

"Pipe down, Marshal," Enberg said. "Or I'll blow your fool head off." He saw Tanner's right hand move toward the pistol jutting from the holster thonged on his right thigh. "You can keep the short gun where it is, too, Tanner, or whatever misery you're feeling is gonna feel like a mosquito bite when I trip this next trigger."

"You . . . son . . . of a . . . bitch!" Tanner grated out, his angry voice low and teeming with frustration.

"Well, now that you've expressed your feelin' about my bloodline, suppose you two hop down out of them saddles. You can take it a little easier than Cook did, but get down off them horses just the same."

The two just stared at him, nostrils flared.

Enberg tripped the shotgun's second trigger, blowing up another clump of gravel in front of the deputies' horses. Tanner's horse bucked once. Jackson's lurched backward and sideways, whickering and staring at the man atop the bluff uneasily.

Enberg lowered the smoking shotgun and pulled Tanner's Army Colt out from behind his belt, and cocked it.

"Dismount. Now," he ordered.

The deputies glanced at each other. Then, returning their enraged gazes to Enberg, they stepped down from their saddles.

"What—you gonna kill us, now, too? Same as Whipple?"

"Don't give me any ideas," Dag said, as he tramped down the hill. As he walked, he used his left hand to break open the shotgun, shake out the spent wads, pluck two fresh ones from his bandoliers, and slip them into the tubes.

He shook the popper closed, then returned Tanner's Colt to his belt and took the shotgun in both hands.

He looked at Cook, who was down on one knee, dabbing at a cut on his other knee with a finger. He glowered at Enberg.

"Over here, Marshal," Enberg ordered, waving his shotgun.

"Why? You wanna kill us all with one blast, spare another wad?"

"You fellas are full of good ideas. Get over here. I won't tell you again."

When Cook had limped over to stand with his two deputies, Enberg said, "Drop your pistol belts."

As Cook unbuckled his shell belt, he said, "So . . . you're headed for Mexico, eh? Hope to meet up with Cougar Ketchum and help him spend that strongbox money?"

"Maybe I will," Enberg said. "But I can tell you this for sure. If I see you three on my trail again, I'm not gonna be near as nice as I was here today. I'm just gonna blow your fool heads off and leave you to the mountain lions."

Cook and his deputies shared skeptical looks.

Cook turned back to Enberg. "What do you mean . . . you're not gonna kill us?"

"You tinhorns aren't worth the trouble." Enberg jerked the twelve-gauge in the direction of Mineral Springs. "Head on back to town and stay there."

"What?" Jackson said, scowling. "You mean *walk*?"

"You can either walk back to town or fly to heaven on golden wings. Your choice."

"Without our guns?"

"That's right. I'm gonna take whatever I think I can use, and them I'm gonna bury the rest out here somewhere. You won't use any of those guns against me again. Don't bother comin' back to look for 'em. You'll never find 'em. Now, skedaddle before I have a change of heart."

The men looked at each other.

Tanner glared at Cook. "You goddamn fool. You're supposed to be the boss now, but you led us right up on him!"

Cook snapped a wild, enraged look at Tanner. "You're the fool who let him escape!" He lurched toward Tanner but Jackson grabbed him by his arms and held him back. Cook huffed and puffed, seething.

Tanner stepped back, raising his fists defensively.

Enberg rolled his eyes. "Get a move on, fellas!"

Cook jerked his arms free of Jackson's grip. Then, cussing under his breath at Tanner, he began walking back in the direction from which they'd come. The others cast indignant looks at Enberg and then followed Mineral Springs's new marshal in the direction of town.

Enberg gathered up their horses into a tight group, then triggered his shotgun in the air over their heads.

The horses galloped off buck-kicking past the three lawmen. Tanner tried to catch one but gave up and merely stood cussing and shaking his fist at the three mounts that would likely beat him, Cook, and Jackson back to town by a good hour.

Enberg grabbed a pistol and a carbine out of the pile at his feet. He also took all three well-filled cartridge belts, as the ammo would likely come in handy. He tossed the rest of the weapons into the brush. He returned to his horses, shoved the rifle into the scabbard strapped to his saddle, and dropped the second pistol and the shell belts into a saddlebag pouch.

There was no telling how much firepower he was going to need once he caught up to Ketchum. Better safe than sorry.

He mounted up and rode on.

Late in the day, he came upon a long mound of dirt and rocks beside the trail. It was marked with a cross hastily fashioned from two chunks of driftwood.

"Oh, no," Enberg said, staring with dread down at the freshly dug grave.

CHAPTER TWENTY-FIVE

Heavy with exhaustion, Enberg swung down from the steel-dust's back and dropped to a knee beside the grave. He placed two hands on the mound, squeezing a couple of rocks covering it, wondering if Emily lay under the rocks and dirt.

Had Cates found her along the travel and given her a hasty burial?

Who else could it be?

Heart hammering, Enberg began removing the rocks from the mounded dirt.

"Please, please, please," he muttered, sweat running down his bearded cheeks as he toiled faster. "Don't let it be Emily!"

When he got all of the rocks removed from the head of the grave, near the cross, he began digging into the dirt with his hands. He worked like a desperate gopher, scooping up the dirt and gravel and tossing it back behind him.

He was already sweaty, sunburned, and filthy from the hard ride south, but he was even sweatier, filthier, and even more sunburned by the time he felt some yielding object as his fingers scratched away at the grave.

Enberg paused. He stared down at the hole he'd dug through the loose dirt. His heart chugged in dread of what he was about to find.

He swallowed, steeling himself, and then continued digging, scraping away the dirt from over and around what felt like a human head. As he worked, the head began to take shape. Gradually, he began to make out the paleness of facial skin beneath the thin layer of dark-red dirt and gravel.

Enberg's heart beat faster and harder as he continued his excavation, quickly but carefully clearing dirt and sand away from the face taking shape beneath him. Finally, he sat back on his heels and heaved a long sigh of relief.

The face in the hole before him was the patch-bearded face of the Mineral Springs gunsmith, Art Winkleman. There was a ragged hole in Winkleman's forehead, about two inches above his right eye. The man's lids were not quite closed, and the waning salmon sunlight glistened dully in the bottoms of his eyes.

Enberg sighed again. "Sorry, Art," he said in vaguely sheepish acknowledgment of his relief at not finding the body of his wife.

He rose slowly, grabbed his canteen off his saddle, and took a long drink, clearing the dust from his throat. Then, wondering how Winkleman had come to be shot—had Ketchum ambushed the posse?—he walked back over to the grave and dutifully covered it.

As he reset the cross, which he'd knocked over during the excavation, he looked up suddenly.

He'd heard something.

He rose from his work, grabbed the steeldust's reins, and led both horses into the chaparral far wide of the trail. He tied the steeldust, who was trailing the pinto, to a mesquite, then plucked his shotgun's leather lanyard from around his saddle horn, looping it over his head and shoulder and taking the deadly popper in both hands.

He walked back toward the trail, climbed a low mound of rocks and cactus, and dropped to his belly near the top. He doffed his hat and stared south along the trail, which he could see clearly from this high vantage.

Gradually, two horseback riders topped a low rise and then

started down the near side, heading toward Enberg. Two more riders appeared behind the first two. Enberg waited, remaining hidden but watching the four riders approach—four men so dusty that they and their horses looked as though they'd rolled in dirt.

The left lead rider appeared to be wearing a bandage around the top of his head. It was slanted down across his right eye. As he and the others neared Enberg, Dag saw a red stain on the bandage, over the man's right eye.

Enberg didn't recognize this wounded rider, but he recognized the man riding next to him. As they drew even with his position and several feet below, he recognized the other two, as well. The right rear rider was pulling a travois on which yet another posse member rode—this one a black man named Owen Tate, who was a hostler at the Arizona Feed & Livery Barn, which Olaf Enberg had long ago established.

Tate groaned as the travois carried him along, rocking him this way and that. His buckskin breeches were badly blood-stained. Enberg saw what could only have been an Apache arrow protruding from the man's lower left leg. The fletched end of the arrow had been broken off, but it looked like no one had been able to extract the tip from the man's leg bone. Apparently, they were leaving that delicate maneuver to the doctor in Mineral Springs.

They were a ragged lot. They looked even wearier than Enberg felt.

And now he had one more thing to worry about.

Apaches.

Apparently, the posse had been ambushed by a group who'd most likely jumped the reservation and was wreaking havoc along the border.

Enberg cursed and looked down at the grave he'd just excavated and recovered, wondering if Winkleman had been killed by Apaches, as well, and if the same group who'd killed him had continued to dog the posse farther south. If so, they might be dogging Ketchum's bunch, as well, which meant even more danger for Emily.

Enberg watched the four riders and Tate dwindle off into the northern distance. Gaining his feet, he was reminded again how exhausted he was. He fell to a knee as he moved back down the rocky rise, and clutched his burning left forearm.

He looked at the horses. He wanted to mount up and continue riding south but fatigue was like an anvil on his shoulders.

He had to pause here, drink some water, eat some of the food Zee had provided, and catch a few winks. He'd rest the horses, as well. The last thing he needed was to blow out his mounts.

He unsaddled the steeldust, gave both horses a cursory rubdown with a swatch of burlap, watered and grained them, and then made a cold camp in a notch of rocks near Winkleman's grave, about fifty feet from the trail. He wanted a cup of coffee in the worst way, but if Apaches were on the lurk, he couldn't risk a fire.

Water and one of the sandwiches Zee had provided would have to do.

He sat down against a rock in his little stone nest also sheltered by a large cottonwood and several mesquites, and dug into a food sack, withdrawing the burlap pouch in which Zee had placed several ham sandwiches wrapped in waxed paper.

He pulled out a couple of pickled eggs and a small pouch of jerky and biscuits, as well. Zee must have gleaned such provisions from the kitchen at the Diamond in the Rough. He didn't know her to cook. Cooking wasn't in her arsenal of man-pleasing talents, and it hadn't needed to be.

One of the sandwiches and two of the eggs went down

quickly, washed down with water. When Enberg had finished the meal, the sun was almost behind the western ridges. It teetered there, a giant pink ball that slowly turned darker and smaller as it passed on down behind a near western range.

Darkness swept like the shadow of a giant bird across the desert.

The air chilled.

Coyotes yammered in the far distance.

Nearby, each tied to a picket pin, the horses snorted contentedly and pulled at small tufts of needle grass.

Enberg lay back against his saddle. As he pulled his hat brim down over his eyes, sleep came as suddenly as if he'd been hit with a sledgehammer.

He was awakened by the night cry of a stalking mountain lion. Born and raised in the desert, he knew the sound well, but it never ceased to chill him. The horses knew the sound, too. They looked around cautiously, nickering.

The sound had traveled far on the cool, dry desert air. The cat was likely stalking prey in the nearby mountains but far enough away that Enberg wasn't worried the cat was stalking him or his mounts.

Still, he rose, grunting at the stiffness in his joints and his sundry other miseries. The spider bite still burned, but not as badly as before. The gunpowder was drawing the venom out. He could tell that the swelling was going down beneath the bandage.

He could use another couple of hours of shut-eye, but the position of the stars told him it was getting along toward dawn. He ate some jerky, drank some water, stretched, gathered his gear, saddled the pinto, and mounted up.

Trailing the steeldust, he rode off at a fast walk, for the moon was down and, while Ketchum's and Cates's trail was reasonably clear, overlaid as it was by the four retreating posse riders and the travois they were pulling, it was still too dark for fast travel without risking the horses.

The sun rose, the heat building fast. The positions of the mountains around him now told him that he was most likely in Mexico, probably having crossed the line around midafternoon of the day before. Now, he not only had to worry about Apaches but Rurales and Federales, as well, who didn't take kindly to *norteamericanos* crossing the border uninvited.

He traveled hard all day, then stopped to cold camp around four. He rose and started out again around midnight, for the moon was high and the trail was clear, and there was no point in traveling during the heat of the desert day if he didn't have to. This way he and his horses would stay fresher for longer.

He rested again for two hours in the middle of the day.

How far was Ketchum going, anyway? He was deep enough into Mexico now that he could hole up anywhere and wait for his trail to cool. Most likely, he was continuing to move because Cates was continuing his pursuit.

Enberg thanked god that he had still not yet discovered Emily's body along the trail. Of course, they could have dumped her anywhere, but Ketchum was probably holding onto her to use her as a bargaining chip against Cates, if and when Cates caught up to the outlaws.

An hour after he started traveling again, he came upon the point in the trail where the retreating riders had entered it, one rider pulling the travois. Enberg left the trail and looked around, finding three more graves lined up side by side on the lip of a dry wash. Near the graves were Chiricahua arrows and spent brass cartridge casings.

There were also several sizeable patches of spilled blood. What looked like crimson paint had been splashed across the branches of a spindly mesquite where one posse rider had likely been shot out of his saddle.

Enberg didn't bother investigating the graves. There was a chance one belonged to Emily, but there was a greater chance they were now the eternal resting places of more posse members.

With four dead and five others on their way to town, Cates was down to only himself and four other men. Cates must still be alive; it was doubtful that any other posse members would have continued after Ketchum without their leader.

Enberg found his and the other riders' trail just beyond where the travois had entered it.

Cates was pushing south after Ketchum, who must somehow have avoided the Apaches.

Cates was a damned relentless man. Enberg would give him that. He wondered what he was most eager to recover—his stepdaughter or his strongbox. Enberg knew the answer to that question. At least, he thought he did.

He continued following the trail southwest, stopped before sundown, and started out again around midnight.

That afternoon, the crackling of gunfire rose from the trail ahead of him.

He stopped the pinto abruptly, and his heart thudded.

Above the gunfire sounded the banshee-like squalling of attacking Apaches.

CHAPTER TWENTY-SIX

Enberg stared ahead along the trail.

The gunfire and the war whoops of the Apaches were coming from what he judged to be about two hundred yards ahead. Now he could see wisps of dust and possibly powder smoke rising ahead and to the right of the trail, to the right of where a giant fireplace hearth of crenellated sandstone jutted two hundred feet above the desert.

His blood jetting in his veins—Enberg had the same primordial fear of Apaches as any other man—he gigged his horses along the trail, pondering the situation. The last thing he wanted was to get tangled up in an Apache fight, but if white men were their quarry, he couldn't very well just sit back on his heels.

He turned the horses off the trail and traced a broad circle around the hair-raising sounds of the war whoops and the crackling gunfire. As he rode, a man's shrill, agonized screams lifted. They were the screams of a white man. Only white men screamed like that, and usually only when they were enduring a good old-fashioned Apache disemboweling or gelding.

Enberg's blood ran cold at the bellowing, panting screams. He was glad when they died about fifteen seconds after they'd started.

He rode around to the southern perimeter of the fight—if you could call what Enberg was now hearing a fight. It sounded like a massacre. He could hear only the intermittent cracks of a single rifle now, beneath the whoops of the Apaches' crazed yowling.

Enberg swung down from the pinto's back and scrambled to the top of a low rise. Pressing his belly to the ground, he looked out from between two flat-topped rocks to stare into the bowl of ground on the other side, toward the east.

Right away, he saw three Apaches making their crouching way up the gradual, boulder- and gravel-strewn slope that aproned down from the base of the sandstone formation that resembled a fireplace. The savages' backs were to Enberg. Near the top of the slope and the base of the chimney-like formation, smoke puffed every six or eight seconds.

A single man with a rifle was trying to hold off the four Apache raiders.

Nearer Enberg, from twenty to thirty yards out away from the base of the rise he was on, eight or nine dead men lay sprawled in bloody heaps. Four were white men.

Which meant there was only one posse rider left.

Enberg studied the Apaches, who continued to make their slow, gradual way up the slope toward the lone rifleman. Two were wielding what appeared to be Winchester carbines, while the other was shooting arrows. They were spread out about twenty yards apart across the apron slope.

The lone rifleman didn't have a chance.

Enberg cursed as he gained his feet and jogged back down the rise. He untied the steeldust's reins from the pinto's tail, and mounted up. He took his shotgun in his hands and adjusted the pistol jutting from behind his belt.

"Let's go!" he urged the pinto, booting it up the rise.

The horse picked its own way around large rocks and boulders. At the top, Enberg paused to study the layout below him once more and then rammed his heels into the pinto's flanks.

The horse gave a shrill whinny and plunged down the slope. It was a violent, lunging descent. Enberg leaned far back in the saddle to keep from being thrown over the pinto's head. When the horse gained level ground, Enberg hunkered low over the horse's windblown mane and rammed his heels into its ribs once more, urging more speed.

At a ground-churning run, the horse crossed the bowl-shaped area at the base of the next rise and then started the climb toward the towering, hearth-like formation. Enberg steered it straight up the slope, the three Apaches growing before him, two on the move up the slope beyond, the other just now shooting his Winchester over the top of a flat rock toward the pinned-down man above him.

As Enberg closed the gap between him and the three Chiricahuas, he veered toward the left-most Apache and took his shotgun in his right hand, thumbing both hammers back and curling his index finger through the trigger guard. The Apache jerked a startled look behind him. His brown eyes grew wider when they saw the big, bearded *hombre* closing on him atop the pinto.

The Apache howled and swung his Winchester around.

Enberg jerked the pinto's reins sharply right, turning the horse nearly sideways. He slid the shotgun across his chest, planted the maws on the Apache, and triggered the left barrel.

Ka-boooommm!

The Apache triggered his carbine skyward as he flew up and straight back to land several feet up the slope, howling. He dropped his rifle and rolled back down the slope, black hair flying wildly around his head, his bare, copper-colored chest basted red with blood.

The other two marauders jerked around toward Enberg.

Dag booted the pinto up the slope at an angle toward the next Apache. The Chiricahua had spied him by now. The

Apache leaped atop a boulder, dropped to a knee, and rammed his carbine's butt against his shoulder.

Dag fired the twelve-gauge one-handed again.

The broad spread of buckshot shredded the Chiricahua's red calico shirt as it hurled him backward. This Indian, too, triggered his carbine wide before falling back against the slope to lay spread-eagle, screaming and quivering as he died.

As Enberg swung the empty shotgun back behind him, to hang down his back by its lanyard, an arrow curled the air six inches off his left ear.

Dag flinched. Looking up again, he saw the Apache who'd fired the wooden missile wheeling and running off across the slope, leaping rocks and tufts of cactus, black hair laced with hawk feathers bouncing wildly across his copper shoulders.

Enberg pulled the Colt Army .44 from behind his belt, clicked back the hammer, and, closing on the Apache, aimed.

He fired, but missed his target as the pinto leaped a large rock.

The Apache swung around as Enberg bore down on him.

The brave opened his mouth to scream. Dag's second shot drilled him in his bare chest, in the dead center of a swirl of multicolored tattoos ringing his breastbone. The Apache stumbled backward, dropping his ash bow at his moccasin-clad feet, then falling and rolling lifelessly down the hill toward Dag and the pinto.

Enberg's horse hurtled the pinwheeling body with an indignant whinny. Enberg checked the pinto down and turned it to stand sideways against the slope. Blinking against his own dust catching up to him, he looked up toward where he'd seen the rifleman.

He could see nothing but brown clumps of rock and occasional tufts of cactus fronting the awesome jut of hearth-like outcropping. Nothing moved up there at the base of the hearth.

No shadows, no smoke, nothing—only a hawk wheeling high in the sky above the general area where Enberg had seen the lone rifleman trying to hold off the Apaches.

Dag shoved his Colt behind his belt, quickly reloaded the shotgun, and rode up the slope. He moved slowly, looking around, wary of being ambushed.

He gained the base of the hearth-like outcropping, which cast a wide stretch of purple shade over him, and looked around, frowning.

"Hey," he called. "Hey, you with the rifle. I'm friendly if . . ."

He let his voice trail off when he heard the single chime of a spur behind him. He jerked his head and shotgun around. A tall, slightly stoop-shouldered man had stepped out from behind a wagon-sized boulder. He was dusty and bedraggled, a bloody swatch cut across the side of his head. Blood dripped over his right ear. His hollow, bruised cheeks were waxen behind a peeling sunburn.

Logan Cates held his rifle on Enberg. He stared incredulously at the horseback rider before him, one eye narrowed.

"Dag," Cates snarled, curling his lip. "What in hell are you doing here?"

"Savin' your bacon, looks like." Enberg tightened his grip on his shotgun's neck. "You'd best drop that rifle, Logan, before I decide to fix my mistake."

CHAPTER TWENTY-SEVEN

Enberg added a mesquite branch to the small fire he'd dared build in a nest in the rocks of his and Logan Cates's camp, about a mile south of where the dead Apaches and the dead posse members lay.

He and Cates hadn't dared take the time to bury the posse men. More Indians could have been drawn to the area by the gunfire.

"How'd you get out of jail?" Cates asked, gingerly adjusting the strip of flannel Enberg had wrapped around the business-man's head, angling it over his bloody ear.

Dag had removed his own head wrap, for the cut on his temple, compliments of Cougar Ketchum himself, had scabbed nicely and the swelling was nearly gone.

Enberg poured a cup of coffee from a rusty tin pot. "Tanner was on night duty."

Cates gave a sardonic snort, picked up his own coffee cup, and blew into it. He was staring at Enberg skeptically as the firelight throbbed around them, reflecting off closely surrounding boulders. Somewhere off in the desert darkness, a night-hunting owl gave its piercing screech.

"What're you lookin' at?"

"I'm wondering if I had it wrong."

"If you didn't," Enberg said, lifting his own cup to his lips, "you think you'd still be alive?"

"They told me you were part of it."

"Didn't Emily tell you different?"

"They had her out back with their horses. Ketchum had been about to pull out when I walked in on them. Someone nearby had heard the ruckus and summoned Whipple, who brought Wilkes, but by the time Whipple got there, Ketchum's bunch was gone."

Enberg sat back against his saddle, stretching his legs out and crossing his ankles. "I don't blame you for believing them," he said, giving Cates a direct look. "After the lowdown things I've done, and climbing back in the bottle. But I'm not a thief, Logan. I never would have turned over the strongbox if they hadn't threatened to kill Emily."

"All right," Cates said, nodding slowly and waving an insect away from his cup. "I had it wrong. I apologize. Tell me something, though. Do you love her?"

Enberg looked off through a gap between two granite boulders, pondering his answer. He turned back to Cates, and said, "In the past, not like I should have."

"What about the future?"

"I aim to make things right . . . just as soon as I get her and your money back."

Cates's mouth corners quirked a faint smile. He reached into his wool coat pocket, and pulled out two cigars. "Here."

He tossed one to Enberg, who caught it across the fire and looked at it. A Cuban stogie with a gold wrapper.

"Thanks for lending a hand back there, Dag. I was out of shells, almost finished. I'd be dead or worse if you hadn't shown up."

"Maybe you're lucky I didn't know it was you I was savin'," Enberg said, and smiled ironically.

Cates said, "I'm sorry I had Whipple lock you up. I was frustrated. I jumped to conclusions." He hiked a shoulder as he scratched a match to life on the side of a boulder. "Whipple's death was an accident."

Enberg sniffed the cigar, which smelled like butterscotch and brandy. It made his mouth water. "A lowly soul like me shouldn't light one of these. Might make me want more."

Cates chuffed a laugh as he rolled his own cigar between his lips, the flame dancing as smoke puffed around him.

"Tell me, Logan," Enberg said, when he'd lit his own cigar and had sunk back against his saddle again to enjoy it, "what's in the strongbox? Must be mighty important to bring you way out here."

"You don't think I would have come all this way just for Emily?"

"I'd like to think you would have. But then there's a lot of things I'd like to think I'd do, too."

Cates blew smoke out his nostrils and narrowed his eyes across the fire at his shotgun rider. "I would have, Dag. She and Gertrude don't get along, but I know each of their stories, and I don't hold either one solely to blame. Emily's as stubborn as her mother, though. You probably realize that."

"She's gotta be stubborn. Otherwise, she wouldn't have stuck it out with me this long."

"As far as what's in the box—pretty much my entire life."

Enberg frowned across the fire.

"I sold a mine near Tomahawk. The gold that's in that box is about all the money not wrapped up in property I have left."

Enberg felt his lower jaw drop. "Holy Christ. Why?"

Cates drew a deep breath. He probed his ear, which was a bulge beneath the bloodstained bandage. He looked at his finger, which had a smear of blood on it, and ran the finger and his thumb together.

"I'm almost broke. Bad investments overseas. I got greedy, overly ambitious. I had some bad advice. It all got away from me. I owe nearly more than I'm worth. Here's the topper."

Cates leveled a frank look at Enberg. "I'm dying. Cancer of the blood. When I rode out to California a few months ago, it was to see a doctor. I'd been feeling weak and my stomach didn't feel right. Gertrude noticed that I was losing weight."

"The doctor didn't help?"

Cates shrugged. "Nothing beyond diagnosing the disease and prescribing something to help me keep weight on . . . for a while. He's prescribed something for the nausea and the pain, as well. I'll be dead within a year, maybe sooner. That's why I sold the mine . . . for a hundred thousand dollars in gold bullion. I wanted to provide for Gertrude. Gold is the best way to provide for someone who, given her own family history and strength of will"—he chuckled wryly—"will likely live another fifty years. She's my legacy, that woman, God help her. And I wanted to provide for her daughter, as well, despite their rocky relationship."

Cates looked narrowly at Enberg and gave a grim smile. "That became all the more important when I didn't think you could provide for her . . . and the baby . . . yourself." He puffed his cigar for a time. "I hoped she'd move back in with her mother."

Enberg tried to digest what Cates had told him. He puffed his cigar for a time, looking out at the night through a gap between the boulders, and then removed the stogie from his lips and tapped ashes into the fire.

"I have to ask you another question, Logan. I'd appreciate a straight answer. Shouldn't be hard. Seems you're in the mood for straight answers."

"I have time for nothing less. No, I didn't have Olaf killed. Olaf and my father were best friends, and it would have dishonored my uncle's good name . . . not to mention my own. Please believe that, and don't ask me about it again. It makes me feel bad for both of us."

"Honor," Enberg said, pensively puffing smoke and staring across the fire at the man who for so long had seemed his rival. "It means a lot—don't it?"

"It's the foundation for the building of every good life. Without it, the structure of that life will fall apart, no matter how well the life itself was built."

Enberg leaned forward, raised his right knee, and draped that arm over it. He looked at his cigar coal. "It seems I've been so jealous of you for so long, Logan, that I overlooked what a good man you are."

"Let's let bygones be bygones."

"I'll second that."

"What're your intentions regarding Emily? Have they changed?"

"Depends on what your intentions are regarding me. Am I still fired? Kicked out of town?"

"No. I've arranged for the line to continue under different ownership. I can arrange for you to keep your job."

"One more chance, eh?" Enberg shook his head ironically.

"You deserve another one more than you realize, Dag. That's really been your biggest problem."

Enberg spat some bits of cigar into the fire, and lifted his coffee cup. He stared down into the coal-black liquid, the surface spotted with tiny gray ashes. "I'm gonna get her back. I'm gonna win her back, if I have to, though I won't blame her a bit if she won't have me." He glanced at Cates. "But I won't take your money."

"After all the sour years—why the hell not?"

"Honor." Enberg sat back and looked up at the stars beyond the fire's short column of gray smoke and glowing ciders. "I reckon we just have to wait and see what Emily wants to do," Dag said. "All *we* can do now is get her back."

"I'll second that." Cates raised his coffee cup and sipped.

CHAPTER TWENTY-EIGHT

Enberg rose at dawn's first blush.

Cactus wrens piped in the chaparral. Rabbits and pocket mice made skittering sounds as they flitted around the nest of boulders in which Dag and Cates had set up their camp. Enberg tossed his blanket aside and reached for his boots, tipping them over to make sure no spiders or rattlesnakes had crawled inside during the night.

He'd had his fill of both.

"Best roll out, Logan," he said, glancing at where Cates lay curled under his blankets on the other side of the cold fire.

When Cates didn't respond, Enberg drew his right boot on and said a little louder, "Logan, it's time."

Still, nothing.

Enberg looked at Cates. The man lay on his right side, head resting against his pillow. His feet clad in gray socks poked out from the bottom of his blankets. He wasn't making a sound. He didn't appear to be moving.

Was he breathing?

Apprehension skitter-hopped along Enberg's spine.

Stiffly, he rose and walked around the fire ring heaped with gray ashes, and dropped to one knee beside Cates.

"Logan?" he said, nudging the man's shoulder. "Logan, are you—?"

He stopped when Cates jerked his head up and blinked, startled. He stared at Enberg as though waiting for the fog of sleep to lift, and said, "What is it? Apaches?"

"No, nothin' like that," Enberg said, exhaling with relief. He canted his head toward the dull gray glow in the east. "We'd best hit the trail."

"Oh. Yeah, yeah—right."

They broke camp, saddled their horses, and then sat down on rocks to quickly eat some biscuits and jerky. "You've been this far into Mexico—haven't you, Dag?" Cates asked as he chewed a muffin.

"A time or two. Pa and I used to come down here, following the old Spanish trails, searching for gold."

"He was bound and determined, wasn't he?"

"He had gold-fever, Pa did. And he just plain loved the desert. There was something about it that called to him. Funny, him havin' come from such a far different place in Norway."

"Must have been the exoticness of it." Taking another bite of biscuit, Cates looked at Enberg. "Where do you think they're heading—Ketchum's bunch?"

"Hard to say. Maybe the Sea of Cortez. With as much gold as they're carrying, they could easily book passage on a clipper ship to take 'em pretty much anywhere they want."

"How far away is the sea?"

"Another two, three days' ride."

"We'd better catch up to them soon, then." Cates stuffed the last of his biscuit into his mouth and rubbed his hands on his whipcord trousers. "Before the Apaches attacked us, we were getting close. Judging by Ketchum's tracks, Bart Moses figured they were no more than a few hours ahead."

Moses had been one of the last of the posse members killed.

"Possible." Enberg nodded. "Maybe we'll overtake them today, then." He rose and corked his canteen as he turned toward his waiting horses.

"Dag?"

Enberg turned back to Cates, who gave him a frank, worried look.

"You realize that . . . Emily . . . ?"

"Might be dead by now?"

Enberg felt as though he'd just taken a long drink of sour milk. He nodded. Of course, he'd considered the possibility. He'd ridden every foot and yard in dread of finding her dead along the trail.

She could have been killed by Ketchum himself or by Apaches stalking Ketchum's bunch. Lord knew there were plenty of ways to die out here.

Cates's bringing up the possibility of Emily's death was like a knife being driven into Enberg's ribs. "Maybe. But maybe not. Ketchum might want to hold her for leverage against anyone comin' for her until he boards that clipper."

Enberg slung his canteen over his saddle horn and turned out his left stirrup. He swung up into the leather. Cates gave a grunt as he attempted to mount his own horse. Enberg couldn't see him clearly, for he was on the far side of his horse from Dag, but it looked as though the man had missed his stirrup.

He sagged against his horse, clinging to the saddle horn with one black-gloved hand.

Enberg swung down from the steeldust's back and hurried over to stand by Cates, who leaned against his paint gelding, blinking rapidly, trying to catch his breath. "You all right, Logan?"

Cates drew a deep breath, and nodded. "Just got a little dizzy for a moment."

"You sure you want to keep going? Maybe you should ride on back to Mineral Springs. I'll go after Emily and the gold myself. I—"

"No." Cates gave him a direct look. It was the look of a proud, determined man. "I can make it."

"All right. Okay, Logan. Don't push too hard, though."

"For chrissakes, Dag," Cates said, heaving himself with a grunt into his saddle. "I've never known you to sound like an old woman before. Come on—let's run those bastards to ground!"

He reined his paint around, and rammed his heels into the horse's flanks, galloping out.

Midmorning, Dag paused to dismount and inspect a pile of horse apples, pinching one between thumb and index finger, checking the texture. A good tracker in his own right, Enberg judged that the late Bart Moses's assessment of Ketchum's trail to be sound.

"They're about a half a day ahead, all right."

Now that Ketchum's trail hadn't been obscured by the posse's trail, Enberg could count the number of horses in Ketchum's group.

"Six riders," he said, walking from one side of the trail to the other and pausing to toe one of the prints in the finely churned dirt. "One of those better be Emily."

He didn't look at Cates, though he could feel the man's eyes on him. He grabbed his reins, mounted up, and they set off once more.

So they could cover a lot of ground quickly, Enberg and Cates both made use of all three horses, allowing one to trail for a time without the burden of a rider, so it could replenish itself. Two hours after Enberg had inspected the horse apple, he and Cates refilled their canteens and watered their horses at a rare water source—a well in the yard of an abandoned estancia, whose mud house was crumbling amidst a thicket of drooping mesquites.

The tracks around the adobe well coping told Enberg that Ketchum had watered here, as well. Not long ago.

They rode hard for the rest of the day, following their quarry onto the southwestern tine of a fork in the old Spanish trail they'd been following. Here the country became more and more rugged, with great gothic cathedrals and variously shaped mesas of wind-blasted, sun-scorched rock looming in all directions. They rested for a time; then, hoping to finally close the gap between them and Cougar Ketchum's bunch, they set out at two in the morning.

There was some treacherous travel along the ridge of a deep canyon and then into the jutting slopes of an isolated mountain range. Finally, just after sundown, they checked their mounts down on a spruce-stippled high-country slope, where the air was fresh and cool and spiced with the tang of evergreen.

Enberg slipped an extra pistol behind his belt and looked at Cates. His trail partner looked extra pale and gaunt, his nose peeling from sunburn.

"You all right, Logan?"

Cates sagged forward in the saddle, but he cracked a sneering grin beneath the brim of his tan Stetson. "There's that old lady rearing her persnickety head again."

Enberg smiled as though complicit with the joke, and said, "Wait here with the horses."

"Where you going?"

"I'm going to check out the top of this slope. One ridge back, I thought I saw a building of sorts up there. If so, we might be shaking hands with Ketchum's bunch soon."

"I'd like to shake their hands, all right," Cates said, hardening his jaws.

"Wait here."

"Dag?"

Enberg turned back to him.

"Don't do nothin' foolish on your own. You've already won your job back. If you still want it, that is."

Enberg smiled with genuine satisfaction. "Thanks, Logan."

He swung his shotgun around to his chest, took the big popper in both hands, and started up the slope. He glanced back to where Cates remained on his horse, slumped forward, chin down, eyes closed. The man didn't look well. The Apache arrow that had cut the groove over the side of his head and his ear, as well as the long trek down from Mineral Springs, had worn him ragged.

Enberg would leave him there. He wouldn't be any good in a fight. In his current state, he'd be easy pickings for Ketchum. Enberg felt it odd that he cared about what happened to Cates, but it was a good feeling. He hadn't cared much about what happened to anyone in a long time.

Not even himself.

CHAPTER TWENTY-NINE

Enberg stopped at the top of the slope and stared ahead through the pines and spruces.

Beyond lay a broad, sun-washed clearing in which a white adobe church stood about forty yards right of a white adobe casa. Two slender pines stood like sentinels before the church's two, large wooden doors, beneath the stone cross jutting from the roof.

To the church's right, the house was like a series of barrack-like boxes of varying levels connected by narrow stone stairways. There were several arched windows and doors and a couple of narrow balconies with tarnished metal rails.

A courtyard beyond a low, stone wall fronted the place. It glistened with greenery and bright, well-tended flowers.

A wood frame and adobe barn lay nearer to Enberg, about fifty yards to his left. A peeled pine corral angled off the barn. Eight horses, two mules, and a donkey milled inside. Chickens roamed around the corral. In fact, they roamed nearly everywhere, strutting around and foraging the straw-strewn ground between the barn and the house.

They were so spread out that something told Enberg they hadn't been put up last evening but had roamed all night.

A rooster stood atop the corral, crowing. Several horses and one of the mules watched it closely, one of the horses switching its tail apprehensively. As far as Enberg could tell, there were no humans out and about in the yard.

Fingering the trigger guard of his shotgun hanging down his chest, he stepped back deeper into the trees and began moving toward the barn, trying to keep out of sight of the house and the church. When the stable was between him and the main yard, he slowly stepped out of the trees, looked around to make sure no one was near, and then jogged to the rear of the barn.

Two doors lay before him. They were closed but didn't appear latched.

Enberg pulled the right door open, wincing at the faint groaning of the hinges. He stepped inside, leaving the door cracked, and looked around. The stables to either side of him, sheathing the main alley, appeared empty.

Flies buzzed around the shuttered windows. The front doors were partway open, and buttery sunlight filtered between them, giving Enberg enough light to see by.

Two chickens pecked in the straw-flecked dirt near the front, near the base of a square ceiling-support post hung with tack and against which a wagon wheel leaned. The stable was neat and relatively clean and in good repair. Cracks in the walls had been freshly mortared.

Someone was taking good care of the place.

Enberg moved along the main alley, between the rows of stables.

He stopped abruptly, having seen something in the periphery of his vision. He turned to his right, and his heart hiccupped painfully in his chest.

Grimacing, he stepped closer to the stall on that side of the alley, and peered over the low door. A man and a girl lay inside, on a low mound of hay.

They were both naked. The man was Ketchum's gang member, Ugly Tom—long and lean and pale with a crucifix of dark-brown hair matted on his upper torso.

The burned half of his face looked like a grisly carnival mask.

The girl was Mexican. She had long, black hair. She might have been sixteen or seventeen, with fleshy hips and thighs and small pert breasts. She wore only a small, gold crucifix around her neck.

The crucifix and its gold-washed chain were covered in the thick, dark-red blood that had run down from the gash that had been cut across the girl's neck, from just beneath one ear to the other ear.

She lay on her side, her back to Ugly Tom, a pool of blood in the hay beneath her chin.

Her open eyes stared at the blood as though in hushed amazement.

Clothes were strewn about the stable. Enberg recognized Ugly Tom's attire. Then he saw the nun's habit lying in a torn and crumpled heap not far from the girl.

Enberg studied the dark, woolen garb. It had obviously been torn from the girl's body. There was no other women's attire in the stable.

A nun.

Enberg shuttled his gaze back to Ugly Tom, who lay on his back, pale chest rising and falling heavily. His right hand was covered in blood. A large, wooden-handled Bowie knife lay within a foot of it.

Hardening his jaws, Enberg quietly clicked the latch on the stable door, slowly drawing the door open. Glancing once more at the young, dead nun, Enberg stopped near Ugly Tom. He glared down at the man, who lay softly snoring, pale chest rising and falling slowly, heavily. A faintly satisfied expression played across his half-burned mouth.

Enberg looked down at the man's crotch.

He lifted his shotgun's lanyard up over his head, letting it hang free. He squeezed the heavy shotgun in both hands, took one more step forward, raised the shotgun back behind his shoulder, and then smashed its broad butt down hard against Ugly Tom's privates.

When Ugly Tom sat up and opened his mouth to scream against the burning agony in his smashed nubs, Enberg didn't let him get more than the first note out before he smashed the shotgun against the side of the man's head, turning his ear to jelly.

Ugly Tom's head bounced off the stall partition, and he flopped back down in the straw, out like a windblown lamp.

Enberg jerked his head up. There'd been a sound in the barn.

A faint warbling . . .

He looped his shotgun back over his head and shoulder and aimed it toward the front of the barn. Again, he heard the sound. It sounded like mice. There was a faint scuttling sound.

But something told him the sounds weren't mice.

Slowly, quietly, Enberg made his way back out of the stall. He strode just as slowly toward the front of the stable, from where the sounds seemed to be issuing. He heard it again—a faint squeak. Then another. It was followed by a very quietly uttered shushing sound.

The sounds were coming from a feed chute in the wall to his left, behind a feed crib and trough.

Enberg strode toward the slatted crib that angled down from the loft, aiming his shotgun at the chute behind it. He cocked both of the shotgun's hammers, then reached forward through the crib and placed his hand on the wooden handle of the chute's clean-out door.

Now there was silence like that of a held breath.

Enberg quickly slid the door up to reveal two nuns in dark habits sitting side by side in the chute, huddled so closely together they were practically on top of each other. One was old and craggy-faced, the other young and round-faced. Both Mexican.

The younger woman pressed her face against the older woman's neck, sobbing while the older woman held her tightly and stared up in horror at the big, bearded man holding the savage-looking shotgun on them.

Enberg raised the shotgun's barrels, depressing the hammers. He held up a placating hand, palm out.

"It's all right," he said, then repeated it in his halting Spanish, adding the order, *"Quedate donde estás y no te muevas!"*

The older nun nodded her understanding.

Enberg slid the chute's door closed, then strode to the barn's partly open front doors. He looked toward the church and then to the house that sat directly across the yard from the stable.

Nothing moved around either building. The silence behind the clucking chickens and cheeping morning birds was unnerving.

A breeze blew, moaning softly and lifting dust and straw in the yard and sweeping it from Enberg's right to his left. A chicken was startled by the breeze; it took off running, clucking angrily.

The image of the young nun with the slashed throat remained lodged in Dag's brain. It was a thin, membranous image overlying his vision of the house. The young Mexican nun's image faded, however. It was replaced by the image of Emily, her throat cut from ear to ear.

Enberg tensed himself and drew a deep breath.

He adjusted the angle of the pistols wedged behind his belt. He took his shotgun in both hands, then, crouching low, took off running toward a small wooden door in the adobe wall surrounding the house.

CHAPTER THIRTY

Enberg dropped to a knee in front of the wall, left of the slatted wooden gate. He nudged the unlatched gate open and peered through the gap.

Beyond lay the courtyard filled with neat plantings of bushes, nut and fruit trees, and flowers. A stone walk angled through the courtyard to a stone staircase that slanted up the front of the casa to two wooden doors painted bright blue.

There didn't appear to be anyone in the courtyard. A cracked whiskey bottle lay at the bottom of the stone steps, as though it had rolled down from above. Enberg looked at the casa's windows overlooking the courtyard. Some of the shutters had been thrown back; some were shuttered. He couldn't see anyone inside, however. The bottle told him there was a good possibility that Ketchum's bunch was as asleep as Ugly Tom had been.

At least, before Enberg had crushed his balls and sent him hurtling to hell . . .

Dag moved, crouching, through the open wooden gate.

He looked around carefully, his thumb caressing both of the shotgun's steel hammers, as he strode along the path. He stopped at the bottom of the stairs. A bearded man lay asleep on the steps about six feet up from the bottom. Enberg recognized him: Josiah Cotton. A border tough often seen with Cougar Ketchum.

When Enberg had been town marshal of Mineral Springs, he'd kicked Cotton out of town for breaking up a saloon and abusing two working girls. Cotton had a reputation as a brutal killer and a rapist.

He lay sprawled back on the steps as though he'd fallen from a balcony above, though he hadn't. He'd just passed out here sometime last night, and dropped his bottle. There were several fresh scratches on his cheeks. Fingernail scratches. His head lay canted slightly to one side. One corner of his mouth was twitching a lusty smile, as though the outlaw were reliving the debauchery of the previous night.

Vaguely, Enberg noted the empty holster on Cotton's left hip.

Enberg mounted the steps.

Cotton must have sensed his presence. He opened his eyes, staring up at Enberg. He stared dully at first. Then his eyes began to clarify and fill with anxiety. As he opened his mouth to call out, Enberg caved in the man's skull with his shotgun.

The outlaw slid several steps down the stairs, rolled once, broke wind, and lay still. Blood and white flecks of brain matter bathed the steps above him.

Enberg continued up the steps to the two blue doors. He nudged one of the doors wide and stepped inside. He stared up in horror at three bodies hanging by ropes from a stone balcony rail above—one Mexican man and two Mexican women.

The man, who had long, thin black hair streaked with gray, wore the worn pajamas of a *peon*. He wore one rope sandal. The other sandal lay on the floor ten feet beneath him. His bare foot was dirty and streaked with blood.

His face was a mask of swollen bruises.

The women, both gray-haired and middle-aged, were dressed in nuns' habits. The habits hung in tatters from their badly beaten bodies.

An elaborately carved eating table lay to Enberg's left, fronting shelves filled with fine glass and china, some of which was broken. There were bullet holes in the shelves and in the adobe wall around them.

The table was littered with quirley and cigar stubs, whiskey bottles, and stone crocks and stone wineglasses, some over-turned amidst pools of spilled wine and sangria. There were playing cards, pistols, some ammo, and gold coins in messy piles.

In the middle of the mess lay the strongbox, its lid thrown back.

The room smelled of roasted meat, stale tobacco smoke, hu-man sweat, and blood. Enberg had never known what fear smelled like, but he could smell it here. The room was fetid with the horror of the previous night, of the hours following Ketchum's appearance at what was obviously a convent.

Enberg could smell the hours of terror and torment that had torn apart this once peaceful mountain sanctuary.

"Emily," a horror-stricken voice kept whispering in Enberg's head. "What of Emily?"

There were other voices outside of his head. Other sounds. He couldn't make out any words or identify the sounds, but they were coming faintly from up the stairs that slanted along the wall on the far side of the room, leading to the balcony above.

Enberg looked once more at the dead man and two dead nuns hanging from the balcony rail. His guts recoiled at their terrified eyes staring around the room as the bodies turned slightly this way and that at the ends of their ropes.

Enberg moved across the room and slowly climbed the stairs, taking one step at a time and looking up the stairs as well as into the room below. The sounds grew louder before him— knocking sounds, groaning sounds.

Enberg gained the top of the steps and looked both ways down the hall, which was pocked with sunlight issuing from the open doors of rooms on both sides of the hall. The knocking sounds issued from along the hall on his right.

He started in that direction.

He saw a shadow move out of a room he'd just passed—a room that a single glance had told him was empty. He should have looked closer. He froze as something round and hard was pressed against his back.

"I'm going to kill you," a throaty voice said.

Enberg turned. Emily stood before him, aiming a Schofield revolver at his belly. She was badly disheveled and sunburned, her hair hanging tangled around her shoulders. She wore the same dress he'd last seen her in, but it was dusty and torn. She glared up at Enberg, studying his face.

"I'm going to kill you," she said again.

His heart thudded. She was looking right at him.

Enberg frowned. "Emily . . . you . . . you . . ."

"I've been waiting . . . to kill you," Emily said, grinding her teeth on the words.

"Emily . . ."

Slowly, he reached out with his right hand and began to close it around the pistol. She jerked it back sharply, taking one step back away from him. Her hand tightened around the gun as she aimed it up at his face. He steeled himself for the bullet.

Then her eyes widened slightly with recognition. Her brows ridged. She lowered the pistol and said in a hushed voice, "Dag?"

Relief washed through Enberg. For a second, he'd thought . . .

"Dag . . . is it you?"

"It's me, honey," Enberg said, and engulfed the girl in his arms.

She sobbed, her body spasming against his, her tears soaking his shirt.

"I'm here. Everything will be all right."

"You came for me!"

"Shh-shh!" Enberg took her by the arm and led her back into the room from which she'd emerged. "Of course I did. I love you, honey. Stay in here, now—all right? You understand? Close the door and lock it and don't open it for anyone except me."

"What're you going to do?"

"You'll know soon enough. Wait here—real silent-like. I'll be back for you."

Emily smiled up at him through her tears. "Oh, Dag . . . I knew you'd come!"

Enberg placed a finger to his lips. "Shhh." He drew the door closed and waited to hear her turn the key in the lock before he moved off down the hall, heading in the direction from which the sounds were still issuing.

CHAPTER THIRTY-ONE

Enberg moved to the door from behind which the sounds were coming.

He knew what they were now. He was close enough. He could hear the woman's complaining groans and the man's lusty grunts. He could hear the creaking of the bed's leather springs and the thumping of the headboard against the wall.

Enberg turned the doorknob. It wasn't locked. The latch clicked faintly.

Enberg nudged the door wide with his right boot and filled the doorway, holding his shotgun straight out from his right side.

The bed lay before him. A naked young woman lay on it, her nun's habit on the floor by a washstand. The pitcher had fallen off the stand and now lay in pieces on the floor near the habit. It had likely been broken during the struggle that had preceded the rape Enberg was now watching.

Dag couldn't see the man's face, because the man had his back to the doorway. He lay atop the girl, hammering his hips against hers. She lay back against the pillow, sobbing and turning her head from side to side in protest of the savage assault.

She couldn't fight the man atop her, because her wrists and ankles were tied to the bed's corner posts with pillowcases.

Suddenly, the man stopped assaulting the girl.

He stared straight ahead as though looking out the open window at the far end of the bed.

Slowly, he turned his head to stare fearfully over his left shoulder at Enberg. Ray McInally's eyes opened wider. They flicked to the shotgun in Enberg's hands.

"Enberg!" McInally shouted, leaping off the bed and turning to face his killer, hands in the air.

Ka-boom!

McInally screamed as the buckshot flung him back against the window.

Enberg tripped the greener's second trigger.

Ka-boom!

McInally was hurled straight backward out the window with another scream and then a crunching thud as his body hit the roof. There was one more, softer thud as McInally's lifeless body hit the ground below.

As it did, Enberg heard the startled, incredulous shouts of male voices rising from behind doors along the hall.

Enberg stepped farther into the room before him, slammed the door, and quickly used his Bowie knife to cut the young nun free of her ties. She watched him wide-eyed from behind a veil of tears, shock from what had occurred rendering her unable to fully comprehend what was happening.

"Did someone say Enberg?" a man yelled from out in the hall.

Enberg pulled the nun off the bed and onto the floor, then shoved her into a closet. *"Permanecer alli!"* He closed the closet door.

"Where'd that shootin' come from?" shouted another man. "Sounded like a shotgun!"

In seconds, Enberg had his shotgun loaded with fresh wads.

He clicked the greener closed and jerked the room's door open.

Two men stood in the hall to his left. Both were dressed only in wash-worn balbriggans but they were both holding pistols—

two apiece. One was about ten feet away from Enberg, nearer the hall's right side. The other stood another ten feet behind the first man and nearer the hall's left side.

"Ah, fuck," said the first man, glancing at the savage-looking shotgun in the big, bearded shotgun rider's hands.

The first outlaw was holding both his pistols low. So was the other outlaw. They hadn't had time to raise them yet. They didn't look one bit happy about that.

Through the open door just off the first man's left shoulder came the squeals of another frightened nun.

"You fellas been havin' a good time, have ya?" Enberg asked. He recognized both of these men, in their early and late thirties, respectively, as members of Ketchum's bunch, though he didn't bother trying to recall their names.

It didn't matter who they were. In seconds, they wouldn't be anyone.

"Who the hell are you?" asked the second man.

"Dag Enberg!" said a familiar voice at the far end of the hall, behind Enberg.

A chill climbed Dag's spine.

Cougar Ketchum was behind him.

Ketchum laughed.

Enberg threw himself back into the room he'd just left as Ketchum triggered what sounded like a pistol. One of the two men in the hall gave a yelp and shouted, "Ketchum, for chrissakes!"

Enberg bounced off the bed and hurled himself back out into the hall. He hit the floor as Ketchum sent another bullet through the air over his head.

Enberg lay on his right shoulder, facing the two men in the hall. The second man had dropped to a knee and was clutching his right arm, which Ketchum must have pinked when he'd fired his pistol.

As the first man jerked his own revolver toward Enberg, Enberg triggered his shotgun and watched the first man's face, neck, and chest turn tomato red as he was slammed back against the frame of his door.

Enberg rolled to face the opposite end of the hall, where Ketchum, also clad only in balbriggans, was down on one knee, triggering his rifle from half inside a room on the hall's right side.

Two bullets thumped loudly into the wood floor in front of Enberg before he squeezed his shotgun's second trigger.

Ketchum yelped and threw himself through the nearest open door.

Remembering the second man in the hall, Enberg rolled back to face him. He dropped his empty greener, jerking both his pistols out from behind his belt. The second man triggered his Smith & Wesson at Enberg. Dag felt the burn of the bullet across the nub of his left cheek.

He triggered both his aimed Colts.

One bullet chewed into the doorframe over the second man's head. The second bullet took the man in the right cheek and whipped his head back and sideways against the doorframe.

Enberg fired again and watched his bullet punch through the dead center of the man's chest. Instantly, all the tension left the second man's body. He shrugged his shoulders, leaned forward, and then, quivering as the life left him, rolled over onto his side.

Enberg whipped around again to face the other end of the hall. He hurled two bullets toward Cougar Ketchum's room, then dropped both pistols, grabbed his greener, broke it open, and quickly plucked out the spent shells.

As he did, he cast quick, desperate glances at the closed door of Ketchum's room.

Silence. No movement.

Enberg clicked the greener closed. He rose to a knee, studying Ketchum's door. Nothing came from that direction except silence. Ketchum might have skinned out a window.

Enberg hurried down the hall. He paused beside the door, then rammed his shotgun's butt hard against the top panel.

"Cougar?"

"I got me a purty li'l nun in here, Dag," Ketchum said, voice pitched with mocking challenge. "If you don't throw that gut-shredder down, I'm gonna cut her purty head off!"

From the door's other side came a weird, strangling, grunting sound.

Enberg stepped in front of the door. He slammed his right boot against the frame, to the right of the knob. The door flew open. Enberg stepped inside and stopped the door's bounce off the wall with his right boot.

Ketchum walked slowly, haltingly, toward Enberg. His left arm and left side was speckled with blood from Enberg's buckshot. Ketchum had a big Bowie knife in one hand, his revolver in his other hand. He had a weird, faraway look in his eyes as he continued to stumble heavily toward the shotgun rider.

Suddenly, he dropped to his knees.

A letter opener in the form of a silver crucifix was embedded in his back, between his shoulder blades. Behind him stood the young, naked Mexican girl who'd rammed it there. Petite, with skin so dark she must have had some Indio blood, she scowled down at the outlaw, lips pursed, black eyes blazing.

She spat in rage and disgust at her attacker.

Ketchum stared wide-eyed at Enberg.

"Why . . . why'd you come, Dag?" he said, frowning as though deeply heartbroken. "We thought . . . we thought . . . we'd lost everyone. We thought . . . we thought we were . . . *rich*!"

"You are rich, Cougar."

Enberg gestured to the girl, who stepped away from Ketchum.

She climbed up on the bed, sat down with her back against the wall, and raised her knees to her chin. She wrapped her arms around her bare legs and gave Enberg a faint smile of complicity.

"You're rich in double-aught buck, Cougar."

He leveled the greener on Ketchum.

Ketchum's eyes brightened fearfully.

"Dag, no!"

He hadn't gotten that last out before Enberg sent his head plummeting off his shoulders and out the window behind him.

Enberg looked at the girl on the bed. "You all right?" He repeated the question in Spanish.

Smiling savagely at Cougar Ketchum's bloody corpse, the girl nodded.

Enberg ran out of the room, and stopped.

Emily stood in an open doorway on the hall's opposite side.

"Is it over?" she asked.

Enberg walked to her, wrapping his wife in his arms. "It's over." He took her by the shoulders, drew her away from him, and brushed a thumb across her freckled cheek. "Are you all right?"

She nodded.

"The . . . baby . . . ?"

Emily lifted her hands to his face, brushing a finger across the bullet burn on his left cheek. "Ketchum's bunch left me alone. I told them I was with child. Maybe they had a shred of honor."

Emily quirked a smile as she gazed up at her husband. "Maybe the real reason they left me alone was because they thought that if they didn't, a certain big Norwegian shotgun rider would hunt them to the ends of the earth, and they'd never have a minute's peace."

Enberg winked at her. "They had that right."

Emily's eyes acquired a faraway cast as she looked into the hall behind Enberg. "But when they got here . . ."

"When they got here, they made up for leaving you alone on the trail."

"Let's do what we can to help, huh?" Emily said, moving out into the hall. She glanced back at Enberg. "And then let's go home."

"Emily?"

"What is it?"

"Cates is dying. He's outside. He was too weak to help in the fight. He's all but broke, but he sold a mine. He's leaving the gold to you . . . and Gertrude."

Emily considered this. Then she turned to Enberg, placed her hands on each of his bearded cheeks, and said, "He left it to Gertrude. We don't need his money, Dag. We'll be fine. You, me, and the baby."

Enberg squeezed her wrists, and kissed her hand. "I couldn't agree more, honey."

★ ★ ★ ★ ★

Two Smoking Barrels

★ ★ ★ ★ ★

CHAPTER ONE

"Dag, did you see what I just saw?"

"I saw it, Charlie."

"Four men?"

"Five."

"I saw four."

"That's because you're older than the Sonora Desert, Charlie, and your peepers are gettin' foggy."

"Why, you disrespectful pup! If you don't think I can still take you in a fair fight—!"

"Shut up and drive, Charlie," said Dag Enberg, shotgun rider for the Yuma Line. "That's what you're good at. Just keep the team on the trail. You let me worry about them *five* skulkers. That's what *I'm* good at."

"If your old man was alive to hear you talk to me like that— his best friend!—why, Olaf Enberg would tan your britches so's you'd walk for a month like you had a full load in your drawers!"

Charlie Grissom, the white-bearded jehu, glanced once more toward the northern buttes where he and Dag Enberg had briefly glimpsed the riders sitting clumped in the shade of a distant butte shoulder, and glanced anxiously at the shotgun man riding on the seat beside him. "How you gonna play it?"

"Like I always play it."

"The leader of that bunch is prob'ly Joe Ted Perrine. I seen him lurkin' around the stage line office last week. I had me a feelin' he might try a hit. I heard the tough-nuts and hard-tails around Mineral Springs got 'em a wager goin' on whose gonna be the first to take down a stage you're ridin' shotgun on.

"Perrine and his cousin, Herman Buckley, always have been the struttin'est cocks of the walk out in this neck of Arizona. I got a feelin' two of them riders we seen was them. If there really was five and you ain't just bein' contrary, takin' after your old man like you do, I'd say there's George Lamb, "Gila River" Tom Tiegan, and Liam O'Malley there, too.

"Gila River busted out of a territorial pen up north, and he's prob'ly been chompin' at the bit to get to ridin' the long coulees again. There ain't no pen that can hold that son of a no-good squawkin' bitch. No, sir, no one likes a good stagecoach robbery like Gila River and Joe Ted Perrine!"

"Did you tell Normandy about the wager?"

"Hell, no."

"Why not?"

Expertly working the six-hitch team's leather ribbons that he held loosely in his gloved hands, Grissom arched a brow at Enberg. "I figured he might hold it against you."

Enberg chuckled. "Why would he hold it against *me*?"

" 'Cause, for whatever reason, I don't think he likes you. I don't think he likes it that part of Logan Cates's deal in sellin' the line to him was that Normandy kept you on as shotgun rider." Grissom scowled. "Now, you know why Cates felt he had to make that deal—so you could keep your job, you contrary cuss—just as well as I do!"

"Ah, hell," Enberg groaned, breaking open the twelve-gauge sawed-off shotgun in his hands and making sure it was loaded with fresh buckshot.

"Sometimes you're your own worst enemy, Dag."

"Where have I heard that before?"

Enberg snapped the shotgun closed and glanced again to the

north. He couldn't see the riders from here, because a mesa had pushed up close to the trail. But the five riders were out there, all right. Likely taking their positions.

Enberg could sense it.

He himself had caused enough trouble in his gnarly past to know exactly what it smelled like . . .

"Hold up, Charlie," he said. "I'm gonna get off."

"What're you gonna do?"

"Take a piss."

"Ah, now, don't do nothin' foolhardy, you crazy Norski!" Grissom warned as he hauled back on the reins.

As Grissom checked down the lunging team, Enberg glanced around once more.

Now there was only rolling desert bristling with chaparral around the coach. He could see no movement to the north, but he knew this desert well enough—he'd been raised in it, after all, by his old Norwegian desert-rat father, who'd come all the way from Norway nearly fifty years ago to hunt for gold—to know that there was a wash that paralleled the trail about a quarter mile north.

The wash was considerably lower than the trail, so it couldn't be seen from Enberg's current vantage. The wash was where the road agents were likely riding, skirting the main trail and taking a shortcut to get ahead of the coach.

Perrine's bunch would likely carry out their ambush another mile and a half farther north and east, where the stage crossed the wash at a place called Bloody Gulch, which had been named after a contingent of cavalry soldiers hauling supplies from the federal storehouse in California to Fort Huachuca had been savagely attacked a number of years ago by Apaches.

When Grissom had stopped the team, the jehu blinked against the dust roiling up around him, and turned to Enberg.

"You're thinkin' they're gonna hit us in Bloody Gulch—ain't ya?"

Slinging his shotgun over his neck and shoulder to let it hang down his back by its wide leather lanyard, Enberg began climbing down from the driver's boot. "That's what I'm thinkin'."

He stepped off the metal ring protruding from just above the Concord's right front wheel, and dropped to the ground.

Grissom glared down at him. "You be careful, blame it!"

Enberg shaded his eyes against the sun with one gloved hand, and grinned up at his old friend—one of his only friends in Mineral Springs. "If you ain't careful, Charlie, I'm gonna think you're worried about me."

"Someone's got to!"

"Sir, please, I don't understand—what is happening? Why are we stopping here?"

Enberg turned to see the sole female passenger, whose name, he remembered, was Lisle Stanton, peering out at him from the rear window, left of the door. Miss Stanton was a pretty young woman, maybe in her middle twenties, with a cameo-delicate face and large, light-brown eyes.

Judging by her fancily cut, burgundy traveling gown and feathered picture hat, she was a young woman of considerable means. What she was doing way out here on this canker on the devil's ass, however, Enberg had no idea.

His job was to see that passengers and cargo made it safely along his assigned stretch of route, between Mineral Springs and Tomahawk, or vice versa. That was his job and only job. Fraternizing with the passengers was just as frowned upon by his new boss, the persnickety Bud Normandy, as it had been by his former boss, Logan Cates, who currently lay on his deathbed in Mineral Springs.

A cancer was eating away at Cates's insides.

Cates might even be dead by the time Enberg returned to the

route's main headquarters in Mineral Springs.

Miss Stanton's beauty rocked Enberg back on his heels a bit, but only for a moment. He was fully aware of the seriousness of the situation and his need to keep his wits about him, though few things could dull Enberg's wits like a beautiful woman.

Beautiful women had been Dag's undoing more than a few times in the past.

"Nothin' to worry about, Miss Stanton," Enberg lied, thinking fast to come up with a reasonable-sounding explanation for his abandoning the coach. "I'm just gonna ride on ahead and scout a stretch of trail that might have gotten washed out during that last hard rain we had."

He turned toward his horse, the wily-looking dun he called War Bonnet, tied to the rear of the coach, but then a man's voice said, "What do you take us for, sir? Fools? There must be some sort of trouble ahead. I've ridden enough stagecoaches to know that they only stop for water, to switch teams at relay stations, and when brigands are on the lurk!"

The dapper gent in a dark-brown suit, and sporting a waxed and upturned mustache, was scowling out from the window opposite Miss Stanton's.

From deeper inside the coach, another man said, "We all heard the driver tell you to be careful—so don't try to pull the wool over our eyes! We're all aware this is outlaw country!"

"Now, now, folks!" Grissom interjected from the driver's box, looking at Enberg and jerking his head toward the shotgun rider's horse, urging Dag to get a move on. "Nothin' to get all hepped up about. Just takin' a little precautionary action's all. That's how we do things on the Yuma Line, yessir!"

"You should run for public office, Charlie," Enberg said, smiling up at the older man. "You're good!"

Grissom gestured angrily. "Get a move on, you ninny!"

Enberg started back toward War Bonnet once more but

stopped again when Lisle Stanton poked her beautiful, elaborately hatted head out the window, her doe eyes as wide as china saucers. The window was too small for the hat. The frame caught it and slid it back and down one side of her head as the pins in her hair loosened. The sun glistened in the thickly coiled, red-brown tresses that now hung in a beautiful, messy bunch down over her left ear.

If Lisle noticed the problem with the hat, she didn't let on. The young woman's gaze flicked boldly up and down the shotgun rider's husky frame as she smiled beseechingly, canted her head a little to one side, and said, "You'll take care of us, won't you, Mr. Enberg? You won't let anything bad happen, will you?"

Strangely, Enberg's tall, broad body, with his thickly bearded face chiseled in the severe planes of his Viking ancestors, suddenly became two identical bodies. The second stepped out of the first. Enberg watched with vague incredulity as his second body stepped forward, wrapped its hands around the girl's beautiful head, tipped her face up slightly, and closed its mouth over her rich red lips.

Enberg could imagine his second self savoring the warm, soft moistness of the girl's lips and the cool playfulness of her tongue moving forward to briefly entangle itself with his own.

"You have absolutely nothing to worry about, Miss Stanton," Enberg said, giving the young woman a courtly bow and a reassuring smile that caused his long, Nordic eyes to slant more than normal. "You got my word on that."

"Dag, damnit, get a move on!" Grissom bellowed from the hurricane deck.

Suddenly, Enberg's second body stepped back into the first one, and he was all one lusty man again, standing about four feet away from Miss Stanton, not having kissed her, but his heart thudding as though he had, his lips still tingling with the sensation of her lips on his.

The girl was still smiling sweetly, beseechingly as before, but a slight flush had risen in her perfect cheeks, as though she was aware of the kiss he'd so keenly imagined.

"Don't get your drawers in a twist, Charlie!" Enberg gave Lisle Stanton a wink and then hurried back to untie his horse, tighten the saddle cinch, and swing up into the leather.

He adjusted the two Colt revolvers he wore wedged behind the wide, brown belt encircling his waist—he didn't use holsters—then touched heels to the dun's flanks. The horse rocketed off the trail and into the chaparral.

Enberg crouched low and tipped his hat brim down over his forehead as he gave the horse free rein to wend its own way through the prickly pear, barrel cactus, and occasional mesquites.

When he started down a long, gradual slope and saw the course of the dry wash angling across the desert before him marked with spindly cottonwoods, desert willows, mesquites, and greasewood, he glanced over his left shoulder to see the dust of the stagecoach trailing off to the east.

Ten minutes later, Enberg dropped down into the broad wash. He halted the dun long enough to spy the sign of five horseback riders trotting from west to east along the wash.

"Told ya, Charlie," the shotgun rider muttered with satisfaction, raking a hand across his bearded chin and clucking his horse on along the arroyo.

Horse and rider followed the meandering cut through the chaparral to the east for nearly a quarter mile and then to the northwest for another couple of hundred yards. Enberg kept a close eye on the prints of the five shod horses scoring the ancient riverbed, making sure he was still on the stage-stalkers' trail.

When he came to a large cottonwood beneath which a wagon-sized boulder humped on the wash's right side, Enberg stopped and swung down from the saddle.

Dag used to hunt this wash for javelinas and deer when he was a kid and living out on the desert with his father, and he knew that the cottonwood and boulder were within a hundred or so yards of Bloody Gulch.

He adjusted the pistols wedged behind his belt once more, slid his shotgun around to the front, and squeezed the wicked-looking popper in both gloved hands. He started walking along the gulch, looking carefully around and pricking his ears to listen.

He didn't want to walk up on Perrine's bunch and get himself blasted. That would be downright embarrassing.

At a break in the scrub to his left, Enberg stopped.

A faint smudge of dust hovered low over the desert to the southwest. The stage had followed the trail wide of the dry wash and was now swinging back to make the crossing at Bloody Gulch, which was probably another fifty yards beyond Enberg's current position.

The shotgun rider continued forward, increasing his step. He wanted to get to the Gulch at roughly the same time as the coach did, so he'd be there when Perrine showed himself.

He followed another bed in the curving wash, and stopped abruptly.

He'd seen a shadow move in the corner of his right eye.

He started to swing around too late.

"No, no, no, Enberg," said a voice pitched low with menace behind him. "You just keep facin' east. That's a good direction for you. If you turn that big popper on me, I'm gonna burn down your Norski ass!"

CHAPTER TWO

"Who the hell are you?"

"Why, it's Gila River Tom, Dag!"

Enberg's heart quickened. He felt like a fool for letting one of the gang get the drop on him. At the same time, frustration raked him. The stage was barreling toward the trap Perrine's bunch were setting for it.

"What the hell you doin' here, Gila?" Enberg asked, trying to keep his voice mild, conversational. "Last I heard you were still shovelin' shit in some pen up north."

"Don't bullshit an old bullshitter, Dag." Boots crunched gravel as the man walked up behind Enberg. "Old Charlie Grissom saw me out by the Diamond in the Rough the other day. He tried to look like he didn't see me, but when I seen that look he got—like he just swallowed beer that had a dead rat in the tub it was brewed in—I knew he seen me, all right. And told you, most like."

Gila River poked a cold, hard gun barrel against Enberg's back, and ordered with quiet menace, "Hold the popper out to the right, one-handed. Any fast moves, and I'll blow a hole through you wide enough to drive that stagecoach through."

Enberg drew a deep breath in frustration, and did what he was told. He didn't see any other option. At the same time, he heard the distant thunder of the stage hammering in from the south, probably within a hundred yards now of Bloody Gulch and Perrine's gang waiting for it. Charlie would have to slow the team to enter the gulch, and that's when the gang would hit him.

Gila River wrapped a gloved hand around the sawed-off shotgun, and lifted the lanyard up and over Enberg's head. He also pulled Dag's Bowie knife out of the sheath Enberg wore on the back of his belt. The outlaw rammed the shotgun's butt against the shotgun rider's back, between his shoulder blades. It was a hard, hammering blow.

Enberg grunted as he stumbled forward, knees buckling.

He hit the floor of the wash with a groan, and rolled once, gasping. His hat tumbled off his shoulder.

The blow had knocked the air out of him.

"You son of a bitch!" he wheezed, trying to work some air back into his chest.

When he rolled onto his side, Gila River stepped forward, aiming Enberg's own shotgun at Enberg's face. Gila River grinned, showing his two prominent and chipped eyeteeth that resembled fangs.

The outlaw wore two pistols in holsters on his hips. He was a good six feet, unshaven, his hair hanging long and greasy to his shoulders. He didn't wear traditional riding boots but high-topped, Apache-style moccasins that he'd rolled down to just below his knees.

The hide-wrapped handle of a Bowie knife jutted from the top of the man's right moccasin.

"You shouldn't call me names, Dag," said Gila River. "We was friends once—remember?"

"We might have tossed back tequila together a few nights, a long time ago, but you and me were never friends, Gila."

"Now, that makes me sad to hear you say it." But Gila didn't look sad. His dark-brown eyes set in shallow sockets in his round, fleshy face owned a mocking glint. "Toss them pistols over there near that rock yonder. One at a time. Use two fingers.

If you use three, I'm gonna blow you in two with your own shotgun. Now, that'd be right embarrassin', Dag!"

He was right. It would be embarrassing. But Enberg's mind was on Charlie Grissom and the stage . . . and young Lisle Stanton . . . now barreling toward the trap the savage Perrine bunch had set for them. There was no telling what the gang of seedy misfits would do once they saw the pretty girl in the coach.

There was also a chance they might shoot Charlie just to get him out of the way. Perrine's bunch was not above cold-blooded murder.

Meanwhile, Dag lay here in the wash, a hundred yards distant, staring at the double bores of his own shotgun down which the savage Gila River Tom Tiegan stared, grinning at him.

"How in the hell did you get behind me?" Dag asked.

"When I seen you pull out of Tomahawk with your horse tied to the stage, I knew what it was for. You're gettin' predictable, Dag. Me an' the boys heard that leavin' the stage and circlin' around behind trouble was how you foiled previous holdups. Well, me an' Perrine is too smart to let that happen to *us*. We ain't half as dumb as most road agents in these parts. No, sir! We let you get a look at us back there, when we was loungin' around in the shade of that butte, waitin' on ya, and then the rest of the gang went ahead while I held back to say hidey."

Gila River laughed and shook his head as he stood about five feet away from Enberg, feet spread a little more than shoulder-width apart, aiming Enberg's own shotgun at Enberg's face. "Dag, you should see yourself. You're the very picture of one miserable son of a bitch!"

The rattling of the stage and the drumming of the team's hooves grew louder. In his mind's eye, Enberg could see the stage approaching the lip of the gulch. As the rattling and the drumming died, he could see Charlie hauling back on the team's ribbons, slowing the horses so they'd enter the gulch at a trot.

Entering the gulch at a dead run would be suicide. The drop was shallow but sudden, and the monsoon rains they'd been having recently could litter the ford with deadly boulders or trees that had been torn out of the banks farther upstream.

Guns began popping.

Enberg gritted his teeth. Charlie was in the gang's whipsaw. Charlie shouted—a muffled, bellowing wail from this distance.

Fury threatened to overwhelm Enberg. He stared at the grinning countenance of Gila River Tiegan, then at the shotgun in the man's hands.

He wanted to make a move on the gun so badly his limbs were quivering, but one sudden lurch would be the end of him, and that wouldn't do Charlie and Lisle Stanton and the other passengers any good.

The shooting died.

"I wonder if they shot ole Charlie," Gila River said. "What do you think, Dag?"

Enberg glowered up at the outlaw holding the shotgun on him. The only reason Tiegan hadn't killed him was because Tiegan wanted to taunt him with the holdup. They were just close enough to hear enough sounds from that direction that Gila River was getting the desired effect.

Enberg's nerves were leaping around beneath his skin.

Dag regretted ever sharing a bottle with Gila River Tom Tiegan.

He and the outlaw had gone drinking, gambling, and whoring together a few times just after Dag had returned from the war. Dag had discovered that his father, old Olaf, had been found dead out in the desert, the cause unknown. He'd been half-eaten by coyotes.

The small fortune he'd made building up the springs into a bustling town had gone to Logan Cates, because Olaf had thought that Dag had been killed during the war. Logan Cates's uncle, Norman Century, had been Olaf's sole business partner. They'd built up the springs together from a mere desert watering hole on a major freight road running up from the border.

In and of itself, that little watering hole in the desert, surrounded by endless miles of bristling chaparral and barren, sun-seared mountains, had been worth a small El Dorado.

In addition to what he'd made on establishing the town, Olaf had hidden a cache of gold out in the desert—the result of years of obsessive, mostly solitary picking and shoveling. But he'd shared with no one the whereabouts of the cache, and he'd left no map to designate its location.

So Enberg had come home to nothing but death and desolation. He'd expected his old man to be alive and to be relatively wealthy, and to have a stake or a job waiting for his son—enough comforts and opportunities to take Dag's mind off of four bloody years of war.

But there was nothing but the town that now mostly belonged to Logan Cates, who'd been Norman Century's sole heir. Everything both Olaf and Norman Century had owned together was now owned by Cates. Olaf's gold was as good as gone.

So Dag, feeling sorry for himself—as he had a habit of doing—had gone on a bender. Like most drunks, he wasn't discerning. He hadn't much cared whom he'd drunk, whored, and gambled with. By hook or by crook, he'd fallen into a rough crowd that had included the known outlaw Gila River Tom Tiegan. Eventually during that drunken time, and predictably, the two had had a falling out.

Enberg couldn't quite remember what it had been about— probably a girl—but it wouldn't have taken much to cause the men to lock horns. They'd both been pie-eyed for nearly two weeks straight, and even sober they were as hot-tempered as broom-tailed mustang stallions.

Down the wash, a girl screamed.

Enberg jerked with a start and turned to stare toward where the outlaws had hit the stage.

"That was a girl's scream," said Gila River. "There ain't a girl on the stage today—is there, Dag?"

He chuckled. He knew very well there was a girl on today's run back to Mineral Springs. The outlaws had obviously scouted the coach before it had left Tomahawk.

The girl screamed again.

A man shouted.

A gun barked.

Enberg turned his anxious gaze to Gila River grinning mockingly down at him.

"If you'll forgive me, Dag," the outlaw said. "I'm gonna have to kill you now, so I can join the festivities. After Perrine has her, I'll be takin' my turn. You're better off dead, anyways. Old Grissom is likely dead, and the stage has been hit. That poor girl—no tellin' what's gonna be left of her after we're done with her."

He clucked and shook his head with mock sadness. "Nah, you don't wanna have to ride on back to Mineral Springs and tell everyone what happened to the stage on your watch."

"I reckon you're right," Enberg said. "Go ahead and shoot me. I got it comin' for the fool move I pulled, not expectin' one of you would have guessed my ploy. But you best use only one wad on me, because after I'm gone you're gonna wanna take care of the snake comin' up behind ya."

Gila River tensed, rolling his eyes to one side but keeping Enberg's twelve-gauge aimed at the shotgun rider.

"Bullshit."

"Right, bullshit. There ain't no snake behind you. A Mojave green rattler, to be exact." Enberg was staring past Gila River's right knee. "Forget I mentioned it."

Apparently, Gila River had the same fear most desert dwellers had of rattlesnakes. He'd probably known more than a few men, as Enberg had, who'd been bit. He knew the misery that such bites caused. The deaths that often resulted.

As much as he didn't want to, he turned his head to one side, then jerked it full around, half-swinging the shotgun around with him. That was the opening Enberg needed to snatch the hideout pistol out from his right boot well.

Heart racing, Enberg raised the ivory gripped over-and-under derringer, but Gila River turned back around to face him at the same time.

"Why, you lyin' sack o'—"

Enberg's derringer barked. At the same time, his own shotgun was triggered by Gila River. His assailant had been rocked back slightly when he'd glimpsed the hideout popper in Enberg's fist, and he'd fired the shotgun's left barrel a quarter of an eye wink too soon.

The brunt of the fist-sized wad blew a dogget of gravel and caliche out of the wash's bed just over Enberg's right shoulder.

Enberg triggered the derringer's top barrel, and watched with satisfaction as Gila River staggered backward, eyes widening in shock. Gila River lowered the shotgun to his side as he took another staggering step backward. When he tried to raise the double-barreled gut-shredder again, Enberg tripped the derringer's second eyelash trigger, aiming straight out and up.

The .32-caliber bullet punched a neat, dark-blue hole in Gila River's forehead, about two inches above his right eye. That tipped his head back, and as he took another shambling step backward, he tripped the twelve-gauge's second barrel straight down in front of him, turning his right boot to red jelly.

Most men would have given an ear-rattling scream with such an injury, but Gila River only grunted as he took yet one more step backward, and fell. The bullet to his brain had rendered him, if not dead, at least unconscious enough that he probably barely registered the obliteration of his foot.

He kicked both feet, sighed, and died.

His right foot looked like someone had dropped a jar of cherry jelly on it. Pale bone shards poked out from the torn leather.

Enberg shoved the empty derringer back into the small buckskin holster he'd sewn into his boot. He crawled over to where Gila River lay on his back, blood soaking into the sand and gravel around his head.

Gila River stared straight up at nothing, one lid a little more closed than the other. There was a dark patch around the crotch of his canvas trousers where'd he'd peed himself.

"Nasty way to leave this earth, Gila," Dag said, grabbing his shotgun, breaking it open, and plucking out the spent, still-smoking wads. As he replaced them with fresh ammo from his bandolier, he said, "Yessir, nasty way to die, but a right fitting one in your case. Good riddance, you son of a bitch!"

He returned his knife to its sheath, donned his hat, rose, and gave Gila River's good foot a savage kick.

He gritted his teeth angrily as he stared down at the dead man, and then snapped the shotgun closed and cast his gaze down the wash, in the direction of the stage. He tensed as he realized that he hadn't heard any sounds coming from that direction for the past couple of minutes. The other brigands had probably heard the pops of Enberg's derringer as well as the thunder of his shotgun, and were likely curious . . .

One or two or all might be heading this way.

CHAPTER THREE

When Enberg had gathered his pistols, he strode slowly, quietly along the arroyo's left bank, staying close to the shade of the overhanging brush and aiming his shotgun straight out from his right side.

As he rounded a gradual bend in the wash, he jerked back.

He'd seen a figure moving toward him—a man cat-footing along the wash's opposite bank.

Enberg dropped to a knee behind a boulder, and waited. He dropped his hat down beside him and edged a look around the boulder. He pulled his head back when the man again came into view—a short, broad-shouldered tough-nut holding a carbine. He wore a funnel-brimmed, weather-stained Stetson and fringed chaps.

Enberg heard the faint trill of a spur and the quiet grind of gravel.

"Gila?" the man said, keeping his voice low and tense. "Gila, you all right?"

Enberg waited, gritting his teeth and listening to the trilling of the spurs growing gradually louder.

The trilling stopped.

"Gila?" the man called again.

Enberg donned his hat and rose. "Gila's seen better days, George."

George Lamb jerked his wide-eyed gaze toward Enberg, who tripped one of his twelve-gauge's triggers and watched the buckshot rip into Lamb and blast him six feet back into the brush on the wash's opposite bank. Enberg jerked his gaze to another man who'd just appeared around the bend in the wash. The man snapped his rifle to his shoulder, yelling, "It's Enberg!"

Dag tripped his second trigger, and the second man, whom he recognized as Liam O'Malley, fired his Winchester wide as he stumbled backward, screaming. He was a good thirty feet away from Enberg. That was too far for a tight grouping of buckshot, but that didn't mean that O'Malley didn't get a good, wide peppering.

A heavy dose of hurt.

He screamed again at the spraying he'd taken, which probably felt like hornet bites over a good half of his body. As he gained his feet, leaving his rifle behind, and started running off down the wash toward the stage, Enberg ran after him, slinging the shotgun back behind his shoulder. He slid one of his Colts out from behind his belt, clicked the hammer back, and, as he rounded a bend in the wash, stopped, aimed, and sent two shots hurling toward O'Malley.

The Irishman screamed as he flew forward, and lay writhing.

Beyond him were three more outlaws and the stage sitting in the middle of the wash, the team prancing anxiously in their traces.

One of the outlaws was holding Lisle Stanton belly down on the ground and was shoving her dress up over her naked bottom. He had one gloved hand clamped down over the back of Lisle's head, pressing her face into the dirt.

The other two highwaymen were standing by a loose group of saddle horses milling nervously by the stage. The men appeared to be shoving something into a pair of saddlebags—loot from the strongbox.

The man trying to savage the girl rose abruptly, closing his fly with one hand and clawing a revolver out of a holster with his other hand. Enberg was jogging down the wash toward the stage, but he stopped abruptly, aimed hastily, and triggered a round that clipped the girl's would-be rapist in his left side, throwing the flap of his canvas coat out.

The man gave a yell and staggered backward.

"Let's vamoose!" shouted one of the two men standing around the loosely grouped horses.

The man Enberg had winged bellowed a curse and, rising to one knee, swung his pistol toward Enberg. He snapped off a shot. The bullet screeched over Dag's left shoulder to plunk into a saguaro behind him. Dag fired at the man he'd winged, but he was distracted by the movement around the stage, and his bullet sailed wide of its mark.

The man on the ground fired another round at Enberg, then heaved himself to his feet and ran toward the other two outlaws swinging up onto their horses.

"Wait, goddamn you, sonso'bitches!" he bellowed.

Enberg saw someone on the ground near the stage crawl out away from it, toward Enberg. It was Charlie Grissom. The driver wasn't wearing his hat, and the sun shone on the pale, nearly bald crown of his head as he plucked a revolver up off the floor of the wash.

The pistol barked, smoke and flames lapping from the barrel.

The man running toward him jerked to a stop, twisted around slightly, and dropped to one knee. He bellowed a curse as he raised his pistol, aiming toward Grissom. Enberg fired his Colt at the same time that Grissom fired his old Remington, and both bullets cut into the howling outlaw, driving him to the ground where he thrashed for a couple of seconds before lying still.

Enberg aimed his Colt toward where the other two riders had been swinging onto their horses, but both men were gone, their dust billowing along the wash behind them, around the stage. The three riderless horses galloped after them, the thuds of the five mounts quickly dwindling to silence.

Enberg ran forward and crouched over Lisle Stanton, who was sitting up and pushing her dress down to cover her bare legs. A pair of pantaloons and silk underpants lay nearby, cut to ribbons. The girl was missing one shoe, as well.

"You all right, Miss Stanton?" Enberg asked, breathless, glancing at Charlie Grissom, who rose slowly, clutching his bloody left arm.

"I think . . . I think I'm all right," the girl said, her eyes wide with shock. She looked around, saw her underwear, and grabbed the torn cloth, bunching it in her fist and sliding it toward her. "They . . . they didn't hurt me too badly, Mr. Enberg . . . thanks to you. If you hadn't come when you did . . ."

The girl gave a shudder and let her voice trail off.

"I reckon I broke my promise—sorry about that," Enberg said, helping the girl to her feet. "Are you sure you're all right?"

She nodded, then squeezed her eyes closed. Now that the shock of the attack was wearing off, emotions were beginning to overcome her. Tears dribbled down her cheeks, but she did not cry. "I'll be all right. I . . . I just need a minute alone, Mr. Enberg," the girl said, her voice quaking as she turned and walked away, holding her underwear up against her chest.

"Please don't wander too far, Miss Stanton."

Enberg strode over to Grissom.

The driver had opened the stage door and the four men inside, all dressed in the garb of businessmen or drummers, began exiting the stage, looking around a little sheepishly. They'd obviously done nothing to help the girl. Anger flashed in their eyes when they saw Enberg.

"Where in hell were you?" said the man with the waxed mustache. Enberg thought one of the others had called him

Blevins. Cyril Blevins, owner of a freighting company. "You're supposed to be the guard on this deathtrap!"

Fury exploded in Enberg. Before he could rein it back, his thick arm was up and his first was flying straight forward, smashing into Blevins's face. Blevins's nose exploded like a ripe tomato. He gave a yelp as he flew backwards and into the arms of two of the other passengers, who regarded Enberg in horror.

Blevins's eyes were glazed with shock as he stared at Enberg over the hands he'd cupped to his nose.

Blood oozed out from between his fingers.

"Christ, Dag!" admonished Grissom.

The two other men led the man with the smashed nose away from the stage, all looking warily back over their shoulders at Enberg, as though he were an escaped circus lion.

"That ain't gonna go down well with Normandy," Grissom said, still clutching his bloody left arm.

"Maybe not, but it made me feel better." Enberg stood glaring at the four men gathered around Blevins. "Did those men do anything to keep Miss Stanton from bein' dragged out of the coach?"

"That's your job!" one of the men bellowed as he helped ease the bloody Blevins to the ground.

Enberg lurched forward, fists clenched. "You chicken-hearted son of a bitch!"

Grissom grabbed Enberg's arm. "Dag, let it go. For chrissakes, let it go!"

Enberg felt the heat of incredulity rise in his cheeks. He turned to Grissom, saw the blood oozing from the hole in the old driver's left arm, and said, "Shit, Charlie," as he ripped his red bandanna from around his neck.

"I pulled my Remy on 'em when they dragged the girl out of the stage," Grissom said. "Didn't get one damn shot off." He shook his silver-bearded head as he looked down at the arm Enberg was wrapping. "Sometimes I think I'm getting too old for this profession."

"You did your job, Charlie. You didn't have any goddamn help. That was the problem."

"Poor girl," Grissom said, scowling off down the wash, where Lisle Stanton had disappeared in the brush to compose herself. "Those sonso'bitches were gonna take turns with her. Likely would have cut her throat afterwards. That goddamn Perrine is the goddamnedest devil I've ever known, and I've known a few!"

"What were they packing in them saddlebags?" Enberg knotted the bandanna around the jehu's arm and canted his head in the direction the outlaws had ridden—Joe Ted Perrine himself and Herman Buckley. At least Buckley was who Enberg thought he'd seen with Perrine by the horses. He'd seen all their faces sketched on wanted circulars hanging in the Wells Fargo office. "It was the loot from the strongbox, wasn't it?"

He stepped back to gaze up at the roof, and a stone dropped in his belly when he saw the strongbox still chained to the brackets but its lid yawning wide. "Shit!"

"They got it, all right—the payroll for Hud Cormorant's Box G-3. Cormorant ain't gonna be at all happy about that, but at least no passengers were killed. I think the girl was just shaken up a little's all."

"You took a bullet, Charlie," Enberg said, hating himself for letting Gila River get the drop on him. His problem was he was getting overly confident in his abilities, and he'd let his guard down.

And now this had happened.

His first stage robbery. If you didn't include the one where Cougar Ketchum had kidnapped Enberg's wife and held her for ransom, the ransom being the cache of gold bullion Enberg's stage had been carrying. Enberg and Logan Cates had trailed

Ketchum's bunch down to Mexico, and had retrieved the stolen loot as well as Dag's wife, who was also Cates's stepdaughter, the former Emily Dayton.

If you didn't include that bit of nastiness, this was the first time a stage Enberg had been guarding had been robbed.

Dag walked out to where the team stood, rippling their withers and stomping and snorting, still jittery from the shooting. Enberg stared off along the trail in the direction that Perrine and Buckley had fled. They'd probably left the trail and were heading either north or south. Probably south, toward Mexico.

Again, Enberg clenched his fists and gritted his teeth. He considered unharnessing one of the horses and riding after the two robbers bareback. He'd like to run them down before they crossed the border, but he knew it was a fool notion even before he turned back to see Charlie Grissom falling back against the stage, eyelids heavy.

He'd lost a lot of blood and was losing more. Enberg had to get him to Mineral Springs.

Dag hurried back to the old jehu. "How you doin', Charlie?"

Grissom was clutching his arm and gritting his teeth. "Just feelin' a little faint's all. Hep me down, hep me down . . ."

Grissom leaned forward to grab Enberg's arm as his knees buckled. Dag eased his old friend down to the ground and gentled him back against the coach's rear wheel.

"We'd best get you back to Mineral Springs, Charlie. The sawbones is gonna need to take a look at that arm." Enberg reached up and grabbed his canteen down from the driver's boot. He unscrewed the cap and, dropping to a knee beside Grissom, gave the old jehu the flask. "Here—take a drink of that. Then we'll get you inside the coach. I'll drive back."

"I ain't hurt that bad. It's a flesh wound. I'll be all right once I've had some water." Grissom lifted the flask and took a drink, though most of the water sluiced out around his lips and dribbled down into his gray beard to carve streaks of mud down his red, leathery neck. It dampened the dirty red neckerchief billowing out across his broad chest.

Enberg helped him steady the canteen. "I can manage the team for the last few miles back to Mineral Springs, Charlie. It's a fairly straight shot, an'—"

"How is Mr. Grissom?"

The girl's voice startled Enberg. He turned to see her standing behind him. Her underwear was no longer in her hand. She must have repaired the garments enough to be able to wear them. Her hair was still a little mussed and some dirt was smudged on her cheeks, but she looked relatively composed.

"He's ornery as usual," Enberg said, rising, giving the girl a gentle smile. "That's a good sign, I reckon. How are you, Miss Stanton?"

"I'm fine, Mr. Enberg."

"Please, call me Dag."

"All right . . . Dag. I like that. It's Norwegian, isn't it?"

"Yes, it means 'Day.' My old man came all the way out here from Norway, found a Norwegian girl, the daughter of a California freighter, and married up with her. I reckon she was fool enough to stay out here with that old desert rat, long enough to have me, anyways. That's why you have this useless hunk of Norwegian hide standing before you now."

"You're not useless, Mr. Enberg. Why, you saved the day!" Lisle's direct gaze met Enberg's. The light danced in her eyes.

Enberg's heart thudded passionately. Immediately, he chastised himself for his attraction to this beautiful girl, and his goatish male yearning to make love to her.

He was a married man, after all, and he'd vowed to both himself and to Emily that he would forevermore be true to her despite his past bouts of untethered lust, which had been directed mostly toward a lovely Mineral Springs doxie named

Zenobia Chevere, or "Zee," as she was more widely known.

"I could have saved the day a little sooner, Miss Stanton."

"That's for damn sure," snorted one of the men administering to Blevins, who sagged weakly against a boulder with his head tipped back and a handkerchief pressed to his nose.

The others were down on one knee around him.

The man who'd made the sarcastic comment jerked his gaze away as soon as Enberg looked at him. Enberg swallowed his anger and turned back to the girl. "Can I help you into the stage, Miss Stanton? We'd better get back on the trail to Mineral Springs. We only have a few miles left, and I need to get Charlie to a sawbones."

Lisle crouched down beside the jehu and placed her fine hand on his shoulder. "Is there anything I can do to help, Mr. Grissom?"

Charlie looked up at her, squinting one eye, a little color rising in his pasty cheeks. "No, I'm fine, Miss Stanton. I been hurt worse fallin' on my way out to the privy at night." He chuckled at that, looking sheepish. "Sorry about that. I know better than to use such barn talk around—"

"Hold on, Mr. Grissom."

Lisle reached into the stage and rummaged around inside a red carpetbag. When she pulled her head out of the stage, she held a small, silver flask in her hand.

Uncorking the flask, she crouched over Grissom once more. "Here—I have a feeling this will make you feel considerably better."

Grissom's face brightened as his eyes settled on the glittering silver flask. "Why, Miss Stanton—!" he said in hushed delight.

"It's tequila."

"You don't say!" Grissom took the flask between his thumb and index finger and, daintily extending one sausage-like pinkie, tipped the flask to his bearded mouth. He took a couple of gurgling swallows, lowered the flask, and smacked his lips.

He winked devilishly at Enberg, then returned his suddenly brighter gaze to the girl. "Say, are you married, Miss Stanton?"

"No, I'm not, Mr. Grissom."

Grissom removed his hat and held it over his heart. "Would you like to be?"

Lisle rose and turned to Enberg, flushing beautifully. "I think he's going to live, Dag."

"Thanks to you, I think he is, too, Miss Stanton," Enberg said, chuckling.

"Please, it's Lisle."

"All right, then," Enberg said, feeling his cheeks get hot as scalding kettles. "Lisle it is . . ."

Chapter Four

While Grissom rode in the box with Enberg, the old jehu was not up to driving. He tried and failed—the burn in his arm was too great. Only a few yards beyond Bloody Gulch, he turned the reins over to Enberg with a bellowed curse.

As Dag drove the six-horse hitch nearly straight east toward Mineral Springs, he vaguely reflected on the deceptive ease with which Grissom usually handled the reins. He made it look so easy that Dag had taken the man's work for granted. Now, as the shotgun rider tried to finesse the six ribbons in his hands and keep the team and the coach on the curving trail without clipping rocks or brush to either side, and to keep moving at a good pace, he was reminded why he usually held the shotgun and Charlie usually held the ribbons.

Driving six horses was a complicated maneuver not unlike the herding of feral cats.

As the team jounced along the trail, the leaders, pullers, and wheelers glanced back at Enberg incredulously. They knew as well as Enberg did that no master was steering them, and they did not take kindly to not having Charlie Grissom holding their ribbons.

Dag felt as though all of his fingers had turned to lead. He was sure that Charlie drove the team instinctively, half-consciously applying pressure to this rein to get the leader to turn a little this way, or pressure to that rein to get the wheeler to hold back a little when starting downhill, and on and on.

Charlie didn't have to think about it. He and the six horses were one. There was an art to driving a team, which only came with time, but as the coach rattled and rocked along the trail toward town, Enberg decided that such a job required more patience and less emotion than that which had been bestowed upon his stormy Nordic soul.

"Shit, Charlie, I don't see how you do this," he growled, flipping the reins between his seemingly jointless fingers, hardening his jaws in frustration. "Why in the hell does Eve keep pulling to the damn right?"

"Because Adam tends to pull to the left, and she likes to show him who the real leader of the team is. Besides, she knows a tinhorn's driving, and she's funnin' with ya. Typical female." Clamping his left hand over his wounded right arm, Grissom lifted his chin to bellow, "Eve, you straighten up and fly right or all you'll get for supper is a handful of moldy hay! I may not be drivin' this heap, but I'm here, and I got my eye on you, lady!"

Enberg was glad to see the town of Mineral Springs take shape before him, the scattered adobe brick and wood-frame buildings arranging themselves in the chaparral. Gradually, the tall false façades of the business district fell into line along both sides of the trail, where the trail became the town's main street.

The largest building in the bustling business district was Mineral Springs's crown jewel. It was Logan Cates's Diamond in the Rough Hotel & Saloon, and it was this garish, sprawling structure that Enberg headed for. The hotel and saloon was also the headquarters for the Yuma Line. Cates himself was usually out on the front veranda, awaiting the arrival of whatever stage was due, but it was not the well-attired Cates who was out there this afternoon.

Holding that position, in a deep wicker chair, was the man whom Cates had sold the line to—the well-buttoned Bud Normandy, who was a few years older than Cates and who

owned a pugnacious disposition and uncompromising demeanor. He was sort of like an old bulldog always slavering at
the chance to get into the pit with another, younger dog just to
prove to all the other dogs as well as himself how tough he still
was—despite his age and considerable girth.

The man's face, in full alcoholic flower, appeared all the red-
der for its contrast to the gray muttonchops that grew long and
bushy down to his jaws and which were shaved into the forms
of arrowheads pointing at his small, thin-lipped mouth.

Save for a white shirt and black four-in-hand tie, he was
dressed entirely in green, the gold chain of his pocket watch
drooping from one green, wool vest pocket to the other. His
delicate pince-nez reading spectacles dangled from his coat
lapel by a red silk thong.

Grissom barked advice at Enberg as the shotgun rider
wrestled to get the team stopped in front of the Diamond in the
Rough without plowing into the boardwalk or taking off one of
the step rails. Try as he might, he couldn't get the team stopped
where he wanted but several feet ahead of the hotel's broad
front porch steps—actually closer to Melville's Drug Emporium
standing just beyond it. He also parked at an odd slant.

"I told you dog-gonnit, Dag," Grissom cajoled, "you can't try
to manhandle Eve. She chafes at manhandlin'. Just ask Adam!
And the wheelers get all nervous if you're all herky-jerky on
their reins. Steady, even pressure!"

Enberg sighed as he locked the brake and wrapped the reins
around the handle. "Well, that's the first and, I hope, the last
time I have to drive this heap, Charlie."

"You ain't the only one!"

"Come on, Charlie—let's get you to . . ."

Enberg let his voice trail off when he saw Bud Normandy
moving toward him along the boardwalk, scowling skeptically
up at him. "What in Christ's name happened?"

"I'll tell you what happened," said a man's muffled, angry voice inside the coach beneath Enberg. "Your shotgun rider not only let the coach get attacked by the special brand of depraved savages you have out here, but he *busted my nose!*"

Dag hadn't recognized the man's voice, because the man had obviously been speaking through a thick handkerchief held to his face, but now he realized the indignant speaker had been Blevins.

"What?" exclaimed Normandy as he glanced from inside the coach to Enberg, who was helping Grissom up out of his seat.

"Uh-oh," Charlie said. "I just hope that clause Cates put in the contract to keep you your job is a sound one."

"Yeah, me, too."

Fists on his hips, Normandy glared up at Dag and Grissom, "What happened? And why did you strike one of our passengers, Enberg?"

"Long story, Chief," Dag said as Charlie climbed tenderly down over the side of the coach.

"There'd better be a short explanation!"

Grissom stepped down to the ground near Normandy.

The jehu said, "We was hit at Bloody Gulch by Joe Ted Perrine. Dag here—"

"What about the strongbox?" Normandy said, stepping back to stare up at the coach roof, shading his eyes with one small, fat hand.

"They took it," Enberg said, as he stepped down beside Grissom.

"Goddamnit, Enberg!" Normandy shouted, turning to the much taller shotgun rider and rising up onto the toes of his black patent leather shoes. "It's your duty to make sure those strongboxes are protected at all costs! If you can't do your job, I'll find someone else who can!"

"Look, Mr. Normandy," Grissom said, wincing at the smaller

man's sharp attack on his shotgun guard, "Dag did all he could. There was five of them an' only two of us, and—"

"Isn't someone going to inquire how my nose came to be broken?"

This from Blevins, who'd exited the stage with the other passengers, including Lisle Stanton. The girl stood nearby, holding her carpetbag and looking anxiously on at the vitriolic little bulldog in the green suit straining at its seams.

"I assure you, sir, I am going to get to the bottom of that, as well," Normandy said.

"I'll just say this about that, Chief," Enberg said, glaring at Blevins. "That greasy little bastard had it comin'!" He saw Lisle standing not far from Blevins, and added with chagrin, "Uh . . . sorry about my language Miss . . . er . . . I mean, Lisle . . ."

Normandy turned to the girl, and his eyes bugged with surprise. "Why, Lisle . . ."

"Hello, Uncle Bud. I decided to surprise you and come a week early." She flicked her coy gaze from Normandy to Enberg, then back to her uncle again.

Uncle Bud? Enberg thought. *The girl was Normandy's niece?*

Normandy grabbed the girl's arm. "Lisle—my god, are you all right?"

She nodded, pursing her lips. "Just a little shaken up is all. I'll be fine after a hot bath."

Blevins stepped forward, rudely breaking up Normandy's reunion with his niece. "I am going to sue this line!" he intoned nasally through the handkerchief he held to his nose.

"What the hell's going on?" Yet another voice was added to the mix of overlying conversations.

When Enberg saw the town marshal, Roscoe Clemens, striding toward the hotel, he glanced at Grissom and said, "Come on, Charlie—let's get you over to the doc."

As Dag took Grissom's arm and began leading him away,

Normandy said, "Enberg, you and I have much to discuss. I'd like to see you in my office at your earliest convenience. That said, you need to know that Logan Cates has taken to his deathbed."

Enberg whipped around in shock, though he wasn't sure why he was so surprised. In the two months since he and Cates had returned from Mexico, where they'd retrieved Cates's stolen bullion as well as Emily, he'd been looking frailer and frailer. At least he had the few times that Dag had seen him. Enberg hadn't noticed his former employer and his wife's stepfather outside of his house on the bluff above the town in a couple of weeks.

Still, Logan Cates's imminent demise was hard to fathom. He'd meant so much to this town. He'd meant so much to Dag Enberg . . .

The town marshal stood beside Normandy now as Normandy, ignoring his niece for the time being, said, "Your wife asked me to inform you of that dour bit of news upon your arrival. She'd like you to join her as soon as possible at the Cates house. That does not mean, however, that this matter is in any way closed. I want to see you in my office as soon as you can get away—sooner rather than later."

Normandy turned toward Roscoe Clemens, and said, "Now, then, Marshal Clemens—we're going to need a posse. The stage was hit at Bloody Gulch by Joe Ted Perrine, and . . ."

Enberg didn't hear the rest. He was leading Grissom across the street toward the doctor's office at the rear of a furniture store, and his mind was elsewhere.

"Well, I'll be hanged," Grissom said as they mounted the boardwalk on the opposite side of the street from the Diamond. "Ole Cates on his deathbed."

"Yeah."

As Enberg led the old jehu along the boardwalk that ran down the side of the furniture store to the rear, where the local sawbones had his office, Grissom stopped and turned to the shotgun rider. "I know my way to the doc's place, Dag. You get on over and see Cates one last time. I'm sure Emily and her mother need you a whole lot worse than I do. And stop feelin' bad about the holdup. There wasn't nothin' you did wrong. So Gila River got the drop on you. You can bet you ain't the first he ever got the drop on, but at least he'll be the last!"

Grissom winked.

"You got that right. At least he's snugglin' with the diamond-backs, the son of a bitch."

"Go on." Grissom jerked his head in the direction of the Cates residence. "The sawbones'll clean this up and sew it for me. After that I'm gonna track me down a fat, young whore, a steak with all the surroundin's, and a bottle of cheap bourbon. I'll be on the mend in grand fashion."

Enberg chuckled. "All right. I'll see you later."

He gave the jehu's good arm an affectionate squeeze and then headed home. War Bonnet had followed the stage back into town, and he was likely standing out by Enberg's stable, waiting to be fed and watered. Finding the horse where he'd expected, Dag quickly unsaddled and tended him, then set off in the direction of Cates's place.

As he walked toward the bluff humping up on the southeast corner of town, the crest of which Cates's Victorian house graced like the cherry atop an otherwise bland bowl of ice cream, Dag pondered Logan Cates, whom he'd held a grudge against for a long time after his return from the war, since Cates's uncle had willed over all of his own as well as Dag's father's holdings to Logan alone. That added up to a good half of Mineral Springs, including the Diamond in the Rough Hotel & Saloon, which had been jointly held by Olaf Enberg and Norman Century, Cates's uncle.

Of course, there had been nothing nefarious about Dag's

having been left out of the will. Because of a telegram the Union Army had sent to Mineral Springs by mistake, everyone in town had thought he'd been killed in the war.

That hadn't been Cates's doing nor his fault.

Still, it had been tough to come home to so little when Cates had so much. But Cates had built up the raw materials he'd been given, and he'd made his businesses run like clockwork. If Enberg had wanted in on Cates's ventures, he'd have had to carve a place for himself.

Instead of rolling up his shirtsleeves and getting to work, however, Enberg had mooned around town, drinking and whoring and gambling and generally feeling sorry for himself. Cates had used his influence to get Enberg the job as town marshal, but Enberg's drinking had caused him to lose the job under the most embarrassing circumstances imaginable—the Mineral Springs bank had been robbed while Enberg had been too drunk to do anything about it. A couple of innocent girls had been killed by the robbers.

By offering Dag a job as shotgun rider on his Yuma Stage Line, Cates had given Enberg yet another chance to build a life for himself in Mineral Springs. Dag almost messed that up a couple of months ago when Emily had been kidnapped by the Cougar Ketchum gang, but he'd made up for it by saving Cates's life down in Mexico and getting the man's money and stepdaughter back.

Complicated.

That was how Enberg would describe his feelings regarding Logan Cates.

And now Cates was dying. Enberg didn't want him to die. A year ago . . . hell, even a few months ago . . . he wouldn't have felt half as somber about the whole affair.

But now, damnit, Enberg felt he'd turned his life around. He'd stopped whoring and drinking and cheating on his wife.

He'd become a good husband to Emily. He'd stopped feeling sorry for himself.

Sure, today was a bitter disappointment, but, like Charlie had said, he'd done his best. He'd done all he could do to keep the stage from being robbed. Sometimes that was all a man could do. His best. He'd make up for what had happened today, just as he'd compensated for his previous missteps.

Aside from his wife, Logan Cates was about the closest thing to family that Enberg had. Cates was like Enberg's older brother. He wanted Logan to live so he could see, years on down the road, how well Dag turned out.

He wanted Logan to live so he could see that the chances he'd given Dag had not been given in vain.

Ahead, Cates's grand Victorian loomed atop the bald bluff, touched with the coppers and salmons of the late-day sunshine. Emily was on the front porch, staring toward Dag.

She waved. Enberg waved to his pretty wife and increased his pace as he started climbing the hill.

CHAPTER FIVE

Enberg had rarely visited Cates's grand house, but the few times he had he'd always felt intimidated. Not only because his own place was a little prospector's shack he'd bought for its back taxes, and wasn't even as large as Cates's woodshed, but because Emily had grown up in houses like this one of Cates, on the East Coast, and now she lived in Enberg's dilapidated shanty.

It made Dag feel like a severely inadequate provider for the young woman.

Emily's mother, the formidable Gertrude, had married Cates after her husband, Emily's father, had died a few years ago. The man, even wealthier than Cates, having hailed from old Eastern money, had been a business associate of Cates. After his death, however, it was learned that he'd been worth less than his debt. Thus the reason for Logan and Gertrude's joining of forces, so to speak.

Seeing the kind of finery his wife had been raised around made Enberg feel bad for Emily, and unworthy of her. He was still amazed that she'd chosen to marry him. Emily lived in Enberg's humble cabin without complaining or encouraging Enberg to find something better for them.

Not even now when she was three months in the family way, with their first child.

"Hi, honey," Enberg said as he gained the top of the sprawling, wraparound porch appointed with several wicker chairs and a wooden, leather-cushioned loveseat that hung from the porch rafters by chains.

"Dag, I'm so glad you're here!" Emily moved to him, wrapped her arms around him, and pressed her cheek against his chest. "This place always makes me feel so odd . . . and sad and lonely. I don't like being here alone, without you. It reminds me too much of being imprisoned in houses like this when I was a child. But Mother needed me. For the first time in her life, she needed me. She sent Albert to fetch me from the cabin."

Albert was Logan's and Gertrude's head butler, a loyal, straight-backed Englishman in his late forties whom Gertrude had brought west with her when she'd married Cates.

Emily looked up at her husband. "He's dying, Dag."

"I know, I heard."

Enberg held his young wife's freckled face in his hands, and brushed his thumbs across her cheeks. He leaned down to kiss her plump lips, then gazed down at her, smiling gently. She gazed up at him, wisps of her long, copper hair dancing around her cheeks in the breeze.

The former Emily Dayton was a pretty girl. Twenty-two years old, she owned the fine, even features and intelligent eyes of a good, strong bloodline, of Old World wealth. That wealth had not spoiled her or made her in the least bit haughty. Emily was the sweetest, most passionate girl Enberg had ever known.

That sweetness and passion came wrapped in a girlish romanticism that made her somehow fragile, vulnerable, and caused her to sometimes be at bitter odds with her mother, who valued restraint, common sense, and the confining, sterile formalities of long traditions.

Emily had been a poetic, dreamy girl raised in a strict home and with the rigidity of a queenly, uncompromising mother and largely absent father who couldn't be bothered with the frivolities of child-rearing.

"Is your mother with Logan?" Dag asked.

"I believe so." Emily reached up and tried to smooth the lines spoking out from the corner of his right eye, frowning. "What happened? You're troubled. Didn't the run go well?" She added, raising her voice with worry. "You weren't held up, were you?"

Of course, given her husband's line of work, that was Emily's constant concern.

Enberg opened his mouth to speak but nothing came out. He might as well have gone ahead and told her. She brought both hands to her mouth in shock and horror.

"Now, Em—it wasn't that bad. No one was hurt. At least, not bad. Charlie got shot, but—"

"Charlie was *shot*? Is he all right?"

Enberg placed his hands on her arms, trying to calm her down. "He's fine. It was a flesh wound. Pinked him in the arm."

"Did I hear someone was shot? Who was shot?"

Enberg turned to see Gertrude standing in the house's open doorway behind Emily. Her silver-blond hair pulled up into an elaborate roll on her head and gathered into a tight bun in back, the bun garnished with a black velvet bow, Gertrude stood frowning out at her son-in-law. "Who on earth was shot, Mr. Enberg?"

Gertrude had never once, as far as Enberg could remember, used his first name. It was always "Mr. Enberg." From the start, that had been her way of voicing her disapproval of Enberg marrying Gertrude's only daughter, whom she'd honed to marry a young man from her own societal and economic station.

Certainly not a big, bearded, raggedy-heeled westerner with the mercurial blood and wolfish demeanor of a full-blood Norwegian coursing through his veins.

Most certainly not a lowly shotgun rider.

And *absolutely* not a lowly shotgun rider who would take her precious daughter away to an ancient, dilapidated prospector's shack on the far north side of town, at the base of a craggy mesa that was home to a slithering nest of Mojave green rattlesnakes!

Enberg wasn't sure how Gertrude had resisted the urge to hire someone to kill him. She certainly had the money. Maybe she still would. Regulators weren't hard to come by. Or maybe she'd do the deed herself. Enberg wouldn't put anything, including cold-blooded, back-shooting murder, past his mother-in-law.

"The stagecoach driver was shot, Mrs. Cates. Charlie Grissom. The stage was hit. But like I was tellin' Emily, Charlie's gonna be all right."

"What was the coach carrying in its strongbox?" If that wasn't just like Gertrude—worrying more about money than human life.

"Payroll for the Box G-30."

"Did the thieves get away with it?"

"So far, but Marshal Clemens is organizing a posse to go after it."

"The choleric Hud Cormorant is going to be hopping mad!" Gertrude drew a tight breath and nervously fingered a jewel-encrusted cameo she wore on a choker around her long, slender neck. "Well, at least the stage line is no longer our worry. I'm glad Normandy has it despite his virtual robbing it from us."

She arched a none-too-happy brow at her daughter. "Mr. Enberg, I suppose you're here because Emily sent for you."

"Of course I did, Mother," Emily said crisply.

Enberg remembered his hat. He doffed it, and held it against his chest. "She said Logan . . . uh, Mr. Cates . . . is dyin'."

"Dying, Mr. Enberg. Dy-innggg. So help me, if I spend the rest of my life out here, I will never get accustomed to the way you westerners speak, clipping the ends off your words as though it's too much trouble to pronounce them all the way through!"

"Good Lord, Mother!" Emily intoned, her freckles standing out against the flush of her fury. "Must you harp even at a time like this? Your husband is upstairs—*dyinnggggg*!"

Enberg had never once heard Emily raise her voice to anyone until he heard her around her mother. Around Gertrude, Emily became a different person. Most of the time she had the demeanor of a playful kitten, but around her mother she turned one-hundred-percent rabid mountain lion.

Enberg himself was almost afraid of her when Gertrude was present. He was nearly six-and-a-half feet tall and weighted nearly two-hundred-and-forty pounds dry as a bone in his birthday suit, but he feared getting between these two women more than he feared inadvertently separating a momma grizzly from her wide-eyed cubs.

By this time, Gertrude had stepped back from the door and impatiently waved Dag and Emily into the foyer but not before reminding Enberg to leave his guns on the porch. He leaned the twelve-gauge against a porch rail, set both his pistols atop the rail, and followed the women into the large, dark foyer that smelled of candles and varnish. A cabinet clock ticked against the wall near the base of the dark mahogany stairs that rose into the shadows of the second story.

"Scrub the dung from your boots and go on up," Gertrude said. "He *has* asked for a word with you, Mr. Enberg. Please do not tarry. He has virtually no strength, and every word he is forced to utter only hastens his end."

She gestured at the stairs and then wheeled to disappear through a doorway, muttering, "As for me . . . I'm going to have a badly needed finger of sherry. Come, Emily—do make yourself useful and pour your dear beloved mother a sherry, won't you? That's the doting child I raised!"

Emily rolled her eyes, tossed her head, then pecked Dag on the lips and followed her mother into the parlor.

Holding his hat, Enberg climbed the stairs. He winced as each boot came down in turn on the carpeted steps. He was a big man, and he'd felt like a bull in a china shop the few times he'd visited the Cates residence. The staircase with its elaborately scrolled rails seemed inadequate for his weight. With each step, the entire case seemed to shake though he had to admit it didn't quiver as badly as the short stretch of steps to his and Emily's cabin loft.

Still, he vaguely worried he was going to turn the Cates's staircase to jackstraws and kindling, and was relieved when he gained the second story. He'd been up here once before, visiting Cates in his home office, and Logan had given him a short tour, so he knew that the main bedroom was behind the door at the far end of the hall. He paused outside the door, listened for a moment, and, hearing nothing from inside the room, tapped with the backs of his fingers.

A choking sound. The sound of a phlegmy throat being cleared.

Then—"Come in, Dag."

Enberg twisted the knob and entered the bedroom slowly, tentatively. The bed was a little to the right, its head abutting the right wall. It was surprisingly high off the carpeted floor, but, then, Enberg figured its height would only be surprising to someone more accustomed to sleeping on rough-hewn military cots.

There was a canopy over the bed. A body lay humped beneath the covers. A gray face and even grayer head protruded from the top of the sheets and quilts. The head looked so small and insignificant, it seemed to barely make a dent in the snow-white pillow beneath it.

On the wall above the bed was a large oil painting behind

glass of the town of Mineral Springs back when there was only the springs itself, a livery barn, and the first version of the Diamond in the Rough Saloon, which had been merely a sprawling tent with some insignificant plank framing and a tented brewhouse flanking it. Three wooden shanties also flanked the sprawling tent. These were the first whores' cribs. The madam had been a cranky old Chinese woman, long dead now.

DIAMOND IN THE ROUGH SALOON was announced on a carefully hand-lettered sign jutting into the street and held aloft by two crooked cedar poles. The painting depicted two old men working out front of the place, near the livery barn. They were murky figures, but they were probably the artist's conception, as directed by Cates's uncle, Norman Century, of Norman himself and Dag's father, Olaf. A similar painting had once hung in Cates's office in the Diamond, so Enberg had perused it before.

"Dag?" came a small, withered, croaking sound. It sounded like the death rattle of a large bird, Enberg vaguely reflected.

He strode slowly, reluctantly up to the head of the bed, his features tense. He hadn't seen Logan in a couple of weeks, and even then he had seemed a ghost of his former self. Now, what would Dag find?

He inwardly recoiled at the man's visage staring up at him from the pillow—the eyes twice as large as they'd last appeared, for the sockets had withered around them. The man's face was angular and cadaverous. It appeared totally lacking in color. What little hair the man had left was the color of old, dried corn silk.

Enberg thought he could probably wrap one hand around the man's neck.

The man, who could not possibly be Logan Cates, but was, twisted his thin, chapped, pink lips into a semblance of a wry grin. "I know I'm lookin' a little off my feed, Dag. Don't worry.

This won't take long. I just wanted a word with you, since this will likely be our last visit. Pull up a chair."

Enberg looked around and saw a brocade armchair against the wall behind him. He dragged it up, involuntarily making a face against the death fetor and coppery smell of blood and the musk of urine that hung heavy in the warm room, which could have done with a good airing out. The drapes were drawn across windows that were obviously closed. Sweat trickled down Enberg's back, beneath his shirt.

Again as though reading Enberg's mind, Cates said in his wheezing little chirp, "Sorry about the smell."

"Don't matter, Logan. Don't worry about it." Enberg sank into the chair, dropped his hat onto the floor between his boots, and leaned forward, resting his elbows on his knees. "How you doin'?"

Cates sighed raggedly. "I've been better." His inordinately large, dark eyes, which were once a much lighter blue, rolled toward Enberg. "Did they tell you I'm on my way out?"

Enberg swallowed, nodded. "Anything I can do to . . . uh . . . make you more comfortable?"

"You could put a bullet in my head." Again, that grisly death grin.

Enberg grunted a chuckle, though there was no mirth in it whatever. He was deeply uncomfortable. He was deeply sad and lonely. He and Cates had only started getting along a couple of months ago, and now Cates was dying slowly, hideously.

"Christ, Logan. I'm really sorry about this. Why in the cryin' fuck did you have to go and get that damn cancer, anyways? Shit, I wouldn't will this kind of end on my worst enemies!"

"Be careful, my friend," Cates rattled out. "Gertrude hears every curse word uttered in this house. She hears nothing else. *Only* the curses."

Enberg gave another wry snort.

"What was she ringing your bell about down there?"

Enberg hesitated. He was reluctant to admit the holdup to Cates, who'd given him so many second chances, but he knew he had to tell him.

"Stage got hit. Bloody Gulch. Charlie was shot. Not bad. But two of the gang that hit us got away with the strongbox."

"Goddamn." Cates wasn't able to put much volume into the epithet. "S-sorry, Dag."

"*You're* sorry? Christ, Logan—I feel like I let you down. Again!"

Cates grunted and made a face as he pushed himself up a bit on the bed. He jerked his head, and said, "Help me here. Lift the pillow."

As Cates lifted his head off the pillow, Enberg pulled it up against the headboard. Cates rested his head and shoulders back against it.

"How's that?" Dag asked.

Cates nodded. He looked at Enberg. "You're gonna get hit. You know as well as I do that the stretch of trail between here and Tomahawk is the nastiest stretch of trail in Arizona. Bronco Apaches, outlaws, *banditos* up from the border. They all gravitate toward that stretch of trail, because it's the easiest place to hit it. That's why I put you on it. You're good at riding shotgun. You'll be a lawman again, Dag. It's just a matter of time. Ridin' shotgun gives you time to file the edge off your emotions and grow back your confidence. When you've done that, you'll be ready to wear another badge."

"I don't know if I want to wear another badge, Logan."

Cates shook his head, as though annoyed by the turn the conversation had taken. "We . . . er, I mean *you* . . . will cross that bridge when you come to it. But getting back to the holdup—it's gonna happen. I know it and Normandy knows it. When you run a stage line in rough country, you come to terms with it. But you hedge your bets with the best men you can get your hands on. And you're one of the best. That was your first holdup."

Cates smiled though his smiles these days looked more like grimaces. "At least it was the first time you were taken by surprise." He was referring to the debacle with Cougar Ketchum. "There'll be more holdups. But there'll be damn fewer than if Normandy had anyone else wielding the twelve-gauge up there on the seat beside Charlie."

Enberg lowered his head and ran his hand through his thick tangle of wavy, red-blond hair. He gave a groan of deep frustration, still replaying in his mind Gila River Tom Tiegan sneaking up on him from behind.

"You're your own worst enemy, Dag. You know that. Get your emotions under control. Don't expect so much from yourself. You want to be a god, but you're just a man. Just like the rest of us. We live and we die. Hopefully, between those events, we're able to do a few things we're proud of. You're a good, capable man. You're a moral man with good instincts. You took a bad turn when you came back from the war, got thrown off your feet. But you've regained your footing now, so don't let this one holdup throw you off."

Cates stared at him through his large, watery eyes.

"All right?" he said, pointedly.

Enberg nodded, and smiled. "All right, Logan." He realized now that he'd needed the pep talk. He genuinely felt better. That really was his problem—sometimes he expected too much from himself. Maybe that was because at times in the past he'd expected so little. Now he was trying to compensate.

He dearly regretted that Logan wouldn't be around to steer him back right in the future. He was going to have to try to get the hang of it himself.

"There's another thing I hope doesn't throw you off," Cates said.

Enberg frowned, curious.

Cates shifted his gaze to something on the other side of the room.

"Fetch me the Bible off the shelf over there, will you, Dag?"

"Bible?"

"Yeah. Don't worry, I'm not going to give you a sermon."

Puzzled, Enberg rose from his chair, plucked the heavy Bible, which was stuffed with papers of various degrees of aged yellow, off a bookshelf beside a heavy oak armoire, and set it down on the bed beside Cates.

CHAPTER SIX

Cates wrapped a hand around the Bible. He tried to pick it up, but couldn't. It was too heavy. Scowling, shaking his head in disgust, he said, "Inside the back cover, there's a folded piece of paper. Take it out."

Enberg lifted the Bible. He saw the quarter-folded sheaf of yellowed notepaper. He pulled it out, set the Bible down, and looked at the paper. On the side facing him the words GIVE TO DAG IF I GIVE UP THE GHOST.

Holy shit. The words had been penciled in a heavy, untutored hand. They were also badly smudged. Still, Enberg recognized the boyish writing and wry, self-deprecating humor.

He looked at Cates, whose mouth corners quirked an ironic smile.

"Pa?" Dag said.

He carefully unfolded the yellowed and brittle piece of notepaper until what stared up at him was a crudely penciled map. His eyes hastily, greedily scoured the paper, noting the squiggly lines that must have signified mountains and the broken, semi-straight line that showed a trail across a bristling desert, between mountain ranges in south-central Arizona Territory. Several familiar features, including mountain peaks, a canyon, a couple of *tenajas,* a well, and a jog of bluffs near the border, had been marked.

There was a dark X at the base of one of these bluffs, near a *tenaja,* or natural rock tank holding rainwater.

Enberg's heart beat heavily. His mouth was dry.

He shifted his wide, shocked gaze from the map to Cates. "Pa's map . . ."

Logan nodded weakly. He spoke slowly, his gravelly, halting sentences punctuated by shallow inhalations. "I happened to pick up my uncle's family Bible yesterday, and started flipping through it, looking for comfort here at the end, I guess you could say. That fell out of it, almost as though it had been waiting for someone to find it."

"So there *was* a map. Pa gave it to your uncle. Makes sense."

"To their way of thinking, it would. To Uncle Norman, that Bible was as good as a safe. I guess I should have thought to look through it before. I was too busy dealing with all his holdings, I reckon." Cates smiled sagely. "There you have it, Dag. The map to the treasure—one of the things you'd hoped to find when you returned from the war."

Enberg stared down at the paper again, his heart still racing, his hands shaking slightly.

Cates was right. He'd at least hoped to have whatever treasure his old man had stashed out in the desert. Olaf Enberg had told Dag that he'd found considerable gold in his desert wanderings and diggings, but he'd never said what form it had been in or where he'd cached it. He'd never told anyone. After Enberg had gone off to the war, Olaf must have scribbled the map and given it to Norman Century, in case Olaf died before his son returned from fighting.

If he returned.

Century had placed the map in the Bible for safekeeping. As tight-lipped as old Olaf had been, Century had apparently told no one else about its existence. And then he'd died a year after Olaf had been found dead in the desert. Century had been claimed by infection that had set in after he'd been struck by a Chiricahua arrow while holding off the Apaches trying to sack the fledgling settlement of Mineral Springs.

"What's the matter?" Cates asked, his voice barely audible now. The strain of the conversation had sapped whatever strength he'd had before Enberg had walked into the room. "I'd have thought you'd be jumping up and down . . . hustling outside to rent a couple of mules . . . and chase after your wealth."

"I don't know," Enberg said. His heart had slowed. Finding the map suddenly felt a little anticlimactic. "I don't know what's the matter, Logan."

He slowly lowered the map, chuckled dryly, and frowned skeptically at Cates. "Suddenly I don't feel all that het up about it."

"You've built a life without it," Cates said. "Probably a better one than you would have had if you'd found it before. Maybe it's best to wait on that cache of old Olaf's . . . continue as you are. Struggle a little more. Struggle is what makes life worth living. Besides, you never liked prospecting. You always hated holes in the ground—remember? They made you claustrophobic. Love your wife and that baby she's going to have. Work. Then, when you feel the time is right, when you've grown into the man you want to become . . . then rig a couple of pack mules and go after it, if you still feel the urge."

Cates turned his head and coughed into a handkerchief.

"Easy, Logan," Enberg said, placing his hand on Cates's bucking shoulder. "I'll get Gertrude."

Cates nodded. Through his coughing, he said, "Tell her to bring my pills."

"I will." Enberg turned and headed for the door. Realizing that this might be the last time he'd ever see Logan Cates again, a man who had turned Dag's life around, he strode back to the bed, wrapped his arms around Cates's spindly shoulders, and gave him a gentle hug. "Thanks, Logan."

Cates nodded, trying to smile, blood dribbling out the corners of his shrunken mouth. "Don't get sentimental on me, you big bastard. My pills!"

Cates was coughing and laughing.

"I'll get Gertrude!"

Enberg jogged out of the room, tears streaming down his cheeks.

When Gertrude had taken Cates's medication upstairs, Enberg told Emily he needed to check on Charlie and then head out to the proverbial woodshed with his new employer, Bud Normandy.

Emily gave a little, affectionate tug on Enberg's sweaty shirt. "What's the matter, Dag? You look as though you've been kicked in the gut. I know Logan looks bad, but . . ."

"It's not just Logan, Em," Enberg said, his mind still foggy from the shock of being presented with the map. "I'll tell you the rest later, all right? I'm worried about Charlie."

"Please remember, darling—you're only one man, and there are more bad men than good men in this world. You're not going to prevent every holdup."

"That's what Logan said." Enberg grinned and pecked her forehead. "Maybe you have more in common with your steppap than you think."

Emily's relationship with Cates had been strained due to her mother. She saw Cates as being led around by his nose by Gertrude, but Enberg didn't blame him for that. Any man would have been led around by Gertrude, if he found himself in the unenviable position of sharing a roof with the woman.

Emily still resented Logan for forbidding her to marry Dag, though it hadn't prevented her from doing so. Enberg had put that whole mess past him in light of all that the dying man had done for him. It wasn't news to him that Emily hadn't.

Maybe she had more of her mother in her than she wanted to believe.

"I'm glad he doesn't hold the holdup against you, anyway," Emily said. "It wouldn't be right."

"Yeah, well, let's hope Normandy feels the same way. How long are you going to stay here, Em?"

"As long as Mother needs me, I guess. I'd like to go home with you, and make you a nice big supper after your harried day, but I'm afraid I'd feel guilty leaving her alone with Logan. The doctor won't be back till this evening."

"Does he have any idea how much longer Logan's going to hold on?"

"He said it could be anywhere from a few hours to a few days."

"I'll check on you later, then." Enberg drew Emily to him, kissed her lips, clipped her chin with his thumb, and headed for the door.

"I suppose you'll be going over to the Diamond, then . . . since you're going to see Normandy."

Turning back to his wife, Enberg said, "That's where his office is, Em."

Emily pursed his lips and nodded regretfully.

Enberg winked at her, went out, and started tramping back down the bluff toward town.

He'd ignored his wife's chagrin at his visiting the Diamond, but he knew the cause of her misgivings. Zenobia Chevere was there—the inimitable Zee with whom Dag had had an affair that would probably still be going hot and heavy if Cates hadn't put a stop to it. Logan had forbidden his employees from "intermingling." Enberg suspected that part of the reason he'd put the kibosh on Enberg's and Zee's trysts, which they'd tried to keep secret, was because Cates himself was secretly in love with the ravishing Mexican girl.

Enberg hadn't been able to blame Cates for that, either, given the beauty of the buxom, chocolate-eyed young *puta,* who had escaped a violent revolution in her native land and come north to make a life for herself in any way she could.

Besides, living with Gertrude would have caused any man to look in another direction for passion, though Enberg suspected that Cates did indeed, *improbably,* love the frigid woman. A relationship forged by necessity for them both, business-wise, had turned to something much deeper, though Enberg attributed that more to Logan's good-heartedness than to Gertrude's. But something caused him to suspect that she loved him, as well.

Zee . . .

Enberg shook the *puta's* image from his mind. He hoped he wouldn't see her in the Diamond. He had enough on his mind to have to negotiate those old feelings, as well. Feelings that, for the life of him and despite his love and devotion to Emily, had not lost their fire.

And now that map. Damn the map. Why did Cates have to find it?

Enberg had nearly been able to wipe that frustration from his mind, as well. He'd been concentrating on his job and on Emily to the exclusion of nearly everything else.

He headed over to the doctor's office to find Doc Miles Koehler just finishing putting the last touches of plaster of Paris on Cyril Blevins's nose. Blevins did not look pleased to see the man who had inflicted such pain on him, but he was hurting too badly to do much but glare around the doctor's plaster-coated fingers.

Both of his eyes were swollen and discolored.

"I sent Charlie over to the Diamond, Dag," said the middle-aged sawbones. "Normandy gave him a room over there, as per my suggestion. Don't want that old geezer sleepin' in one o' them dirty whores' cribs he usually throws down in, down by the wash. Risk of infection. Normandy agreed to give him a night for free. That's where you'll find him, all right. Likely chugging the whiskey like it's the last batch, knowin' Charlie!"

"The old codger gonna be all right, Doc?"

"He'll be fine as frog hair. Just a flesh wound. He's had a few of those in his day. Doubt it will even slow him down after tomorrow."

The doctor chuckled and shook his head.

"Thanks, Doc."

"Oh, Dag?"

Enberg turned back to the examination room.

"Normandy told me if I saw you to make sure you made a beeline for his office over at the Diamond." The doctor scowled and shook his head again. "He didn't seem real happy."

Blevins managed a satisfied smile at that.

"All right," Enberg said with a sigh, and went out.

He'd been entertaining the notion of heading home and leaving the meeting with his boss to tomorrow, after Normandy had had time to cool down. And to give the posse time to run down Perrine and Buckley. Now, it looked like he'd better see Normandy *pronto.*

Enberg drew another calming breath as he crossed the main street of Mineral Springs, wending his way through late-day supply wagon traffic, and headed up the steps of the Diamond in the Rough's broad front porch. Business in the place was already picking up, as it often did around three.

Enberg learned from one of the two bartenders on duty which room Grissom had been given, and headed for the stairs. He'd check on Charlie first and then visit Normandy.

He paused near the bottom of the stairs when Zee came through a door flanking the broad horseshoe bar. Inwardly, Enberg winced. He hadn't expected to see her out this early. She usually didn't show herself until after seven or so in the evening. She was holding a tray with a glass and a bottle of beer on it.

Zenobia Chevere looked customarily gorgeous, her near-black hair shining, her dark eyes glistening, her mostly-exposed Mexican-brown skin looking cool and flawless and eminently irresistible. Her bare legs were long, firm, and slender. Her breasts were both tucked back and pushed up by the lacy black corset she wore under a sheer red wrap. The deep valley between her bosoms was dark and inviting.

She moved forward. Enberg's feet held him where he was, though he wanted to beat a hasty retreat from the girl, even if it made him look foolish. But, then, every man around Zee came out looking foolish in the end.

"Why do you scowl when you see me?" Zee asked him, pursing her lips and wrinkling her brows in a pout as she stopped just off his right shoulder.

The top of her head came up to the middle of that arm. The shadow of his tall, broad body encompassed all of her. She was small and curvy and brown and supple, and every time he saw her, he remembered how it had been, making love to such a bewitching sorceress.

He remembered the cries she'd made, the way she'd tasted . . .

"Just because you don't love me anymore doesn't mean you can't be civil," Zee added.

Enberg glanced around, feeling guilty for standing this close to her, as though Emily might see. But of course, Emily wasn't here. A few of the customers were watching, however, and they likely remembered the storied trysts that had somehow not only become known but legendary, given the forbidden quality of the meetings as well as the passionate natures of both participants. Dag no longer liked being seen with her. If it got around and Emily found out . . .

"I'm going upstairs," Enberg said, and started climbing the steps.

"So am I," Zee said, still pouty and falling into step beside him. "I am bringing this beer to Charlie."

"Christ," Enberg said.

CHAPTER SEVEN

"What is wrong with you, anyway, *querido*?" Zee asked as she climbed the stairs to Dag's left. "There was a time you couldn't keep your hands off me."

Enberg gained the second floor landing. He glanced over his shoulder to make sure no one was watching from below, and then grabbed Zee by her arm and swung her around in front of him. She gasped. The bottle of beer tumbled off the tray, but Enberg grabbed it. The glass fell to the floor with a muffled thud on the carpet, but did not break.

Enberg pressed Zee up against the wall. Zee stared at him, her eyes wide with fear. It was then that Enberg realized he had his right hand around her throat. Quickly, he removed it. Zee's breasts rose and fell sharply.

"Whoa!" she said with a nervous laugh. "What—now you want to kill me?"

"Shut up, goddamnit, Zee!" Enberg looked around. Thank god there was no one else in the hall. "Stop with the games. You know what you're doing. You can't help playing them because of who you are, and what we once were, but all that is over. You know it's over. You even encouraged me to move on, you bitch!"

An embarrassed flush rose beneath Zee's natural tan. It started at the tops of her breasts and rose up through her neck and into her heart-shaped face.

"I know." She looked down with chagrin. "I am sorry. I can't help missing you, Dag. At the same time I am grateful that you moved on, that you married Emily and that all is going well for you."

"I think about you all the goddamn time," Enberg said through gritted teeth. He was breathing hard, his eyes devouring her.

"I wish I could say I wish you didn't. But you've moved on . . . to happiness . . . and I'm still here where I'll be for a few more years, until the lines grow long in my face and my tits start to sag. At least . . . at least I know you still love me. Or at least *want* me."

"Of course I want you. What man wouldn't? But we can't be seen together anymore. We have to agree that when you see me or I see you—*one of us* walks the other way. I can't stand the torture of being this close to you, Zee, and I don't want Emily to find out. I love her, goddamnit. She's my wife, and she's going to have a baby in a few months!"

"I know, I know." Zee gazed up at him, her lips parted, breasts rising and falling, causing the corset to move with them.

Her lips were plump and rich. He could feel her breath gently puffing against his neck. She smelled like cherry blossoms and sandalwood. Before he knew what he was doing, he was kissing her. She wrapped her arms around his neck with a groan, and entangled her tongue with his. She pressed against him, and he could feel her bosom swelling against his chest.

Oh, god—to spend just one more night with her. One hour!

But he couldn't do that to Emily.

He tried to pull back away from Zee, but she clung to him, groaning, mashing her lips against his. He reached up and grabbed her hands and lowered them and then shoved her back against the wall. He could feel her warm saliva on his lips. His denims were tight across his crotch, and a high-pitched wail of desire resounded in his ears.

"That can't ever happen again," he said, clearing his throat.

"But we both want it to so bad!" Zee said, stepping into him and wrapping her arms around his neck again.

He was powerless to stop her from pressing her lips against his once more, and snaking her warm, wet tongue against his. He hadn't realized that he'd heard the soft tread of footsteps on the stairs until a girl's voice said, "Oh!"

Enberg shoved Zee back away from him and turned to see Lisle Stanton standing at the top of the steps, staring at him in wide-eyed shock.

"Dag!" the girl said, her lower jaw hanging. She'd obviously bathed and changed her clothes since her arrival in Mineral Springs. She wore a sporty yellow frock with a short, yellow jacket, and her hair was pulled up into an elegant bun atop her head. The bun was held in place by an ebony barrette studded with what appeared to be pearls.

Enberg just stared at her, bells of embarrassment tolling in his ears.

"I . . . I'm sorry," Lisle said, glancing from Zee to Enberg and then whipping her head forward. She crossed the hall and continued on up the next flight of stairs to the third floor.

"Shit!" Enberg raked out, glaring at Zee standing before him with her back against the wall.

"Who is that?" Zee asked, her voice pitched with jealousy. "She's . . . pretty."

"Never mind. I gotta go."

Enberg turned away from her, but he'd suddenly forgotten where he'd been heading. Zee grabbed his arm and swung him back to face her.

"Dag, I can't lie with another man without seeing you!"

He didn't want to tell her that when he was with Emily it was often the same way for him. He didn't want to think about it or acknowledge it.

He remembered where he'd been heading when he'd run

into her. His voice was quivering, his hand shaking, as he lifted the beer bottle up in front of Zee's face. "I'll take this to Charlie. Go back downstairs, or . . . get anywhere but where I am."

"Dag!" Zee called desperately behind him.

Ignoring her, willing himself not to turn his head to face her, to see her in all her desperate longing that mirrored his own, Enberg continued on down the hall. Finally, he heard her give a sharp Spanish curse, and then her footsteps faded behind him as she went back down the stairs, and he heaved a long sigh of relief.

Still, his feet felt as though they'd gone to sleep and his pressing need to lie with the beautiful young *puta* was still a stab-like pain in his loins.

He found the door he was looking for. Muffled, garbled sighs came from the other side.

Enberg frowned, tapped once, and said, "Charlie? Room service."

" 'Bout time!" Charlie's voice barked.

Enberg gave a snort and opened the door. Grissom lay on the bed to the right. He looked at Enberg and said, "It's a bonded fact you can't get good help no more. Set it right here on the table, boy." He grinned and jerked his head at the small lamp table beside the bed.

Then he went back to grinning and sighing up at the ceiling. A girl was under the bed's single sheet, bobbing her head up and down, over the old man's waist. Enberg could see her naked silhouette through the spindly sheet. She was making wet sucking sounds while Charlie groaned and sighed.

Enberg gave another wry snort as he carried the bottle across the room and set it down on the table beside Grissom. "Don't expect a tip for such slow service, boy," Charlie grunted, wincing with delight at the whore's ministrations.

"I take it you're on the mend."

"The pill roller done a nice job on my arm." Grissom winced and stretched his lips back from his chipped, tobacco-yellow teeth. "And Rosie's puttin' the finishin' touches on the doctorin'. A good French lesson is the best elixir known to man," he added through a dreamy sigh.

"I'll leave you two lovebirds alone." Enberg headed for the door.

"You do that, boy. Next time put a little hop in your step, and you might earn a tip!" Grissom wheezed a delighted laugh.

Enberg rolled his eyes as he stepped into the hall and drew the door closed behind him.

He paused. Now for his visit with Normandy.

"Ah, shit," he said, craving a sip of the beer he'd just taken to Grissom. He had a deep urge to head on downstairs for a shot of tarantula juice, but he'd given up drinking. It had a bad effect on him. It mixed about as well with his one hundred percent Norski blood as it did with pure Apache blood.

Like fire and kerosene.

It was a lit match tossed into a powder keg.

It had caused Cates to fire him from his position as town marshal.

Enberg cursed again as he tramped back down the hall and made his way upstairs to the third floor. Cates's old office, which was now occupied by Bud Normandy, lay at the far end of the hall, behind the door marked with a gold nameplate. Like Cates's, Normandy's name was etched in ornate cursive.

Enberg sighed and knocked on the door.

"Who is it?" came Normandy's voice.

"Enberg."

"Come."

Enberg opened the door and entered the room. He stopped just inside the door, frowning.

Lisle Stanton stood behind Normandy's desk, beside

Normandy. They were both looking down at several open books spilling papers. Normandy was saying, ". . . and this one I found all alone in a file drawer, but I can't make heads or tails of the accounts in it. If you can straighten all these out for me, Lis, I'd be forever grateful."

"Don't worry, Uncle Bud," Lisle said, closing one of the books. "I'll get right on it. The office you set up for me will be more than adequate."

"Are you sure you don't want to wait until tomorrow, dear?" Normandy asked. "After all, you just got here, and the last leg of your journey was quite trying."

He cast an accusing glare across the room at Enberg, still standing inside the open door, kneading the brim of his hat in his hands. He'd removed his shotgun from around his neck and shoulder, and leaned it against the wall by the door. Enberg's ears warmed with chagrin.

"I'd like to get the books organized this evening so I can start bearing down on them tomorrow. I'd just as soon not sit around and think about the holdup." Lisle closed the books one by one, gathered them up in her arms, and straightened, smiling winningly, a trifle coquettishly across the room at Enberg. "There you are again, Dag. Odd how we keep running into each other!"

Enberg's ears grew hotter.

"I see you're on a first-name basis with my shotgun rider," Normandy said with vague reproof in his tone as well as in his eyes.

Lisle moved out from behind Normandy's desk and strode toward Enberg. She was a lissome girl, and her eyes sparkled with good-natured jeering. "This man saved my life, Uncle Bud. That does indeed put us on a first-name basis."

She paused in front of Enberg and gazed up at him, keeping her voice low as she said, "I hope your . . . um . . . conversation with the pretty *senorita* went . . . um . . . well, Mr. Enberg."

The burn of embarrassment moved into Dag's cheeks and swelled his tongue so that he could find no way to respond.

"What's that?" her uncle asked, scowling behind his desk. "I can't hear you, child."

Lisle glanced over her shoulder at Normandy. "Oh, nothing, Uncle Bud. I was just thanking Mr. Enberg again for his help. If he hadn't come along when he did, those depraved owlhoots might have finished what they'd started and dragged me all the way to Mexico with them, to finish me off!"

"Oh, Lisle!" remonstrated her uncle.

She gave Enberg an unabashedly flirtatious wink and walked around him to the door, saying, "I'll check in with you first thing tomorrow, Uncle Bud." She went out, drawing the door closed behind Enberg.

"Never mind her, Enberg," Normandy said, slacking his broad, stocky frame into the high-backed leather chair that Enberg was more accustomed to seeing Logan Cates in. "She's a bit feisty. But smart as a whip. Excels in accounting—entirely self-taught. Her folks were having trouble keeping her on a leash back in San Diego, so I said, 'Send her to Mineral Springs. I can put her to work straightening out all of Cates's old accounts. That should keep her out of trouble until she's at least forty!' "

"I had no idea she was your niece."

"No, she wouldn't have said. She might have thought she'd been given special treatment. That's Lisle for you. I was a little surprised to see her myself. I wasn't expecting her till next week. She must have really been chomping at the bit for a change of scenery." Normandy paused, thoughtful. "Uh . . . Enberg . . . ?"

"Yes, Mr. Normandy?"

"You will remember that's she's my niece, won't you? And that she's entirely off-limits . . . ?"

Self-righteous indignation burned in Enberg. "What are you saying, Mr. Normandy?"

"I've had you investigated, Enberg."

"Why?"

"Sit down."

"I'll stand."

Normandy half-rose from his chair, his broad, round facing turning red, the snow-white muttonchops standing in sharp contrast against it. "Sit down, Enberg!"

Enberg clenched his fists, barely able to keep his wolf on its chain. He had a feeling, however, that he'd met his match in that regard. The challenging, enraged expression on Normandy's face told Dag that, despite his agreement with Cates, this man was spoiling for a reason to fire him. With Cates near death, there would likely be little to stop him.

Enberg unclenched his fists, drew a deep, calming breath, and sagged into the visitor chair angled before his boss's desk.

Normandy retook his own chair, sitting back in the tall chair and resting his arms on the wooden chair arms. He regarded Enberg stoically for a time, his jaws hard, and then he brushed a beringed right hand across his mouth, and said, "When Cates insisted with such vehemence that I keep you on, to the point that he even had it written into our agreement, I decided to investigate your history. I wanted to know why it was so important to Cates to not only keep you on but to have it wedged into the contract for my buying the stage line. He could have just recommended you, verbally, and left it at that. I no doubt would have kept you on and asked no questions. But the lengths he went to raised my suspicions."

Silently, Enberg groaned.

"I learned all about you. I learned who your father was. I learned about your war experiences. Quite a gallant war record. The trouble for you started, it seems, once you got back home to Mineral Springs and found your father dead and none of his holdings willed to you. Everything had gone to Cates, as per Cates's uncle's will."

Silently, Enberg groaned again as Normandy continued to count off Dag's transgressions on his fingers—the drinking and whoring, his ill-fated stint as town marshal, the bank robbery he'd been too drunk to foil, his proscribed relationship with Cates's prize whore, his dalliance with and then marriage to Emily Dayton despite Cates's and Gertrude's protestations.

The nasty business with Emily's kidnapping and Dag's turning over Cates's prize strongbox to the kidnappers.

"Oh, yes," Normandy said, as though making one concession, "you did help in retrieving the strongbox. Yes, I suppose that was the least you could do, since you got yourself and your pretty wife tangled up in that affair in the first place. But, then, it was also said that you killed the Mineral Springs city marshal, though no charges were brought against you. The man was bitten by several diamondbacks while trying to arrest you, so I guess you couldn't *officially be held accountable.*"

"They were Mojave greens," Enberg said, staring at his right knee, crestfallen.

Normandy cupped a hand to his ear. "Say again . . ."

"The snakes that killed Geylan Whipple—they were Mojave greens."

"I stand corrected." Normandy paused. "And . . . today. The robbers got away with Hud Cormorant's payroll money. Would you like to be the one to explain that fiasco to Hud Cormorant?"

"I will if you want."

"Don't use that defiant tone with me, Enberg! Unlike Cates, I am not a man you can toy with. As of here and now, I am suspending you until further notice."

Enberg leaped out of his chair. "Hey, wait a minute!"

"No, you wait a minute, Enberg!" Red-faced, Normandy

pointed an angry finger across the big desk at Dag. "I suspect that your reputation as a formidable shotgun rider is far overblown. Probably to the point where outlaws in this nefarious neck of the Arizona Territory have targeted you as well as the runs you are on to prove that they can take the big man down. I can't afford that kind of trouble. I have a stage station to run—one that was not kept in the best condition, either staff-wise or book-wise! It's going to take me a while to get this line in order. And while I'm doing so—with the help of my niece whom you are to steer far clear of, I am going to reiterate!—I will ponder your fate. Until I've come to my decision on whether or not to keep you on or give you your walking papers, you are suspended, and that is that!"

CHAPTER EIGHT

Dag fairly bounded out of his chair and strode to the door. He swung the twelve-gauge around his neck and shoulder, shoving it behind him. He opened the door without saying another word to Normandy, and went out.

In the hall, he leaned back against the door and drew a deep breath, trying to calm himself. But his fists were clenched tightly at his sides. His jaws were as hard as anvils.

He'd had to get out of Normandy's office quickly. Fury was welling in him to a dangerous degree. A nearly inaudible voice of reason whispered into his ear, beneath the roaring caldrons of liquid fire: "Get out. Get up and walk out of the office before you leap over the desk and kill the man."

Enberg turned away from Normandy's closed door and staggered as though half-drunk down the hall toward the stairs. Desperate thoughts raced through his mind.

Suspended.

That meant he wouldn't be getting paid until Normandy made up his mind about whether to keep him on or to fire him.

Suspended.

Most likely, he was fired. Normandy had already spelled out his case against the shotgun rider. Nothing was going to change his views. He'd uncovered the raw facts and interpreted them in all the wrong ways, but in the ways he'd wanted to, when he'd set out on his fishing expedition. To Normandy's way of thinking, Enberg was a hot-tempered fool and, in some cases, as in

Geylan Whipple's case, a killer.

Nothing would change what Normandy thought about him.

Enberg was out of another job—a job he'd grown to like and had taken pride in. One he'd thought he'd keep because of Cates's finagling. But now Logan was on his deathbed. There was nothing he could do. Enberg could possibly fight for his job, but there was no winning when a man like Dag fought a man like Bud Normandy.

What would Enberg tell Emily? She was pregnant. In a few months, Enberg would have another mouth to feed. Where could he find another job? After all of his former trouble, who would hire him? His reputation had taken a debilitating beating. One of the other saloons, maybe an ale barn or a little whorehouse on the poor side of town, might hire him to tend bar or to swamp the place out, but he doubted he could endure the indignity of that.

His pride as a man had taken another devastating hit.

Emily Dayton's husband working in a saloon when he'd once been a town marshal and a shotgun rider. A son of one of the town's two founding fathers—self-made men—languishing away in a saloon . . .

He supposed he could go out looking for his father's treasure, but Emily was pregnant. She needed him here. Besides, he was broke. He needed a stake to afford the time to go out and *find* that gold!

Even if he found a fortune, no amount of money could buy a man's pride back.

Frustration and fury were a toxic tide inside of Enberg. Slowly, he dropped down the stairs, his eyes wide and staring, seeing nothing but Emily's face when he told her the news. Seeing nothing but the faces of the other townsfolk glancing at him and whispering among themselves.

"There goes ole Dag Enberg. Olaf's no-good son. The apple sure fell a long ways from the tree on that one!" Ironic chuckles and open laughter.

He had been fired for no good reason from a job that had given him back his dignity. That lone fact was growing into a large, black cloud inside of Dag, pushing aside the optimism and possible wealth of his father's mine and causing the fires of fury to rage just behind his eyes.

His heart thudded heavily and his jaws ached from being clenched.

In his mind's eye, he imagined shoving his fist through Bud Normandy's fat face. Of getting the man down on the floor and hammering him until there was nothing left but ground meat.

A drink.

Enberg needed a drink.

Why not a drink? He'd promised Logan he'd stay off the stuff to keep his job. Well, he'd stayed off the stuff and he'd lost his job. And Logan was dying.

He needed a drink to not kill Normandy, to not hang for murder. He needed a couple of stiff shots to clear his mind and to concentrate more on what he had ahead of him than what he'd so unjustly been robbed of. He needed a clear mind to think through the possibilities of his father's hidden gold and of his future with Emily and their child.

His feet feeling a little lighter, he headed for the large, horseshoe-shaped bar and bellied up against it. The barman, Wade Underhill, was drawing ale for two dusty cavalry soldiers likely from Fort Bowie and out scouring the country for reservation-jumping Apaches. Apaches were always jumping the reservations. When Underhill finished with the soldiers, he wiped his hands on the towel hanging over his shoulder, glanced at Dag, and said, "Glass of buttermilk, Enberg?"

He'd said it with the usual, faintly mocking curl of his upper lip.

He reached under the bar for the buttermilk that Enberg had taken to asking for instead of ale or whiskey.

"Fuck the buttermilk, Wade. Bourbon," Enberg said. "The good stuff. The bottle. One glass. Tell Normandy to take it out of my time."

Underhill's expression changed. "I . . . I thought you was on the wagon, Dag."

"Fuck the wagon. The wagon broke down and dumped me off into a tall pile of hot sheep dip." Enberg slapped the bar with more vigor and more loudly than he'd intended to, causing several surprised faces to turn in his direction. "Set me up, Wade. Come on—I got a whole pint of trail dust gummin' up my tonsils. I'm goddamn parched!"

With a leery arch of his brows, Underhill turned to the back bar. He reluctantly lifted a labeled bottle off a shelf, and, sharing a meaningful glance with the other apron working the current shift, set the bottle on the bar in front of Enberg.

The barman grabbed a shot glass off a glistening pyramid beside a two-gallon jar of pickled hogs' feet, and set the glass down on the bar near the bottle.

"Are you sure about this, Dag?"

"Sure as shit in the nun's privy." Enberg laughed.

Underhill winced, glanced at the bottle, then looked at Enberg again. "Why . . . why don't you take it home?"

"Do what?"

"Why don't you take it on home with you, Dag?" Underhill said, faint beseeching in his low-pitched voice as he leaned over the bar toward Enberg. "Drink it out on your stoop. It's a nice evenin'."

Enberg scowled at him, nostrils flaring, as though he were deeply offended. "I'm gonna pretend I didn't hear that, Wade."

"Ah, shit!" Underhill was very much aware of Dag's reputation. He didn't want him to get drunk and tear up the place and half of the other clientele.

Enberg grabbed the bottle and the glass, hit the apron with another belligerent glare, and headed for a table on the other side of the room. As he often did when he was furious, he was starting to see the face of his antagonist in the faces of others around him. It was something he couldn't control after it had gone to a certain point, and it had come to that now in the sullen, surly Norski's anger-addled mind.

He knew deep down he shouldn't pry the cork from the bottle, that eventually the whiskey would only compound his already churlish disposition. But at the moment he could fathom only the comforting burn and soothing flush of those first few drinks.

He ignored the wary glances being tossed his way by the late afternoon crowd. A glance at the clock behind the bar told him it was a little after six p.m. A long night ahead. He slacked into the chair, set his shotgun on the table, pried the cork from the bottle with his folding knife, and filled the glass.

He gazed down at the amber liquid.

It no longer looked like whiskey.

It looked like an elixir set down here by some eminently benevolent god intending to sooth the unjustly traumatized shotgun rider's nerves, to set his mind at ease. To soothe the hurt of the wrongful firing, to distract him from needling, guilty thoughts about providing for his family, from his lust for Zee, and from the death of his friend and prime benefactor, Logan Cates.

Enberg grinned, picked up the shot between his thumb and index finger, both of which were shaking a little with anticipation, and carefully lifted the glass to his lips. He dipped his tongue into the whiskey and savored the burn. He trickled some of the busthead back across his tongue and into his throat. He followed that with the entire rest of the shot, and swallowed.

The bourbon plunged into him, bottomed out. The heat swelled inside him. The elixir began working its magic, muffling the war drum of his heart and nerves. By the third shot, a warm glow oozed through every pore and muscle and stretch of sinew.

He sat back in his chair, doffed his hat, and refilled his glass.

He was halfway to the bottom of the bottle, and the room was filled with a gauzy twilight haze through which he was blissfully grinning, staring at nothing but only feeling the numbing effects of the tangle-leg percolating inside him, when he turned to see the comely Zenobia Chevere coming down the stairs.

Her bare legs were long and brown.

Zee held the hem of her wrap above the tops of her black stilettos as she made her graceful descent.

"Ah, look—there she is!" Enberg vaguely heard a man raise his voice above the growing din.

The voice was like an annoying black fly buzzing around Enberg's head.

He flared his nostrils with annoyance. Envy began its old stirrings deep inside him.

He sensed all the men in the room turning to gaze lustily toward the staircase down which the Mexican goddess was descending. As Dag himself continued to watch Zee's graceful descent toward the Diamond's main drinking hall, bending each long, beautiful leg in turn, her breasts jostling alluringly inside her corset, ancient male lust began spreading its wings and warming his loins.

His eyes were riveted on the beautiful creature before him. His heart broke out of its alcohol stupor to hammer the back of his breastbone.

Zee glanced around the room, smiling her intoxicating smile.

As she turned her head slowly to take in the entire room, her eyes found Enberg. They held on him. They flicked to the bottle on the table before him. And then, three steps from the bottom of the stairs, she stopped her descent.

Zee stared across the smoke-hazy room into Enberg's eyes.

He stared back at her, his heart hammering a war rhythm against his ribs. His eyes raked her up and down, feasting on her. His tongue was thick. A clenched fist of knot-solid male need was lodged in his throat.

A well-dressed man had peeled himself away from the bar to stand at the bottom of the stairs, smiling unctuously up at Zee. Like the rest of the male crowd, he'd obviously been awaiting the regal seductress's emergence from her chamber.

The man was speaking to Zee, his lips moving. But her eyes were on Enberg. The smile faded from her lips so slowly that the change was almost unnoticeable.

An apprehensive tightness replaced it. Zee's left hand anxiously squeezed the banister rail beside her.

The well-dressed gent turned to follow her gaze. He frowned apprehensively at Enberg, who was rising heavily from his chair. Dag donned his hat, swung the shotgun behind his shoulder, and picked up the bottle. As he took one heavy step toward the stairs, Zee's eyes snapped wide with an old recognition and fear.

She swung around and stumbled a little as she rushed back up the carpeted steps.

Enberg increased his pace as he crossed the room, stumbling into chairs, tripping over table legs, knocking over bottles, and rattling glasses.

"What the hell?" intoned an indignant customer, grabbing a bottle before it tumbled to the floor.

Ignoring the man, Enberg continued toward the stairs, his eyes on Zee frantically climbing the steps and glancing nervously back over her shoulder at him. Her sashaying backside was round, firm, and beckoning.

"No, Dag!" she cried, the plea nearly lost beneath the crowd's low roar.

She turned her head forward as she gained the top of the stairs and then disappeared down the second floor hall. Enberg gained the bottom of the stairs and hurled himself up the staircase, taking two and three steps at a time, stumbling and pushing up off the steps with his left hand. His right hand clenched the rail.

"Hey, what's going on here?" yelled the well-dressed gent, glaring up at the big, red-bearded man rushing up the stairs.

Dag gained the top of the stairs and bounded down the hall.

Ahead of him, Zee ran down the hall toward her boudoir at the end. She'd kicked out of her shoes. She was running barefoot. She glanced over her right shoulder to see the big man racing toward her.

She screamed and lunged for her door.

CHAPTER NINE

Zee fumbled with the doorknob as Enberg strode toward her, boots thundering on the hall's carpeted floor and causing the mantels of the bracket lamps to rattle.

Zee cursed as she struggled anxiously with the knob then pushed the door open, bolted inside, and swung it closed. She didn't get it latched, however, before Enberg shoved it open, pushing Zee back away from it as though she weighed no more than a scrap of paper.

Zee screamed as she stumbled backward toward the foot of her canopied bed.

"Get out of here, Dag!"

Enberg grinned and held up the bourbon with two fingers. "I brought a bottle."

He closed the door and turned the key, locking it.

"Get out of here, Dag! *Now!*"

"All right, then—we won't drink. I've had my fill for a while, anyway." Enberg ran his feverish gaze up and down her spectacular body. "Let's get down to brass tacks."

"You're drunk. Get out!"

Enberg set the bottle on a small table by the door. He set his shotgun across the arms of a chair. He set his pistols and Bowie knife on the chair. He removed his hat and tossed it away. He strode toward Zee who continued backing away from him, staring up at him as though he were a grizzly that had escaped its cage.

"Please, Dag," she said, her lips trembling. "Don't do this."

Enberg stopped before her, caressing her bare shoulders lightly with the backs of his hands. His bulky shadow swallowed her.

"Dag," Zee said, thinly, tears streaming down her cheeks as she gazed up at him. "Please . . . turn around . . . and leave!"

Enberg grinned down at her. He planted a kiss on her forehead and then began unlacing her corset, drawing the strings out of the eyelets almost violently, the laces making whipping sounds as he freed them.

Finally, he peeled both sides of the corset back away from her breasts and flipped it over his shoulder. Zee sucked back a sob as she crossed her arms on her breasts. Enberg knelt before her. He nuzzled her crotch and then, kissing her legs, he slowly peeled her ruffled, silk panties down her thigh and calves, and left them on the floor around her small, bare, brown feet.

He straightened, his shadow engulfing her once more, and removed the jewel-studded comb from her hair, letting the dark tresses tumble messily down around her shoulders and swirl across her arms to lie in wisps against the edges of her full, upturned breasts. He brushed his thumbs across her nipples, smiling with satisfaction as they hardened and stood out against the broad areolas.

Zee tightened her arms on her breasts, and, her hair now partly hiding her face, loosed another sob.

"There, now," Enberg whispered, and kicked out of his boots. "That's better."

As he undressed before her, his heart thudding, a fire raging in his loins, Zee backed slowly away from him, keeping her arms crossed on her chest. Enberg sat down on the blanket-draped steamer trunk at the foot of Zee's bed, and peeled his wash-worn, summer-weight underwear down his muscular legs carpeted in a thin mat of red-blond hair, and kicked the underwear across the room.

When he stood and turned once more to Zee, she stood near the open top drawer of her dresser, aiming a pearl-gripped derringer at him.

She had the gun in one hand. Now she removed her other arm from her breasts and wrapped that hand, too, around the pistol. Gritting her teeth, she cocked it.

"Get out," she said through the thick screen of her dark-brown hair.

Naked, his swollen shaft jutting redly before him, Enberg strode over to her. He pressed his chest against the barrel of the extended derringer.

"Go ahead," he dared her.

Zee sobbed, tears running down her cheeks, dampening the screen of her mussed hair.

Enberg laughed, crouched, and picked her up in his arms. He carried her over to the bed and tossed her onto it.

"You bastard!" the girl cried. As she bounced atop the bed, she triggered the derringer. The bullet plunked into the wall abutting the hall.

Enberg laughed again. He threw himself onto the bed. Zee tried to scuttle up against the headboard to get away from him. As she did, she swung the derringer at him. Laughing, Enberg ducked and the gun flew out of her hand to hammer the same wall that the bullet had plunked into.

He grabbed Zee's right ankle and dragged her back toward him.

"*Bastardo!*" she cried, punching his shoulders and kicking at him. "You can't, Dag! You can't! You're *drunk!*"

"You want it as bad as I do, *chiquita*. You said as much not a half hour ago."

He separated her legs with his own, pinning her arms back on the bed. She was breathing hard, writhing around beneath him. Her breasts rose and fell sharply behind the dark screen of her hair. Her lips were plump and pink and mounding up out of her mussed hair.

Enberg kissed those rich lips through the hair. He pressed the head of his jutting member against her muff. She was moist and hot. He could feel the petal-like folds of her flesh opening for him.

She stared up at him, sharp javelins of golden light dancing in her eyes.

Enberg nuzzled her breasts, running his tongue down her hot, sweaty cleavage. He released her hands and, as he plunged into her, she wrapped her arms around his neck, snaked her legs around his back, and ground her heels into the back of his thighs.

"Bastard!" she cried. "Oh, you dirty rotten bastard!"

Enberg laughed.

He hammered against her. She bucked up against him, no longer sobbing but mewling and groaning. She closed her mouth over his shoulder and bit down hard. The pain was bittersweet, enflaming his desire.

The bed squawked and barked furiously for a time, and then, lifting his head toward the canopy, Enberg loosed a vicious snarling, wolf-like growl as he shoved his hips taut against hers, and spent himself inside her.

Zee placed her feet down flat on the bed and lifted her pelvis up, grinding against him and tossing her head violently from side to side.

They shivered together, grinding together, causing the bed to jerk and sputter, like a boat tied on a short rope, for nearly a minute.

Zee sighed and dropped her ass down onto the bed.

She was covered in sweat.

Enberg lowered his head, panting, and rolled away from her.

He realized that people were thumping around in the hall outside Zee's room. Men were consulting each other in anxious tones. Finally, boots thudded louder. Someone pounded on Zee's door.

"Enberg? Enberg? Get out here, Enberg. It's Roscoe Clemens, town marshal!"

"Mierda!" Zee cursed, bringing both hands to her face.

Feeling drunk now as well as spent, Enberg climbed off the bed and stumbled over to the door. He punched it twice and bellowed at the upper panel, "I'll be out there when I'm good and ready!"

"Shit!" Zee said from behind her hands.

She rolled onto her side, facing Enberg, and drew her knees to her belly. She wrapped her arms around her head as though to shut out the sounds from the hall.

"You'll get out now, Enberg, or I'll break this door down and haul you out!"

Zee removed her hands from her face and yelled, "Don't break the door! He's coming!" She looked at Enberg, who was staggering around drunkenly, the rage inside building once more. "You have to go, Dag. Hurry—before they break the door!"

"Sonso'bitches," Enberg said, slurring his words. He turned to the door and bellowed, "I'll come out when I'm good and ready!"

"Ay, yi, yi," Zee said, placing her hands over her face again, curling tightly into the fetal position. "Oh, you stupid bastard!"

Clemens yelled from the other side of the door, "Are you all right in there, Zee?"

"Si," Zee called. "I'm all right. Don't break down my door!"

"Tell him to hurry up or I'm gonna have to!" Clemens returned.

"Hurry up, Dag!" Zee said. "I don't want them breaking my

door. I don't want them coming in here. You're a *lunatic!*"

Enberg laughed and, hearing the marshal and several other men milling around in the hall, he started to dress. He took his time, chuckling to himself, cursing, then laughing and bellowing insults at the door.

His mind was swathed in the heavy, emotional fog it always was when he drank. Only a shadow of his sober, rational self remained, small and insignificant and cowering in a corner of his brain, like a defenseless child, looking on in horror at his crazy, drunken self and dreading what he'd do next, dreading the price he'd pay for it.

Hating himself.

Finally, dressed, he set his hat very carefully on his head, shoved his pistols behind his belt, returned his knife to its sheath, swung his shotgun behind his back, and glanced at Zee, who had crawled under the covers and was burying her head beneath a pillow.

"*Hasta luego, senorita,*" Enberg drawled as he twisted the key in the lock.

Zee did not move or say a word.

Enberg opened the door. A small cluster of men formed a ragged semicircle around him. One was Normandy, who pulled a cigar out of his mouth to bellow, "You're fired! I'm having you arrested, you son of a bitch!"

Enberg lunged toward Normandy, raising his clenched right fist. He intended to smash the man's face to pulp, but someone jumped him from behind, grabbing his arm and pulling it back with the rest of him. It must have been one of Roscoe Clemens's three deputies.

Clemens faced Enberg, a five-pointed star on his brown leather vest. He was nearly as tall as Enberg, but about five years older, and leaner of frame.

"You're under arrest, Enberg!"

"Bullshit!"

Enberg threw the man off his back and smashed his fist into Clemens left cheek. Clemens flew backward. The other men converged on Enberg—all except Normandy, who back-stepped so quickly he almost tripped and fell. He lost his cigar and stooped to retrieve it. But then the next man whom Enberg smashed with his fist went flying into Normandy, and they both fell in a bellowing heap.

One of the deputies clawed iron from his holster, but Normandy yelled from his back on the hall floor, "No shooting!"

"Grab the sonofabitch!" shouted Clemens, climbing to his feet and retrieving his hat, a wing of mussed, gray-blond hair in his right eye.

Two deputies jumped on Enberg. They weren't nearly as big as Dag, and he shrugged one off easily, punched the other one, and then stepped over Normandy and stumbled off down the hall toward the stairs. He was grinning now, feeling exhilarated, from both his sex with Zee and the fight.

When he was filled with whiskey, he loved nothing more than sex and a fight, not necessarily in that order.

Men stormed him from behind, and two more went flying. One punched Enberg in the back of the head and then in his ear, grunting as he hammered away at the big Norwegian. Enberg hardly felt the blows. He returned both to the man's mouth, smashing the man's lips and sending him stumbling back into the others, his mouth a bloody mess.

Enberg swung around, laughing, and continued on to the stairs. As he started down the steps, he yelled to Underhill, who was still working behind the bar, "Another bottle, Wade. That first one went down like communion wine!"

Underhill merely stared up at him, towel on his shoulder, fists on his hips, slowly shaking his head.

A good-sized crowd had grown in the main drinking hall. And every wide-eyed face was turned toward Enberg.

Boots thundered on the stairs behind him.

"I got him!" shouted one of the deputies.

The man threw himself onto Enberg's shoulders. Dag flew forward, the deputy on his back piggyback style and whooping and hollering loudly. Enberg hit the steps, and he and the deputy rolled together to the bottom.

Dag climbed to a knee. So did the deputy, who threw himself on Dag again. Two more lunged at him from the stairs. They threw him onto his back but he managed to fight them off, blindly swinging his fists and bellowing, his voice filling the saloon like the Norse god Odin blowing on a ram's horn.

Vaguely, as he was swinging his fists like a windmill dancing in a hurricane, he heard Clemens say as he reached over the bar, "Wade, hand me that bungstarter!"

Enberg smashed his bloody fist against one more bloody face and turned to see Clemens stepping toward him. The man's pale blue eyes were slitted, and he gritted his teeth beneath his mustache as he swung the bungstarter like a baseball bat toward Enberg's head.

That was all she wrote.

CHAPTER TEN

Enberg could hear the echoing clang of a key turning the bolt in the cellblock door. He heard the heavy door squawk open on its iron hinges. A boot clacked on the stone floor, and Roscoe Clemens's echoing voice said, "Enberg, you got a visitor."

Lying on his bunk, staring up at the stone ceiling, Enberg said dully, "No visitors."

"It's your wife."

Enberg grimaced as he continued staring. He knew he'd have to see her sometime. It might as well be now, four days after the humiliating dustup at the Diamond in the Rough Saloon. Emily had no doubt heard all of the grisly details, including his time in Zee's room.

By now, everyone in the county had probably heard about it.

Clemens's heavy footsteps sounded in the cellblock, growing louder as he approached Enberg's cell, which was halfway down the corridor between the two rows of cells, four on each side. Another, lighter pair of footsteps accompanied those of the town marshal.

Enberg groaned, wincing at the ache that lingered in his head from his unceremonious collision with Clemens's bungstarter. The doctor had sewn the five-inch gash in his temple closed with catgut, and Enberg fingered the bristling cut now as he sat up and dropped his feet to the floor.

Clemens stopped at his cell, and looked down at Emily standing before him, and then at Enberg sitting on his cot. "Can I get you two a cup of coffee? I boiled a pot about a half hour ago, so it's fresh."

"No, thank you, Marshal," Emily said, gazing grimly through the bars at her husband, who had not yet looked into her eyes. "I won't be here long. I have a stage to board."

Now Enberg looked at her. Clemens, who still had a bruise on his left cheek and a little discoloration around that eye—compliments of Enberg's right fist—glanced at her and then at Enberg. Then he stepped back away from the cell.

"All right, then. Just give a yell when you're through here, Mrs. Enberg."

"Thank you, Marshal Clemens."

When Clemens had strode on back into his office and had locked the cellblock door, Enberg rose wearily from the cot and turned to face his wife. No words came to him. He had no idea what to say to her.

She spoke first: "How's your head, Dag?"

Enberg shrugged a shoulder.

He saw she was clad in a powder-blue traveling gown with a ruffled white shirtwaist and matching, feathered hat. She wore white gloves on her slender hands, which she'd wrapped around the bars of his cell door.

Enberg didn't recognize the dress. Gertrude must have bought it for her recently. Enberg reached out to place one of his hands on one of hers, but she removed her hand from the bar before he could touch her.

"Em, where are you going?" he asked, reaching out through a dullness that lingered in his brain. He wasn't sure if it was a result of the dawdling effects of the whiskey or the craziness that followed its consumption or the battering he'd taken from Clemens's bungstarter. Or guilt and humiliation.

Or the self-hatred he felt.

Probably a combination of all of those things.

"You heard that Logan passed?" Emily said quietly.

Enberg nodded. He'd heard the news about Logan the morning after his embarrassing display over at the Diamond, which one of Clemens's deputies had informed him had been humorously dubbed "Enberg's March," after General Sherman's March to the Sea.

Dag had heard that no less than seven men had been treated by the doctor for various injuries, including several broken ribs and two broken noses. There was one dislocated jaw and countless broken or missing teeth. One of Clemens's deputies, Blaze Pyle, was hobbling around on crutches and snarling at Enberg like an angry bobcat whenever he had to bring food to the prisoner who'd so abused him.

To Enberg's everlasting dismay, that night would likely live on in legend in Mineral Springs.

Ironic that Logan Cates had passed that same night. Or early the next morning, anyway . . .

The funeral had been yesterday, while Enberg had been lying here in his cell staring up at the cold stone ceiling, as shocked and disgusted by his own actions as was everyone else around town. What made it worse was Cates's passing within only a few hours of Enberg's display.

So, that had been Enberg's way of honoring his only friend and benefactor . . .

"You said you had a stage to board," Enberg said. "Where are you going?"

"Gertrude and I are going to San Diego. My mother has a sister there."

"How long are you going to be gone?"

"I don't know. Probably until after the baby's born."

The news was no real surprise to Enberg, in light of his behavior. He was sure that Emily had heard the most ghastly part about that night in the Diamond—about his attack on Zee in her boudoir. He could see that deep injury in the flatness of his wife's gaze and in the tautness of her features.

She looked, in fact, as though she'd been laid up with a physical illness—a little withered, ashen.

He wasn't surprised to hear that Emily was leaving, but the information was still an anvil being lowered onto his shoulders.

"Till . . . till the baby's born, huh?" he said, the words raking out on a deep sigh.

"Yes, till the baby's born. After that, I'm not sure what I'm going to do. I might stay out there."

The anvil on Enberg's shoulders grew heavier. "I see."

"I'll send you a letter, to let you know when the baby has come," Emily said. "I suppose you deserve that much, since you are the father."

"Christ, Emily," Enberg said, a tremor in his voice, "I'm so, so sor—"

"No!" Emily scolded him. "Don't you dare say it. You have no right to say you're sorry. After what you did, you have no right to say anything to me at all." She paused. "Look at me, Dag."

Enberg raised his eyes to her face. She hardened her jaws as she said, "I am carrying your child!"

She'd enunciated each word of the sentence so an idiot could understand what she was saying.

A flood of tears washed over Enberg's eyes. They streamed down his cheeks.

"Em," he said around the fist-sized knot in his throat. "Please, Em . . . don't go. You . . . you and the baby . . . are all I have."

Emily's eyes were as hard as flint. She flared her nostrils as she said, "Goodbye, Dag," and swung around toward the cell-block door.

"Emily, please don't go!" Enberg sobbed, squeezing the bars of his cell door in his fists and pressing his broad face up taut against them. "I love you, goddamnit! *You're all I have!*"

He stared in horror as she retreated along the corridor. She stopped at the door and said through the barred window, "I'm ready, Marshal Clemens."

She did not look back even once as Clemens opened the cell-block door and stepped back to let her enter his office. Clemens glanced in disgust at Enberg, shook his head, and then followed Emily into his office and locked the door behind him.

"Goddamnit!" Enberg shouted, his voice booming around the cellblock.

He sagged down onto his cot and sobbed uncontrollably, like a child, for a long time.

He was cried out and lying back on his cot, staring at the stone ceiling, when the key rattled in the lock of the cellblock door again. Clemens sauntered down the corridor.

The marshal stopped and said a few words to the jail's only other prisoner, a little Mexican named Tobi, whom Clemens had jailed for stabbing another man in the stomach during a knife fight the previous night. Then Clemens continued mosey-ing down the corridor until he came to Enberg's cell.

He held a ring of keys in his hand.

He stared through the door at Enberg, who stared back at him dully.

"What're you lookin' at?" Enberg growled.

"Seven kinds of a fool."

"That what you come down here to tell me?"

Clemens shook his head. He chose one of the four keys on the ring, and stuck it into the lock of Enberg's door. He turned it, making a harsh ratcheting sound, and the door sagged on its hinges.

Enberg pushed up onto his elbows. "What's goin' on? You

gonna take me out back and shoot me? You'd only be doin' me a favor."

Clemens grinned. "I'm not in the mood to do you any favors. You about caved my face in with that ham-sized fist of yours." He drew the door wide, and let it fall back against the cell wall. "Get out."

He turned slowly and sauntered back down the corridor.

Enberg stared at him, incredulous. He looked at the yawning cell door. Then he looked at Clemens again as the man unlocked the cellblock door, opened it, and stepped through it into his office, leaving the cellblock door yawning as wide as the door to Enberg's cell.

"What the hell?" Enberg said, grabbing his hat off the floor.

He set the hat on his head, then rose from the cot. He strode slowly to the door, half-wondering if a trap had been set for him.

He knew that Clemens had summoned the circuit court judge, who was riding down from Tucson, so Enberg could stand trial for disorderly conduct and assault. Normandy had wanted to pin rape on him, too, but apparently Zee had refused to press charges.

The judge wasn't due until Monday. It was only Friday.

Was Clemens so miffed at Enberg for giving him that gash on his cheek that he intended to shoot him "trying to escape"?

Enberg walked through the open door and into the corridor. He stared warily up the corridor toward the open cellblock door. Was Clemens sitting inside his office with a double-barreled shotgun resting across his thighs, waiting for Enberg to make his escape, so he could blast him to kingdom come?

"Pssst-pssst! Hey, Enberg?"

This from the little Mexican, Tobi. He stood at his cell door, staring up at the much taller Enberg through the bars. Tobi was just a little over five feet tall, and he wore a goatskin vest and baggy denim trousers with hide-patched knees. He was as dark as Apache, with long, Apache-dark hair. He was grinning.

He kept his voice low, as though afraid someone might overhear him. "What was she like?"

"What was who like?" Enberg grunted.

"Zee!" Tobi grinned again. "I've always wondered. They said you two really went at it the other night!" He chuckled through his teeth.

"Shut up," Enberg said, and took a step forward.

Then he felt bad. A little man like Tobi would never be able to afford a night with a whore of Zee's caliber. She was much lusted after, dreamed about. A beautiful, forbidden princess residing high in her velvet-curtained castle.

Even if a man could afford her intoxicating services, it didn't mean she'd lie with him. Zee was discerning. It added to her mystery, her appeal.

Enberg turned back to Tobi, frowning through the bars at him.

"Forget her," Enberg advised the young Mexican. "She ain't nothin' to get all het up about. The girls in the Mex cribs are a better value."

Enberg winked. Tobi smiled like a gambler acquiring inside information on a rigged house.

Enberg strode forward, a sick, flu-like feeling coming over him and making him dizzy as he remembered the other night with Zee. Christ, he'd been an animal. He was damned lucky he hadn't killed her. He remembered her derringer and wished like hell she'd killed him.

But she never could have done that.

Damn her . . .

Still, he remembered her body. As drunk as he'd been, he himself would be damned if that memory—the image and feel of her sprawled out on that bed beneath him, his manhood impaling her—didn't evoke the stirrings of another arousal.

He walked boldly through the open cellblock door now, hoping that Clemens would be waiting for him with the shotgun. He felt a little crestfallen when he saw the town marshal merely kicked back in the swivel chair behind his roll-top desk, boots crossed on his cluttered desk top, near an ashtray in which a half-smoked black cheroot smoldered.

He had no shotgun resting across his thighs, its hammers eared back, ready to blow a pumpkin-sized hole in Enberg.

In fact, he wasn't holding any kind of weapon. His pistol jutted from the holster on his right hip.

"What the hell's goin' on?" Enberg said.

Clemens reached for his cheroot, knocked ashes from its tip, stuck it into his mouth, and took a long drag. "I'm letting you out till the judge arrives on Monday," he said as he blew smoke out his nostrils. The cigar smoke smelled a little stale.

"Why? What about Normandy?"

"It's my goddamn town, Enberg. Normandy doesn't own me."

"Normandy owns everybody Cates did. Ain't that how it works?"

"Not as far as I'm concerned. Normandy might have hired me, but I answer to the town council." Clemens grinned a sly, catlike grin. "Besides, Normandy left town. Rode out on the same stage your wife and her mother rode out on. Headin' for Tomahawk. He'll be gone for three days."

"I still don't understand why you're letting me go."

"Because I think you'll likely suffer just as much back at that empty cabin of yours, knowin' your wife is on the stage rollin' away from you, as you will here. Besides, it's the start of the weekend, and I got a feelin' I'm gonna need every cell I got."

Enberg reflected that the marshal was probably right. He'd probably suffer far more in his empty cabin filled with reminders of Emily than he would here. It would be a very long weekend, indeed.

"Your guns and that Bowie knife are gonna stay here with me," Clemens added, jerking his head toward the gun rack on the office's far wall. "And if you got any more at home, you'd best not let me catch you totin' any of 'em."

"What's the word on the posse?" Enberg asked him. "Any sign of Perrine and the strongbox?"

Clemens shook his head. "The posse came back empty-handed. Perrine scoured his trail, as I knew he probably would. I was in Kansas when Perrine robbed the Territorial Bank in Hays, and the bastard disappeared like smoke on the wind. I'm gonna go out and have a look myself just as soon as Homer gets back from his rounds." He gave Enberg an accusatory glance. "I'm a little short-handed, don't ya know!"

"Sorry about that," Enberg grumbled, running his hand down his face in chagrin.

"You should be. You'll be lucky if the judge don't send you to the territorial pen for that stunt. I'm recommending he give you a month hard labor, swamping out saloons right here around Mineral Springs, but Judge Calhoun is a might set in his ways."

"Why would you do that?"

Clemens took another deep drag on the cheroot, and shook his head. "I really don't know. Go on—git out of here. Don't let me catch you anywhere near one of the saloons this weekend. You stay home and take stock. Be back here at nine a.m. Monday morning to see the judge. Nine a.m. sharp!"

"All right. Thanks, Clemens."

"Get the hell out of here, Enberg!"

CHAPTER ELEVEN

Enberg left the town marshal's office.

He looked around, blinking, unaccustomed to the bright sunlight of the early afternoon. Everything looked a little surreal to him now on the lee side of the big trouble. A life-changer, the dustup had been. The world looked different to him now. He felt oddly disoriented in it, not quite sure how to go on. There was no point in thinking farther ahead than Monday, however.

Tuesday he might very well be heading for the territorial penitentiary in a jail wagon.

He started across the street, glancing both ways to make sure he wasn't going to get run down by one of the half-dozen or so wagons in town stocking up on ranching or mining supplies. That would be the cherry on trouble of the Big Trouble. With his luck, the wagon probably wouldn't even kill him.

As he started to cross the street, he saw the cemetery on the far east end of Mineral Springs. The markers were strewn across a low hill bristling with prickly pear and Mormon tea, and studded here and there with widely scattered mesquites.

Logan . . .

Enberg felt an urge to pay a visit to the man's grave. He'd missed his funeral, after all. He should pay his respects.

He swung to the east and began walking along the south side of the street, tramping over the short stretches of sun-grayed boardwalks fronting the adobe brick or wood-frame business establishments. As he made his way eastward, he passed several men and a few women. No one spoke to him. Most gave him looks of lingering, vaguely accusatory interest.

Guiltily, he kept his gaze down, fingers stuffed into the pockets of his faded denims.

When he gained the far east edge of town, he followed the narrow, stone-lined path that snaked up the side of the butte around tufts of cactus and occasional mesquites. As he walked, he looked around for a fresh grave.

He saw one on the cemetery's southern slope, not far from the crest of the hill. He swerved to the right of the trail and angled up the hill to stop and look down at the freshly mounded red dirt and rocks flanked by a single palo verde tree.

There was no marker yet. When Enberg had left the jail, he'd heard the clanging raps of someone chiseling stone. That would likely be the undertaker working on Logan's marker. This was undoubtedly Logan's grave. Enberg had heard of no other recent deaths, and he could see no other fresh graves anywhere around the humble little sun-beaten desert boneyard.

He stood guiltily looking down at the fresh mound of dirt and rocks. As he did, he regretted being here. In lieu of the horrible trouble he'd caused, which would have no doubt been endlessly disappointing to Logan Cates, he felt somehow disrespectful and unworthy of being here at Cates's place of final rest.

On the other hand, he didn't want to go home to an empty cabin.

He dropped to a knee and stood staring down at the grave for a long time. He thought he should say something to Logan about what he'd done, but he could find no words with which to speak to a mound of red gravel and rock. Logan wasn't here. He was gone. Enberg was alone here in this cemetery.

In this life.

There was no one here to forgive him.

He himself wasn't about to. Whoever *he* was. He had no idea.

He realized now with a cold chill on such a hot day that he was a stranger to himself.

Finally, he tossed a handful of pebbles on Logan's grave, hearing the rattling clacks as the gravel settled amongst the rocks. The sun beat down on him. A cicada was buzzing loudly. He looked off beyond the town toward the long stretch of desert between the town and a long, craggy mountain range humping up out of the chaparral, like the back of slouching dinosaur.

The stolen strongbox floated up from the depths of his unconsciousness.

He wondered where Perrine and Buckley had taken it. He felt an urge to go after them. It was they, after all, who'd started this new bout of trouble for Enberg.

If they hadn't hit the stage and stolen the payroll money, Enberg wouldn't have gotten fired and drunk himself crazy the other night, and Emily would not currently be on today's stage, heading west, away from him. He himself would be on that stage, riding shotgun for Charlie Grissom.

All would be well with the world.

Those thoughts sounded too pat to even his own ears, for some reason. But he decided to hold on to them. After all, it was far easier to blame a pair of gutless owlhoots for Enberg's troubles than to lay all the blame on himself.

He rose and turned away from Cates's grave. He'd taken only three steps when he stopped abruptly.

Zee sat on the ground before him, leaning back against the palo verde. She held a yellow parasol that matched her yellow dress cut in the Mexican style, leaving her shoulders bare. Her hair was pulled up behind her head. Gold rings dangled from her ears.

"Christ," Enberg said.

"Don't worry—I didn't follow you up here," Zee said. "True, I saw you heading this way, but I was already strolling this way myself."

"You should have headed in another direction. You're the last person I want to see right now."

"Feeling sorry for yourself again?"

Enberg doffed his hat and swabbed it out with his elbow. "Why the hell not?"

"Your fate is at the mercy of the gods—is that how you see it, Dag?"

"If it makes me feel better—why not?" Enberg set his hat back on his head and scowled at her. "Why did you follow me? Christ, I raped you the other night!"

Zee chuckled. "It wasn't anything I hadn't wanted ever since you met Emily, you damn fool. I baited you into that, and you took the bait. I tried to stop you—sure. For the benefit of my own conscience. I knew you were drunk. But I didn't really want you to stop."

"Why not?"

"Because you're the most thrilling thing in my life." Zee looked away and chuckled ironically. "Isn't that sad?"

"It is sad."

"You should leave here once and for all. Now that Emily is gone, and you've lost your job, you should leave. If you don't, we'll kill each other."

"Maybe that would be a fitting end for both of us."

"*Si* . . . but way too melodramatic."

"Besides," Enberg said, "I'm gonna get her back. It's Emily I love. I don't love you."

"Bullshit, Dag."

Enberg frowned. "What?"

"You love the *idea* of Emily. A good woman who you could raise a family with. That isn't going to happen for you, Dag.

Just as marrying a good man and raising
cards, either."

"Why isn't it?" It was a serious quest
inkling she was onto something he himsel
he wasn't quite sure what it was.

"Because we both have a craziness ins
craziness and wildness that makes us no go
do is ruin and disappoint other people. Lo
family in Mexico just when they needed
hacienda was being attacked and they were a
safety"—tears glazed her dark eyes—"and
alone. I honor their memory by working as a

A tear rolled down her cheek.

Enberg squatted before her and brushed
cheek with his thumb. "Don't cry. For some
cry is almost harder on me than seeing Emily

"Only because it's so unlike me," Zee s
caustic chuckle.

Enberg looked around, picked up a couple o
and tossed them away.

"Guess what?"

"What?"

Enberg tapped his shirt pocket. "Cates foun
treasure map in Norman Century's family B
looking through the Bible the other day, o
comforting words, I reckon, when he came ont

"I know."

Enberg looked at her, dubious.

Zee said, "He found it a long time ago."

Enberg just stared at her in disbelief.

"His uncle told him about it before he died
about it for years. Since way back before you ret

Her words were like a bucket of cold water th

face. His impulse was to disbelieve her. "No. You're
Besides, why would Logan tell you about it?"

10 else was he going to tell things to? Gertrude?" Zee
dry laugh. "Don't worry—we never slept together. He
never have been disloyal to Gertrude in that way, but
)esn't mean he told her his most private secrets. He told
at Century had the map and that your old man told him
s it on to you when you returned from the war. When
)ne, including Logan, thought you had died in the war,
was no dilemma. When you returned, however, there was
nma."

don't get it—what dilemma? I can't believe Logan wanted
iche for himself. He would have gone after it if he had."

: shook her head. "He didn't want it for himself. He didn't
you the map because he didn't want you to waste your
trying to find it. He knew the map would mean a lot to
out it would probably only get you killed."

don't get it—*why?*"

e shrugged and opened her hands. "Apparently, Logan's
: thought your father was crazy. A sun-addled desert rat.
n himself believed that was true. After you left for the war,
father stopped coming to town. Whenever Century and
n went out into the desert to find him, he seemed crazier
crazier, talking to himself and telling wild stories that
dn't have been true. He said he heard voices—that spirits of
ent, long-dead Indians spoke to him and told him where
' buried Spanish treasure. He lived like a wild animal out
e in the desert. He lived like an Apache—a blue-eyed, blond-
:ded Apache."

nberg was still staring at her in astonishment. Slowly,
)elievingly, he shook his head. "Why . . . why didn't Logan
me about any of this?"

Because he didn't think you would believe him. Because

. . ." Zee looked around, as though searching for the right words to continue. Haltingly, she said, "Because . . . he said that you were—"

"Too much like him," Enberg finished for her. "He thought I was crazy in much the same way old Olaf was crazy."

Zee said nothing. She didn't have to. Her response was in the directness of her dark-eyed gaze.

Zee reached forward and placed her hand on his bearded cheek. "Go live in the desert."

"What?" Enberg glowered at her, puzzled. "Logan didn't think the treasure is really out there."

Zee shook her head. "Not that treasure. But the treasure of solitude. Go live in the desert and raise wild horses or something. Find yourself a wild Apache wife who can rein you in and bear your children. You don't belong in town. You're wild, Dag. As wild as the wildest of wild stallions." She stretched her lips back from her fine, white teeth. "That's why I am so addicted to you."

Enberg's heart thudded with old lust. He looked down at her cleavage. He could see her distended nipples through her dress. Her red lips were erotically swollen. He remembered the other night, how her legs were tangled around him, how she bucked up against him, shook her head like a mare in season.

She removed her hand from his face and drew back a little, but he placed his hand on the back of her neck and started to draw her head toward his. Dag said, "What the hell? Emily's gone. She's not coming back."

"Oh, you want a repeat of the other night, eh?" Zee used her left forearm to break his hold on her. "Don't try it again, lover. Next time my derringer won't miss."

"Come on, Zee. You want me as much—"

"*Si*," Zee said, nodding. "But I like my silk sheets and having a roof over my head and food in my belly. Normandy thinks you forced yourself on me the other night. Which you did, though I'll admit I didn't fight very hard, and I enjoyed every minute of it more than I would admit to anyone except you. But I won't let it happen again. If Normandy knows I still carry a torch for you, lover, he'll fire me. I'm not about to go work in the cribs down by the wash or work as a fry cook. I like my life even if it's a cage I live in. At least, it's a pretty one."

She jerked her head to indicate the hazy, rocky mountains humping up in the north. "Go. Leave here. Build a life for yourself away from town. You're crazy as I am crazy, but the difference is I can keep my wolf on a leash . . . at least most of the time. You can't. You never will. You got it from your father, who probably got it from his father. Some people are just like that, Dag. Crazy. They don't fit in. They're no good to anyone and should live alone . . . out in the desert."

Enberg chuckled. "You think I should find an Apache girl, huh?"

"*Si*. Find yourself an Apache. She might tame you."

"You'd be as jealous of her as you were of Emily."

"Yes, but I wouldn't have to look at your handsome face every day." Zee blinked slowly, pursed her lips, gave her head a slow dip. "And I would know that you were all right."

She sighed, gave him her hand, and, rising, he pulled her to her feet. "I am going to go back to the Diamond now. You stay here. I don't want anyone to see us walking together."

She rose onto her tiptoes and kissed him sensuously, nibbling his lips. She pulled away, smiling coquettishly.

"God, you're a bitch," he said.

Zee swung around, batting her eyes and rocking her hips in shameless flirtation. "Goodbye, Dag."

Enberg watched her saunter down the knoll, twirling her yellow parasol.

Snarling with needling desire, he turned away from her and

stared toward the mountains. He dug the map out of his shirt pocket, unfolded it, and looked at it.

Was he looking at the mad conjuring of a sun-addled desert rat?

Most likely.

He'd known long ago that his father was crazy. Now he realized that in many ways he'd become his father. The apple *hadn't* fallen very far from the tree. He started to bunch the paper up in his hands, but stopped.

He wouldn't tear it up. It was the only thing he had to remember his old man by. After all, old Olaf had scribbled it for him. It was a last message of sorts, one that Olaf himself had most certainly believed to be true.

Who knew? Maybe it was.

Probably not, but maybe.

Anyway, Enberg wouldn't throw it away.

He folded the map back up and returned it to his pocket. Then, since he had nowhere else to go, he walked on down the knoll's west side and headed on back to his cabin.

He walked to the far western edge of Mineral Springs, crossed the wash sheathed in willows, and saw the low-slung cabin standing before him, at the base of the high, slanting mesa that spread a cool, purple sheet of shade over the shack. The place looked even more forlorn than it had before.

Emily was gone. She probably wouldn't be back.

Enberg had no idea what he was going to do with himself.

The judge would likely take care of that problem on Monday morning, so he wouldn't have to think too far ahead just yet. Maybe Zee was right. Maybe, like his father had done, he should just head off into the desert. Find a crazy Apache girl to father his children.

Thinking about his father believing that he'd heard the voices of ancient Indians telling him about hidden Spanish treasure,

Enberg headed for the shack. He was at the small, sunken patch of ground fronting the door when he spied movement in the corner of his left eye.

He whipped his head in that direction. His lower jaw hung in shock.

Joe Ted Perrine was stumbling out of the willows, hatless, holding a long-barreled revolver in his right hand. He appeared battered and bloody, sweaty and dusty. Badly sunburned. His hair hung in his eyes. "Hello, Enberg. You ready to die, you son of a bitch?"

The stage robber stretched a snakelike grin and raised the pistol.

Chapter Twelve

Enberg tripped the door latch and dove into the cabin as Perrine's revolver gave a wicked belch. Enberg hit the floor by the table. The bullet tore wood slivers from the doorframe.

"Enberg!" Perrine bellowed.

Again, the revolver crashed. Boots thudded as Perrine ran toward the cabin.

Enberg kicked the door closed and gained his feet as the outlaw's revolver popped again. The bullet plowed through the spindly plank door near Enberg's left shoulder. Enberg quickly dropped the locking bar over the steel bars, to keep the shooter outside.

"Enberg, you get out here, goddamn you! I'm gonna kill you, you son of a bitch!"

The outlaw's shadow passed in front of the window just right of the door. Enberg threw himself down behind the table as Perrine fired a round through the window, breaking out the glass. He fired another round, and that bullet clanged off the wood stove behind Dag.

He kept his head down, but looked toward the cabin's front wall from beneath the table. He couldn't see Perrine's face from this angle, but he could see his shadow moving around on the other side of the window.

The man fired two more shots, both bullets plunking into the eating table above Dag. The shooter's shadow moved to the second window in the front wall, and he blew that window out, as well.

Fear had Enberg's gut in a cold grip.

With both windows out, Perrine would be in here in less than a minute.

Dag considered his weapons. Both pistols and his shotgun were in Clemens's office. They were all he had. Christ!

No, wait.

The old cap-and-ball Colt Navy that he'd used during the war was upstairs, in a drawer of the night table.

"Enberg, get out here, you bastard. I'm gonna blow you to goddamn kingdom-fucking-come!"

"Why are you so mad at me, Joe?" Enberg shouted as he swung around and crabbed on hands and knees toward the stairs that led to the loft. "You're the one that stole the strongbox and made me look like a damn idiot!"

As he climbed the stairs on his hands and feet, keeping his head down, he saw Perrine poke his head and revolver through the near front window. Perrine looked around, then turned his head toward the stairs. "Hey, where you think you're goin'?"

He triggered two rounds. One bullet clipped a riser to Enberg's left, within six inches of his cheek. The other bullet thudded into the wall over the stairs, eight inches above Enberg's head.

Perrine was a pretty good shot—Enberg would give him that.

"You done killed my whole gang, 'ceptin' Buckley, but now he's dead, too! Since I'm close behind him"—Perrine pitched his voice with quiet menace as he aimed his pistol through the broken window, tracking Enberg up the stairs—"I decided to take you with me, you big ugly son of a bitch!"

He fired two more shots. But both bullets sailed wide.

Enberg was in the small loft over the kitchen now, where Dag's and Emily's bed shared close quarters with a dilapidated dresser and a tin-topped washstand. He crawled to the small box table he'd nailed together from shipping crates. His pistol was on the second shelf of the crate, beneath three pairs of clean socks and a pair of legless summer underwear.

He pulled out the old cap-and-ball and quickly checked its loads.

All the chambers were charged, the nipples capped. He'd never seen a reason to keep an unloaded gun around. An unloaded weapon was as good as no weapon at all. He supposed it was a notion he'd carried over from the war and, before that, from right here in Mineral Springs when the Apaches attacked every two or three nights, bound and determined to keep the town from growing to fruition.

"Enberg!" Perrine shouted in a lilting singsong. "Get your ass out here. Face me like a man!"

Still on his hands and knees, Enberg crawled over to peer through the loft's pine rail and into the kitchen. Perrine was waiting for him, two revolvers aimed now in Enberg's direction, through the window.

Enberg dropped as he glimpsed flames lapping from the two barrels.

One slug plunked into the bed behind Enberg while the other snapped a spool running vertically between upper and lower rails.

"Almost, Joe!" Enberg shouted, gritting his teeth as he poked the old Colt through the rail and fired.

Perrine fired a quarter wink after Enberg had, and, lowering both pistols, he sent both slugs slamming into the top of the kitchen table. Perrine dropped one of the guns on the kitchen floor and stumbled backward, raising a hand to his left temple.

"Oh," he said as though in surprise. "Oh, shit . . . you son of a *bitch*!"

He disappeared from Enberg's view, stumbling backward

into the yard.

Enberg hurried down the stairs. He removed the bar from over the door, jerked the door open, and stepped outside, aiming the cap-and-ball out before him. Perrine was down on one knee, half-turned away from Enberg. He'd heard the door open, and he turned now, snaking his right hand pistol under his left arm, hastily aiming at Enberg, who dropped the old Colt's hammer on another cap.

The old Navy thundered, smoke smelling like burnt powder wreathing it and its shooter.

Perrine triggered his own pistol far wide and fell backward with another shrill curse. He lay belly up on the ground, arms and legs spread, chest rising and falling sharply, belly expanding and contracting wildly.

Enberg cocked the Colt once more and walked out to stand over his attacker.

"What in the hell are you doing here, Joe?" He glanced around for Buckley. "I figured you'd be dancing with the *senoritas* in Mexico by now . . . and spending Hud Cormorant's payroll."

"Ah, Christ . . . I should be . . . doin' just that," Perrine said through sharp breaths. Blood oozed from the hole Enberg had drilled in his chest and from a previous injury farther down on his left side. His left thigh was also bloody. "B-but me an' Buckley ran into Apaches when we was about to start circlin' back south."

"Apaches?"

Perrine jerked a nod, wincing against his misery. "We stopped to cover our trail. Three braves rode up on us out of nowhere, drilled an arrow through Buck. I got on my horse but one Injun with a Winchester was too good a shot. Drilled me twice, the red-skinned son of a bitch. Hit my horse, too. He dropped just outside of town."

"Why'd you come back to Mineral Springs?"

"It's the only town out here." Perrine chuckled in spite of his obvious agony. "I figured they wouldn't follow me into town. I figured I'd get the sawbones to sew me up, but first I was gonna drill you and steal one of your horses. Drill you for what you did to Gila River and the others."

Enberg could smell the alcohol mingling with Perrine's sweat and blood fetor. The man had made his foolish attack on Dag because, to fight the pain of his injuries, he'd gotten good and drunk. Good and drunk and mean and angry.

Enberg understood too well the mixture.

"Goddamn Apaches," Perrine grunted, blood and snot now dribbling out of his nose. "Seen all kinds o' Injun sign. Bunch of 'em musta jumped the reservation at San Carlos. Red bastards."

"Where's the loo—?" Enberg cut himself off when, turning his head toward the willows from which Perrine had emerged, he saw the saddlebags on the ground, at the edge of the bushes.

Enberg walked over, his heart beating hopefully. He dropped to a knee beside the bags, unbuckled the leather straps, and dipped his hand into the pouch. Out it came with a fistful of banded greenbacks.

Dag cast a grin to Perrine, and said, "Well, thank you mighty kind-ly . . ." He let his voice trail off.

Perrine lay unmoving.

Enberg shoved the wad of greenbacks back inside the saddlebag pouch, draped the bags over his shoulder, and walked back to stand over the outlaw, looking down. Joe Ted Perrine lay with his eyes lightly closed. His chest was still.

"As I was sayin'," Enberg said, "I thank you mighty kindly, Joe. You made what had looked like a total nightmare of a day just a tad bit brighter."

Suddenly, the grin faded from Enberg's bearded face. His

blue eyes widened slightly as he turned to stare toward the mesa rising in the north. His heart quickened as he remembered what Perrine had said about the Apaches.

"Seen all kinds o' Injun sign. Bunch of 'em musta jumped the reservation at San Carlos."

"Shit," Enberg said, his heart beating even faster and harder.

He swung around and headed back into the cabin. He set the saddlebags on the kitchen table while he hurried around the shack, stuffing trail supplies into his own saddlebags.

He prepared his bedroll, tying it closed with strips of rawhide, then went out and turned the bolt home in the cabin's front door. Ten minutes later, he'd saddled War Bonnet and had tossed both sets of saddlebags over his hind end.

Enberg swung into the saddle and gigged the mount into a gallop, bulling through the brush and across the wash and tracing a circuitous route back into the heart of town. He pulled up in front of the jailhouse to find Roscoe Clemens standing out on the boardwalk fronting the stone and wood-frame structure, talking to one of his deputies, Blaze Pyle.

Pyle's right ankle was in a cast, and he had a crutch under each arm. Pyle was in his early thirties, a former cowpuncher who'd gotten kicked in the head by an angry steer during branding last September, and had decided to hang up his *riata* and give a shot at law-dogging on the local level.

He wore the scar of the steer's hoof on his left temple, low enough that you could see part of the red indentation below the crown of his hat. He and Clemens turned as Enberg rode up to the office, and Pyle pointed an angry finger at the former shotgun rider.

He said through gritted teeth, "You broke my ankle, you son of a bitch!"

Ignoring the man, Enberg swung down from the saddle, grabbed the saddlebags containing the Box G-30 payroll money, and strode up onto the boardwalk.

Clemens scowled at him. "What's going on, Enberg? Is that a pistol you're totin' behind your belt? I told you—"

Enberg tossed the town marshal the saddlebags, which Clemens caught over one arm. He regarded the bags as though he'd just been tossed a rattlesnake for his stewpot.

"That's Cormorant's payroll. Joe Ted Perrine paid me a little visit earlier."

"Perrine?" both the marshal and his deputy exclaimed in unison.

Clemens said, "Was that the shootin' I heard from that direction? I thought maybe Frank Darabont was shootin' rattlesnakes up on the mesa."

"It was Perrine, all right. He and Buckley were ambushed by Apaches. Perrine came to my place to settle up with me and take one of my horses. His was shot out from under him."

"Apaches?" both the marshal and his deputy again exclaimed in unison, with even more fervor.

"He said he saw the sign of a bunch of 'em. That means the stage might be in trouble. Hand over my shotgun and pistols, Clemens. I'm gonna ride west and have a look-see."

"Shit," Clemens said, worriedly smoothing his mustache with his right hand. "Them soldiers told me the other day that a grandson of Geronimo had stirred up a passel of Chiricahuas, and they . . ."

"Clemens, my guns!" Enberg urged. "I gotta get after that stage!"

"You ain't goin' nowhere, you sonofabitch," Pyle said. "You broke my ankle. The judge is on his way to . . ." He let the statement die on his lips when Clemens strode past him into his office.

"Hey, Marshal, what're you doin'?" Pyle said, following both the marshal and Enberg into the office. "You ain't gonna give this crazy bastard his guns back—are ya? After what he done to my ankle? Why, I'm an officer of the law!"

"Oh, shut up, Blaze." Clemens had grabbed his ring of keys off a spike in a ceiling support post. "Hobble over to the livery barn and tell Edgar Montaine to saddle my horse. *Pronto!*"

Clemens poked one of the keys into the padlock securing a log chain over the open gun rack mounted on the office's far wall, above the potbelly stove.

"But, Marshal," Pyle objected, frustrated as hell, "he broke—"

"If those Apaches have their way, you're gonna end up with a lot more than a broken ankle, Blaze. And if they don't do it, I will. Now *vamoose!*"

That set the deputy scramble-hobbling out the office door and down the street toward the Mineral Springs Federated Livery and Feed Barn.

Clemens tossed Enberg his shotgun.

"You go on ahead," Clemens said. "I'll be behind you."

"Just you?" Dag said as he broke open the gut-shredder and thumbed a wad down each tube. "If there's as many Apaches out there as Perrine seemed to think there were, we'll need—"

"A whole posse, I know. I'll have Pyle organize one behind me. I'm gonna round up my other deputies. Hopefully, we won't need 'em. A small contingent of soldiers from Fort Huachuca passed through here yesterday, patrolling the stage line and checking on settlers. Maybe we'll run into 'em."

Enberg slung the loaded shotgun behind his back and accepted both pistols from Clemens butt-first. "That makes me feel a little better, anyway. Not much, but a little."

Hurrying toward the open door, Enberg stuffed both his pistols behind the wide brown belt at his waist.

"Oh, Enberg?"

Clemens's voice swiveled Dag's head back around. The marshal was scowling at him while he punched fresh brass into a Winchester carbine he held upside down on his desk.

"If you run out on me, you son of a bitch, I'll hunt you down and gut-shoot you. The returned Box G-30 loot and the Apaches notwithstanding, you still got you a mighty big come-uppance for the other night, and I'm gonna see you go before the judge with your hat in your hands."

Enberg nodded. "I wouldn't have it any other way!" He hurried outside and across the boardwalk.

He swung up onto his horse, turned it west, and touched spurs to its flanks.

CHAPTER THIRTEEN

Nearly an hour after he'd left Mineral Springs, Enberg checked down the sweat-lathered dun in a crease between bristling desert hills, and swung down from the saddle. He ground-reined the gelding in a wash that ran through the crease, loosened the horse's saddle cinch, so it could breathe without restriction, and patted the mount's neck.

"Stay, fella."

Enberg swung his twelve-gauge around in front of him as he stepped up out of the wash and, holding the shotgun by its neck, began climbing the western slope beyond, weaving around boulders and brush and cactus clumps. Near the top of the ridge, he glanced around for rattlesnakes, then doffed his hat and dropped to his knees.

He climbed a little farther toward the top of the ridge, and stopped when he could see down over the ridge crest to the other side, where the Gonzalez ranch lay in a shallow bowl between the butte Enberg was on and another, lower dike of red sandstone farther west.

The Gonzalez ranch was the first relay station on the trail west from Mineral Springs to Tomahawk. Run by Tio Gonzalez and his wife, Lenore, as well as their three daughters, one son, and two hired men, the *rancho* was little more than a long, low-slung, mud-brick cabin flanking a windmill and stone stock tank. There was also a long, mud-brick barn and a woven oco-tillo corral where Gonzalez's own and the stage line's horses were housed. Behind the corral lay a small stone chicken coop.

Enberg held very still while he studied the small *rancho*, holding the shotgun down beneath the crest of the ridge, so the sun wouldn't reflect off the barrel and give him away to whomever was below. His heart thudded insistently, warily.

Ten minutes ago, he'd heard from the *rancho's* direction a brief patter of muffled gunfire and what had sounded like a girl's scream.

Nothing moved among the humble buildings below. The hot breeze picked up, lifted a dust devil in the middle of the yard, and shepherded it several feet before it died against the stock tank, whose blades clattered softly against the faultless, blue desert sky.

Nothing moved.

No people. No horses. Nothing.

There were no sounds. Not even bird sounds. The Gonzalez family raised chickens, but there was no sign of a single chicken anywhere in the yard.

Enberg had experienced the wake of an Apache attack before, and the silence and stillness were what had struck him the most poignantly. It was as though for a time, the attackers sucked all the energy out of a place. They were like a wildfire.

A human wildfire. But unlike a wildfire, there was no elemental indifference in an attack by Chiricahuas. They rampaged with the rancor of a demon straight out of the devil's own hell.

There were no bodies in the yard. That was funny. If the Apaches had indeed attacked the *rancho,* there would have been bodies strewn around.

Finally, deciding to take a closer look, Enberg whistled for his horse. When the dun had climbed the ridge, Enberg tightened the cinch, swung into the saddle, and, holding his shotgun before him in both hands, started down the slope. He held War

Bonnet to a slow walk, giving himself time to look around more thoroughly as he approached, time to detect Apaches possibly lying in wait for him.

Finally, he rode into the yard, War Bonnet's hooves thudding softly and lifting little puffs of dust and hay flecks and horse and chicken shit that had been finely ground by the iron-shod wheels of many Concords.

He dismounted near the stock tank and dropped the dun's reins. He was about to slip the horse's bit from its mouth, so it could drink freely from the hay-flecked water in the stone tank, but suddenly the dun jerked its head and whickered anxiously.

"Easy, easy," Enberg whispered, turning his gaze toward the cabin.

It must have been over ninety degrees out there in the direct sunlight, but apprehension walked cold fingers across the back of the big man's neck.

"Stay here," he told the horse. "Stay quiet."

Looking around anxiously, holding the shotgun straight out from his right side, Enberg walked slowly toward the casa. He clicked both hammers back. The front door yawned wide, tapping against the roadhouse's front, mud-brick wall when the breeze nudged it.

The wooden stand that usually held a large clay pot for washing had been knocked over, and the pot lay cracked on the ground beside it. A looking glass usually hung from the wall over the washstand, but the mirror was gone. Only the rusty nail remained.

A low ringing lifted in Enberg's ears as he approached the yawning roadhouse door that was a black rectangle before him. He approached a little to one side, so he wasn't in a direct line of fire from inside. Finally, he stepped abruptly into the darkness, stepped to his right, and pressed his back against the wall, tightening his finger on the shotgun's triggers.

Flies buzzed around him in the oven-hot place. He could smell the coppery odor of fresh blood. As his eyes adjusted to the deep shadows, he saw where the stench was coming from.

Seven or eight blue-clad soldiers lay on the floor or sprawled across tables or overturned chairs. A woman with silver-streaked, dark-brown hair lay on the floor near one of the tables. She was Lenore Gonzalez, clad in her traditional cotton dress and embroidered green apron, though there was little green left in it.

An arrow protruded from the middle of Lenora's chest, between her pillowy breasts. She seemed to be staring straight up at the soldier who lay atop the table above her, the soldier's head and arms dangling off the table's end, as though he'd been reaching out to the woman either for help or to offer help.

Three arrows fletched in the traditional method and design of the Chiricahua Apache bristled from his back.

Enberg noticed that a whiskey bottle had been overturned on one of the tables, and that on the floor were several small stone jugs that Tio Gonzalez used to serve the *bacanora* he fermented and distilled in a brick shed behind the barn.

Slowly, holding the shotgun in both his sweating, gloved hands, Enberg made his way around the room, making a sour expression at the grisly scene before him. He counted eight dead soldiers, the dead woman, and a dead girl—Ramona Gonzalez. She'd been stripped naked and obviously raped several times before one of her ravagers had cut her throat. Her underclothes lay in a pile beside her body, which lay slumped forward over a bench of one of the room's long eating tables.

Blood ran down the insides of her plump, brown thighs. It lay in a thick pool beneath her hanging head, from the gash in her neck.

"Christ," Enberg said.

It had been a while since he'd seen the results of an Apache attack. Growing up, they'd been a part of his life. A horrific one. To this day, the word Apache or Chiricahua still turned his nerves to jelly. He'd not seen anything during his four years of war that compared to the savagery of the southwestern Indians.

He knew this was their land, but, Christ . . .

When he'd circled the kitchen, eating, and resting area of the Gonzalez casa, he moved through a curtained doorway to the back and down a long corridor on both sides of which sleeping cubicles were curtained off for the Gonzalez family. He checked all of these and found no more bodies.

There was a storage area near the rear of the house. Off the storage area was a door. The door stood open, the glass broken out of the pane in its upper panel. There was a bloody handprint on the frame to the right of the door.

Enberg stepped out through the door and cringed when he saw another body. This was a male, though how he made that determination he wasn't sure. There was so much blood that the dead man looked more like a side of beef than a human being.

The blood was the result of the dead man's belly having been cut open with a knife or a hatchet. The man's guts had been pulled out—several feet of them—and used to strangle him. The bloody guts were looped around the dead man's neck. His hands were crossed on his chest, just beneath his chin, and his eyes bulged nearly out of their sockets. He was making a hideous face, tongue sticking out of his wide-open mouth.

The man was Tio Gonzalez.

Even in death, Gonzalez seemed to be utterly horrified by his hideous end.

Enberg found another dead girl and a dead boy out here, beyond the lumpy, bloody figure of Gonzalez. The girl lay naked, her throat cut. The boy bristled with no less than eight Chiricahua arrows, two of which protruded from his eye sockets.

Enberg's guts rumbled at the grisly sight, and he thought for a moment he was going to be sick. But then he was distracted by sounds coming from beyond some mesquites and a saguaro straight ahead of him, beyond a two-hole privy and a large, L-shaped stack of firewood.

Again clutching the twelve-gauge in both his hands, he moved past the dead Gonzalez boy, past the privy, past the woodpile, and into the mesquites. He'd just brushed past one of the mesquites when he stopped and dropped abruptly to one knee, blood quickening.

Ahead, lay a wash. Two Chiricahua braves were moving around in the wash. They were staggering a little, as though drunk, and conversing in their guttural tongue. They were chuckling.

One wore a girl's cotton dress, a bizarre sight to behold, given that he had distinctly masculine facial features and was also wearing the Apache's traditional red flannel bandanna. His long, black hair was partly braided and liberally greased. The dress came down only to the brave's knees, revealing his deerskin leggings, which were turned down at the tops, and his pointed-toed deerskin moccasins.

The other brave wore a pair of girl's underpants over the top of his head, like a dusting cap. He had a bow slung over one shoulder and a Sharps Army carbine slung over his other shoulder. He wore a war hatchet from a belt around his waist. The belt was a black Army belt with a gold U.S. buckle. The brave held a small stone jug, which he just then hoisted to his mouth, turning to give his back to Enberg.

He and the other brave were watching a third brave bucking against the naked backside of a girl bent over a small boulder on the wash's far side. As they watched, the brave wearing the dress grabbed the jug away from the brave wearing the girl's underwear on his head. In their drunken tussle, one fell down while the other staggered away, doing a little victory dance while holding the stone jug above his head.

Enberg slipped off into the mesquites and quickly crossed the wash about fifty feet east of the drunk Chiricahuas. He circled the small boulder over which the girl was bent, and stole up on the rock slowly, stealthily, crouched so low that he was virtually crawling.

The rock was sheathed in mesquites.

Enberg moved up to it until he could see the face of the girl, but not the face of the brave toiling behind her. The brave's face was obscured by a mesquite branch. The girl's head—the head of the third Gonzalez daughter—jerked forward and back. As Enberg moved still closer to her, he saw that she wasn't blinking. He also saw that the rock she was bent forward over had been brightly painted with the blood that had oozed down from her slit throat.

Enberg gritted his teeth as he moved more quickly toward the rock. With his left hand, he grabbed the branch that was obscuring the Apache's face. With his right hand, he lifted the twelve-gauge and clicked back the left hammer.

He thrust the branch aside, revealing the sharp-featured, dark-eyed face of the grunting Apache. He had a mole the size of Enberg's thumbnail off the right corner of his thick-lipped mouth. The brave's eyes snapped wide in shock when he saw the bearded, blue-eyed Norksi bearing down on him with the gut-shredder, whose bores must have looked as wide as two rain barrels set side by side from that distance and in that predicament.

As the raping Apache opened his mouth to scream, Enberg thrust both barrels into his mouth. He tripped the left trigger.

The brave's head exploded like a pumpkin-sized tomato, eyes and ears flying in opposite directions. The rest turned to jelly. As what was left of the Apache's body dropped like a sack of potatoes, the other two stared in shock at Enberg's bloody shotgun as well as the blood and brain-splattered face of the big man wielding it.

They both leaped into drunken action, reaching for weapons.

Enberg triggered his second barrel.

The two Chiricahuas were close enough together that the single blast peppered them both, sending them stumbling and screaming back into the brush. Enberg stepped forward around the rock and the dead Gonzalez girl draped over it, and grabbed his pistols. One of the Apaches, bleeding from the dozen or so buckshot wounds spread across his head and torso, scrambled clumsily to his feet, howling and jerking the war hatchet from his belt.

Enberg stepped calmly into the wash, aimed one of his Colts, and punched a .44-caliber round through the brave's head, just above his right eye.

The other brave had taken the brunt of the buckshot. He was writhing around, screeching and trying to gain his feet. One of his eyes hung half out of its socket, dangling by the optic nerve. Enberg aimed both Colts, fired, and watched in grim satisfaction as the Apache was punched back onto a patch of prickly pear where he lay convulsing wildly as he died.

Dag looked around, listening.

Except for the faint gurgling sounds issuing from one of the soon-to-be dead Chiricahuas, dead silence.

No others seemed to be around. If they were, they'd be here by now.

Enberg turned back to the Gonzalez girl. He took her gently by her shoulders and laid her down on the ground beside the rock. Her dark-brown eyes stared up at him with faint beseeching.

"I'm sorry, girl," Enberg said, his voice quavering a little with emotion.

It had been a long time since he'd seen this much carnage. He'd hoped he'd never see it again. He brushed his fingers lightly down the dead girl's face, closing her eyes. He wished he had time to give her a decent burial, but that would have to wait.

His primary concern was the stagecoach. There were most likely many more marauding Apaches where these three had come from, and they might have gone after the stage.

If they hadn't run it down already.

Enberg jogged back around to the front of the stage relay station. He could tell by the moccasin tracks in the yard that there had been more Apaches here than only the three he'd dispatched. The others had likely headed up the trail. They must have run off all of the station's horses as well as the soldiers' mounts.

He strode quickly over to the stock tank at the base of the windmill, and dunked his head in the tepid water, scrubbing the brave's blood and brains from his bearded face with his hands. When he thought he'd gotten most of it off, he placed his hat on his head, swung the shotgun behind his back, and grabbed the nervous dun's hanging reins.

He'd just turned a stirrup out, when the beat of several sets of galloping hooves rose in the east.

CHAPTER FOURTEEN

Enberg stepped away from his horse, and swung the shotgun around to his front, taking the big popper in both hands and resting his thumb across the hammers.

But then he saw Roscoe Clemens and two deputies galloping down the eastern ridge, rounding a curve in the trail and loping into the yard. Clemens and the two deputies drew rein before Enberg, the deputies giving Dag the wooly eyeball. Bill Bragg and Cal Mundy obviously still had their necks in a hump over the other night. Mundy had a bandage over his nose, and Bragg had several scabbed cuts on his face, and one eye was partly swollen.

Clemens's eyes were raking the station house. The lawman's gaze swung toward Enberg, dropped to the double bores of the twelve-gauge that were still streaked with blood and white flecks of brain matter.

Clemens scowled. "Apaches?"

"Eight soldiers dead inside. The Chiricahua must have snuck up on 'em like they do, and hit 'em before they knew what was happening. Lenore Gonzalez and one daughter are inside. Dead. Tio, their boy, and two more daughters are dead out back . . . with three dead Apaches. The two hired men are likely around here somewhere. Dead, I'd wager."

"There must have been more than three Apaches."

"I'm betting the others are headed for the next station. They might be after the stage. Since it isn't here, I figure it must have left before the Gonzalez ranch was hit." Enberg had swung up into the leather. "I'm gonna head for the Rebel Canyon Station."

He didn't give voice to what was needling him the most—the possibility that the Apaches had hit the stagecoach *first, before* they'd come here. If so, he'd probably find the stage between the Gonzalez *rancho* and Rebel Canyon. Emily and her mother were aboard that coach.

"Hold on, goddamnit, Enberg!" Clemens said.

With the nervous dun prancing around beneath him, Enberg turned to the town marshal. "You'd best go back to Mineral Springs and send a telegram to the sheriff in Wilcox. And another one to Fort Huachuca. We're gonna need help!"

With that, he touched spurs to the dun's flanks and began lunging westward along the trail, noting several sets of unshod hoofprints on the trail before him. The unshod prints obscured the wheel tracks of the stagecoach that had probably traversed this country two, maybe three hours ago.

The Apaches' tracks obscured the tracks of the unshod wheels, but the wheel tracks were still intermittently visible.

Those glimpses were reassuring, even though Enberg knew they didn't mean the coach hadn't been overtaken by now. Charlie Grissom was a good driver, but not even he could outrun bronco Apaches on mountain-bred mustangs.

Hoofs sounded loudly behind Dag. He turned to see Clemens and his deputies catching up to him.

Clemens rode up on Dag's left, and narrowed an eye as he said, "I'm the town marshal, Dag. Unofficial sheriff's deputy. That means I'm leadin' up this posse. I make the decisions. Before I send for help, I want a clearer picture of what we're up against . . . and I want to find that stage!"

The stage had Clemens worried, too. No wonder. The man's unofficial boss was aboard. Enberg wouldn't have given a plug nickel for Normandy's life, but the possibility that Emily might have come to harm was a cold, tightly clenched fist around his heart.

Emily and his unborn child.

She'd left because of him. If she . . . they . . . died because of him, he'd never forgive himself.

Enberg whipped his rein ends across the dun's withers, urging more speed. The horse obliged him, stretching out and lowering his head.

Enberg could hear War Bonnet's lungs working like a bellows beneath the saddle. He was pushing the horse too hard, but he had to push this hard. If the Apaches had already overtaken the stage, he'd likely be too late to save Emily, but that didn't mean he wasn't compelled to try with every fiber of his body.

He soon left Clemens and his two deputies well behind.

War Bonnet fairly flew up the trail, as though he understood his rider's worry and plight. The horse's hooves tattooed a harried, rataplan rhythm on the hard-packed trail. A thick cloud of dust rose behind.

Twelve miles separated the Gonzalez *rancho* from Rebel Canyon. Having ridden this route nearly a hundred times over the past year and a half, Enberg knew every twist and turn in the trail. Every rock and cactus, every tree, every catclaw clump, every upward thrust of dike and bluff to either side of the trace.

When he saw the sprawling, half-dead cottonwood in which an old eagle's nest perched in a high V among the tangled branches, he knew the station was just over the next rise.

As he peered toward the ridge, his heart gave a painful lurch.

Several puffs of thick, gray smoke were rising from beyond the next hill to unspool against a sky that was turning dark green now as evening approached. That smoke could merely signify the supper fire of Mrs. Wormwood, the wizened old bird who ran the place with her two sons and a half-breed Kickapoo

Indian, but something told Enberg it meant something far darker.

His poor horse was blowing hard. The last rise slowed it considerably. Halfway to the crest, Enberg leaped down from the saddle, dropped the reins, and ran to the top of the hill. As he stared down the other side, his heart tore loose from its moorings and dropped into his belly.

Mrs. Wormwood's L-shaped adobe brick house was on fire, flames licking from the windows. What got the bulk of Enberg's attention, however, was the stagecoach sitting in the yard about thirty feet in front of the house—between the house and the large, burning barn.

There was no team hitched to the Concord. The luggage boot had been emptied. Luggage and a single strongbox were on the ground. The contents of the luggage were strewn in a ragged semicircle around the coach. The lid of the strongbox stood open.

Enberg broke into a run down the hill, heart pounding. He kept remembering the grisly scene he'd been confronted with back at the Gonzalez *rancho*. Would he find a similar scene here?

Would he find Emily inside Mrs. Wormwood's burning station house?

Enberg fairly flew into the yard. He leaped an open steamer trunk, spilling women's clothing, then crossed the porch and ran into the cabin, his eyes instantly watering as the smoke hit him.

He cupped his hand across his mouth as he moved forward, into the broad front room, which was flanked by the kitchen. To the left was a makeshift parlor area with a large braided rug and several sticks of rough-hewn furniture.

Flames licked at the window curtains, the window frames, and the furniture, but because the building was constructed of whitewashed mud brick, there wasn't enough fuel for a roiling blaze. There was mostly smoke and the fetor of kerosene, which the attackers had probably tossed around from gas lamps.

"Emily?" Enberg called as he moved around the smoky cabin, one hand cupped over his nose, the other hand holding the twelve-gauge. "Charlie?"

He moved through the back rooms—three small bedrooms; Mrs. Wormwood's larger, neat bedroom with an oil painting of Christ above the bed; a storage room filled with airtight tins, cured meat, and barrels of meal; and a pantry—and found no one.

No one living, no one dead.

"Emily?" Enberg yelled as he moved back through the house toward the front, tears streaming down his face from the roiling gray smoke.

He entered the kitchen as Roscoe Clemens crossed the porch and ducked through the doorway, a Winchester in his hands. Clemens looked around.

"There's no one here," Enberg said as he brushed past the lawman and stepped out onto the porch.

It was nearly dark now. The yard of the way station was filled with cool purple shadows. Smoke billowed up from the large, burning barn on the other side of the U-shaped yard. The barn was built of logs and lumber and likely filled with straw and hay. It provided better fuel for the flames than the cabin did.

Enberg stepped between Clemens's deputies and into the yard, looking around, seeing scuffed unshod hoofprints as well as the prints of Apache moccasins.

Clemens stepped out into the yard behind Enberg, holding his rifle on his hip and looking around warily. "You suppose the Apaches rode off with everybody?"

"Without spilling a drop of blood?" Enberg said, incredulous. "Not likely."

Dag walked around, studying the large mesas that rose in the north and the south. He stepped away from the smoking cabin to stare past it to the north, where a brushy arroyo meandered between the steep red walls of table-topped mesas. Beyond lay several rocky ridges.

Clemens sniffed the air as he walked up to Enberg. Keeping his voice low, the lawman said, "Apaches, all right. I can smell 'em."

"You've fought Apaches?"

"Most of my life. I was born in New Mexico. Soldiered out here. I was stationed at Fort Buchanan during the War Between the States. There were more rattlesnakes than soldiers at Buchanan during the war. We were pestered for three long years by Coyoteros. Believe me—I know what Apaches smell like."

"Like the inside of a bobcat?"

"You got it."

Enberg studied the ground again. "Looks like the Apaches headed off behind the cabin."

"The white folks must have tried to make a run for it."

"Let's find out."

Quickly, Enberg removed his spurs and left them on the ground. Clemens followed suit. As Dag moved forward, heading for the arroyo, Clemens beckoned to his deputies, who didn't look all that eager to follow their boss into the brush behind the station house.

"Spread out," Clemens told his men quietly behind Enberg. "Keep your eyes and ears skinned."

"Gettin' dark, Roscoe," said Bragg, his voice trembling a little as he paused to unstrap his own spurs from his boots. "I don't like fightin' 'Paches in the *daylight*."

"Ever done it before?" Clemens asked him.

"No."

"How do you know, then?" Clemens said.

Despite his anxiety over the stagecoach's fate, Enberg felt his lips quirk a slight smile. He'd found himself taking a liking to Clemens. He seemed a rung or two up from the last couple of Mineral Springs town marshals—himself not included, of course.

Enberg followed a pair of moccasin prints into the brush. Those prints were getting harder and harder to see as the dark-green light quickly leached out of the sky, and the ground grew murky with ever-thickening shadows.

He stopped when a coyote yapped from a rise ahead of him. There were three quick, ululating barks followed by one more a half-second later. The yaps were returned from another rise ahead of Enberg, on his left.

Enberg glanced at Clemens, who was walking slowly along about fifteen feet to Enberg's right.

"Them weren't coyotes," Clemens said softly.

"Nope," Enberg agreed, and shouldered past a ragged mesquite as he moved deeper into the arroyo.

The short hairs on the back of his neck were prickling.

Chicken flesh rose around those prickling hairs when some bird that was not a bird piped just ahead of him, maybe twenty feet away.

Enberg stopped and dropped to a knee, as did Clemens. Enberg glanced at the lawman, who parried the glance with a grave look. Dag held up his hand, indicating for Clemens to hold his position, then regained his feet and crept ever so slowly ahead, until he could see a dark-brown figure crouched in the brush straight ahead of him, not ten feet away.

A deerskin quiver bristling with ash arrows hung down the Chiricahua's broad back clad in red calico.

Enberg drew a deep, calming breath.

He licked his lips and reached back to slide his Bowie from its sheath.

He had to move as quietly as the Indians did, or he and the three lawmen would be goners. He'd been taught by old Olaf to move as quietly as an Apache over Apache terrain. Anyone who couldn't do that, white man or red, didn't last long in Apacheria.

Enberg stole up behind the crouching warrior.

He got so close he could smell the rancid stench of javelina grease, sweat, and smoky deerskins.

Dag cupped one big hand over the Chiricahua's nose and mouth and tipped the Indian's head back, muffling a startled grunt and exposing the neck. The Apache gave a violent lurch as Enberg slid his razor-edged Bowie knife across his victim's throat, feeling the blood wash like warm syrup over his knife hand.

CHAPTER FIFTEEN

Enberg held the Indian's head down fast against the ground, keeping his hand pressed over the brave's nose and mouth. He gritted his teeth as the brave, wide-eyed in horror, fought him feebly as his life poured out with the blood geysering from the gash in his neck.

The brave kicked and flailed at Dag's hand with his own.

Enberg gritted his teeth, looking around, hoping no other Apaches were close enough to hear the panicked thrashing.

Finally, the Apache fell still against the ground, eyes rolling back in his head.

Enberg looked around once more and then cleaned his Bowie knife with sand. He wiped his hands off on the ground. He returned the Bowie knife to the sheath on his belt, and slid the twelve-gauge around to his chest. He glanced down at the dead brave. He'd probably been stationed here to make sure that the marauding party's quarry didn't circle back to the station yard.

That meant that Emily and Grissom and the others were likely still alive. And somewhere ahead.

Enberg saw a shadow move on his far right. He turned to see Clemens moving up to flank him from about ten feet away. He glimpsed the two deputies moving up behind him on his left, both men keeping about fifteen feet between them. It was getting so dark now that Dag could see only their murky silhouettes against the brush, which bent as they moved through it.

Enberg looked at Clemens again, then at the deputies. He

canted his head to indicate up the draw, and continued moving.

Fifteen minutes later he found himself climbing a steep slope over strewn boulders. There was a mere thimbleful of light left in the desert sky, which would have made movement through such broken terrain dangerous to near deadly, even if Apaches hadn't also been on the lurk out here . . . somewhere.

How many warriors, there was no saying.

Dag could no longer see Clemens moving along to the south of him, nor the deputies to the north. Not only was it dark, but the arroyo had become more broken and choked with more brush, cactus, spindly trees, and boulders. At one point he heard a crunching sound and a sharp intake of breath to his left.

He stopped, wincing. One of the deputies had likely stepped in a cactus patch.

Enberg crawled up the sharply slanted surface of a slab-sided boulder leaning against a low, steep rise. He was about to step off the boulder and onto the top of the rise, when he stopped suddenly and dropped to a crouch.

Something had moved in the inky darkness below him.

There was the faint crunch of gravel beneath what was most likely a deerskin moccasin.

Enberg watched the shadow drift away from him, up the draw.

He stepped off the boulder and stole down the other side of the rise. He took half a dozen steps, moving straight up the arroyo floor, which was rising toward the dike looming blackly in the east, and stopped again.

A man-shaped silhouette had just stepped out from behind a boulder. Ambient light touched what was probably the shaft of an arrow being nocked to a bowstring.

Enberg started to raise the twelve-gauge in his hands but stopped himself. There could be no noise, or he'd have the entire marauding party on top of him in minutes.

Instead, he reached for the Bowie again, sending it hurling end over end. The knife gave a silver twinkle as it arced up and then down. There was a crunching thump.

A man grunted.

There was the soft clatter of a bow and arrow being dropped.

Another, softer, gurgling grunt. Then a thud.

Enberg hurried forward. He dropped to a knee beside the dark figure sprawled facedown before him. There was a hump in the brave's back. The brave's moccasin-clad feet moved as though he were trying to run in place.

Enberg shoved the brave onto his back. The Bowie's hide-wrapped handle jutted from high in the brave's chest. The dark eyes blinked rapidly.

The Indian was making low gurgling sounds, flopping his arms, trying to scream. Enberg placed a boot on the Indian's chest, just below the knife, and yanked the Bowie out with a grinding, sucking sound.

He swiped the blade across the Chiricahua's throat. He stepped back as blood spewed.

The brave fell silent. He jerked as he bled out, dying fast.

Enberg cleaned the blade on the Indian's leggings, and, holding the Bowie in his right hand, as it had become his weapon of choice out here, he continued making slow, stealthy progress up the debris-littered arroyo. He wasn't sure of his war plan. He supposed it was to kill as many Indians as he could until he found Emily and the stage passengers, as well as Mrs. Wormwood's gang from the station.

Finding them out here was probably as unlikely as finding a needle in a haystack, but what could he do but keep looking? He supposed he'd just keep moving and just keeping killing Indians until the sun came up ahead of him, and he'd have an easier time of tracking the group from the station.

A shrill scream rose from far away on Enberg's left.

It rose again. Again. And again, each time a little quieter and more miserable than the last.

It was followed by two gunshots. Rifle shots.

Enberg waited, his heart drumming in his ears.

He waited for nearly a minute, pricking his ears, listening. But no more sounds came.

The scream had been a white man's scream. An Indian's scream was more like an animal's wail. This had been a white man dying hard. One of the deputies. The other deputy had probably gone to render assistance. He'd likely died for his efforts.

The silence in that direction was as heavy as mud.

Enberg removed his hat and scrubbed his forehead with his shirtsleeve. It was chilly out here, but he was sweating. His shirt was basted with cold sweat against his back.

He donned his hat and continued moving forward, meandering slowly and quietly around tufts of ocotillo and yucca. He'd gained higher ground than before, and while the terrain was gently rolling, it was generally flat and spiked with chaparral.

There was no moon, but the stars offered enough light that he could see maybe ten, fifteen feet around him. The night was eerily quiet.

Enberg had moved for another twenty minutes when he stopped again and looked to his right. He'd heard something.

Clemens?

Another Chiricahua?

He dropped to a knee, squeezing the Bowie in his right hand.

A man's rattling voice said, "Fuck . . ."

There was a crunching thud as though the man had fallen.

Enberg lightened his grip on the knife, rose, and began stealing quietly in the direction from which the voice had come. He stepped between two broad chollas, careful not to rake an arm against the savage cactus, and moved past a large, cracked boulder.

Just beyond the boulder, starlight shone on the bald head of a man on the ground—a stout, broad-shouldered figure with a white beard. The man's hat lay crown down beside him.

Enberg dropped to a knee beside the fallen man. "Charlie, you ugly son of a bitch—is that you?"

Grissom jerked his face up in surprise. "Dag, you scared a good two years off my life, you big whore-fuckin' Norski lummox! What the hell are you doin' out here?"

"Do-si-doin' with your Apache friends."

"I just turned a little jig with one myself."

Grissom rose a little on his knees. Enberg saw the ten inches of fletched arrow protruding from the man's chest, near his left shoulder. Dag looked behind the silver-bearded jehu and saw the tip of the arrow with its strap-iron blade—preferred by the modern Apache over the stone tips of their ancestors—glistening in the starlight.

"Shit, Charlie. Shot a few days ago, and now *this*?"

"Stop your goddamn cussin'. Your pa raised you better'n that!"

"You should have stayed home!"

"Who in the hell are you to—?"

"Shut up, you old fool!" Enberg hissed, gazing into the darkness beyond Grissom. "Where's your dance partner now?"

"I skewered the bastard with my Green River knife. He's either dead or nursin' one hell of a bellyache."

Grissom chuckled but then his head dropped and jerked a little as he groaned.

Enberg pulled the old jehu's head up by the back of his shirt collar. Keeping his voice low and soft, he said, "Where are the others?"

"In a little shack on the other side of Carl's Mountain."

"What the hell is Carl's Mountain?"

"That big rocky butte to the north. Mrs. Wormwood calls it Carl's Mountain. Her husband dug a mineshaft in there. Built a stone cabin backed up to the shaft. That's where she and the rest of the bunch from the way station is holed up. I saw the Apaches comin' when we was still on the trail, and told that old woman, Wormwood. She led us all into an escape tunnel ole Carl had dug twenty years ago behind the station house, for skinnin' out when the Apaches attacked. The tunnel emptied out not far from here, about halfway between the station house and Carl's shack."

"Emily's with the others?"

"Hell, yeah. Her and her mother. That damn Gertrude keeps givin' me the hairy eyeball."

"That's just her way of sayin' she fancies you, Charlie."

"Dag, tell me something . . . ?"

Enberg wrapped an arm around Grissom's waist and began hoisting the big, heavy man to his feet. "What's that, Charlie?"

"How is it you get all the good-lookin' women? I figure you must be three-legged—am I right?"

"Shut up, you old peckerwood, or I'll pull my pants down an' show ya!"

Grissom wheezed a miserable laugh and made a sour expression.

When he'd steadied his friend on his feet, Enberg said, "What are you doin' out here? How come you're not with the others?"

"I couldn't stand sittin' around in that damn shack, waitin' for daylight. I come out to kill me some Injuns. Todd Vincent's out here somewhere, too."

"Todd Vincent?" Vincent was an alcoholic game hunter whom Cates had hired to shoot meat for the Diamond in the Rough's dining room. He also cut firewood during the winter for various folks around town.

"Normandy hired Todd to replace you as shotgun guard."

"That bastard has no respect for the position," Enberg lamented, looking around cautiously.

He squinted and pricked his ears to listen for a time. Then, relatively sure no Apaches lurked in his and Grissom's close proximity, he turned to the graybeard. "Lead me back to Carl's shack. We gotta get you tended, Charlie, before you bleed out dry as an old boot."

"All right, all right. Give me a second. Gotta catch my second wind."

Grissom drew several deep breaths, then managed to stagger heavily off to the east. Dag followed him, looking around cautiously. They came to a game trail, and Grissom followed the trail to the north and east. As they rounded a bend in the trail, Grissom tripped over something, grunted a shrill curse, and fell facedown.

"Charlie!" Dag rasped.

"Clumsy bastard!" Grissom chastised himself.

Crouching, Enberg saw what the jehu had tripped over. A man lay in the trail. Three arrows protruded from his chest and neck. Another protruded from his crotch. His throat had been cut from ear to ear.

"Oh, no," Enberg said.

Grissom sat up, breathing hard. "Who is it?"

Enberg stared down at the heavy-lidded eyes. "Clemens. God-damnit." Oddly, the local lawman had become a friend. Now, another friend was dead.

Enberg helped Grissom to his feet again, and again they started moving, climbing a gradual rise with strewn boulders and clumps of wiry chaparral. They made their way around the east side of the flat-topped bluff rising darkly before them, blotting out the stars, and then started to climb more sharply.

Grissom had to pause every few steps to catch his breath.

When he paused once more, about halfway up the bluff's apron slope, Enberg said, "Where's the shack?"

"Straight up. Should be, anyways. I can't see fer shit out here."

Just then, a man's voice bellowed, "Oh, ya red bastard son of a bitch!" There was the heavy, crushing report of a shotgun. It sounded like two barrels being triggered at the same time. The reverberations bounced around the canyon, and dwindled. Enberg had seen the red flash up the slope about thirty feet and to his right.

The echoing blasts were followed by a high screeching sound. A keening wail that dwindled quickly to silence.

"Shit!" said Grissom.

"What in the hell was that?" Enberg said, his pulse quickening as he stared up the slope.

That shotgun blast was going to bring every Apache in southern Arizona.

"Sounded like Todd."

"I'm gonna check it out."

Enberg strode quickly upslope in the darkness. He'd moved only ten feet when a shadow slid out from a large boulder before him. Enberg raised the twelve-gauge but held fire.

The figure shambling toward him was a white man.

Todd Vincent came down the slope, chin dipped toward his hands crossed on his belly. He stopped about six feet upslope from Enberg, and looked slowly up.

"Who . . . er . . . you?" he said in a pinched, distracted voice.

"Dag Enberg. What the hell happened?"

"An Injun just . . ." Todd sobbed. "One o' them dirty devils . . . just killed me!" He lowered his hands and there was a wet plopping sound as the man's guts spilled onto the ground at his boots. "Cut me with a cavalry saber," Vincent said through another, louder sob. "But I blasted him clear to the Happy

Huntin' Grounds for his troubles!"

He fell forward. Enberg caught him and eased him to the ground where he lay quivering atop his steaming innards.

A rifle barked downslope, beyond Grissom. The bullet screeched off a rock to Enberg's left. A wild yapping rose from various points in the murky darkness.

"Shit!" Grissom yelled. "Here they come!"

CHAPTER SIXTEEN

Enberg ran down the incline, draped one of Grissom's arms around his neck, and began half-carrying him up toward the shack he could not yet see atop the bluff's apron slope, at the base of the dark ridge.

The Apaches gave their eerie, yapping cries. As they converged on the base of the slope, the yapping grew louder. Rifles crashed and bullets spanged shrilly off rocks around Enberg and Grissom. Dag would have returned fire, to hold off the Chiricahua swarm, but he didn't want to give away his position any more than Todd Vincent already had.

When he heard running footsteps closing on him from behind, however, he had no choice.

"Keep headin' uphill, Charlie," he said as he released the jehu.

"Ah, shit," the graybeard muttered as he hobbled heavily, breathing hard, up the slope, one hand around the fletched end of the arrow sticking out of his chest.

Enberg pressed his back against the upslope side of a boulder. The Apaches' running footsteps grew louder. He decided there were two pairs of running feet, two pairs of straining lungs. One of the Chiricahuas was making low guttural sounds, like a wolf on the attack, as he ran.

Enberg waited.

Then he stepped out away from the boulder, aiming the twelve-gauge out from his right side, clicking both big hammers back. When he saw the jostling shadows with their long, buffeting hair glinting in the starlight, he cut loose with the left barrel.

Ka-booom!

The first brave threw away his carbine and went flying.

The other brave stopped abruptly, crouching.

Ka-booom!

The second brave turned a backward somersault in midair before disappearing in the darkness.

Enberg swung around and ran up the slope as the mad yapping grew louder and madder, and rifles cracked in the darkness behind him. Ahead the slope flattened out.

The stone shack appeared before him—milky white in the darkness, a faint ambience dancing thinly beyond the windows on each side of the plank-board door. The door was open, and two women were helping Grissom into the cabin.

A slender man stood nearby, aiming a pistol down the slope toward Grissom, a red bandanna billowing around his neck. "Best hurry, Mr. Grissom—you got one comin' up behind ya!" the man yelled.

"That's Enberg—don't shoot him," Charlie said, glancing behind him and adding whimsically despite the gravity of the situation, "you'll just be cheatin' some hangman!"

"Shut up and get in there, you old fossil," Enberg said as, gaining the top of the slope, he dropped to one knee and, facing the incline dropping away into the stone-studded darkness beyond, he broke open the twelve-gauge and quickly replaced the two spent wads.

More Indians were running up the slope, sort of fanned out among the rocks and piles of slag likely dumped there by old Carl Wormwood—a prospector he'd never met but only heard about. He'd died before Enberg had returned from the war.

The man who'd called out to Charlie moved over to kneel beside Dag. "Where's Todd?" he asked.

"Dead."

"Oh, lordy!"

"Friends of Todd's, were you?" Enberg said as he clicked the twelve-gauge closed.

"Oh, no, I wouldn't know him from Adam's off ox," the young man said, his voice trembling slightly. "I'm just driftin' through, followin' my star, I reckon. I just don't like seein' no one give up his ghost. Especially to an Apache *on the thirteenth day of the month.* That's the worst kinda luck a fellow can have. Oh, lordy, I see 'em comin'!"

The odd young man tore off three quick shots with his old Schofield revolver, evoking a guttural cry in the darkness. Enberg saw three figures running up out of the darkness. He made them disappear with twin blasts of the twelve-gauge.

As the resounding echo of the blast rocketed skyward, fading, Enberg heard a rifle clattering onto rocks.

"Let's head inside!" Enberg said, rising.

"Best idea I heard all night," the young man said, and ran crouching up the slope ahead of Dag.

Enberg followed the young man into the dimly lit cabin and drew the door closed behind him. He turned to the sandy-haired young man in a wool shirt and leather chaps standing to his left, dimly lit by candlelight.

"Who are you, anyway?" Dag asked.

The kid's eyes were wide and he was breathing hard. He wasn't wearing a hat. A wing of sandy hair hung down over one hazel eye. He wasn't really a kid—maybe late twenties—but there was something guileless about his manner that made him seem younger.

He stuck out his hand. "Galveston Penny."

Enberg shook the young man's hand, which was earnestly firm but not overly so. "Dag Enberg."

"What're you doin' out here, Mr. Enberg? I mean, not that I

mind, it's just that . . ."

"Dag!"

Enberg turned to see Emily climb up from where she'd been sitting against the stone wall. Tears streaming down her cheeks, she ran to her husband, hugged him tightly, and pressed her face against his chest. Enberg engulfed the young woman in his arms and pressed his own cheek against her head, loving the feel of her body against him at last.

"Oh, Dag!" she sobbed. She looked up to gaze at him lovingly, with relief in her tear-flooded eyes. He wasn't sure how she'd react when she saw him again, and he was pleased indeed. "I'm so glad to see you!"

"I'm so glad to see you too, honey. Are you all right?"

Emily nodded. She was dusty, and her dress was rumpled, but she otherwise looked fine. "Somehow, I knew you'd come. I knew you'd find me!"

"You bet I did. And I'm gonna get us outta here soon."

"How do you propose to do that, Enberg?"

This had come from Bud Normandy, who stood a ways behind Emily. His niece, the lovely Lisle Stanton, sat on an old, timeworn, ladder-back chair behind him, smiling as though she too were relieved to see the big, red-bearded Norski.

Lisle said nothing but she kept her eyes on Enberg. In light of Emily's also being here, Lisle's gaze made Dag feel a little uncomfortable, sheepish, though he had plenty of other, more important things to worry about. He hadn't known until now that Miss Stanton had accompanied Normandy on his journey to Tomahawk. He supposed her uncle had wanted her along to inspect the accounting in the line's outlying offices.

Enberg wasn't sure, but he thought he saw Emily follow her husband's fleeting gaze to Lisle. Enberg swept those insignificant concerns out of his mind for the moment, and turned to Normandy, who added, "That canyon down there is swarming with Apaches. How did you make it through? And . . . say, aren't you supposed to be in Clemens's jail?"

"You land your crazy ass in jail again, Dag? Good for you. I was afearin' you was startin' to get soft now that you got yourself hitched."

Eldora Wormwood cackled where she stood holding a long-barreled, double-bore shotgun in her crossed arms, to Dag's right. Her two sons, Leo and Tony, were each standing at a front window, both holding Winchesters. So did her half-breed hired hand, the Kickapoo whom Enberg knew only as Rides the Clouds, or Rides for short.

Short and stocky, his gray-streaked hair pulled back in a loose ponytail, he held an old infantry-model Sharps carbine.

Mrs. Wormwood, as everyone called her, was a frail-looking little wisp of a woman given to men's worn range attire. Her grizzled, pewter-colored hair flowed in tangled locks to her shoulders. She might not have weighed over a hundred pounds. Dag doubted she was much over sixty, but that those had been hard-earned years told in every deep line and wrinkle. Mrs. Wormwood's hard mileage notwithstanding, she was as tough as an ironwood knot, and as straightforward as a grizzly sow with two cubs in her fold.

Dag knew not to cross her, as did most men who'd known her for longer than five minutes.

Normandy, however, seemed not to have gotten the message.

"Please, don't encourage him, Mrs. Wormwood!" Normandy turned his scolding gaze on Enberg. "This man is due to stand trial . . ."

"Balderdash, you simple fool!" Wormwood intoned at Normandy, who was her height but twice her breadth. "Dag here was born and raised in this desert. Just like my boys and the Injun, Rides. Now that they're all together, we can just sit back and let 'em figure a way out of this bailiwick."

She turned her bright, light-brown gaze up to Enberg tower-ing over her. "I for one was just startin' to get a little worried. My Carl's old mine shack is a nice hidey-hole, but I had a feelin' the Apaches would find us sooner or later."

"It was that goddamn Todd Vincent's shotgun blast that brung 'em," complained Grissom from where he sat back against the wall, favoring the arrow in his chest.

"It ain't good to speak ill of the dead, Mr. Grissom," Galveston Penny politely admonished the old jehu.

"Mr. Grissom!" As though she'd just now seen that Charlie was injured, Lisle rose from her chair and crouched down beside the graybeard. "Good Lord—how did this happen?"

"I reckon I ain't as young . . . and don't move as quiet-like . . . as I once did," lamented the driver.

Enberg turned to Emily, who still had her cheek pressed against his chest. "How's your mother, honey?" He saw Ger-trude sitting down on the floor near where Emily had been sit-ting. The woman, clad in soiled traveling attire, just stared into space, as though she were in a trance.

"She hasn't said a thing in the past hour. I'm worried about her, Dag. She just stares."

"You'd best go to her."

Enberg guided Emily back across the shack.

A gun cracked at the front, and Enberg and everyone else jerked with a start as they turned to where Galveston Penny stood by a front window, smoke from his pistol wafting around him. "Thought I saw an Injun. Reckon it was just a bat or some-such," the drifter said a little guiltily. "I think they're all con-vergin' at the bottom of the slope. Prob'ly gonna wait us out. Maybe wait for daylight."

Enberg nodded, then dropped to a knee beside Gertrude.

"How you doin', Mrs. Cates?" he asked the woman.

She did not respond, but merely sat staring.

"Mother, Dag's here," Emily said with concern.

Gertrude's eyes went to Enberg. She sort of looked her son-in-law up and down, but Enberg couldn't tell if she recognized him or not. Then she went back to staring off into space, as though her mind were a million miles away.

To Emily, Dag said, "She'll be all right once we're out of here. She's just real scared, honey. I'm sure that's all it is."

Emily cast her worried gaze from him to Gertrude.

Enberg rose and looked around the room. There were six people from the stage and four from the roadhouse. Emily, her mother, and Lisle Stanton couldn't be expected to help hold off the Chiricahuas, who would likely keep threatening the shack despite the braves they'd already lost. Probably *because* of those they'd lost, and because their honor would not let them give up a fight unless the odds were overwhelmingly against them, they'd keep fighting.

That meant Enberg and the other men and Mrs. Wormwood, who had lived out here most of her life and was accustomed to fighting Apaches, would have to somehow hold them off and find a way out of the shack.

Enberg looked around again, this time inspecting the shack itself. Two candles offered the only, watery light, which probably couldn't be seen from very far down the slope. The cabin was outfitted with a sheet-iron stove, a cot, some makeshift cupboards, and a washstand. The floor was hard-packed earth with rails running through it from two heavy timber doors in the rear wall.

Enberg toed the dusty rails that had been used to haul the slag out of the mineshaft, in an ore car. He went over and ran his hand across the dusty, timbered doors that covered the mineshaft, and turned to Mrs. Wormwood.

"How far does the shaft run into the mountain?"

The old station mistress turned to her sons. Leo, the oldest, who was a little younger than Dag, said with a shrug, "Prob'ly a hundred yards, maybe more. He blasted on it for years, Pa did. I helped. So did Tony."

"Don't even think about it," drawled Mrs. Wormwood in her throaty, masculine voice. "That whole shaft is one big rattlesnake nest. Mojave greens. Carl busted into the nest. The boys here found him a few hours later, swollen up like a foundered bull. He was a small man, but no normal-sized coffin would hold him."

"Poor ole Carl," lamented Grissom, who'd been a friend of Carl Wormwood.

All eyes had turned toward Eldora Wormwood. Even Gertrude appeared to have heard the grisly tale, if dimly.

"You step foot in there now, you'll be pissin' venom down your leg inside of three minutes," Mrs. Wormwood warned Dag.

She looked at Emily and Lisle. "Pardon my French, girls. I was a God-fearin' woman once, lived by the Bible. But a woman coarsens, and her tongue gets a little blue out here . . ."

CHAPTER SEVENTEEN

"There must be an air shaft," Enberg said, sliding his gaze from Mrs. Wormwood to Leo and Tony, who were keeping one eye on the night-cloaked slope fronting the cabin.

"Sure," Leo said, swallowing. "There's an air shaft. But . . . like Ma said . . ."

Mrs. Wormwood shook her head darkly. "None of us would make it ten feet. When Carl busted into that nest, them vipers came out of there, slitherin' and hissin' every which way. Like Satan's vipers oozin' up outta hell's bowels! I wouldn't let the boys pull the body out. I did it my ownself. Loaded him into the ore car and used a torch to scare away them slitherin' devils while I rolled him out. That was three years ago. There's probably double, triple the number of snakes in there now."

Galveston Penny gave a shudder of revulsion and turned away from the window. "I reckon we're just gonna have to shoot it out."

"I reckon." Enberg didn't like that idea.

True, they had the high ground here. They could stand against the Chiricahua for a time. But, depending on how many Apaches they were dealing with, eventually they'd run out of ammunition.

Enberg wasn't sure which was a better to way to die. By Apache or by rattlesnake? He decided it would likely be slow and painful either way—six of one, half-dozen of the other.

Enberg crouched beside Grissom, on the other side of the

jehu from Lisle Stanton, who was pressing a handkerchief and a bandanna against the man's entrance and exit wounds. Enberg caught her gaze, then quickly slid his own to the bright, pain-wracked eyes of the stage driver.

"Gonna have to get that arrow out of there, Charlie."

"Ah hell—don't worry about me, Dag. You best go up and help keep them Chiricahua at bay."

"It's pretty quiet out there now," Enberg said. "I got a feelin', like Penny said, they're gonna make us sweat for a while, maybe attack around first light."

"I reckon you're right. After all, you was raised half-Apache your ownself," Grissom said with a chuckle, glancing first at Lisle kneeling off his right shoulder, then at Dag kneeling beside his left one.

Lisle smiled and looked at Enberg again. He wished she'd stop looking at him. He didn't like how it made him feel. Emily apparently didn't like it, either, because she came over and knelt down beside Lisle and said, "I'll help my husband, Miss Stanton. You should go sit down. You look tired."

Lisle glanced at Dag, who did not return the look. Then she turned the bandanna and handkerchief over to Emily, rose, and walked over and sat down on the chair near her uncle again.

She stared worriedly toward the shack's front windows—one on either side of the door and around which the Wormwood boys and Galveston Penny were crouched, watching, listening, waiting . . .

The Kickapoo, Rides, squatted against the wall, an old Springfield rifle resting across his thighs. Dag couldn't remember ever hearing the man say anything. He said nothing now.

"You want somethin' to chomp down on, Charlie?"

"That's all right," Grissom said. "I'll chomp down on my tongue. At my age, it's as tough as whang leather." He glanced at Emily, and grinned his devilish, vaguely, habitually flirtatious grin.

"You're gonna be all right," Emily told him. "Dag knows what he's doing—don't you, Dag?" She looked at her husband a little dubiously.

"Sure, sure," Enberg said without conviction.

He took hold of the point of the arrow and broke it off.

"Oh, boy!" said Grissom through a raking grunt, squeezing his eyes closed.

"Now, I'm gonna pull it out, Charlie."

"Give me a minute, will you Da—ah, Jesus, that smarts!"

Enberg held both ends of the dripping arrow up in front of Grissom. "All done. Now, you'll heal."

But Grissom didn't say anything. His head was resting back against the shack wall, and his eyes were closed. He'd passed out.

"He's bleeding an awful lot," Emily said, wincing as she held the cloths against both wounds, front and back.

"We're gonna need some more cloth."

"Here." Emily lifted her skirt and ripped off a long strip of cambric from the bottom of her white chemise. "This will help." She tore the strip in two and stuffed the wads into the wounds.

Looking around for more cloth, Enberg's gaze had settled on a banded steamer trunk sitting beneath a square wooden eating table, to the right of the heavy timber doors covering the mine-shaft entrance. There might be medical supplies in there.

He went over, dropped to a knee, and pulled the trunk out from under the table. He lifted the lid and stared down, his lower jaw instantly hanging.

"Holy—!" Reminding himself that ladies were present, he cut himself off.

"What is it?" Galveston Penny walked over and stared into the steamer trunk. "Holy—!"

"Yeah," Dag said, staring down at the half-dozen or so sticks of Magic dynamite. They were in a loose bundle bound with twine. Rummaging among the sticks and a mouse nest fabricated from an old shredded newspaper, he discovered two burlap pouches containing blasting caps and fuses. In one corner of the trunk was a rusty, steel push box for detonating the dynamite.

Mrs. Wormwood had come over to stare down at the trunk with the two crouching men. "Hmmm . . ."

Enberg poked his hat back off his forehead. "That's what I say."

"We could light the fuses and toss the sticks down the slope, I reckon," said Galveston.

Enberg touched a finger to each dark-red stick, counting them. "There's only five. Them Injuns'll likely be spread out. We might get 'em all with this many sticks, but we might not. Might just piss-burn 'em really good. They could pin us down here a good long time." *Waiting to drag us out one by one and slow-roast us over a low fire,* he added only to himself.

"What do you suggest?" asked Mrs. Wormwood. "You wanna blow us all up, Dag—save the Chiricahuas the trouble?" She laughed a deep-lunged, croaking laugh.

"No," Enberg said, thinking it through. "But I could slip back into the mineshaft and crawl out the air vent. I could work around the Apaches. Ain't there a steep ridge just across the bottom of the slope? A rocky one? I could throw down on 'em from there."

He thought he'd seen one humping up against the stars.

"Yep," said Leo Wormwood, keeping his voice low. Neither Wormwood boy was much of a talker. Dag figured their mother did most of their talking for them. Living way out here, they probably had minimal use for words.

Angrily impatient, Eldora said, "What did I tell you about the vipers in that shaft, you big, good-lookin' rascal?" She knocked on Dag's head as though she were knocking on a door. "You got anything but rocks in there?"

"That could be debated a spell," Dag said, considering the five sticks in his hand. "If I had a torch, I might be able to make it through the shaft. Maybe the snakes are asleep this late. I know I'd rather be." He looked at the boys, whom he figured probably knew the shaft nearly as well as their father had. "Can a man my size make it through the air vent?"

The two young Wormwood men looked at each other, and then Leo, who did most of the talking on the rare occasion talking was needed, said, "Prob'ly."

"Dag, no—please," Emily said, staring up at him, worry in her eyes. "Listen to Mrs. Wormwood."

"Someone better," Eldora said.

"I don't see that we have much of a choice. We're pinned down in here pretty good. Eventually, we'll run out of ammo. I know how the Chiricahua work. They'll draw our fire until they bleed us dry, and then come . . ."

No need to finish the thought. He glanced at Emily and then at her mother, who was watching him now as though a part of her was listening from somewhere behind her glazed stare.

"I'm gonna give it a shot." Enberg squeezed his wife's arm. He never thought he'd see her looking at him again like she was looking at him now. It warmed his heart despite the direness of their situation. "I'll be all right, honey. I have to give it a shot. I don't see as I . . . or we . . . have any other option."

Emily drew a deep breath, steeling herself against the possibility of her husband's demise. Enberg was relieved to see that she still loved him in spite of his regrettable actions the other night. She might not have wanted to, and he likely still had some talking to do to get her back into his life, but she loved him.

"How far inside the shaft is the air vent?" he asked the Wormwood boys.

Leo Wormwood shrugged a shoulder. "Good ways. Around the dogleg. Maybe fifty, sixty yards."

"All right. I'm gonna need a flame. A torch."

Mrs. Wormwood walked over to a small stack of sticks near a slightly larger stack of split firewood. "Carl an' the boys used these mesquite branches for torches. They wrapped 'em in burlap. There." She pointed to a small peach crate stuffed with what appeared old flour sacks. "There's kerosene in this can."

She lifted the rusty tin can by its wire handle, giving it a shake. Liquid sloshed around inside.

"All right," Enberg said. "That'll do."

"I'll go with you," offered Galveston Penny.

There was a buzzing sound. The buzzing grew quickly louder.

The arrow whistled through the window left of the door, narrowly missing Leo Wormwood, before it made a long, dark arc through the candlelit shack and thudded into one of the timber doors, quavering loudly.

Emily and Lisle Stanton screamed.

"Everybody keep your heads down!" Enberg yelled, dropping to his knees and pulling Emily down beside him.

Both Wormwood boys fired rifles through their respective windows.

"Hold your fire, hold your fire!" Dag ordered. "They're just tryin' to get us to pop off all our ammo, like I said they'd do. Everybody just stay down and keep away from the windows. Only shoot if you got a clear shot at one o' them devils!"

Enberg looked at Galveston Penny hunkered down beside him. "You stay here. If I don't make it, these folks are gonna need all the help they can get fightin' off them Apaches. And I saw how you handled that Schofield outside. You're good."

Penny gave a bashful shrug.

343

"When are you going to go?" Emily whispered, squeezing his forearm desperately.

"I'll wait until just before false dawn. I'll need a little light, or there's no point in goin'. Dark as the bottom of a well out there. I'm betting the Apaches'll attack a little after dawn. They're prob'ly stayin' close together now, since they know where we are. I reckon I'm just gonna have to hope they're in a fairly tight group. If I play my cards right, I should be able to take out most of 'em with those five dynamite sticks."

"If you play your cards right," said Eldora Wormwood.

"If not," Enberg said, "well, at least I'll have their flank when they storm the cabin. They likely won't be expectin' anyone to work around behind."

"I just hope there's not too many of 'em," said Galveston Penny.

Enberg sighed. "Yeah. Me, too."

Eldora Wormwood nodded sagely, darkly, as, leaning back against the wall, her shotgun resting across her thighs, she took out a small, curved pipe and packed it with tobacco.

Keeping his head low, Enberg blew out the candles. Darkness engulfed the cabin.

Dag sat back against the wall, near the trunk containing the dynamite, beside Emily.

Lisle Stanton sat down against the cabin's right wall, beside Normandy, who hadn't said much since Enberg had entered the shack. Normandy was a businessman. Out here, he was totally out of his element and had very little to say. He looked nearly as stricken as Gertrude did, sitting back against the wall, near Eldora Wormwood, who quietly, pensively, puffed her pipe and sent its aromatic smoke drifting through the shack.

The Wormwood boys sat near the windows, occasionally lifting their heads a little to cast cautious glances down the slope.

Galveston Penny sat near the Wormwood boys, in the cabin's front corner, Lisle on his left.

Rides squatted where he'd squatted all along, saying nothing.

An hour trickled by.

Around one a.m., according to Enberg's watch, an eerie chortling rose from the slope outside the shack. It was the Chiricahuas singing their coyote-like songs of war. The songs had a dual purpose, Enberg assumed. One was to build up their own courage. The other was to scare the living hell out of their quarry.

Immediately, Enberg felt the tension rise in the shack. It was like a low whining sound.

"It's all right," Dag said quietly. "They're just tryin' to rankle us."

"They're doin' a damn good job," said Normandy, sitting against the wall and resting his arms across his raised knees.

Lisle reached out and placed a reassuring hand on her uncle's shoulder. The girl had sand. This was the second tight spot she'd been in since coming to Mineral Springs, and she was far from unglued. Enberg wondered what her story was. He was curious, but he'd likely never know. He didn't want to get close enough to her to learn any more about her, because he'd seen the way she'd looked at him. For his part, he couldn't deny an instinctive male pull in her direction.

But he wanted no more trouble with Emily. He loved his wife.

It was going to be hard enough to win her back the way it was. At the moment, she needed him. After this was over—if they lived through it, that was—she'd have time to remember his considerable transgressions.

That said, not long after the Apaches had begun their caterwauling, Emily moved closer to Dag. She wrapped an arm around his neck and sank down onto his lap, burying her face in his neck. She sniffed him and rubbed her forehead against his bearded cheek, but she didn't say anything.

Her silence was a pouting, scolding remonstration even while she snuggled intimately against him. Knowing women as well as he did, Dag sensed that she wanted to be close to him for a sense of security. But he also knew that his young wife was making sure Lisle Stanton knew who he belonged to, even while keeping Dag himself wondering if he really did have her back.

The night wore on. It was like a black cat taking its time padding across a broad, open field under cover of choking darkness.

Eldora Wormwood puffed her pipe.

Emily dozed, snoring softly, in Dag's lap, causing his right leg to go to sleep.

Along the dark slope beyond the shack, the Apaches sang their promise of slow death and bloody victory.

Chapter Eighteen

"You be careful, now—you hear me?" Emily said, and kissed Dag's lips. She gave his tunic a hard tug. "You got a come-uppance due you, Enberg, and you better be around to receive it!"

This was the first time since they'd been reunited that she'd mentioned what he'd come to call in his own mind the "Big Trouble," and the back of his neck warmed with shame. "I will, honey. I promise."

Enberg glanced at the others, who were pretty much maintaining the same positions they'd been in all night.

It was now around four-thirty. Dawn light would begin to wash into the eastern sky in an hour or so. The Apaches would probably attack then in force and fury. They'd draw their quarry's fire, and, when Dag's bunch had fired off all their ammo, they'd bust into the shack and begin their brand of slow, painful torture.

Enberg had seen the results of that torture before, and he wanted no such thing for Emily or Lisle or Mrs. Wormwood, not to mention himself and the other males in his party, even Bud Normandy.

On hands and knees near the two stout doors at the back of the shack, Enberg returned his wife's kiss. "I love you, Em. Whatever happens, you remember that."

Emily didn't reply. She merely held his gaze with a stern, commanding gaze of her own.

"You be careful, you big galoot," ordered Eldora Wormwood quietly.

"Yeah, Dag," said Lisle Stanton. "Be careful, okay?"

Galveston Penny pinched his hat brim. He'd helped Dag fashion a burlap rucksack with which to carry the dynamite, caps, and fuses. The rucksack now hung down Dag's left shoulder. He had his shotgun slung over his right shoulder. His two pistols jutted up from behind his belt.

He held his unlit torch in his left hand, keeping the right one free for his pistols or twelve-gauge or Bowie.

Enberg gave the young drifter a two-fingered salute, then rose and pulled on one of the door's steel handles. The door scraped open loudly on its heavy hinges, causing dust to waft from the ceiling around it. Immediately, stale, pent-up air rife with the smell of bat guano pushed against Enberg, almost sucking the oxygen out of his lungs.

"Oh, god—it smells awful in there!" Emily exclaimed in a pinched voice, crouched nearby.

"Ah, hell—it smells like freedom!" Enberg gave his wife one last parting grin, and then stepped into the mine, pulling the heavy door closed behind him.

He hadn't wanted to light his torch until he was inside the mine, so the Apaches wouldn't see the light and know he was up to something. He struck a match on the shotgun's lanyard and touched it to the kerosene-soaked burlap wrapped and knotted around the end of the slightly crooked green mesquite stick in his hand.

He held the flame high—at least, as high as he could. The ceiling was so low that he had to crouch. Even then, the crown of his hat scraped against the chipped stone.

To both sides and above, the dark walls and ceiling pocked with white stones and gravel closed in around him. He'd never cared for tight confines. They made him feel buried alive. He'd put that anxiety out of his mind when he'd made his decision to head out through the air shaft.

He'd never understood how prospectors like his father were able to work so many hours in dank, dark caverns like the one he was in now. That was why he had joined old Olaf on his gold-seeking expeditions only a few times, but had chosen instead to stay around Mineral Springs, tending the springs and the livery business.

His old man hadn't minded wriggling around in the deep, dark earth. Maybe it had something to do with his large size, or maybe his vivid imagination, but Dag didn't like it a bit. Especially when you threw rattlesnakes into the mix . . .

Enberg waved the guttering flame around, but the flickering umber light revealed no vipers slithering near him. He was glad about that. If he'd seen snakes this close to the entrance, he might have lost his nerve and turned back, making a fool of himself.

Eldora Wormwood's husky voice whispered jeeringly in his ear: "You step foot in there, you'll be pissin' venom down your leg inside of three minutes . . ."

Enberg crouched, listening. When he heard no rattling and continued to see no slithering movement in the walls or ceiling or along the floor, down the middle of which the narrow steel rails for the ore car stretched, he began edging forward, his lower back already beginning to ache from having to bend so low.

As he remembered, Carl Wormwood had been a much smaller man.

Enberg walked along, brushing the flame along the ceiling, shuttling his gaze from left to right and back again, noting white streaks of bat guano and the occasional rubble fallen from the walls or ceiling. Occasionally, he kicked a discarded airtight tin, which rattled his nerves as it banged off his boot and rolled away along the floor.

He heard the intermittent mouse or rat screech and scuttle away from the light, sliding its red ambience along the tracks.

The tunnel made a slow curve to the right. He'd just made the curve when what appeared to be two copper pennies glistened in the torchlight to his left. He stopped and recoiled in horror when he saw the rattlesnake coiled tightly, staring up at him, flicking its forked tongue and button tail.

"Ah, hell!"

Enberg pulled his Colt from behind his belt and blew the beast in two writhing parts. The rocketing crash of the revolver in the close confines was like two open palms being slapped over his ears, which instantly started ringing.

He turned to his right in time to see another serpent just then pulling its ugly tail into a crack between two boulders bulging out of the wall. Enberg gave a shudder; then, recocking the Colt and holding it out in front of him in his right hand, he continued forward.

He could smell the rattlers now, so he must have been getting close to the nest. He'd stumbled upon rattlesnake caverns before, and each one had owned the smell of rotten cucumbers.

Ahead was a gap in the left wall. Staying to the far right, which wasn't far since the cavern was only about six feet wide, he glanced into the gap. That must have been where Carl, beginning an intersecting tunnel to follow a gold vein, had picked into the nest. Dag could see nothing in there now but shadowy angles and rubble heaped halfway to the ceiling—and that's just what he wanted to see.

No rattlesnakes.

A rat peeped somewhere ahead of him. He saw the little shadow scurrying along the floor before disappearing beneath one of the rails of the narrow steel tracks.

He strode forward, continuing around the curve, and brushed

past a rusted ore car half-filled with ore. An old torn shirt hung from the side of the car, and a rusty pickaxe poked up from one corner.

Enberg walked on until he came to another gap—this one in the mine's right side. He shone the light into the gap. It was a flue of sorts, chiseled from about halfway up the right wall and into the ceiling. It angled away into a stygian darkness that Enberg's torch wouldn't penetrate.

Apparently, the vent curved and angled its way toward fresh air.

Needing air down here to continue his work, Carl must have blasted and chipped out the vent from above as well as from inside the tunnel, and hauled out the rubble with his ore cars. He'd likely followed a natural fissure in the rock.

Enberg shoved the burning torch farther up the vent. He could see about seven feet beyond him. Still, he couldn't see much but shadows. He swirled the torch around, listening for that dry rattling of a piss-burned viper, but heard nothing.

Good.

There would be no easy way to climb up the vent, he saw. He just had to try to kick and claw his way up through the narrow cleft the best way he could . . . while holding the torch.

He ground one foot against a side of the vent and pulled himself up into the cleft with his right hand, holding the torch with his left. Hoisting and kicking himself upward, he shoved his head and shoulders back against the side of the vent opposite the side where his foot had been.

That would be the best—maybe the *only* way—to climb the thing while holding the torch. To sort of kick and claw and writhe his way up, levering himself against the sides. That shouldn't be too hard, because the vent was only about five feet wide. At least, it was that wide as far as he could tell . . .

He continued kicking and pushing and pulling himself up the

vent, using his legs and arms and shoulders and even the back of his head for leverage, grunting and cursing with the effort. He knocked gravel and rock chunks off the sides of the chute and heard them plunk onto the tunnel floor below.

Occasionally, he let the torch get too close to his face and nearly set his hat on fire. The smoke made his eyes run.

When he was about ten feet up from the bottom, he sort of braced himself between the walls and lifted the torch high to see where in hell he was.

The vent narrowed some about five feet up. He looked around. The walls were close upon him, and he could have sworn they were getting closer. He could almost see them sliding toward each other like the two halves of an iron vise, intending to squash him to mush or worse—trap him here forever!

The torch made it hot as a furnace in here, but a chill ran through Dag.

His breathing grew rapid, and his heart started hammering his ribs almost painfully. A cold sweat broke out across his forehead. His limbs stiffened up, as though his arms and legs suddenly had iron rods in them.

"Oh, shit!"

The shaft began to slide and pitch around him.

Sweat dribbled down his cheeks and basted his shirt against his back.

He heard a faint scratching sound. Something moved in the upper periphery of his vision. He looked in horror to see a snake making an S curve as it slithered out of a crack in the shaft wall and moved down the shaft toward him, testing the air with its tongue.

Enberg screamed and jerked back.

At the same time, he automatically thrust his right hand toward the snake just as the viper lunged at him. He had no idea how he did it, but he caught the beast around the neck, and, with another scream that he was none too proud of—high-pitched and girlish as it was—he thrust the snake straight down away from him. He watched it tumble out of sight.

It hit the mine floor with a thud and immediately lifted an indignant ratcheting snarl loud enough to be heard even from this distance.

More movement just above his line of vision.

Another snake was poking its nose and slithering tongue out of the crack.

"Oh, no you don't!" Enberg bellowed, sliding his Colt from behind his belt.

He clicked back the hammer, slammed the pistol barrel into the crack, against the serpent's nose, and fired.

He clicked the hammer back, and, yelling, fired again.

The blasts were oddly muffled by the rock, but they still echoed around Dag, causing the shaft's walls to reverberate. The smell of cordite mingled with the stench of rotten cucumbers.

Something stabbed Enberg's left shoulder. It felt like a sharp, rusty knife buried to the bone. The pain was keen—hot and heavy.

Burning.

He jerked his head to the left to see a Mojave green rattler sinking its fangs into his upper arm. Its copper eyes were dull and vacant, like two chips of fool's gold set into a flat, diamond-shaped chunk of flint.

"Christ!" Enberg jerked his shoulder away from the snake, ripping his flesh free of the viper's grip.

He revolved in the tight confines, shifting his feet and shoulders, aimed his revolver, and fired two rounds at the snake. He didn't know if he hit the beast or not, but it suddenly was no longer there. It must have pulled its head back into the crack from which it had come.

The slugs were fractured by the stone wall he'd fired them into, and one of the ricocheting fragments dug into his right side, about midway between his hip and his shoulder.

Damn fool, he vaguely told himself, far beneath the panic that raged in him like a typhoon in a bottle. He was lucky he hadn't been hit with more than just the one fragment.

Or maybe he had. At the moment, he wouldn't know. The shaft was spinning and his ears were ringing and his blood was jetting through his veins at a million miles an hour.

He dropped the torch and began scratching and clawing at the shaft walls, crabbing up around the dogleg in the cleft. Now he could smell fresh air. He kept climbing blindly in the darkness, panicking, bells tolling inside his head.

Scratching.

Fumbling.

Clawing . . .

Losing ground and then desperately regaining it.

Upward he went, loosing rocks and gravel. He skinned his head on what felt like a tree root angling into the vent. He kept climbing. Glancing upward, he saw a ragged-edged patch of gray. It must be full dawn, which meant he'd taken longer in the mine than he'd intended.

He continued scratching and kicking and clawing his way up the vent, gritting his teeth against another possible snakebite. He barely registered the heavy, aching feeling in his left shoulder. All he could think about—if you could call it thinking—was getting the hell out of the snake-infested hole.

The gray circle grew above him.

The air smelled like sage and creosote.

It was touched with the smell of rancid javelina grease and sweat . . .

Enberg's brain had just told him what that last mix of odors likely belonged to before he stuck his head up out of the hole and reached out to grab something with which to hoist himself the rest of the way out of the ground.

Instead, something grabbed *him*.

Enberg stared up in hang-jawed shock at the large, red hand knotted with twisted white scars grasping his own right hand as though to shake it. As though the other hand belonged to an old friend Dag hadn't seen in a long time, and here they both were, meeting again on some city boardwalk, say, or on a railroad platform outside a depot building.

A Chiricahua.

Ah, shit.

Chapter Nineteen

There was a grunt that Enberg didn't think had come from himself, and then he was wrenched up out of the hole by the powerful Apache who'd grabbed him. He lay belly down atop the hole, his legs still dangling over the sides of the vent.

Looking up, he saw the large Chiricahua warrior towering over him. The man, maybe roughly his own age, appeared as large as a bear standing there silhouetted against the gray dawn sky. He wore a faded blue cavalry tunic with sergeant's stripes on the sleeves, and a blue cavalry hat with a badly frayed brim. A saber dangled from the wide, black leather belt encircling the warrior's waist.

Long hair hung down from under the hat, framing his oval-shaped, severely chiseled face. He held a feathered ash bow in his right hand. A quiver of arrows poked up from behind his right shoulder.

A string of bear claws dangled low across his chest clad in red and white calico.

The Chiricahua stared down, slant-eyed, at Enberg, his hair billowing in the dawn breeze. He grinned, showing a mouthful of dark, crooked teeth.

He grunted a long string of words in his own tongue, pointing a scolding finger at Dag, and then gritted his teeth as he drew one moccasin-clad foot back and rammed it forward into Enberg's belly.

The savage blow pummeled the air out of Dag's lungs.

When he saw another kick coming, he rolled toward the Apache and wrapped both his arms around the ankle the warrior kept on the ground. The Chiricahua hadn't expected the move, and it foiled the man's second kick, causing him to stumble backward.

Enberg jerked forward on the Indian's ankle, and the warrior fell to his ass with a grunt.

Mindless of having only half his wind and trying to ignore the heavy burning in his swelling left arm, Dag scrambled to his feet. But not before the big warrior had regained his own. Enberg was just rising from a crouch when the Indian hurled his large, bear-like body at him, grinning in delight.

Indians loved hand-to-hand. Nothing honored a Chiricahua as much as beating an enemy senseless and then using a skinning knife to evoke ear-piercing screams for hours.

Enberg hit the ground on his back. The Indian went rolling over his head, whooping savagely.

Knowing he had no time to waste trying to recover from any of his aches and pains, Enberg again began scrambling to his feet, clawing his Colt from his belt. The Indian lunged forward, kicking the revolver out of Dag's hand. It flew up over Dag's head to thud onto the ground behind him.

Dag bulled forward. He lifted the big Apache up off the ground and backward, slamming him against a boulder.

The two rolled to the ground, the whooping and hollering Apache on top of Dag. The Indian head-butted Dag twice before Enberg got both hands up over the Apache's face and pushed his head back. The Apache screamed as his head went farther and farther back. Dag thought he was about to snap the Chiricahua's neck, when his attacker smashed his left knee hard into Enberg's groin.

Dag released his grip on the Indian's face as waves of agony rolled through his belly. He felt as though his balls had been smashed on a railroad track with a sledgehammer. For several moments, all he could see was a red veil of throbbing misery.

The Indian quirked his thick lips in a devilish smile as he reached back over his right shoulder, plucked an arrow from his deerskin quiver, and thrust it straight down toward Dag's neck.

Enberg's agony was tempered by his fear of bloody death.

He managed to grab the Indian's hands clutching the arrow when the strap-iron blade, honed to a razor edge, was six inches from his jugular. Still, the Indian literally had the upper hand. Down the blade slid . . . farther, farther. It shook as the four hands wrapped fast around it shook. Dag lowered his fearful gaze, tracking the blade's progress toward his jugular vein.

At the last second, he funneled all his waning strength into a hard left push. The blade scraped painfully across his shoulder before embedding in the red sand and gravel. Enberg gave a bellowing cry of conjured strength and smashed his right fist twice against the Apache's jaw.

He hit the man so hard he felt the jawbone give, then saw it sag low in the man's leathery face. The Indian's eyes glazed, stunned, as he rolled off of Enberg, who wasted no time in reaching for a pistol. But both his Colts were gone, as was his shotgun. He'd lost them in the fight. He could go for his knife, but his right foot seemed handier. Quickly, he reached into his right boot well, plucked out his over-and-under derringer, and pressed the barrel against the cowering Apache's left temple.

Pop!

Pop!

The brave jerked, twisted around, and fell backward, both heavy legs curled beneath his bulk.

The sound of running footsteps rose somewhere near Enberg. He wasn't sure where they were coming from.

Bells of agony were still tolling in his head, and the ground pitched and rolled around him.

Finally, staggering to his heavy feet, he looked down a slope covered in red slide-rock, and saw three braves sprinting up from the canyon below—about forty yards away and closing fast. Others were moving toward him from farther back along the canyon, which twisted narrowly between two high, rocky ridges.

Enberg had no idea where he was in relation to Carl's mine shack, and at the moment he had no time to worry about it. The running footsteps were growing louder.

Enberg saw his twelve-gauge lying on the ground. He staggered over to it, picked it up, and swung around just as the first of three nearest Apaches gained the top of the slope, howling. The brave had an arrow knocked to his bow. The brave stopped abruptly, and sent the arrow hurling toward Enberg. As Dag felt the shuddering pain of the arrow tearing into his upper left thigh, he eared back both his shotgun's hammers, centered the barrels on the chest of the Apache who'd fired the arrow at him, and . . .

BOOM!

The young brave's chest turned bright red as he flew back down the hill.

Enberg staggered toward the brow of the slope. The other two Apaches were running toward him, leaping and lunging, long hair dancing across their shoulders.

Enberg squeezed the shotgun's second trigger and curled his upper lip as the wide spread of double-aught buck sliced into the upper torsos and faces of both braves, sending them screaming and dancing backward. They fell and rolled.

Yet another Apache, twenty yards behind the others, stopped and raised a Spencer carbine. The Spencer cracked, the smoke tearing away from the barrel.

The bullet screeched over Dag's right shoulder. He tossed away his empty shotgun, looked around desperately, then picked up one of his fallen Colts. While the Apache quickly cocked the Spencer again, Enberg aimed and fired.

He was so weak, his vision so blurry, that his first four shots merely plumed dust around the brave with the carbine. His fifth shot blew the Indian's lower jaw off.

The Chiricahua, who'd been dodging Dag's bullets, tumbled down the steep slope, loosing slide-rock in his wake. Dag aimed carefully and fired again, finishing him.

The others—a good dozen or so, Enberg could tell through the watery haze of his fading vision—were storming toward him down the deep, narrow canyon.

"Ah, hell."

Stiffly, the Chiricahua arrow bristling from his left leg, his left arm now swelling up to the size of a good-sized tree branch, Enberg limped stiff-legged over to where he'd dropped the burlap rucksack. Quickly, he pulled out the five dynamite sticks, wrapped them with a single long fuse into a single bundle, then capped each of the five sticks.

He shoved a fuse into one of the detonator caps.

"Ah, hell," he said again as he heard the whooping and hollering Apaches sprinting up the slope from the canyon floor.

Enberg limped painfully over to the crest of the slope. He pulled a match out of his shirt pocket, scratched it to life on his belt, and touched the flame to the dynamite fuse.

He raised the five sticks and the sizzling fuse high above his head, grinning.

"Come and get it, you red-skinned *sonso'bitch-ezzzz!*" he bellowed.

He was a goner. But there was one last thing he could do.

He could take the Chiricahuas howling off to hell with him.

"I'll introduce you red devils to Ole Scratch!" Enberg bellowed, laughing crazily and waving the dynamite sticks and lit fuse high over his head.

The first of the dozen or so Apaches sprinting up the slope stopped suddenly. He stared wide-eyed at the dynamite with the sputtering fuse clenched tightly in the fist of the big, red-bearded, crazy-looking white-eyes standing on the crest of the slope. Apparently, the Apaches were familiar with dynamite.

Yelling and gesturing wildly, the Apache wheeled and started running back down the hill. The others stopped and looked up the hill in Enberg's direction, and then they too wheeled and ran back in the direction from which they'd come—down the long, angling canyon floor between the two tall, steep ridges.

"Cowards!"

Enberg cocked his right arm, leaning far back and down, and then brought it back up with a fierce grunt. He slung the dynamite bundle as far as he could down the slope. It hit the incline and rolled, smoking and sputtering and bouncing along about fifteen feet behind the crowd of leaping and bolting red men, as though it were a loyal dog trying to catch up to them.

The blast was like a giant hiccup issuing from the earth's bowels.

The dynamite suddenly erupted in a giant puff of black smoke and a cherry-colored flash. A full second later, the concussion of the blast threw Enberg backward as though he'd been punched by a giant fist. He hit the ground and rolled, screaming against the fiery pain in his snake-bit arm and arrow-pierced leg.

He rolled onto his back and stared up at the sky.

"Shit," he said.

The blast had probably taken out a few of the Apaches. Likely, the others had been far enough from the blast that they were unscathed. Their ears probably hurt, but otherwise they were undoubtedly just fine. They'd likely head back this way in a minute.

"Damnit all," Enberg croaked out, feeling around for one of

his pistols. He could at least deny the Apaches the fun of torturing him—likely skinning him alive and getting creative with his innards.

They'd beaten him. The red devils had beaten him.

Emily and the others would still die . . .

Enberg continued to claw around for his gun, then stopped.

A low rumbling sounded. The ground beneath Enberg quivered. It felt like it did when a train was pulling into a station.

But they weren't within a thousand square miles of a railroad line . . .

An earthquake?

Enberg lifted his head to stare out over the canyon. As he did, his jaws loosened in fascination as a large boulder maybe as large as a Concord coach or a double-hole privy shuddered itself free of its precarious perch along the side of the ridge on the canyon's left side, fifty yards down from the top.

The boulder rolled onto its face. Then it rolled forward again, dust sparkling lemon in the light from the new sun billowing up around it.

The boulder rolled again.

Again.

And again, picking up more speed with each heavy roll.

Other boulders of various shapes and sizes also stippling that steep ridge began rolling, as well. Those giant boulders appeared to have been tossed like craps by some malicious giant standing atop the ridge crest.

All along the side of that northeastern ridge, dust rose like smoke from a gigantic fire. The sound was like that from a cyclone Enberg had once seen tearing up trees and pioneer shanties up on the Texas Panhandle.

The ground shuddered ever more violently beneath him.

He switched his gaze to the right and saw that boulders on

the opposite ridge were also falling, kicking up a great cloud of roiling dust.

The boulders were leaping over each other and smashing against each other in their hurry to get to the bottom of the canyon. Beneath the roar of the crashing boulders, Dag could hear the shrill screams of the Apaches those boulders were just now smashing on the canyon floor.

Turning the marauders to red jelly and shredded deerskin.

Enberg grinned at the thought as he rested his head back against the ground. "There ya go," he muttered. "Take that, savages."

His eyes widened when he saw boulders that had been perched on the ridge directly above him also falling—bounding toward him like huge wooden blocks from a child's giant toy set.

Enberg didn't feel any particular emotion about those boulders tumbling toward him. He was going to die, anyway. Might as well be smashed by a hundred-ton boulder than just lie here in the worst kind of misery, waiting to bleed out.

He heard something beneath the thundering cacophony of the rockslide.

"Dag!"

It was Emily.

"Dag!" she called again, louder this time. She was getting closer.

"Dag!" she screamed, even closer on his right now.

Enberg looked straight up to see his copper-haired, freckle-faced wife staring down at him in horror. "Oh, Dag!" she cried.

Then Galveston Penny was crouched over him, hands on his thighs. "You still kickin', pard?"

The Kickapoo, Rides, was there, too—staring stonily down at Enberg.

Enberg tried to respond but no air found its way across his

vocal chords.

Galveston looked up at the boulders hammering toward them. "Let's get him out of here before that whole mountain comes down on us!"

"No," Dag wanted to say, but couldn't find the words. He was half or three-quarters gone. "Leave me here. Just let me lie here and rest until one of them boulders turns me to jelly. Oh, please, just leave me!"

He didn't think he could endure the agony of being moved.

But they didn't leave him.

Galveston Penny and Rides reached down and wrestled his big, hulking frame up off the ground. Rides and Emily each carrying an ankle and Galveston Penny hefting him by the shoulders, they awkwardly hustled him around the shoulder of the mountain and out of the path of certain death.

Enberg must have passed out from the pain and blood loss, because the next thing he knew he was inside the stone mine shack sharing up at the face of his beautiful wife and the equally beautiful Lisle Stanton staring down at him, their eyes wide with worry.

Bud Normandy stood crouching over the women, peering down between them at Dag. Eldora Wormwood's face appeared, then, too, beside Normandy's. She was puffing her pipe and, like Normandy, she was slowly, fatefully shaking her head.

"Damn you, Dag!" Emily cried, sandwiching her husband's big, bearded face in her hands. "Don't you die on me, you simple idiot!"

She laid her head down on his chest, and sobbed.

"Ah, hell," Enberg thought he heard himself say. "I love you, too, honey."

CHAPTER TWENTY

Enberg didn't die

But over the next several weeks he often wished he had.

Especially during his ride back to town on the "padded" bed that Emily and Galveston Penny had fashioned for him and Charlie Grissom out of cedar bows.

There was no amount of soft bedding save for a billowy cloud straight out of heaven that would have eased his aches and pains on that seemingly endless journey back to Mineral Springs aboard the stage, which had only been a little scorched by the fire that had eaten away at the Wormwood station house. Charlie Grissom lay groaning on the coach roof beside him.

During that ride back to Mineral Springs, every fiber in Enberg's snake-bit, arrow-pierced, Apache-beaten body had screamed out in the worst kind of agony.

He hoped he hadn't sobbed and bawled like a spoiled brat who hadn't gotten the Christmas toy he'd wanted, for Emily had ridden up on the coach roof beside him, holding his hand. But as awful as he'd felt, he'd probably bawled his lungs out.

He didn't know. He'd mostly been unconscious—aware of only his misery.

He didn't *want* to know how big a fool he might have made of himself up there, in front of his pretty, long-suffering wife whom, it seemed, was going to take him back into her life despite his unspeakable sundry transgressions.

The scene he might have made aboard the coach wasn't

something he liked to think about as he recovered in his room in his mother-in-law's house, where both Emily and Gertrude had insisted he stay while he healed. Enberg himself hadn't been in any condition to have much say about squatting in his mother-in-law's digs. Especially during the first weeks of his recovery, he'd needed nearly twenty-four-hour care, and Gertrude certainly wasn't going to move out to Enberg's own crude shack at the base of that snake-infested mountain to help care for him.

And Emily couldn't do it alone.

However, Dag was a little surprised by Emily's being so agreeable about moving back into Cates's house with her mother, when she'd wanted so long to escape the place. But it seemed that now in the wake of Cates's death, as well as her own near-death experience at the Rebel Canyon Station, the strain between Emily and Gertrude had eased.

At least, they were no longer going at each other like two bobcats locked in the same woodshed.

Enberg had no idea when Gertrude had recovered her wits after the attack, for he must have been entirely or at least partly unconscious when she had. All he knew was that when he himself had recovered his own wits enough that he knew where he was and that it wasn't heaven, Gertrude was back giving orders around her house and Dag's recovery room with her customary, unyielding flair.

In light of the attack and the severity of the injuries Enberg had incurred while saving them, Gertrude and Emily had postponed their trip to the West Coast. At least, temporarily. Dag had no idea what would happen in the future. He had no idea if Emily would go back home with him once he'd fully recovered. He sure as hell wasn't going to live with his mother-in-law!

During his long hours of slow healing, one thing he learned

was how to take each day as it came . . .

That's what he was doing now as he sat out on the large veranda of Gertrude's house, nearly two months after his tussle with the Apaches, tilting his head back to take the midafternoon sun. He welcomed the healing rays deep down into his battered soul.

He was perched in a wicker rocking chair, clad in his long-handles and socks and with two heavy quilts draped over him like mourning shrouds. He didn't need the quilts, but Emily had insisted he be well covered, as it was winter in the desert. Even in southern Arizona the afternoon breeze could sling a bone-penetrating chill down from the mountains.

Enberg was well on his way to being fully healed. His snake-bit arm had swelled up like a side of beef, though it had now returned to near normal despite a lingering acid-like burn from time to time. The Chiricahua arrow had missed his bone and arteries, and the wound had escaped infection. But he was so glad to have his young, pregnant wife back—at least for the time being—that he objected to nothing she did or said.

Emily, whose belly was bulging beautifully now, could have ordered him to haul water up from the well on his hands and knees, clad in only his birthday suit and a fool's cap, and he'd have said, "How many buckets do you want, honey?"

"Dag, honey, what on earth are you snickering about out there?"

Enberg's ears warmed when he realized he'd been laughing out loud at the reverie, and that Emily had heard him. Her footsteps rose behind him now as she walked out of the house and onto the porch in her high-button shoes.

"Ah . . . oh, nothin', honey. Just . . . just some old joke I heard once, is all."

"I hope all this boredom isn't making you daffy, Dag," Emily said, tucking the quilts a little tighter around him. "Are you warm enough? Would you like to come back inside?"

"Nah, I'm doin' fine, Em. Doin' fine. Love the fresh air." The truth was that Emily was keeping the house so warm for him that, before he'd convinced her to let him come outside, he'd thought he was close to passing out.

"How 'bout some hot tea? Nothing better than hot tea to help you heal." Emily kissed her husband's cheek.

"Sure," he said. "Why not?" She hadn't allowed him a cup of coffee in weeks. Coffee was his favorite brew—right up there with beer and whiskey—but for some reason Emily had it in her head that coffee was too harsh for a man in Dag's condition.

So he'd been practically force-fed tea since he'd started being able to drink anything at all.

"I've got the water heating on the stove right now," Emily said, rubbing a loving hand up and down his forearm, over the quilts. "Should be just about to boil. I'll run and check."

She kissed him again as she rose. Before she turned away, Enberg stole a look down the bodice of the loose pink dress she wore. He loved his wife's freckled breasts with their large areolas and responsive nipples, and he couldn't wait to snuggle with them again. Emily hadn't allowed him to make love to her since he'd been injured, because she also had it in her head that sex might also be too harsh for a man in his condition.

Which meant it was nearly all he could think about, and his loins were fit to burst.

The big Apache and the rattlesnake hadn't killed him, but the lack of coffee and sex would be the death of him yet!

The clomps of a horse and the rattle of a buggy rose along the trail that led up the bluff to the Cates house from the sunshine-bathed town below.

"Who have we here?" Enberg said, turning his gaze toward the trail.

Emily stopped at the house's open door. "Company?"

As the horse and buggy approached, Enberg saw Bud Normandy in the front seat, handling the reins. Bud Normandy was customarily clad in his clown suit and bowler hat—this time the primary color was orange. Lisle Stanton rode beside him, looking radiant in a dark-purple frock and flowered picture hat, her thick, dark-brown hair curling over her shoulders.

Enberg tipped his head a little to see the two men riding in the buggy's second seat, behind Lisle. The weathered Stetson and red-and-black plaid wool shirt and broad, open, cleanly shaven face of one of the men bespoke Galveston Penny.

The other was the big, stoop-shouldered Charlie Grissom, who wore his traditional, torn and forever-dusty wool coat over a battered buckskin tunic. His thick beard fairly glowed like freshly fallen snow against his leathery, dark-red face. Looking customarily sleepy, Charlie rode slouched back in the buggy's leather seat, as though he were out for a Sunday ride, one thick arm and ham-sized hand hanging down over the side of the carriage.

He'd fully recovered from his arrow wound, though he'd resumed driving the stage only a week ago. Normandy had insisted the oldster take it easy for a while, so Grissom had been holing up and having a fine ole time with the *putas* down by the wash.

Emily walked out to the edge of the porch. As Normandy drew up to one of the two wrought-iron hitching posts, she said, "Well, well, to what do we owe the pleasure, Mr. Normandy?"

She cut an ironic glance at Dag, who gave a low snarl at that. He no longer had time for Normandy. However, the man's unexpected visit began to lift Dag's hopes that maybe he had decided to reinstate Enberg as shotgun rider for the Yuma Line. He wasn't sure he wanted the job back after the wrongful firing, but he had to make a living. He didn't think he could endure the humiliation of swamping saloons.

"Good day to you, Mrs. Enberg," Normandy said as he set the buggy's brake and rose from his seat. He smiled his broad, businessman's smile. "You're looking as lovely as ever, I see."

Normandy said nothing more as he waddled around to the other side of the buggy and helped Lisle down. As he did, the lumbering Charlie Grissom and the more fleet-of-foot and younger Galveston Penny unencumbered themselves of the sleek little contraption, as well.

Normandy followed Lisle up the porch steps. Enberg shared a shy glance with the girl and then tried not to look at her again. She was a pretty girl, and he no longer trusted himself around pretty women—beyond his wife, of course.

He'd found other women to be as dangerous as any Apache or rattlesnake . . .

Doffing their hats and looking as shy as whores in church, Grissom and Penny came up the steps, as well. They looked vaguely uncomfortable, sober-faced as they were.

The grandeur of the Cates place obviously had both men cowed. Enberg knew how they felt. It had always cowed him, as well. He felt a little embarrassed at having moved into such ostentatious digs, even if it was only temporarily. He also felt that by moving in here, even though it had been at Emily's insistence, he was accepting charity from his mother-in-law.

He didn't like that one bit, either.

"Please, do come in for some tea," Emily said, thrusting an arm toward the front door. "I'll rouse Mother. She's lain down for a nap, but . . ."

"That won't be necessary, Emily," Normandy said. "We just drove over to have a word with your husband. We won't tarry."

"Oh," Emily said. "Well . . . well . . . I'll just go inside and leave you all . . ."

"That won't be necessary, either," Normandy said, holding

his orange-checked bowler in his beringed, pudgy hands. "You have every right to hear what I have to say to your husband, Mrs. Enberg."

"Oh?" Emily said, sounding a little concerned.

Hell's bells, Enberg thought. Now what? He didn't like the somber way his visitors were looking at him. Even Lisle looked a little uncharacteristically demure, gazing down as she was and sort of nibbling her upper lip.

Dag suddenly felt as though he were about to be run out of town on a greased rail. Why, the ungrateful son of a bitch! But then, he doubted Normandy had ever felt grateful to anyone for anything in his entire moneyed life.

"All right," Enberg said, growing impatient. "Let's have it, Normandy."

"I've come here to introduce you to my new shotgun rider." Normandy glanced at Galveston Penny flanking him. "Come up here, Mr. Penny."

"Uh . . . hiya, Dag," Galveston said, flushing a little as he stepped forward, running his hand around the crease in his hat crown. "Since I was just ridin' the grub line an' all, and didn't have nowhere else to go . . ."

"Yeah, well you more than proved your mettle out there in that canyon," Enberg said. "You're good with a gun and cool under pressure. Normandy would be crazy not to hire a man like you." He narrowed an eye at the businessman, and pitched his voice darkly. "What about me?"

"Yes, regarding you," Normandy said. "You're still fired."

Enberg's cheeks started to burn with anger. He closed his hands around the arms of the whicker rocking chair. "That's what you came up here to tell me? Hell, I already knew I was fired!"

"Yes, you *were* and *are* fired. You're still fired. There's no doubt about it."

The fires of rage burned even hotter in Dag. Emily placed a calming hand on his shoulder, but it did no good. "Why, you little . . ."

"But I'm naming you town marshal."

Enberg scowled. He wasn't quite sure he'd heard the man.

He tipped an ear. "Say again."

"I'm naming you town marshal, Enberg. Well, I can't quite say that *I alone* am naming you town marshal. But I, as did Logan Cates, have considerable influence with the six members of the town council as well as the Mineral Springs mayor. So I managed to convince them that there is no single man anywhere in the territory . . . and probably not anywhere on the entire western frontier . . . better suited for the job. No man more capable than you, Dag . . . if you, uh, don't take umbrage with my calling you Dag, of course . . . ?"

Normandy reached into his coat pocket. He extended his closed hand to Enberg, and opened it.

Emily gasped.

A five-pointed town marshal's star lay in his open palm.

Enberg stared at it, speechless.

"Go on, Dag," Lisle said, smiling radiantly at the ex-shotgun rider. "It's all yours. You earned it. Without you, none of us would be here."

Normandy cleared his throat. "That's not to say that now—as before—the job doesn't come with a few conditions. Namely, that, you . . . uh . . . well . . ." He glanced at Emily, and winced, reluctant to continue with Enberg's wife present.

"Yeah, I know," Dag said, looking up at his wife with chagrin. "I'm to mind my manners . . . and act like a married man. One who loves his wife. And I do. More than anything, Em."

Emily flushed and looked down.

"There you have it, hoss," Charlie Grissom said, his blue eyes twinkling beneath the brim of his big hat.

"Yes," Lisle said. "There you have it." She looked at her uncle. "Shall we go, now, Uncle Bud? And leave the Enbergs alone to ponder their future here in Mineral Springs?"

"I reckon we shall, my dear," said Normandy, offering Lisle his arm.

Lisle gave Dag a fleeting, admiring glance over her right shoulder. Enberg looked quickly away from the pretty girl, as though her gaze were a snake poking its venomous head out of a mine wall.

"Gonna miss you as my right-hand man, hoss," Grissom said when Normandy and Lisle were heading back to the buggy. He offered Dag his hand. "But congratulations just the same."

They shook.

"Congratulations, Dag," Galveston Penny said, extending his own hand to Enberg. "I never thought I'd live to see the sort of thing you did back there in that canyon . . . all by your lonesome."

"Ah, hell—it wasn't hard," Enberg said, looking at Emily. He smiled. "It wasn't hard at all."

"Oh, Enberg?" Normandy had helped Lisle back into the buggy. Now he turned to the porch. "I've also named Mr. Penny as your part-time deputy. Since Blaze Pyle's ankle hasn't quite healed yet," he added a little wryly, "and he is the only lawman we have left in Mineral Springs, I thought you could use an extra hand until you could hire some other men yourself."

"I could," Dag said, smiling up at his new friend. "Thanks. I think we'll get along just fine, Galveston."

"Me, too." Penny pinched his hat brim to Dag and Emily, then tramped off down the porch steps.

Charlie Grissom gave Dag a soft, affectionate punch, and then followed the younger man into the yard.

When the buggy had wheeled away, Emily extended her hand to Dag.

"What—you wanna shake my hand, too, Em?"

"No," Emily said, shaking her head. "I want you to see if you can win me back." She glanced at an upstairs window behind her, and added, "Before Mother wakes up from her nap."

Enberg frowned, puzzled, studying his pretty wife. A slow smile shaped itself on his face. His blood warmed in his loins. "Really, Em?"

"I'll warn you—it's not going to be easy. Not after what you've done, you bad, bad, man."

"No," Enberg said, throwing the quilts aside and slowly rising from his chair. "No, I reckon it won't be. And you know what, Em?"

"What?"

"I wouldn't have it any other way." Enberg laughed as he leaned down and swept his wife up in his arms.

"Oh, Dag—*be careful*!"

Holding her taut against him, Enberg kissed her hungrily and feasted his eyes on her swollen bodice. "Careful ain't in my vocabulary, Em. You know that!"

Laughing, he carried his pregnant wife into the house and upstairs to their bed.

ABOUT THE AUTHOR

Western novelist **Peter Brandvold** has penned over 90 fast-action westerns under his own name and his penname, **Frank Leslie.** He is the author of the ever-popular .45-Caliber books featuring Cuno Massey as well as the Lou Prophet and Yakima Henry novels. The Ben Stillman books are a long-running series with previous volumes available as ebooks. Recently, Brandvold published two horror westerns—*Canyon of a Thousand Eyes* and *Dust of the Damned.* Head honcho at "Mean Pete Publishing," publisher of lightning-fast western ebooks, he has lived all over the American West but currently lives in western Minnesota with his dog. Visit his website at www.peterbrandvold.com. Follow his blog at: www.peterbrandvold.blogspot.com.

The employees of Five Star Publishing hope you have enjoyed this book.

Our Five Star novels explore little-known chapters from America's history, stories told from unique perspectives that will entertain a broad range of readers.

Other Five Star books are available at your local library, bookstore, all major book distributors, and directly from Five Star/Gale.

Connect with Five Star Publishing

Visit us on Facebook:
   https://www.facebook.com/FiveStarCengage

Email:
   FiveStar@cengage.com

For information about titles and placing orders:
   (800) 223-1244
   gale.orders@cengage.com

To share your comments, write to us:
   Five Star Publishing
   Attn: Publisher
   10 Water St., Suite 310
   Waterville, ME 04901